TRIPPED
by love

LJ EVANS

This book is a work of fiction. While reference might be made to actual historical events or existing people and locations, the events, names, characters, places, and incidents are either the product of the author's imagination or are used fictitiously, and any resemblance to actual persons, living or dead, business establishments, events, or locales is entirely coincidental.

TRIPPED BY LOVE © 2021 by LJ Evans

All rights reserved. No part of this book may be reproduced, or stored, in any retrieval system, or transmitted in any form or by any means, electronic, mechanical, photocopying, recording, or otherwise without the prior written permission of the publisher of this book.

Published by LJ Evans Books
www.ljevansbooks.com

Cover Design: © LJ Evans Books
Cover Images: © Unsplash kiwihug and Deposit Photos ninanaina / MaslovaLarisa / Olga_Bonitas / barvart
Content & Line Editor: Evans Editing
Copy Editor: Jenn Lockwood Editing Services
Proofing: Karen Hrdlicka

Library of Congress Cataloging in process.
ISBN: 978-1-962499-07-1

Printed in the United States

https://spoti.fi/3FtVhPe

Breathe by Jonny Diaz
Old Friends by Chris Stapleton
Flavor by Maren Morris
On Me by Thomas Rhett, Kane Brown, Ava Max
I Save Me by Diane Warren and Maren Morris
I Won't Let Go by Rascal Flats
Sugar by Maren Morris
Whiskey Sunrise by Chris Stapleton
The Way You Take Time by Joe Buck
The Thing That Wrecks You by Lady A
Yeah Boy by Kelsea Ballerini
Kiss Her by Eric Van Houten
Bigger Man by Joy Oladokun and Maren Morris
Shade by Maren Morris
Somebody Like You by Keith Urban
Hard Lesson Learned by Kenny Wayne Shepherd
We're Not Friends by Ingrid Andress
Hold You Tonight by Tim McGraw
To Hell and Back by Maren Morris
Better Than I Am by Keith Urban
With You by Keith Urban
One Call Away by Charlie Puth
I Do by Susie Suh
Better Than I Used to Be by Tim McGraw
Just For Now by Maren Morris
Whiskey and Rain by Michael Ray
Let's Make Love by Tim McGraw w/ Faith Hill
Take Your Breath Away by Josh Melton
Make it Rain by Thompson Square
Glass by Thompson Square
Just by Being You (Halo and Wings) by Steel Magnolia
Life Ain't Fair by Canaan Smith
Not Losing You by Maddie Poppe
Blessed by Thomas Rhett
It's Your Love by Tim McGraw w/ Faith Hill
H.O.L.Y. by Florida Georgia Line
My Boy by Elvie Shane

Dedication

*For all the single moms who deserve
a happily ever after all their own.*

Chapter One

Cassidy

BREATHE
Performed by Jonny Diaz

"Mama!" My heart leaped, and joy filled me as Chevelle's little voice echoed through the quiet of the restaurant's kitchen a few seconds before chubby arms wrapped around my legs. I braced myself with a hand on the stainless-steel counter and smiled down at my gorgeous boy. Love soared through my chest, growing and expanding like it had every day since I'd found out I was pregnant, and even more since he'd been placed in my arms.

"Well, hello, Snickerdoodle." I kept one dough-filled hand on the counter and leaned over to kiss the top of his head. The dark curls were soft against my lips as the scent of baby shampoo and apple juice filled my senses. I wanted to pull him to me in the tightest hug known to humanity, but it would have to wait until I finished the prep of the sourdough rounds.

"Sorry," Tristan said, hurrying forward, out of breath. Her softly tanned skin was flushed from racing after my son, and she brushed at a wisp of dark-blonde hair that had escaped her bun held up by two paintbrushes she'd likely forgotten were there. "He just took off, and he's getting fast."

I chuckled. "The other day, he made it from the bathtub to the kitchen before I'd gotten off the floor."

"Don't even try to make me feel better. We both know it has more to do with my waddle-walk than his pace," she said, putting a protective hand on the belly protruding from her soft T-shirt.

My brother's and Tristan's faces glowed with happiness these days after trying for two years to get pregnant. I'd watched their struggles to conceive with a guilty conscience, knowing just how easily Chevelle had come into existence. Too easily—through contraception and a spattering of sex—while they'd lived practically attached limb to limb, fighting for a baby.

I kissed Chevelle's head one more time. "I'm almost done, buddy. Then, we can go home."

Tristan eyed the finished bread that I'd sliced and was letting cool. I chuckled. "Go ahead. You know you want to."

She grimaced. "Nah, I promised Hannah I'd be ready for her next pizza experiment, and if I eat now, I won't have room for another four hours with this critter pushed up against my rib cage."

"What's her latest?" I asked.

"It's pesto, apple, and smoked gouda, I think?" Tristan said, nose squishing together.

I couldn't have hid my smile if I tried. Even though Hannah—at the mere age of seven—was almost as good on the piano as my country-rock legend of a brother, Brady O'Neil, she hadn't let it consume her. Instead, she divided her time, spending almost as many hours in my kitchen as she did in Brady's studio next door.

Chevelle tugged on my leg one more time before sitting down on my feet and holding on for dear life. I knew exactly what he wanted, and it made me hurry through my last task. I placed the last of the bread in the proofing containers before attempting a monster walk toward the sink with Chevelle riding on my foot. I pretended to groan. "Tristan. Help. I have a gremlin attached to me. It's going to eat me."

Chevelle giggled—a boyish, baby giggle that made me smile.

I was almost to the faucet when he tugged at my knees with just enough force to send me careening sideways toward the sink. I hadn't expected it, and with nothing to grab onto, I landed on the rubber mat placed over the sealed concrete flooring, bringing Chevelle down on top of me. He laughed, thinking it was all part of the game. I gasped as pain shot through my elbow and shoulder.

"Cass!" Tristan was at my side, pulling Chevelle off of me in a heartbeat.

"I'm fine," I told her. I inched my way toward the counter and pulled myself up before turning to Chevelle, who was wiggling in Tristan's arms. His dark-brown eyes were full of laughter, and his cheeks pushed up into his eyes from the width of his smile—a smile that reminded me of my brother's much more than his father's.

"You are quite strong, monster," I teased, tickling his stomach and leaving a trail of flour on his dark-blue shirt covered with his favorite animal—dogs.

I turned and washed my hands.

"You sure you're okay," Tristan asked, brow furrowing.

"Only my pride got wounded," I told her.

I was resigned to it—the hits to my ego that came from being so weak. I was leaps and bounds stronger now than I'd ever been in my life, but I was still one of the frailest twenty-five-year-olds around. I had my extra X-chromosome to thank for it.

But I wouldn't let the poor-me feeling overtake me today. I had a good life. Not only did I have my precious little boy, but I also had Brady, Tristan, and my parents, who'd all give a right arm for me. Or a left. Or both arms. Brady had already proven it by giving up an enormous chunk of change to help me start my restaurant.

I dried my hands and reached for Chevelle who was still trying to escape Tristan's grasp. He came easily, and I finally got to give him the tight squeeze I'd been dying for since the moment he'd walked in. The kind of hug that made him grunt and giggle before snuggling up against my neck with his little hand squeezing the bottom of my T-shirt sleeve like he had since he was a few weeks old. The smell of him surrounded me again, soothing me in a way that made me forget completely about the pain in my left arm.

Tristan, however, was still looking at me with concern in her eyes.

I didn't have to force the smile I turned to her. It was honest and heartfelt. "I'm good. Truly. Go before Brady comes in search of you. Then, I'll never get out of here without being hauled to the hospital for an X-ray."

She grimaced. "Just be grateful Arlene wasn't here, or the ambulance would already be on its way."

I laughed, but my heart fell, knowing it was the truth.

Tristan left by the back instead of the door on the

second floor that joined my Golden Heart Café to their *La Musica de Ensueños* Studios, which meant Brady was already in the car, waiting. I was lucky he hadn't appeared at her side, demanding what was taking so long. The only time he could stand being away from her for more than a few moments was when he was lost in his music, and that was something he did less now than ever before. Falling for Tristan and convincing her that she deserved a second chance at love after she'd lost her Navy SEAL husband had changed my brother's life.

Sometimes, I ached for that same kind of devotion. For someone to put me at the center of their world not because I needed to be watched over like my parents seemed to think, but because they couldn't bear to keep their hands off of me. Then, I would remember I barely had time to breathe after taking care of Chevelle and running the restaurant, and I knew I had no time for love or men.

After putting the finished loaves away one-handed with Chevelle still clinging to me, I made one last pass through the restaurant to ensure everything was ready for our morning rush. I paused in the archway between the kitchen and the dining space, and pride filled me, joy traveling through my veins as it did every time I stopped to really look at what I'd built.

There was a fountain in the middle of the room, and while it had been turned off for the night, the water still glistened and sparkled. An enormous Tree of Life soared out of the water's base, the trunk etched with animals, plants, and carved hearts. The long metal branches and metallic-colored leaves stretched up to the ceiling. Windchimes dangled from the limbs, and when the air conditioning kicked in, like now, they blew softly. It was a barely noticeable sound when the restaurant was full, but when it was empty, the melodies were calming. Sweet. The fairy lights I'd weaved through the boughs were the only lights still on, and they cast a shimmering glow over the darkened room. It was beautiful. A stunning art piece that most new restaurants would never have been able to afford, but it had been a gift to me from my parents. I was pretty sure Brady had given them the idea after I'd drawn it and nixed it from the original plans. I hadn't wanted him to cough up more money for a simple decorative piece.

The renovations on the café had been costly enough—money I wasn't sure I'd ever be able to repay him. The guilt ate at me even knowing Brady didn't want me to pay him back. The restaurant wasn't in the red anymore, and I was grateful Chevelle and I could now live on the little profit there was, but it didn't leave much in my checking account at the end of each month. Once in a blue moon, I was able to write Brady a teeny-tiny check that he fought taking, insisting the restaurant had been a gift.

I shut off the lights, hit the alarm, and left through the front door with Chevelle half asleep in my arms. I knew I couldn't let him pass out yet. There was no way he'd go down on time tonight if he snoozed at five o'clock in the evening.

I turned on the sidewalk and almost ran into a couple of college kids in Wilson-Jacobs sweatshirts, laughing and joking. "Oh, are you closed?" the girl asked, disappointment radiating from her.

"Sorry, we're only open for breakfast and lunch," I told her. My stomach twisted because I knew I'd be able to pay Brady off sooner if I stayed open for dinner, but I couldn't afford to hire extra chefs or the management I would need to keep those kinds of hours. And there was no way I'd be able to stay on my feet from five in the morning until nine or ten at night—not if I wanted to keep my health and have even a few hours for Chevelle. He already had so little of my time as he was shuffled back and forth between Tristan and my parents.

"I told you," the boy said, throwing an arm over the girl's shoulder as if it was the most natural thing in the world.

She pouted, and he kissed her temple. A sweet move that made my chest ache. I'd never really had that—tender caresses from someone looking at me like I was everything they wanted.

"What are we going to do for food now?" she asked.

"Well, Mickey's has great wings," I offered. "And if you really want vegan, Artfully Thai just outside town has some great options. Or if you're looking for something sweeter, Sweet Lips is still open."

I didn't wait for a response, heading down the sidewalk. They yelled, "Thanks," in unison as if they were one instead of two. Something Brady and Tristan often did as well, completing each other's sentences and speaking the same words. The ache in my chest grew.

"Mama. Treat?" Chevelle said, raising his head and patting my face. The mention of Sweet Lips Bakery had hope lighting up his deep-brown eyes.

I smiled at my dessert-obsessed little boy. "I have cookies at home. You can have one after dinner."

"Momos?" he asked, bringing a smile to my lips at the adorable mixed-up word he used for the s'more cookies that were one of my Golden Heart Café specialties. Originally, I'd made them for Hannah and her friend, Kiran, but then they'd become a hit at the restaurant.

Creating new items was my true joy, playing with how flavors and textures blended together and how you could use healthy alternatives to make classic dishes. At a minimum, it was a way to keep my mind—which was forever on the go—busy. But it also meant my menu was constantly changing, keeping it fresh and unique.

"Yep, Momos, just for you," I said, bringing his chubby little fingers to my mouth and kissing the tips. "But dinner first."

He nodded and went back to snuggling my neck as I made my way to my Prius that was in the last stages of its life. I buckled him into his car seat, shut the door, and then got behind the wheel, watching as the couple went down the wooden sidewalk with the guy twirling the girl as if they were dancing. They were only a few years younger than me but seemed so much freer.

I rolled my eyes at myself. The melancholy was ridiculous. I'd gotten everything I'd truly wanted. My boy. The restaurant. I didn't need more.

I left behind the postcard-perfect brick-and-ivy buildings of Grand Orchard's downtown, driving a handful of blocks to the small Craftsman-style house I owned next door to my parents. It was yet another thing I had Brady to thank for, but I loved it almost as much as the restaurant. The deep-green siding and white shutters with rustic brown trim brought the forest feel of the café home with me. Like the Tree of Life had tagged along with us.

I'd just barely gotten us into the house when my cell phone rang. I answered without checking. "Yes, I'm home. No, we don't need anything."

Silence on the other end for a moment. Then, a deep chuckle erupted that hit me in the belly, licking its way down and making my already wobbly legs even more unsteady.

"I'm not Arlene," Marco's voice filled the line like he could fill a room with his mere presence. He didn't laugh often. Usually, I was lucky to get a twitch of his lip or, on occasion, a full smile that could wipe away someone's memory, but full-on laughter from him was as rare as a hot day in January in upstate New York.

"Sorry, but you have about thirty seconds before she calls, and if I don't answer, she'll rush over," I said as I put Chevelle down. "Go put your shoes in the basket."

He was growing like a leaf, but his uneven gait was still all toddler. It tugged at my heart that felt strangely bruised tonight. I watched as he half-sat and half-collapsed next to the basket near the back door and focused on taking off his shoes with a little furrow to his brow and tongue sticking out.

"Just making sure we're still on for tonight," Marco asked, and the question itself made me pause.

I couldn't remember the last time Marco and I hadn't worked out together after Chevelle had gone to sleep. Our daily routine was why I was stronger than I'd ever been before. He only ever missed them when he was traveling with Brady.

"Why? You got big plans or something?" I asked, trying to ignore the stab of jealousy that soared through me at the idea of Marco having plans that didn't relate to his position as Brady's bodyguard. Plans that might have involved a woman. Not that I'd ever seen him with a woman. Not in the entire seven years I'd known him.

"Plans?" he asked as if the idea itself was a surprise. "No. I'll be there."

Relief I didn't have a right to had me loosening my death grip on the phone. I'd only been eighteen when Marco had first shown up at Brady's side in Grand Orchard, and we'd barely conversed during the first few years. But ever since he'd started working out with me, we'd become friends. Or…maybe not friends…but something more than mere acquaintances. Or perhaps it was all in my head, and I was simply a project to him—a coach and his trainee. His boss's sister who needed some beefing up.

My phone buzzed with another incoming call. "'Kay. I gotta go. That's Mom."

"See you at seven-thirty."

He hung up, and I switched over, trying to get my pulse to calm down so Mom wouldn't think there was something wrong. So she wouldn't rush over to find out what I was hiding. So I could get through the night before starting my day all over again at four thirty in the morning.

Chapter Two

Marco

OLD FRIENDS
Performed by Chris Stapleton

I tapped my phone to my forehead, silently swearing at my own ridiculousness. It was bad enough that I found my way to the window in the apartment over her parents' garage at five o'clock each night, knowing she'd be driving in. Calling had been over the top. Normally, I just made sure she and Chevelle got into the house okay, but there'd been an aura of sadness about her today that had me dialing before I'd even really thought it through.

In the fading sunlight, her hair had glinted with golds and whites, shimmering like a halo around an angel. The two ever-prevalent buns she needed to keep her long, thick mane out of her face had been losing their battle with tendrils escaping everywhere. The flowy skirt and Golden Heart Café T-shirt she'd had on were her standard uniform—some unique combination of seventies flower child and modern—but it also hid her willowy limbs and lean frame from the world.

While I hadn't been able to see them, I knew her feet were shoved into orthopedic shoes most people would deem ugly-as-sin. I had a love-hate relationship with them because I knew they helped her stand on her feet all day in the kitchen, but I also knew they made her feel undesirable when she was anything but.

That was when I cut my thoughts off.

No way I could desire her. Not only because she was my boss's sister, but because I could never be the person she deserved at her side. My silent vigil and training her would have to be where the story ended. I'd make sure she had the strongest muscles possible and ignore the way she looked in a workout tank that showed off silky skin and shorts that clung to her hips.

My phone shook in my hand with a text from my partner. Trevor and I headed the Garner Security protection detail for Brady O'Neil. When he was touring, the team quadrupled in size, and the owner, Wayne Garner, took on a larger role, but whenever we were in Grand Orchard, he left Trevor and me in charge.

> *TREVOR: Ghost and family are home for the night. A reporter from* The Exhibitor *was sniffing for news about The Painted Daisies album he's producing. I had to kick the guy off the property. Told everyone to keep their eyes peeled.*

Brady's code name was based on the single off his second album and went back to a time when I'd just come onboard with Garner, and Brady had had a real-life stalker on his tail. I'd barely known what I was doing then, having gotten into the protection business right as my military career had ended in a fiery storm.

Tripped by Love

ME: *Thanks for the heads-up.*

I yanked off my uniform of black on black on black, locked my two Glocks in the gun safe, and changed into workout gear. I had two hours to fill before I could ease through the backyard and over to Cassidy O'Neil's house. The workout I did with her was never enough to keep me in the shape required for my job, but then, it had been designed for her and not me. I headed out onto the street for a run. After I came back from her house, I'd burn myself out with more weights until I was so tired that my memories couldn't haunt me. I might sleep then. A handful of hours at best, but it would be enough to get me through.

The first few blocks, I kept my pace slow as I cruised by the edge of Wilson-Jacobs College. The apple trees lined the campus's stone paths, and the heady scent of their fading blooms saturated the air. The sounds of crickets and a boom of bass coming from the dorms carried through the midnight-blue sky as it started to fade into black. A few stars began flickering into sight, and the temperature dropped.

As the old stone buildings covered in moss and ivy disappeared behind me, I had a decision to make. Curl my way through town or head out into the orchards. It was an easy choice. I skipped the red brick and wooden sidewalks that screamed small-town America and pounded my feet along the pavement toward the trees and farms. While upstate New York was very different from where I'd grown up in Texas, both places were capable of humidity that sank into every crevice. Tonight, there was only a hint of it in the air as May wound its way into June.

As if I'd sent out some kind of bat signal to her by thinking about Texas, my phone rang, and

Maliyah's wrinkled face appeared with a video call.

"*Hola, Tía*," I answered, stepping off the side of the road and into the soft dirt that surrounded the orchard.

"You're out running," she said.

"I'm not even out of breath. How could you know that? I could just be taking a leisurely stroll."

Her lips twitched. "You? Leisurely? Besides, you always go running before you work out with Cassidy."

I was getting predictable if even Maliyah knew this about me. I needed to shake things up. Break the routine. But that meant breaking my workouts with an angel, and my chest seized at the thought.

"How are you?" I asked, changing the subject.

"I'm fine. Jonas is fine. We're all fine. Stop worrying."

My lips twitched more. "You called me, *Tía*. So, who's really worrying?"

She waved a finger as if she was scolding me. "When are you taking a vacation?"

"Why? What's wrong?"

"I just told you everything is fine. I didn't ask because there's anything going on. I asked because you work too hard. Constantly protecting someone else is no way to live your own life."

I didn't respond because I couldn't. This was an argument we'd had for years now, and neither of us would change our views.

Instead, I changed the subject. "Did you take your meds today?"

"Yes. Jonas puts them in one of those daily pill containers for me, and then he watches me like a hawk while I swallow them before he leaves for school," she replied, rolling her eyes. "I'm supposed to be the parent, not him. That boy is even more serious than you were at that age."

Guilt washed over me as I realized how long it had been since I talked to Jonas, especially when I knew he was living my teenage nightmare for real. After losing my parents and being placed with Maliyah, I'd walked home from school every day, afraid I'd find her gone, and that was before her heart episode. The fear that she'd disappear from his life for good had to have been weighing on Jonas. I needed to check in with him soon.

Before I could dwell on my failings with my foster brother—like she knew I would—Maliyah launched into an update about everyone in her life, including Maria Carmen and her enormous family who treated Maliyah as if she was one of their sisters. The tightness in my muscles eased slightly when Maliyah broke into laughter while explaining Maria Carmen's disgust with her firefighter son who was dating three women at the same time. After all the worry I'd put Maliyah through—after what had happened to her because of me—hearing her laugh was always a relief, and she knew it.

"I told her she should be happy because at least she has the chance of having grandchildren someday with Álvaro playing the field and not living like a monk," she said as she stared into my eyes through the screen, her meaning clear. "Maybe you need to go on vacation to some Caribbean Island and find a beautiful lady to hook up with." She winked, her hazel eyes sparkling with mischief before she wiggled her chestnut-colored eyebrows to emphasize her point.

A choke of laughter got stuck in my throat as

images of Cassidy spread out on the Caribbean sand filled my head: in a bikini, with the sunlight bouncing off her smooth skin, and her honey-colored eyes tempting me to kiss every inch of her body.

I barely held back a groan.

"I need to finish this run," I said, and Maliyah sighed.

"We're not done with this discussion, *mijo*. And I expect to hear from you sooner than the end of the month. Do you understand?"

More remorse tore through me. I was lousy at keeping up with them.

After I hung up, I ran longer than normal, trying to beat the regrets out of me. Trying to forget my mistakes and the sadness in Maliyah's eyes when I'd shown up on her doorstep with my dreams in shambles.

While burning myself out normally worked to stop the swirl of memories, it failed tonight, and they were still haunting me as I opened the back door of Cassidy's home with the key she'd given me. We'd started working out together after she'd had Chevelle, and for the first year, it had been in my apartment above her parents' garage or in their backyard if the weather cooperated. But after she moved, we'd converted one of the bedrooms into a home gym. We'd finagled a floor mat, treadmill, rower, and weights into the tiny space.

When I walked into Cassidy's house, the sweet smell of chocolate hit me. She must have baked, even though she'd barely gotten home from the restaurant. She cooked like other people breathed. As if it was effortless. As if it was just something you did while standing.

The kitchen was neat, and the dishwasher was running with the stove light on, casting the farmhouse-style cabinets and sink into shadows. I made my way through it to the open living room beyond. It was completely feminine, full of modern colors and patterns that were splashed all over the walls and furniture. It was like seeing Cassidy's flowered skirts morph into a living space. The pictures on the walls were mostly of Chevelle, but there were a handful of the entire O'Neil family, and one of Cassidy at the restaurant, smiling like she'd won the lottery. And I guessed she had in a way. Brady had funded it all for her, but I also knew how hard she worked to try and pay him back.

When I got to the open doorway of the home gym, my heart stopped. She was bent over, stretching with her rear-end facing me in shorts that lined every curve. That made my body respond instantly and harshly, in a way that required me to adjust myself before entering the room in my own exercise shorts, which were fairly loose but still wouldn't hide the enormous hard-on the image of her had caused.

"You going to join me or just stand in the doorway like a weirdo," she said without ever looking up from her legs.

I cleared my throat. "Don't stretch too much before warming up."

She unbent herself to shoot me an eye roll. "This isn't my first day at the rodeo. What is with you today?"

Her hands were on her hips as if she was ready to scold me, and all I could think about was how I wanted to feel the entire length of her tucked up against me. She was tall, five foot eleven when barefoot, and while I still had three inches on her, the slight difference meant I'd barely need to tip my chin to kiss her.

I turned away from her, toward the shelf in the corner, and set down my water bottle and towel in order to give myself a chance to clear my head. To think about the last sequence of footwork we'd done the day before. To think of anything but kisses and curves and hard-ons.

I didn't hear her cross the mat, and so I jumped when her long fingers hit my bicep. I turned my head to look down at her hand before I let my gaze slowly trail up and over all her exposed skin to eyes full of concern. Her brows were furrowed, and before I could prevent myself, I rubbed at the space between the delicate arches with my thumb.

"Don't get frown lines because of me. I'm fine."

Her eyes searched mine, honey ones mixing with my brown ones that were so dark they could be black in certain lights. As if I was a demon without a soul. Sometimes…I wondered if I was.

I stepped back before I did something stupid, like let my finger land on her soft-pink lips…before I let my mouth settle on hers. As I moved away, I glanced at the treadmill that was already down. "You starting there?" I asked.

She shook her head. "No, I already did fifteen on it. Chevelle crashed early. I guess he ran around after Molly half the day."

Molly was Brady and Tristan's fox terrier, and Chevelle loved the dog like almost nothing else.

"Weights, then," I said, moving over to the two sets on wheels in the corner. I turned the dial to the level she used most and pulled the weights off the rack. I handed them to her. "Squat raises?"

Her eyes were still squinty, assessing me, but I ignored them. Instead, I shoved the weights in her direction.

She took them with a sigh. I returned to the second rack, dialed in my amount, and pulled them off. We faced each other in the middle of the mat and went to do the first repetition, but as she raised her arms, pain streaked across her face.

I closed the minimal distance between us, jerking the hand weight from her.

"What the hell?" I asked, voice lowering, fear coasting over me. We'd been working out for two years, and the only time she'd ever looked like that was when she'd done something outside of the gym to hurt herself.

She rubbed her left elbow, continuing all the way up to her shoulder. I dropped the weights and gently pulled her arm toward me. There was a bruise forming above the joint.

"What happened?" I demanded.

Her face closed down, and she brushed me off, stepping away from me much like I had a few moments ago when she'd gotten too close. When she'd gotten under my skin.

"What always happens. I fell. It isn't a big deal." Her voice was full of frustration. Anger. She hated being weak. But she was a hundred times stronger than she'd been when we'd started this.

"Where did you fall?" I asked, trying to stay calm. To not freak out like Arlene did whenever she heard or saw Cassidy injure herself. Cassidy's mom protected her with a fierceness that bordered on obsessive, but I knew it was born out of love. A love

I understood because, once upon a time, my parents had felt the same way about me.

"In the restaurant's kitchen. Chevelle was on my leg…we were playing…I just lost my balance."

Likely she'd hurt herself worse because she'd done whatever she could to fall in the opposite direction of Chevelle. But it meant she'd hit the unforgiving cement floor. I reclosed the distance she'd put between us, tugging at her fingers gently.

"Let me see." I couldn't help the soft beg that littered my tone. Her eyes widened, but she didn't pull away. I felt her arm, probing gently at the elbow, my time as a corpsman coming back easily and readily to me. "I'm pretty sure it's not broken, but just in case, we should ice and elevate it to keep the swelling down. You definitely shouldn't be lifting weights."

"How could you possibly…it doesn't matter. I just want to work out and push past it." Frustration weaved its way through her words again.

"Cassidy, I get it. You don't want to be injured, but you are. Pushing this will only end up with you at the hospital with Arlene hovering over you." I used her mom as a weapon because I could. Because I wanted her to stop and take care of herself, and the easiest way to do that was to threaten Arlene's stifling overprotection.

Her eyes flashed. "Don't use Mom against me."

My lips quirked because she'd called me on it. "Then don't be stubborn. Ice the goddamn elbow."

She lifted my fingers from her arm and moved away again, heading toward the door this time. She tossed back, "Fine. But when it's all better in the morning, you're going to be the one feeling like you overreacted, not me."

I followed her as she made her way into the dimly lit kitchen. Relief mingled with disappointment wafted through me. Calling off our workout meant I wouldn't be able to touch her. I wouldn't be able to watch as her muscles flexed and bent. I'd have to go back to an empty apartment, staring out the window at the lights in her bedroom that called to me more than the stars in the sky.

Chapter Three

Cassidy

FLAVOR
Performed by Maren Morris

The restaurant's kitchen was buzzing with noise and action. Cliff and I were chopping at a fiery pace as we scrambled to substitute items on our menu with things we had on hand. My order from one of the farms had been delayed, and while we were missing ingredients we sorely needed, I refused to serve any dish that was decreased in quality or taste because of it. I fought daily against the image people had of "health" food. They expected it to be bland, dry, and cardboard-like just because it was good for you. I loved surprising them. I loved when they found more flavor in my meatless products than those loaded with it.

Being a farm-to-market restaurant meant my menu was changing constantly with the seasons and availability. It also meant I was never bored with what I was cooking and got to experiment on an almost daily basis. The downside was I had to plan for things to go awry occasionally. Like today.

My bigger problem at the moment was that I wasn't in the best shape for the challenge. Not only did my elbow and shoulder still ache like someone was constantly yanking at them, but I also hadn't slept well. It usually took a long time for my brain to shut off once I landed in my bed at the end of the day, but last night, I'd been haunted by Marco's hands on me as he'd held the ice to my arm. I'd been haunted by the scent of spice surrounding him as he sat close enough for his breath to coast over my neck, and his heated gaze watched my chest rise and fall with my arm angled above my head. It had all been a tantalizing hint of what it would be like if we were actually tangled together for a very different reason.

The appealing visual of us skin to skin had burned itself into my mind. I wanted to feel and taste the contours of his abs that I got peeks of as we lifted weights together. Most of the time, I thought the desire was one-sided. He usually treated me like some recruit in the military he'd once served in and never talked about. But occasionally…occasionally, I saw a flicker of flame in his eyes, and it always kept me awake after seeing it. Made me wonder if there could ever be something more to the spark that drifted between us.

Even though Marco had been in our lives for years, what I knew of him was barely more than I'd known the first time we'd met, because he never talked about his family or his past. Instead, the pieces of knowledge I'd gathered had come from seeing him in action, protecting Brady, pushing me, and playing the hero when I slipped on the ice.

Willow's voice brought me out of my thoughts. "Hey, Cass, one of the customers wants to talk to you."

I slid two dishes that were ready to be served out the pass-through toward her. If it had been Laney telling me a customer wanted to see me, I would have rolled my eyes because Laney couldn't handle someone saying their coffee needed creamer, let alone a more strenuous complaint. But Willow was not only my best waitstaff, she had an innate sense of how to deescalate things—a sense that she was honing as a restaurant management major at Wilson-Jacobs.

I sighed. We were in the middle of our breakfast rush, and I still had recipes to switch out with new ingredients. I didn't have time to be pacifying anyone. But it was part of the gig. Part of owning and managing a restaurant. One of the parts I disliked.

Willow smoothed a hand over her long, red ponytail, looked out to the crowd, and then back to me. She leaned in and said as quietly as she could through the open window, "I think he's some bigwig. He's got a suit and that look, you know."

My eyes followed hers to the corner booth that was barely visible from the kitchen under the dripping branches of the Tree of Life.

"What's he upset about?" I asked, wiping my hands on a towel.

She frowned. "That's it, I'm not sure. He kept saying how much he liked everything. He ordered five different dishes."

I'd seen the orders come in and thought it was a family. He'd ordered some of my regular items that, thankfully, we'd had all the ingredients for, but I'd also had to substitute his carrot pancakes with zucchini.

"You explained about the order change?" I asked.

She nodded.

I looked back at Cliff, who was my second in command. "I need five minutes to take care of a customer. You got this?"

He eyeballed the orders and the dishes being prepped before giving me a thumbs-up. Cliff had more experience in restaurants in one pinky than I did in my entire body, but he'd never once treated me like I didn't know what I was doing.

I washed my hands, dried them on a towel, and headed out into the restaurant.

I had to stop twice before I got to the booth in the corner as locals greeted me, asking about Chevelle or my parents. The man there was an older gentleman, not quite in his sixties like my dad, but still with wrinkles around his eyes, mouth, and forehead. Like he'd carried too many expressions on his face throughout his life. His hair was almost pure snow with hints of a soft brown that must have once been barely a shade over blond, and he had eyes such a startling blue that they stood out against his pale, white skin.

"Hi, I'm Cassidy O'Neil, the owner. Is there a problem?" I asked.

Surprise flitted over his face as he glanced over me. I was used to it. People—who weren't local—were always astonished by how young I was. They'd ask to speak with my boss as if I was dense and hadn't heard the request to talk to the person in charge.

"No. No problem, Ms. O'Neil," he said, a smile widening his face.

Willow was still hovering nearby, and I shooed her away. She left with some reluctance. Her curiosity had been piqued, and she'd definitely demand the scoop when I returned to the kitchen.

"How can I help you?" I asked, keeping my smile

plastered on.

"I think…we might be able to help each other," he responded.

That did wipe my smile away, but he didn't seem to notice it. Instead, he waved to the seat across from him. "Please, won't you sit and give me five minutes of your time? I know it's your morning rush, so I won't keep you long."

His glance took in the full tables and the line waiting outside. The weekends might have been our busiest time, but Friday mornings weren't far off. Locals came in before work or school, and tourists, who'd come for the apple blossom season, showed up excited to kick off their long weekends.

I slid into the other side of the booth.

"The recipes you use to make your food, are they yours? Or do you have a chef who creates them for you?" he asked.

"They're mine," I told him.

"You haven't borrowed them from someone else? Used something one of your line cooks have created?"

I shook my head, eyes narrowing. Was someone suing me, thinking I stole their recipe?

"They're mine," I said, unable to keep the note of defensiveness from my tone.

"That's good. Very good." He smiled, reached into the inside pocket of his suit, opened a little case, and took out a business card. "My name is Lance Ralley, and I own Earth Paradise Distributions."

The name jiggled at the back of my brain, but I couldn't quite place it.

"We're a growing health food company. We produce, market, and sell alternative and earth-conscious food items to grocery stores around the globe. Do you know Wandering World Chips?"

I nodded. They were a potato chip alternative made from turnips and other vegetables. Air fried. Made from ingredients supposedly grown on sustainable farms. They sold off shelves as fast as they came in because the production was so limited.

"Well, I'd like to discuss the possibility of buying your recipes for distribution. Maybe create an entire line based on your Golden Heart menu." He waved his hand at the half-eaten food on the table. "The pomegranate-and-acai coffee cake was fantastic, as well as the soy chorizo quiche. And those s'more cookies…out of this world."

I stared at him, trying to put his words into some sort of order in my brain.

"I don't understand," I finally said. "We're a tiny restaurant. There's no way we could make enough for you to sell to grocery stores."

He chuckled and nodded as if I was a small child in need of soothing. I'd done it myself when Chevelle was frustrated with something he couldn't do.

"Right. We'd buy the recipe and produce it in my facilities."

My heart thudded. He wanted to buy my recipes? Just the idea of it was overwhelming. I had no idea how to negotiate something like this or if I even should. What were the downsides to it? What could go wrong? He seemed to read my reticence and pushed forward.

"You'd be involved every step of the way, of course. Any changes we needed to make to the original recipe to produce it for a mass market would have to be approved by you. We'd use the Golden

Heart name, and you'd have a say in the branding. We'd give you a one-time fee for the recipe purchase and negotiate a percentage of the products sold from there."

It sounded like…someone's dream. Maybe not mine, but someone's. To have the food they created become a household name sold around the world. I didn't have those kinds of dreams. I had dreams about cooking for the people and the town I loved. His offer sounded…big. Like it would take time I already didn't have. That might cut into my already precious hours with my son. But a whispered thought filtered into my conscience. *You might be able to pay Brady back.*

When I still hadn't said anything, Lance chuckled. "I can see I've left you speechless. But my offer is legitimate and heartfelt. You're one of the first farm-to-market, health-centered restaurants I've wanted to come back to in a very long time."

"You've been here before?" I asked, stunned.

"Once a month for the last three months."

I didn't recognize him, but that didn't mean a thing. During the two tourist seasons, which were centered around the apple trees blossoming and then later in the fall around harvest, people flooded the town and the restaurant. I'd never be able to keep their faces straight even if I didn't spend the majority of my time in the kitchen while my staff handled the floor.

"I'm not asking you to agree to anything right here and now," he continued. "I'd like to set up a meeting with you, your investors, your lawyers, and my team."

"I'm not sure…" I wavered, even though I couldn't articulate what was actually holding me back.

"I understand it's a lot to take in. Is there a number I can call other than the restaurant's main line?" he asked.

I eyed him, trying to decide if I should give a complete stranger my cell phone number. He never lost his smile, even while I gave him continued silence. Instead, he stood, placing cash on the table next to his bill.

"Or you can call me." He tapped the business card he'd left behind. "But I'm warning you, if I don't hear from you by the end of the week, I will be calling the restaurant. Repeatedly. I've been told I can be dogged when I see a worthy cause. I can make us both a lot of money, Ms. O'Neil. I promise you that."

He walked away, and I sat there, dumbfounded. Wheels turning. Heart pounding. A glass shattering brought me back to my senses. I turned to see that Laney had dropped a coffee cup as she watched Brady saunter across the restaurant toward me—a normal reaction from her, and many others, who regularly gawked at my brother whenever he appeared. He practically oozed rock-star charisma as he approached with his shaggy, blond hair styled to perfection, scruff littering his chin, and a muscled body he showed off in torn jeans and a faded ABBA T-shirt. Today, he had a beanie on his head and Chucks on his feet, but he was equally as comfortable in a cowboy hat and boots when he was on tour.

Brady slid into the seat Ralley had vacated.

"Can I get you anything?" Laney asked, voice wobbling as she appeared at his side even though this wasn't her table. Brady didn't notice her drool, just like he rarely noticed anyone's anymore. These days, the only person who drew his eyes was his wife.

"Just a coffee, please," he said.

Laney nodded, pushed her dark hair behind her ear, and all but skipped away.

"Should I be worried?" he asked, frowning and snapping the leather bands on his wrists like he always did when deep in thought.

"What?" I asked.

"You're sitting down in the middle of the morning rush. Did you hurt yourself worse than you let on yesterday when you fell?"

I groaned. I wasn't sure if it was Tristan or Marco who'd told him about my mishap.

"No, Mom," I said with a little growl. It was one of the ways I got him to back off—taunting him with Mom's overprotectiveness. I waved the business card at him. "I had to meet with a customer…"

Brady frowned. "Do I need to send Marco or Trevor to deal with it?"

I couldn't help but laugh. "No. And what? Is your security team a hit squad now? Would Marco even agree to that?"

"He was military. He knows how to kill."

"You're ridiculous. No. This guy…" I slid the card to him. "He wants to buy my recipes. Produce them to sell in grocery stores."

Brady's eyes widened. "Really?"

He picked up the card, read it, and then his frown returned.

"Seems fishy."

"Because my food isn't good enough to be mass-marketed?" I said, half-tease, half-hurt.

"Cass, you know that's not what I meant at all.

Your food is amazing. No, it's just weird that some stranger walks in, happens to eat your food, and then says he wants to offer you some kind of deal. What did he ask for upfront? Some kind of down payment?"

"You're so cynical," I said. "He didn't want me to give him anything. He wanted to pay me. And he said it was the third time he's come back."

"Did he ask you to sign something?"

"I'm not stupid, Brady. No. He said he wanted to meet with me, my investors, and my lawyers. He asked me to call him, but he said if he didn't hear from me, he'd call the restaurant."

Brady looked down at the card, thoughtful. "I'll have Lee poke around a bit. See what he comes up with."

Lee was Brady's business manager, and he'd kept Brady in line since he'd first signed a record deal. He'd been there through all the ups and downs of Brady's career, including the stalker and the media storm that had tried to turn his relationship with Tristan into some sort of tragedy. Brady trusted the man with everything in his life, and it was Lee who'd helped Brady and me find a handful of successful restauranteurs to guide us as we'd created the business plan for The Golden Heart Café.

I swallowed hard, wanting so badly to not need my big brother to come in and rescue me again. To save me from getting hurt. But this was what I got for burying my pride and asking Brady to back the restaurant for me to begin with. Now, I had no choice but to continue to let him be a part of it. It was his money and reputation on the line, even more than mine in many ways. If something went wrong with a deal like this, it could splash back on him and his career. Everyone knew he'd invested in The Golden Heart. If we put the brand out there, it would be like putting his stamp of approval on it.

My gut was torn.

Maybe it was too risky. Maybe it was too much to take on. Maybe I needed to stick to my small dreams and the comfortable life I was making for Chevelle and me. We didn't need anything more. Did we?

Chapter Four

Marco

ON ME
Performed by Thomas Rhett, Kane Brown, and Ava Max

Brady stormed back from the restaurant through the secret door on the second floor with eyes blazing, and my heart fell. Was Cassidy worse this morning than last night? Should I have insisted on her going to an urgent care for an X-ray? He'd raced from the studio to check on her when Tristan had let it slip that Cassidy had fallen the day before.

Tristan's eyes widened at the concerned expression on his face, eyes darting from me to Hannah and back to Brady.

Hannah was at the piano, playing a piece with no music in front of her. I thought it was a new song she and Brady were writing together, but I wasn't sure. Her blonde hair was bent toward the keys, and her flowered shawl was slipping from her shoulders. The top hat she'd worn almost daily for the first year after her great-grandmother had died had been left at home today.

"Is she okay?" Tristan finally asked.

"What? Oh, I guess," he said distractedly. "She said she was fine. But this guy"—he shoved a business card in my direction—"was there saying he wants to buy her recipes and produce them for grocery stores. I need you and Lee to check him out."

Tristan pulled out the paintbrush she'd stuffed into her bun and twirled it. "This is incredible news. Why are you upset?"

"I just don't like people poaching off her. You know Cass. She's all sunshine and rainbows. I don't want anyone to take advantage of her."

I barely held back my retort as I took the card. Cassidy was one of the most positive people I knew, but she was also incredibly smart. Savvy in a way her family tended to overlook. She didn't need everyone huddling about her like she was ten instead of a grown-ass businesswoman.

It didn't mean I wasn't going to run this guy and his company through every background check we could find. Maybe even send it out to Nash, a former Navy SEAL who'd worked briefly for Garner. He still had ties to the military that I didn't.

Hannah's fingers crashed to a stop, and she looked up with golden eyes to Brady and her mom. If you didn't know that Hannah wasn't Brady's child, you'd think she was. They were all golden, just like Cassidy. With hearts just as big. Just like the name of Cass's restaurant, even though I knew that wasn't the reason she'd chosen it. When you looked at them all together, they reeked of love. Of belonging. Of family.

Sometimes, seeing it caused an ache in me that was hard to stifle. An ache that felt large enough to swallow me whole. My parents and I had blended together that way. Completely dark to this family's light, but still glowing with adoration. With true affection. I'd missed them every day of the last fourteen years. Losing them at fifteen and being placed into foster care—into homes where love was not on the table—had been eye-opening. It had made the love I'd found with Maliyah and her rowdy, extended family a gift. But it had still never felt the same. It had never felt like the love standing in front of me.

I suddenly needed air. I needed to escape before the black hole that had embedded itself into my soul after that last night at the fair made me implode.

"Josh is downstairs," I said. "I'll just run back to the office and start on this."

I left without looking back. I heard Brady say something to Hannah. I heard the music pick back up, and I kept going.

Josh gave me a curt nod as I left the studio before crossing Main Street and heading to the stairs on the side of Sweet Lips Bakery. Since Brady had made Grand Orchard his home base, opened the studio, and invited a number of famous musicians to record here, our team in town had grown large enough that we'd needed office space to accommodate us. We rented the rooms above the bakery because it gave us line-of-sight to *La Musica de Ensueños* even when we didn't normally need it.

When I opened the door with my key card and thumbprint, Trevor's head swiveled around from the nearest desk. He was blond and lithe, just like the trio across the street, except his pale-blue eyes were a contrast to the warm browns of the O'Neil family.

"What's up?" he asked, frowning because I rarely

left Brady's side during the day unless he was tucked away at home.

"We need to create a file on this guy," I said, handing the card to Trevor and explaining who he was.

Trevor nodded, turned to his computer, and started typing in details. He didn't even look up as he said, "Garner wants to check in with us regarding our security plans for The Painted Daisies."

In a few days, Brady was bringing The Painted Daisies into town to record their next album. The all-female band had burst onto the music scene in the last year and were known for causing mayhem everywhere they went. Not only because of the fans and anti-fans that followed them across the country, but because some of the members were trouble on wheels themselves. The Garner Security team that normally protected the band would be onsite as well as our team, but we were planning for the worst and hoping for the best.

Trevor's fingers paused, and he frowned at the computer screen.

"What?" I asked, doing my damnedest to keep the panic from my voice at the thought of some schmuck trying to weasel into Cassidy's life.

I moved behind him and looked down at the screen.

"Espionage charges?" I couldn't keep the shock from my tone. That was the last thing I'd expected.

"Corporate espionage, not the national security kind," Trevor said. "I'll dig some more."

Brady would flip. Cassidy would be disappointed.

"Don't say anything to Brady until we have all the facts," I said. "We don't want him to overreact."

Trevor chuckled. "Brady? Overreact when it comes to Cassidy? What could you possibly mean?"

I didn't return Trevor's smile. It wasn't a joke to Cassidy. She hated the way her family coddled her almost as much as she loved them for it.

My phone rang, and I glanced down at it, fully expecting to send it to voicemail, until I saw Jonas's face on the screen. As part of the generation who knew how to text but not how to carry on an actual phone conversation, he rarely called. My remorse filled as the promise to myself from last night returned, and I stepped away from Trevor's desk to head for the privacy of the conference room.

"Hey, Jo-Jo. What's up?" I greeted.

A sniffle came from the other end, and my heart fell. "She had another episode." His words struck me in the gut. "She's alive, Marco. But they've got her wrapped up in wires and machines."

Goosebumps littered my skin in a way they rarely did. I took a deep breath, held it, and then exhaled.

"What have the doctors said?" I asked as every single muscle in my body tightened, ready to do battle against an enemy I couldn't fight.

"No one will tell me," he responded as his sadness turned to anger and frustration that I couldn't blame him for.

"Can you give them my number? Have one of them call me? That way we'll get the facts."

"Fine. But they should tell me. I'm not a kid."

He was, but I remembered being sixteen and thinking I was already a man. It took years for me to figure out that I wasn't. It took situations that were out of my control and standing up for things I believed in before I realized I hadn't really known what being a man was before. Even then, I'd still failed.

"You're not. But they see a number attached to your face and nothing more," I told him, trying not to wound his pride more than it was. "Is she awake?"

My stomach twisted, thinking of Maliyah's happy face sagging with pain. Guilt almost rendered me frozen as I thought of what she'd looked like the last time she'd been in the hospital for her broken heart syndrome—because of me. What would happen to Jonas if this continued? Would Child Protective Services let him stay with her if she kept having these episodes?

"I stepped out to call you when she fell asleep," he answered.

"What happened?" I asked.

"I came home from school and found her at the bottom of the stairs. The EMTs said she hadn't been there long, otherwise she might not have…" He couldn't finish it as a sob overcame him.

We both sat in silence while I allowed him to get control of his emotions, fighting a desire to cry myself. I blinked back tears, my grip tightening on my phone as my other hand formed a fist with my nails biting into my palm.

"She said she was taking her meds," I said quietly. Plans started flying through my brain. I'd need to catch a flight to Austin. I had to work on a coverage plan with Trevor. I had to talk with Cassidy…

"She is. I watch her take them every day." His voice grew stronger, tucking away his actual feelings.

I hated that he felt like he had to put a front on with me, but it had always been this way between us. The first time I'd come home on leave to find him sitting on the back step, he'd fucking saluted me as I'd walked up in my camos. It had made the pain stretching through me that day even worse because, at that moment, I'd been nothing more than a rat in the henhouse. The soldier turning on his military family.

"I'm coming," I said. "I don't know how long it'll take me to get there, but I'm on my way. Who's there with you?"

"Maria Carmen and Julianna. They both said I could stay with them, but I'm okay at the house," he replied, defensiveness in every word. He was more than old enough to be on his own for a night, but I could almost guarantee one of them would badger him into going home with them until I showed up.

"I'll call when I have a flight, but if she wakes, will you call me so I can talk to her?"

"Sure."

He sounded broken. Jonas's life had been nothing like mine. I'd been loved and cherished until the accident that took my parents from me. Jonas had been an afterthought to a mom focused on her next high. Maliyah was the first person to be utterly devoted to him, and now she might disappear.

"It's going to be okay, Jo-Jo," I said quietly.

"No. It's really not." And he hung up.

My gut and chest twisted a notch tighter, making it difficult to breathe.

"Fuck," I said to the ceiling and thumbed open my phone's browser, looking for flights out of Albany.

Chapter Five

Cassidy

I SAVE ME
Performed by Diane Warren and Maren Morris

I kissed Chevelle's forehead, and he didn't even wake as I set him in the crib. Normally, I put him to bed before he was fully conked out so he could learn to fall asleep on his own, but I'd been exhausted tonight, unable to get up from the glider in the corner where we'd been reading together. I'd almost fallen asleep along with him.

In addition to the tired seeping through my bones, my elbow was still sore. Icing it had eased it some. Enough that I was determined to make up for my lost workout session by doubling my efforts tonight. If nothing else, it would wear me out and hopefully cast me into a deep, dreamless sleep where I wouldn't think about Marco, the money I owed Brady, or Lance Ralley's offer.

I took the baby monitor with me, shutting the door to Chevelle's room and making my way to my own. The soft lemon-and-white décor soothed me. Like stepping into a field of daisies. Normally, I felt like I could breathe here, but today, the hamper almost overflowing with clothes only made me feel more overwhelmed.

I tossed my long skirt and The Golden Heart Café T-shirt at the pile and searched for a clean pair of workout shorts and a tank. The restaurant was closed on Tuesdays, so I'd have time to do laundry then. I'd just add it to the endless list of things I had to do. Sometimes, all I wanted to do was play with Chevelle, snuggle in bed, and sleep our day away, but that was rarely how my days off went. Still, I was living the exact life I'd wanted—chosen—and it would be ungrateful to gripe about it. Maybe I hadn't really understood what I was signing up for, but I'd signed on the dotted line, and I wouldn't give it up now.

I'd just changed and gone to fill my water bottle in the kitchen when the doorbell rang. It was followed almost immediately by a sharp knock, as if whoever it was couldn't be patient enough to see if I'd answer the first before doing the second.

I didn't get many visitors. Most people I knew walked in my back door with their own key. Mom and Dad. Brady and Tristan. Even Marco.

I made my way to the front door. It was a beautiful piece, carved from old apple trees and lined with tempered glass along the top that didn't allow me, even as tall as I was, to see out. I took a peek through the peephole instead. The image was blurry and contorted, but it was enough to send my heart into my throat. A knock resounded again, and I couldn't help the startled jump it caused. I balanced myself on the wall with a hand as my legs tried to buckle.

"Cassidy?" his smooth voice called through the wood, scattering my skin with goosebumps. Not the good kind. Not the kind that Marco caused by skimming a finger over my arm even accidentally.

This was all disgust.

Disgust with me. Disgust with him.

What did he want?

I took in a deep breath, held it, and then slowly exhaled. I tried not to let the tremble in my fingers show as I flipped the locks and opened the door only wide enough for him to see me. It was far from an invitation to come in.

He looked exactly the same as he had the last time I'd seen him. Dark-brown hair perfectly pressed, square chin with a dimple in it. Gray eyes hidden behind glasses that were hardly needed but added to the scholarly look he so desired. He was in a suit that had to have cost a pretty penny—maybe even more than his monthly salary at Wilson-Jacobs had once been. It was a deep navy with a gray striped shirt underneath and a tie that echoed his eyes.

He looked me over much as I was him, taking in my bare toes with lack of polish, my skinny legs dressed in workout shorts that barely covered anything, and my workout tank that was both bra and top. I had no layers of armor to shield myself from him. I was bare in a way I didn't want to be. On display when I'd promised myself he'd never see any part of me again.

"Cassidy." He nodded, eyes squinting slightly.

"Clayton," I said with a calm I didn't feel. Inside, I was panicking. Why was he here? What did he want? It certainly wasn't me. It wasn't the little boy I'd tucked in bed with his favorite blanket and a stuffed dog he called Hippo.

"Can I come in?" he asked.

I didn't move. I didn't open the door any farther. "What do you want?"

"I'd prefer to talk inside." He glanced both ways down the street furtively. As if he was ashamed to be standing on my doorstep. As if it was costing him every ounce of pride to be here.

"Now isn't really a good time," I told him.

His eyes narrowed. He'd never liked it when I'd disagreed with him. Never liked it when I hadn't easily acquiesced to whatever he wanted...commanded. In a list of regrets in my life, he was at the top while also being at the bottom.

I couldn't completely regret him when I had Chevelle.

"When would be a better time?" he asked.

I groaned internally. Did I want him to come back? Did I want to see him a second time and risk my parents seeing him here? No way in hell. But if I knew Clayton at all, he'd keep rapping on my door until he'd said whatever it was he wanted to say.

"Never," I tossed out but swung the door wider, took a step back, and waved him inside.

He hesitated but then brushed past me. I closed the door, stepping around him and turning to watch him absorb my house with the same scrutiny he gave to his students' assignments. Full of disdain and condescension. Nothing ever good enough. I was grateful he'd never been my professor.

I tried not to see the room through his disapproving eyes, but it was hopeless. Toys from Chevelle were still scattered around the space that I hadn't had a chance to pick up. The furniture was mostly secondhand because I'd been determined to fill my house with things I could afford rather than more money from Brady's or my parents' pockets. None of the pieces were in bad shape, but they clearly weren't new, and they were in patterns I knew would drive him crazy. Mix-matched. Florals and paisleys and stripes in rainbow hues that made me think of more flower fields and blue skies.

Clayton's house had been gray and white and black. Sterile. Modern. The interior had been a complete contrast to the exterior of the old home. It had been another reason he'd wanted to leave Grand Orchard. To escape the quaint feel of the town and the college, even though Harvard had its own old-school charm.

"What do you want, Clayton?" I repeated through gritted teeth.

He turned, schooling his expression and pushing up his glasses on his nose.

"You. The baby," he said.

I laughed. Harshly. Not only because it was insane to think he'd come back after two years to try and resuscitate a relationship that had hardly existed to begin with, but also because I didn't believe him. The Clayton Hardy I knew had no wish for relationships or children. He only cared about his name and the prestige it carried.

He looked away and then back at me, jaw clenching. "I've taken a summer professorship at Wilson-Jacobs just to have the chance to spend time with you and the baby."

"What happened to Harvard?" I asked.

"Nothing. I'm still there. I'm on track for tenure, just like I planned."

"But you decided to come back to Grand Orchard…for me?" I scoffed.

"You and the baby."

"What did I have? Do you even know? Is it a boy or a girl?" I demanded.

He had the decency to look chagrinned. "I didn't look far enough ahead, Cassidy. I didn't see what I was giving up."

I snorted. "You gave up an occasional fuck. That was all you lost."

"Why are you being difficult? Isn't it simple? I'm the father. I'm here. I want to make a go of it with you and the baby. Did you have a boy or a girl? Can I see him or her?"

He'd clearly expected to just show up and for me to go weak in the knees with relief at having Chevelle's father there at last. As if I'd been pining away, miserable without him. As if I'd be grateful that he suddenly deemed me necessary in his life. I narrowed my eyes at him.

"What? Does Harvard expect you to be a family man in order to gain tenure? Too many female students clogging your office hours? Are there whispers about you there like there were here?"

"I can't help it if I'm good-looking. I've never slept with a student," he growled.

"You slept with me."

"You weren't my student. You'd graduated. It was completely different."

I laughed sarcastically. "I'd literally just graduated. I'd walked across the stage that day and gotten my diploma."

He stepped closer, and I stepped back. "Cassidy, give me a chance. Let me spend time with you and the…" He looked around at the toys littering the floor and the pile of baby clothes I hadn't folded yet. "You and my boy."

"Good deduction, Professor. But it isn't going to happen. Not now. Not ever."

"I'm just asking for a chance. Don't be so…"

"Bitchy? Defiant? Angry? Which word would you like to use?"

His jaw was ticking repeatedly. He shoved his hands into his pockets as if to keep me from seeing how they'd tightened into fists. He turned away, toward the windows.

"Spending time with my son…with you…it's the least you can give me."

The least I could give him! Fury filled me, and I would have snapped back, but suddenly, a strong arm looped around my waist from behind, drawing me into a muscled chest. A chest I knew even if I'd never been tucked up against it in quite this way. As if I belonged to it. As if the arm was claiming me in a single, possessive scoop.

"I don't think I like the idea of my girlfriend spending time with the shitty-ass man who left her with money for an abortion and nothing else," Marco's deep voice barreled through the room, coasting over my ear and my cheek and causing Clayton to flip around, startled.

Clayton's eyes squinted, taking in the arm around my midriff. Taking in the wide breadth of Marco's stance and the muscles that rippled beneath his workout gear.

"Who's this?" Clayton demanded.

"Like I said. I'm her boyfriend, and you're the asshole who's leaving."

My heart flipped and twirled with the stupid wish

that the words were true. That somehow, I'd be lucky enough to claim this stunning man as my own. That his possessive, protective grip was something I was used to.

Clayton glared—one I returned, and one I figured Marco was also returning even if I couldn't see his face. It didn't surprise me when it was Clayton who relented first. He stalked toward the door, opened it, and then looked over his shoulder at us.

"I'll be back in a week, and I'll be here all summer. I have a right to see my son, but I want to see you both. Maybe you should figure this out before I return," he said, his eyes landing on Marco's arm before coming back to my face. He was pissed. Angry that whatever plan he'd had going on in his mind had been thwarted with Marco's appearance. With my lack of submission.

The door slammed behind him.

I sagged in relief, my heart pounding as much from Marco's length tight up against mine as from the confrontation with a man I was ashamed to have let in my life.

I pulled away, and Marco let me. The loss of his touch hit me stronger than any loss I'd ever felt from Clayton. This loss made me want to step back into Marco's embrace and see if he could hug me as tightly as I hugged Chevelle. Until there wasn't even a breadth of space between us.

I couldn't meet his eyes. I was afraid that not only would he see the longing in me, but that I'd see disappointment spreading over his face because I'd once let that weasel into my bed. I couldn't bear to be less in Marco's eyes than I already was.

"What the hell was that?" he asked, and instead

of stepping away, he closed the distance again. He put a finger under my chin, drawing my gaze to his. I saw anger there, but I also saw fear tangled with another emotion. One I wanted to call yearning but was probably just concern. Still. It made me gasp. A little breath of air that drew his eyes to my lips.

"I don't know," I said, shaking my head, but so entranced by Marco's skin touching mine that it was hard to think.

"He's really Chevelle's father?" Marco asked.

"Sperm donor. Not a father," I said, my chin raising.

As if it suddenly hit him how close we were and just how much he was touching me, Marco stepped away, all his emotions shuttering behind a blank face that was square and beautiful. As if he was an ancient Aztec god come to life. Black hair shorn short like the military man he'd once been, the bristles echoing the ones scattered across his chiseled cheeks and sharp chin. Heavy brows sheltered his dark-brown eyes that flickered with the emotions his face was trying to conceal.

"He wants to know Chevelle. Wants you?" His voice deepened as if the idea was enough to hurt him. My heart flipped wildly with the hope that maybe there really was more to Marco's and my arrangement than just being workout pals. Maybe the feelings I held at bay were also buried in him.

The image of the couple from the day before, spinning down the sidewalk together, hit me, but instead, it was Marco and me. Could we be that? I shook my head. It was ridiculous. A dream I couldn't risk wishing for not only because I knew better than to expect him to desire me, but because I didn't have time for anything in my life but Chevelle and the café.

"I hardly think that's his real plan," I finally spoke. "He was very clear he never wanted children—and certainly not with some backwater nobody."

Marco's eyes flicked to the door and back to me, his tall frame straightening, tightening as if he was ready to do battle.

"Just ask it," I said.

His eyes widened a hair, nostrils flaring slightly.

"What?"

"Ask me why I was with that pompous, arrogant asshole."

It was a dare I wasn't sure he'd give in to. Because if we were merely gym buddies—if I was merely a project he was overseeing—then he shouldn't care why I'd been with Clayton Hardy, Esquire of Jackasses. But Marco had shown up. Defended me. Claimed me in order to do so, and now I wanted to know if he'd go further, even when I knew I shouldn't tempt it. I ached to know if he'd come out from behind his armor to show that there was more to him…to us.

Chapter Six

Marco

I WON'T LET GO
Performed by Rascal Flats

I could still smell her all over me. The scent of chocolate and sweetness from her kitchen that seemed to hover around her like a cloud. I could still feel the soft skin at her waist that my hand had slid over as I'd tucked her up against me, claiming her even when I knew better. When I knew it was dangerous to do so because I'd find it difficult to walk away and let her go…

And now she was daring me. Daring me to ask about her and the shitty excuse of a human being who'd just stormed out her door with a half-assed threat that I wasn't even sure she'd realized. Not because she was clueless or rainbow-eyed like her brother had insinuated earlier, but because Cassidy couldn't see how any man could desire her, want her for their own. She saw herself as a mother, a sister, a daughter, and a chef. She didn't see herself as a woman to be worshipped.

I swallowed hard, trying to bury the hatred I felt for a man I'd never set eyes on before. Trying to hide the way her body had made mine come alive, tingling from the tips of my fingers down to my toes.

Maybe it was because I'd already had my emotions knocked off center with Jonas's call. Maybe it was because I'd spent years denying every feeling I'd had for her. But her dare caused the words to rip from deep inside me like skin being torn apart by shrapnel.

"Why were you with him?"

Her eyes widened with one eyebrow arching in a perfectly delightful way. She hadn't expected me to give in. To cave. To ask. She raised her chin again—the second time she'd done it—defying me to judge her. To deny her.

"I thought he didn't see me as someone less than anyone else. As someone struggling every day to overcome her challenges. I thought he just saw a pretty woman he could screw, and I wanted that. To be just another pretty face," she said.

I hated him more.

Hated him with a vengeance that would have had me picking him up by his collar and tossing him from the house if he'd still been there. Because I was damn sure he'd taken advantage of her. He'd seen through her to the tender spot she hid away, carved from her childhood challenges, and used it to sleep with her. I could guarantee he hadn't seen her the way I did. Strong and brave. Whole. Unbroken. Because far from being less, Cassidy O'Neil's challenges had made her more.

"You're not just another pretty face," I growled out, my voice deeper than I'd ever heard it in my entire life. But she took my words wrong. She thought I meant that she couldn't escape her hypotonia and extra X-chromosome. She tried to back away, and I grabbed her wrist, capturing her, holding her close when I should have been walking away.

"You'll never be just a pretty face, Cassidy. You can't be. You're so much more than that. You're a beautiful, resilient human who outshines the rest of us. It's us that are less. Not you."

Tears sprang to her eyes, and I hated myself for them.

I closed mine to shut them out and said, "I'm sorry…I shouldn't have—"

Her finger on my lips stopped the rest of my words.

"Don't you dare take it back," she said quietly, and I risked looking at her. There were tears there still, unshed, and she was blinking fast to hold them back, but there was also a look of awe on her face, as if I'd quoted Shakespeare or some goddamn sonnet. "Those are the best words anyone has ever said to me."

I groaned. I couldn't help it. I hated with every fiber of my being that no one had told her these things before. That everyone in her world saw her as needing help…fixing. I'd started working out with her once I'd heard from Brady that she was trying to increase her strength, but it wasn't because I thought she needed to change. It was because I wanted her to see how much she could accomplish. How strong she already was.

Before I could really take in what she was about to do, she was hugging me, squeezing me so tight that it caused air to escape my lips. I hesitated, and then I wrapped her in my arms and hugged her back with the same vehemence. With a force that folded our limbs together until it was hard to know where hers left off and mine began.

I couldn't remember the last time I'd hugged

someone.

Maliyah was good at patting me on the shoulder and kissing a cheek. Jonas was at the stage where men didn't hug men. The last time I'd slept with a woman, it had been a fleeting, one night of passion where hugs weren't on the list. Affection hadn't been the purpose. So instead of breaking the hug when she loosened her grip, I held on, tightening my arms even more. She laughed softly, squeezing back again.

Then, I had to let her go. Not only because if I kept holding her, I'd want to do more than just hug her, but because I had a plane to catch. Hours' worth of flight time and layovers before I'd arrive in Austin in the early morning.

So, I stepped away, and she let me.

"He'll be back," I said, returning us to the reason we'd been entwined to begin with.

She sighed, placing a hand on her forehead and rubbing. "The summer term doesn't start for another week. I have time to figure it out."

"You don't have to figure it out alone. I'll be here."

Her lips quirked. "Well, he does think you're my boyfriend."

I grunted in reply. It wasn't my finest moment. I hadn't really thought my words through, when I was known for doing just that. For being careful. Methodical. Planning everything to a T. Something feral and animalistic had taken over me when I'd seen her taut frame and heard his demands.

Her smile slipped away as if something else had crossed her mind. "Don't tell Brady. Or my parents. God…can you imagine what they'd do?"

It stabbed at me even when I knew they'd be right to freak out. Cassidy O'Neil deserved someone much more than a dishonorably discharged corpsman who played at being a bodyguard.

"Don't worry," I said. "I have no intention of telling Brady I pretended to be your boyfriend for all of two seconds. I'd like to keep my job…and my balls."

Her mouth fell open. "Not that, you big lunk. I mean about Clayton being here and wanting to see Chevelle. Brady would probably hire a whole other detail just to surround the house and then drown me in lawyers."

Knowing she hadn't meant me pretending to be her boyfriend didn't lessen the pinch to my heart, because I still knew the truth. She was an angel, and I was a flawed mortal.

"The lawyer thing doesn't sound like such a bad idea," I told her.

"There's no dad listed on Chevelle's birth certificate. He'd have to ask for a DNA test. I mean, Chevelle's his…but…" She trailed off, uncertainty filling her, and I felt like a jerk for causing her to worry. But she probably did need to think about it if Chevelle's father was trying to insert himself into the picture.

She raised her arm, tightening her ponytail, and it raised her breasts in a way that was hard to look away from. "I feel like I need to burn off twenty years of stress. Ready to get your ass kicked on the mats?"

She needed to burn off stress and worry, and I couldn't be there for her. It twisted my stomach more than it had already been twisting since my phone had rung with Jonas's face appearing on my screen.

"I can't stay," I told her. She looked crestfallen. "I have to go to Austin."

"Austin? Texas?"

I nodded and spoke words I hadn't breathed to anyone, not even Trevor. "My foster mom was hospitalized because of a heart condition."

Cassidy's face was full of surprise. "You…you were a foster kid?"

There was a stigma to those words that most people associated with them. Cassidy hated people judging her because of her Triple X and hypotonia. I hated people expecting me to have some sad, sob story about being in foster care. Sure, it hadn't been great before I'd been placed with Maliyah, but no one had abused me. No one had stolen from me. I'd just moved around a lot until she'd opened her home and taken me in.

"Only for three years…after my parents died," I told her.

"What…what happened to them?"

I swallowed the lump in my throat that would always be there when talking about the moment my world changed. "A truck driver fell asleep at the wheel. Crossed over the divide and hit us head-on."

"God…I'm so sorry," she said. "Us…you were in the car?"

I gave a curt nod. I didn't want to talk about them or the accident, not when my emotions were already so raw.

"I was lucky to have *Tia* Maliyah," I said and meant it.

"She's your aunt?"

My lips twitched. "No. She's no relation at all.

It's just what I call her. She doesn't really have any family of her own either. She was a foster kid, too. But she's surrounded by a group of people from her church and her community who act like she's their family."

I'd just told Cassidy more about my life in two minutes than anyone had known about me in years. I was one-hundred-percent certain Garner knew about my family from his background check when he'd hired me. I was sure Trevor had looked me up as much as I'd looked him up back when we'd been trying to figure out who the insider was giving Brady's stalker intel, but I'd never openly mentioned my situation to either of them.

"I'm hoping to be back by Sunday or Monday at the latest," I told her and headed toward the back door and the SUV I had parked, ready and waiting to take me to Albany.

"Marco, she had a heart attack. Take all the time you need. Brady won't care. No one will. Be where you need to be for those that love you."

I didn't correct her words about being loved or about the heart attack. It hadn't been one. It was takotsubo cardiomyopathy. A heart weakened—broken—by stress, and I'd been the first to break it. Still, Cassidy's words struck a chord that was hard to shake off. After I'd stayed silent—after I'd been court-martialed—I'd sworn an oath to myself that I'd always be there to protect the people who needed it most, no matter what it cost me. It was the reason I'd gone to work for Garner. To be in the line of fire, shielding others. But I'd also promised myself I wouldn't bring anxiety to Maliyah's door again, which was why I'd stayed away as much as possible. In the process, I'd left Maliyah and Jonas unguarded.

Alone. I'd failed her again while thinking I was doing the right thing.

As I stepped out the door, I looked back at Cassidy. The kitchen light was shining behind her, turning those golden strands into the halo that often surrounded her. She wouldn't tell her family about the asshole showing up, but now that I knew, I'd have to keep a watch on her even more. I needed to make sure Clayton didn't pull anything fast or shady. I had to come back as much as I needed to go.

"Will you text me if you hear from him again?" I asked, heart screaming.

The only time we talked or texted was when we were discussing our workouts. Me asking this crossed some line that would be difficult to push ourselves away from once Clayton disappeared again.

She nodded, and I turned away, only to be halted by her soft voice.

"Marco?"

I looked back.

She hesitated as if considering what she wanted to say before finally saying, "Travel safe."

I had a feeling those weren't the words she'd planned, but I couldn't expect more. I couldn't want more. This was already too much.

Chapter Seven

Cassidy

SUGAR

Performed by Maren Morris

I gave up on the idea of working out as soon as Marco left. I resorted to icing my elbow for the second night, downing five cookies, and then collapsing in bed where sleep evaded me. My mind raced with everything that had happened in a span of twenty-four hours: Marco's hands on me, Clayton's veiled threats, and Ralley's offer.

Sleepless nights weren't anything new for me. The nonstop nature of my brain had been a problem since I was a kid. It had made school difficult and studying even harder. But just like the night before, it was Marco who haunted me the most as I lay looking at the ceiling. The truths he'd finally given me about his past and his family, along with the glimpse of affection I'd seen in him for his foster mom, made me greedy to know more, while, at the same time, I ached for what he'd gone through.

So, it was no surprise that when I did finally fall asleep, it was still Marco who drifted through my dreams. Just like he was the first thing to pop into my head when I woke. He filled my thoughts as I got ready for my day and as I met Mom at the back door, coming in with a cup of coffee in hand.

Even at five in the morning on a Saturday, my mom was dressed in tailored jeans and a button-down. She was in good shape for a woman who'd hit sixty, but her hair that had once been the same dirty-blonde color as mine was now littered with white she didn't bother to hide. While Brady and I got our light-brown eyes from our father, our mom's were a pale gray, like storm clouds fading away. Her face was lined with wrinkles, but she still looked younger than her years, regardless of the fact she'd spent twenty-five of them agonizing over me.

"You look exhausted, *cailín deas*," she said, the Irish-Gaelic term for sweetheart rolling off her tongue as it had since I was a baby. I forced myself to remember how lucky I was rather than snip back at her that she looked tired, too. After all, I was the reason she was up so early. She came over every morning, whether or not college was in session, to watch Chevelle for me while I went to the restaurant. During the week, by the time she had to journey off to Wilson-Jacobs for her classes in Celtic studies and the diversity of the Gaelic languages, Tristan was there, picking my son up. My family had circled around me and Chevelle to make sure we had the support we needed. Not all single moms could say the same.

With the school year almost over, Chevelle would spend the entire day with my parents while I was at the restaurant. They were raising him almost more than I was, if I was to count the hours he was with them versus me. It increased the ache I already felt in my chest this morning, growing to proportions that felt hard to keep inside, but I had to. Otherwise, Mom would take it as a sign that I was breaking down, for sure.

So, as her eyes continued to take me in, squinting as if she could see some unknown harm, I turned so that the invisible bruise on my heart and the very visible one on my elbow wouldn't be seen.

"I'm fine," I told her.

"Maybe you should give the workouts with Marco a break for a few days. Give yourself a chance to catch up on some rest," she suggested.

I almost laughed because I'd missed two in a row, and there was no way I was missing more, whether or not Marco was there with me. The workouts were the reason I could stay on my feet all day at the restaurant. They gave my poor muscles a fighting chance. For more reasons than I could count, Marco being there each night, surrounding me with his gaze and his scent, were my moments of peace at the end of my long days.

I kissed her cheek instead of replying. "I'll text you when I'm leaving the café."

"We're taking Hannah and Chevelle out to Romero's after lunch. They've still got chicks and bunnies running all over the place," she said.

The Romero Farm was one of the biggest apple orchards in the area, but they also had a farm full of animals that all the schools and families in the area took their kids to. I tried not to feel even more guilty that it was my parents who were taking Chevelle and not me. It was a normal, grandparent type of activity. Something they might have done even if he wasn't with them so much, but I was going to miss out on all his joy. The way his eyes would light up at the animals and how his little feet would stumble after them.

"Sounds like fun," I said.

"If you get done early, you could join us," she responded.

"I'd like that. I'll have to see how the day goes."

I was out the door and on my way to the restaurant before she could really respond.

Cliff and Willow were waiting at the door when I got to The Golden Heart, both sipping on coffees and looking like they wished they'd had a few more hours of sleep as well. While we did as much prep for our mornings as we could each afternoon, the daily deliveries of fresh produce meant we had plenty to keep us busy until we opened at six. My mind filled with the tasks at hand, and it wasn't until the morning rush had died down into a trickle that Marco came back into my head.

He had to have been in Texas by now.

Before I thought better of it, I took out my phone and sent him a text.

ME: How's Maliyah?

It took a few minutes before he responded back. Maybe it was because we'd never engaged in how-are-you kind of conversations. All our texts had been about workouts and schedules. If I scrolled back through our chain of messages, there was not a single one that asked about something that mattered to him personally.

MARCO: Feisty. Ready to go home even though the doctors aren't letting her out of their sight for a few more days. She had a mild stroke along with the heart episode.

Sadness filled my veins for him as I tried to push aside the selfish thought that now he wouldn't be able to come home any time soon. He'd have to stay a while to take care of her. *Where he should be*, my brain chimed in. But my soul was miserable at the thought of not seeing him again for weeks—maybe longer. Maybe he'd have to stay there permanently. Maybe he'd have to give up his job as Brady's bodyguard altogether.

I tried not to let that thought take the air out of my chest, but it was almost impossible. My heart grieving for something that might not happen. Grieving not only for all of us, but for Marco because he liked his job. He was built to protect others.

What would I say to Clayton when he showed up and asked where my boyfriend had disappeared to? He would know we'd lied. He'd see it as a weakness he could exploit.

I hated myself for making it about me when this was about Marco and someone he cared about.

> *ME: Is she going to be okay?*
>
> *MARCO: They expect her to make a full recovery, but it could take longer than the last time.*

I debated my next question for too long. Typing, deleting, typing again.

> *ME: How are you holding up?*

He didn't reply, and I had to go back to the kitchen as the lunch wave started to roll in. It didn't stop me from wondering if the brave man I knew was actually crumbling inside and afraid to let it show. He protected everyone else, but who was there to protect him?

♪ ♪ ♪

My brother's living room was full of activity. The sounds and voices seemed to bounce off each other, making my tired head ache. Hannah was at the piano, a soft tune dancing from the keys while, behind her, Chevelle tugged on a dog toy in Molly the terrier's mouth. She play-growled, and he giggled. Mom and Tristan were oohing and ahhing over nursery room images. Brady and Dad were discussing which of the bands who'd just played at the annual music festival he and Tristan ran should be invited back. The similarity in their frames and bent heads would have screamed their relationship even if you hadn't known they were related. Dad was simply an older, more wrinkled version of my brother.

While I loved every single one of them, the competing noises only increased the pain that had started behind my eyeballs somewhere mid-afternoon. I should have said no to dinner at Brady's. I should have told Mom I'd pick up Chevelle and take him home, but if I had, they all would have been worried that something was wrong. I'd been lucky no one had mentioned my fall at the restaurant to Mom yet, and I didn't want to give them a reason to tell her now.

Outside the front window, one of Brady's protection detail moved on the porch, the shadow changing the way the fading sun came in through the glass. The sight of the bodyguard only made my chest squeeze tighter, worry coasting through me because Marco still hadn't responded.

"Cass?" Brady's voice called me back from my thoughts as he landed on the couch beside me. I turned from the window to smile.

"Yeah?" I asked.

"You're far away tonight," he said, which caused all the grown-up eyes to land on me. Mom's brows furrowed while Dad's went up.

"Just a lot on my mind," I said, trying to ease everyone's concern.

"Is it about Lance Ralley? Marco and Trevor haven't gotten back to me about him yet, but Lee said he hasn't uncovered anything negative about him or Earth Paradise."

"What's all this?" Mom asked.

I glared at Brady, punching him on the arm before reaching up to flick his ear. He tucked it up against his shoulder, hiding it from me with a grin. "Sorry, I didn't know you hadn't said anything."

"There's a man who wants to buy my recipes and produce them for grocery stores," I said.

Mom and Dad looked stunned.

"Well…that's…that's…" Mom blustered away, but it was Dad who filled in the missing words.

"That's wonderful, Cassidy," he said. "What's the offer look like?"

I shrugged. "I don't know yet. Brady was having him checked out before I agreed to meet with him again. I'm not sure I could even manage it on top of everything else."

Chevelle came running over with Molly chasing him. He landed in my lap, and I tugged him up into my arms. He put his chubby hand covered in dog slobber on my cheek, and I tried desperately not to react. "Mama, I hungry."

Tristan laughed. "Me too, my friend, me too." She looked at Brady. "When's the food getting here?"

Brady left my side and was at Tristan's in a heartbeat, kissing her belly, tugging her hand into his. "It should be here any minute."

All through high school and college, I'd never really cared if my friends had a boyfriend and I didn't. I'd been focused on getting through school with grades I could stomach even when learning came hard. I'd also understood I was the tall, gangly friend who hadn't come into her own and would never lose her awkwardness. I knew I wasn't ugly, and I didn't dwell on my looks a lot, but I also hadn't expected guys to come running after me. I'd been okay with being on my own. But somewhere between the casual screwing I'd done with Clayton and now, I'd found myself aching for someone to be mine in the way Tristan was Brady's.

The way Marco had pulled me into his arms the day before, declaring me his with a possessive growl, had been everything I wanted, even when I'd known he was saying it for Clayton's benefit. I wanted it to be true. I wanted Marco to be my boyfriend.

But it was impossible, for all the reasons we both knew.

I was his boss's sister. I was too busy with a restaurant and a toddler who already didn't get enough of my time to even consider a relationship. It would be unfair to any man to try and fit him into the tiny, free moments I had. And yet, I couldn't stop my soul from wishing for it.

Before I could lose myself in another woe-is-me moment that I was so unused to dwelling on, the doorbell rang, the food was delivered, and we were all sidetracked by dinner. But later, after I'd tucked Chevelle into his crib, with Hippo clutched tight to his chest, the ache came back. The loneliness returned, and my thoughts drifted back to Marco.

I pulled my phone from my pajama pocket and hovered a finger over the call button on his contact information, worry and want warring inside me.

Then, I placed the phone on the charger next to my bed, pulled the covers over my head, and pretended to lose myself to sleep.

Chapter Eight

Marco

WHISKEY SUNRISE
Performed by Chris Stapleton

I shook Jonas's shoulder gently, and he sprang to his feet, alert, as if he was warding off an attack, before his shoulders slumped, realizing it was just me.

Before today, I hadn't seen Maliyah or Jonas since right after Thanksgiving. Six months. Too long. In that time, Jonas had grown another two inches, so he was now six feet tall. His once scrawny shoulders had started to fill out as if he'd been lifting weights, but there was still an awkwardness to him because he hadn't finished growing into his size thirteen feet yet. His soft-brown hair needed a cut, and the edges were curling over his ears in a gentle wave that some teenage girl was sure to find as swoony as the dark-green depths of his eyes.

"Let's go back to the house," I told him quietly.

He glanced to where Maliyah was sleeping, her wrinkled face slouched in a slumber that actually made her look older rather than younger. When she was awake, she was almost always smiling. Add that to the ever-present twinkle in her hazel eyes, and it usually cut a decade off of her. Now, it was clear gravity and life had taken their toll. The gray was showing at her roots she normally kept dyed a brilliant chestnut, and her lean body seemed to have less muscle than I was used to seeing her with. She'd always been fit and thin, but now she just looked frail.

Jonas and I made our way out of the hospital, leaving behind the antiseptic smell and beeping machines to be thrust into the heat, humidity, and noise of a city that had come alive on a Saturday night. We weren't that far away from the music clubs that would be swarming with people ready to get their fill of drinks and dancing. I could almost feel the bass of the music drifting through the cement and over the air to us.

We crammed our tall frames into the subcompact rental car I'd picked up at the airport. It felt like a piece of shit after driving the Escalades and Cadillacs that littered Brady's detail, but it was enough to get us from the hospital to Maliyah's home that sat just past the old district and the freeway. It was an area of town filled with the community Maliyah loved. The people who were like family.

To some, her house might have looked rundown. It needed a paint job, and the grass was practically dead, but I knew the inside would be spick and span. It would smell like the Pine-Sol she cleaned with as well as the sea of spices she used when cooking.

"Want to tell me why you think she was stressed enough to cause another cardiomyopathy episode?" I asked as I dumped my duffel at the foot of the stairs. I wanted to hear it from him and not just Maliyah. I wanted him to get the weight off his chest so I could reassure him that the blame wasn't his.

Tripped by Love

Jonas ran a hand through his shaggy waves, looked down and then out, and finally, with shoulders sagging, said, "She was upset with some of the people I've been hanging out with." He sank onto the steps. "I... This is my fault."

I sat down next to him. "I'm the one who broke her heart first, Jonas. You being a normal teen, getting up to normal mischief...that isn't what did it."

He looked up at me, wide-eyed, and we bonded over shared guilt and grief.

"She wants you to come to Grand Orchard with me for the summer," I told him, and his face shuttered like blinds being drawn to hide the fear he felt at being sent away. Afraid of being passed once again from home to home. "It's not because she doesn't want you. But she's going to a rehab clinic for a few weeks, and then she's going to live with Maria Carmen for a few more. I think knowing you're with someone who will care about you will make her feel better. Will allow her to concentrate on getting stronger so you can be together again when the school year starts."

We'd sent Jonas out to get food for us while Maliyah and I had talked. She needed to get her full range of motion back on her left side and needed to make sure her heart was back in line before she'd be able to come home. Even then, we were both worried that Child Protective Services might flip out about her health and take Jonas away completely. It would be the worst thing possible for him, especially if, like she and he had both told me, he'd already gotten in with the wrong crowd.

"I can help her here. I can cook and clean. Hell, I'll even mow the goddamn lawn. She's been asking me to. I just got caught up with the end-of-the-year stuff," he said, bargaining to stay, his fears from his childhood coming back to haunt him.

I brushed his shoulder.

"This isn't because of anything you did or didn't do, Jo-Jo."

He grimaced at the nickname. My guess was he thought he was too old for it. What I wouldn't give to have my mom call me *peque* one more time. At fifteen, I'd always turned a famous shade of red when she said it anywhere outside the confines of our house.

"What the hell would I do in Grand Orchard?" he scoffed.

"I have a TV and a game box, just like you do here," I teased, bumping his shoulder. "I'm sure Brady could find something to keep you busy at the studio."

His eyes lit up at the idea, but he tried not to show it. He'd been messing around with a guitar on his own for a while now. He'd had a few private lessons and had been playing in the school band up until Christmas. Maliyah said he'd dropped it in order to pick up an art class instead. Either way, Brady and Tristan would likely be a good influence on him in a way I'd never be. Knowing both of them, they'd let Jonas into their studio with open arms because they loved talking about the art they created.

Jonas's phone buzzed for the millionth time since I'd arrived this morning with little sleep and a heart full of anguish. He glanced down at it. I was pretty sure it was someone he liked in the want-to-kiss-you kind of way, because he had that look on his face. Enthralled. Anxious.

"I can't leave," he said, shaking his head.

"Someone counting on you?" I asked, shifting my head toward the phone.

His eyes hit the door and then the ground before he shrugged. "She'd say no if you asked her. She's got a boyfriend…but he's no good, Marco. I know he'll talk her into…" He trailed off, eyes pained, heart on his sleeve.

"Your being here isn't going to stop that," I said quietly.

He grimaced. "I know. I just…want to be here if I have to pick up the pieces, you know?"

I got to my feet, picked up my bag, and then looked back down at him. "Just give it some thought. I'm worried that if CPS catches wind of this, they'll stick you somewhere else until *Tia* gets back on her feet. I'd rather you be with me than anywhere else."

I didn't mean it as a threat, but I could see it struck him that way when it hit him that he could end up in a group home while Maliyah healed. He'd been bounced around for a year after he'd been taken from his mom before ending up with Maliyah, and now he'd been with her for eight years. She would have adopted him by now if Jonas hadn't been waiting, with some twisted hope, for his mom to get out of jail.

I left him to his thoughts, knowing that if I pushed, it would just send him barreling away, and headed up the stairs. The room Maliyah had set aside for me had never really felt like mine even when it was littered with things that belonged to me. Since leaving for basic training, I'd been back here infrequently—bouts of days or weeks. Since joining Garner Security, I'd been back even less. I always took the holiday shifts so people with parents and siblings, or spouses and children, could spend the time they needed with their loved ones. It wasn't that I didn't care about Maliyah and Jonas. It was just that I knew they didn't need me. Maliyah had made a family for herself long before I'd come around, and they were always there for her and Jonas whether I was there or not.

The twin bed felt too small when I crashed down onto it. I took my phone out to charge it and accidentally thumbed open the messages. Cassidy's note was the last one I'd received. The one where she'd asked how I was doing. I hadn't known what to tell her. Hadn't known if I should have told her the truth, which was that I felt responsible and sad and was aching to return to her and Grand Orchard. I felt like I was abandoning her right as Chevelle's asshole father had shown up, but I also felt like I couldn't leave before things were settled here. I'd regret that just as much as not being there for her.

I was torn in a way I hadn't been since the night I'd refused to conduct the code red my commanding officer had handed down to me. Body split with loyalty going in two directions.

I shook my head away from that thought and back to the message sitting on my phone. It had been shitty to not respond when she'd put herself out there, especially when I'd been the one to blur the lines we'd established.

I tapped open the message box.

> *ME: Sorry. There was a lot going on. Don't worry about me. I'm fine.*

It was then that I looked at the time and grimaced. It was ten o'clock here in Texas. That meant it was eleven there, and she'd be in bed, trying to get some sleep before starting her day at four-thirty again. I hoped she had the phone on silent.

I felt worse when she responded.

> *ANGEL: I'd be lying if I said I wasn't worried.*
>
> *ME: I'm sorry. You were probably sleeping. Go back to bed.*
>
> *ANGEL: I was in bed, but I wasn't sleeping.*

That hit me in all the wrong ways, making me hard and uncomfortable. The idea of her in bed…long limbs tangled in sheets, wide awake. The things I wanted to do to her in those sheets. The places on her body I wanted to kiss her.

> *ME: Did Clayton bother you again?*
>
> *ANGEL: No. I haven't seen him since yesterday. He said he wouldn't be back until summer term started. I just have a lot on my mind. The offer from Ralley and feeling guilty about not having enough time for Chevelle. And this…friend…of mine whose foster mom is in the hospital. I've been worried about him.*

I inhaled sharply.

> *ME: Is that what we are? Friends?*

I shouldn't have asked. I knew it. Fucking blurring the lines even more.

> *ANGEL: I like to think so. But maybe I'm just your latest project?*

I could see the hurt in her golden eyes even when she wasn't there. I knew her chin would go up, and her shoulders would go back. If I was right in front of her, she'd try to hide. But then, if I was in front of her, I highly doubted she would have said any of this to me.

ME: You've never been a project.

ANGEL: Then, what does that leave?

It was a dangling dare left for me to pick up. One I couldn't pick up. So many reasons not to left hanging between us.

ME: Friends. We're friends.

It hurt to lower the wall even this much, because I was afraid that once I gave a little, the rest would come tumbling down after it, including all the emotions I had hidden behind it.

ANGEL: Well, friend, if I don't try to get some zzz's I'm not going to be able to function at the restaurant tomorrow.

I hated that I'd kept her this long, even if it was clear she'd already been awake.

ME: Sleep well.

ANGEL: Marco?

ME: Yeah?

ANGEL: Never mind…just…sleep well, too.

It was going to eat away at me a little, not knowing what she'd really wanted to say, just like the night before when I'd left her house. We weren't close enough for her to bare her soul, but it was all I wanted her to do. I wanted every little thought. Every concern. Every smile.

Then, I thought of Jonas, and his buzzing phone, and the girl he liked who had a boyfriend, and I chuckled. He and I weren't as far apart as I sometimes felt.

♪ ♪ ♪

When Jonas and I got to the hospital the next day, Maliyah was sitting up with knitting needles in her hands while trying to demonstrate something to Maria Carmen who was at her bedside. Maria Carmen had aged more gracefully than Maliyah. Her black hair was hardly streaked with gray, and her tan skin was almost wrinkleless, whereas Maliyah's hair that had once been a deep auburn bordering on chestnut had very little left that wasn't gray when it wasn't dyed, and her wrinkles were deep and lined. I didn't know if the differences were on account of their genetics or if it was the lives they'd led.

Maliyah had been in and out of foster homes from the time she was five. She'd been taken away from her parents who'd been drug dealers. One of the last foster homes she'd been at had been next door to Maria Carmen's house, and the two women had become fast friends. So much so that Maliyah had lived with Maria Carmen's family her last year of high school and right on through college where she got her degree in social work.

"Until you can knit without dropping a stitch again, you're staying with me, end of story," Maria Carmen huffed. Her eyes caught sight of us and lit up. "*Mijos!*"

She came over and patted me on the cheek before slinging her arm around Jonas's shoulders. "You ate last night?"

I held back my snort.

"Yes, *Tía*," Jonas said, and he didn't hold back his eye roll.

"Don't you worry about Maliyah. We are going to have her on her feet and running wild before you know it," Maria Carmen said, giving Maliyah a warm smile.

Jonas disentangled himself from Maria Carmen and went to Maliyah's bedside. "You want me to go with Marco?"

Maliyah's eyes shot to me and then back to Jonas. She patted his hand, and when she talked, one side of her mouth was stiffer than the other. Not quite keeping up. It could have been so much worse—the stroke and her heart stopping—but it was still the second occurrence of cardiomyopathy in less than eight years.

"I'll be at the rehab clinic for a while," she said.

"I can stay at the house on my own. I'm not a baby," he said, but the tone almost belied his words.

My phone buzzed.

> *TREVOR: Everything is good here. Stop worrying.*

I wanted to laugh because he knew me well enough to know it had been the first thing on my mind this morning. Brady's detail. His family counting on me. Cassidy.

ME: Thanks. I'm hoping to be home soon.

Austin was where the people who knew me best were at—or at least the people who knew my history. All of it. The good and the ugly. Yet, I couldn't help feeling like Grand Orchard really was my home.

I sent the next text before I could stop myself, repeating Trevor's words to Cassidy.

ME: Stop worrying about me. I'm fine.

ANGEL: You really mean fine as in faking-it-so-nobody-sees-the-pain, right? I know that kind of fine.

I snorted, and it drew the eyes in the room to me. Maliyah's knowing ones lit up.

"Who you texting?" she asked.

"Trevor…about the detail," I said, shoving the phone away.

I couldn't get her hopes up. There would never be anything between Cassidy and me. Nothing more than this little bit of friendship we'd carved out.

Chapter Nine

Cassidy

THE WAY YOU TAKE TIME
Performed by Joe Buck

Irma was chasing Chevelle around the displays in Sweet Lips, and he was giggling. Her gray hair was sticking up at odd angles as if she'd been pulling at it all day. That usually meant she was trying to decide which inventory to rotate out of her antique shop down the street.

It was Tuesday, and I'd spent the majority of the day catching up on household chores, playing with Chevelle, and doing some of the restaurant business that I could do from home while Chevelle had napped. Closing the restaurant one day a week was the only way I'd kept my sanity in the last two years. But it was never enough time to feel like my long list of to-dos was shortening.

I watched with a smile as I handed Helen a check across the counter. Helen was a soft, round ball of goodness, just like her baked goods. When I'd first opened The Golden Heart Café, I'd arranged for all the sweets to be from her bakery and concentrated on the other menu items. But over the last two years, I'd slowly started making a lot of things on my own, and now our roles were almost reversed—she included many of my baked goods in her display cases. But somehow, I'd never been able to master the creation of pies, and Helen's were the only ones I served at my place.

Helen's daughter, Belle, poked her head out of the back. "Is that Chevelle's sweet giggle I hear?"

She came around the counter, and Chevelle gave up on Irma to run to Belle, knowing she'd give him a treat. Almost every store owner on Main Street knew Chevelle's weaknesses. Irma was always sending over stuffed animals she found in her picking efforts across the state. Her husband, Floyd, was always carving him simple toys. Helen and Belle were always giving him soft candies. Even Patty at the hair salon knew that Chevelle liked animals and had a special cape she'd bought just for him when she trimmed his hair.

My heart swelled. There were a lot of people who would have found the familiarity of a small town frustrating—invasive. For me, it felt like we were surrounded in love. A cushion that could catch us if we fell. People who had, quite literally, picked me up off the ground before when I'd stumbled.

My phone buzzed.

MARCO: How was your day?

My heart flipped. Such an innocuous question and yet one that lit me up, making my stomach curl with joy. Since he'd left on Friday, Marco and I had been texting almost daily. At first, it had been stilted, as if neither of us was sure how to proceed, but then it had eased into a friendliness that had been addicting. I was constantly stopping myself from sending him a new one.

> ME: *Tuesdays are always a blessing. We're at Sweet Lips, at the moment.*
>
> MARCO: *Did Belle give him a caramel or fudge?*

I smiled, loving that he knew exactly what my world looked like.

> ME: *Fudge. How was Maliyah's day?*
>
> MARCO: *They moved her to the rehab clinic.*
>
> ME: *That's good news, right?*
>
> MARCO: *Yep. For her. But I'm not sure the people at the clinic agree. You should have seen the way she was ordering them around.*

I laughed. From the little things he'd said, I imagined Maliyah as one of those people who whipped everyone around them into shape with a smile, a tease, and a firm hand.

"Who's put that beautiful smile on your face?" Irma asked.

I looked up at her, flushing. Embarrassed for a reason I couldn't explain. Like a teenager who'd been caught staring at her high school crush.

"No one," I said, shoving the phone in my pocket.

"Ooh, Cassidy has a secret boyfriend," Irma told the others.

Belle looked over with a wide smile. "You do? You can tell us. Who is it?"

"It's Assad, right?" Helen said with a dreamy look on her face. Assad was my brother's public relations manager. He was dark from head to toe, always had a perfect drop fade with curls on top, and wore designer clothes that would make a fashion model drool. He also had enough energy and charisma to charm the shyest of people into talking. Helen was old enough to be his mom if not his grandma, but she adored him. Literally fawned over him whenever he was in town to meet with Brady. He lived in New York City the rest of the time and wasn't likely to ever make a small town like Grand Orchard his home.

"It isn't Assad. I promise, he's all yours," I told Helen, and Belle laughed.

"Don't encourage her," Belle said, shoving a shoulder gently into her mom's.

"Okay, Snickerdoodle," I said, bending down to pick up Chevelle. "We gotta jam from this pop stand and get you home for dinner and a bath."

His face and fingers were covered with chocolate fudge.

Belle laughed again. Something you heard a lot when you were in Sweet Lips.

"Sorry. Here," she said, handing me a napkin.

I wiped the majority of it from his face as I headed for the door, calling back, "Thanks, everyone! I'll see you later."

My phone was buzzing again, and I waited until I had Chevelle tucked into his car seat before looking at it.

BRADY: Lee set up a meeting with Lance

Ralley, our lawyers, and his people for next Tuesday. That'll work for you, right?

My heart stutter-stopped, worry and nervousness flooding my veins. Even taking the meeting seemed like a huge step toward a big, black unknown. A doorway into a world I couldn't see, had never imagined, and wasn't sure I wanted. Lee had said that Lance and Earth Paradise seemed on the up and up. The company was growing and was known for giving back to conservation and global warming charities.

ME: It's fine. Thank you for setting it up.

It was just another thing I owed my brother for. I was grateful—overwhelmingly so—but felt like such a user. As if I was a leech, doing nothing but draining him. It wasn't true, and if I'd been able to do the same for him, I would have. But Brady would never need anything from me. He had more money than most people could imagine, a family who loved him, and a team of people that looked after his every need.

BRADY: Stop beating yourself up. I didn't do anything. I made a couple of calls.

ME: I wouldn't have this opportunity to begin with if you hadn't funded The Golden Heart for me.

BRADY: I feel the need to tickle you until you scream, "Give!" Don't be ridiculous. I'm glad to be able to do something for my family. Mom and Dad don't let me do diddly-squat. What else am I supposed to do with the gazillions I've got squirreled away?

ME: Give it to charity.

BRADY: I do that too. A lot. Dani and Nash have been able to quadruple the number of families that From the Ashes has trained and relocated because of me.

ME: Way to be humble.

BRADY: You started it.

ME: I gotta get home before Mom flips her lid, thinking I crashed and am lying in a ditch somewhere.

BRADY: Shit. Go.

I put the phone in the center console and drove home, talking with Chevelle the whole way about nonsense. About Hippo and dogs and what we were having for dinner.

Mom was waiting on the back porch when I pulled in, and I barely resisted banging my head on the steering wheel. If I did, she'd definitely think something was wrong. As I opened the door, she crossed the yard to lift Chevelle from his seat.

"*Mhamó!*" Chevelle said, using the Irish form of grandmother that she'd taught him as he snuggled against her chest. My boy gave the best snuggles.

She kissed the top of his head and smiled over at me. "He's covered in chocolate."

"Belle," I said by way of explanation. "What's up?"

"You rarely leave the house on Tuesdays. Just making sure everything is good."

She followed me in the back door, setting Chevelle on the floor and watching as he removed his shoes with a toddler-like clumsiness.

"Mom—" I started, only to have her cut me off.

"I know. I'm overbearing, overprotective, and worry too much. I am trying. It's just a twenty-five-year-old habit that's hard to break," she said softly.

It was a huge acknowledgment for her. It tugged at my insides to know she was at least trying to stop treating me like I was fragile and would break if the wind hit me the wrong way.

My phone buzzed again, and I glanced down, expecting it to be Brady. A little thrill went through me when I saw Marco's name again.

> *MARCO: Speaking of ordering people around. You were out on a Tuesday when you normally stay home. Did this make Arlene call the National Guard?*

I couldn't help the gurgle of laughter that escaped me. Mom's eyes narrowed.

"Just Brady," I lied before she made more of it than I wanted, even though my entire being was filled with joy at his simple words—the tease.

"Okay, well, I'm off. I'll see you both in the morning." She kissed Chevelle, patted me on the shoulder, and headed out the back door toward their house. The gate swung shut behind her, and I shot off a return text.

> *ME: It was a close call.*

For the next few hours, the smile Marco had brought stayed on my face. I made Chevelle and myself dinner, gave him a bath, and rocked in the glider while reading his favorite stories and letting his sweet essence surround me. I wished that instead of having one day off, I had twenty. That I wasn't always handing him off to someone. And yet, I was also eager to get back to the restaurant to create more recipes. I'd had a new idea for a cookie flitting around at the back of my brain after paying Helen for her caramel apple pie. It would take quite a few rounds before I could perfect it, which only ended up making me feel guilty again because my brain had flowed away from Chevelle even when I had so little time with him.

I kissed his sweet cheek, ruffled his hair, and made sure he had Hippo tucked up against him before shutting off the light and leaving the room with the baby monitor in hand.

I changed into my workout clothes and hit the treadmill for a few minutes, my brain flying away with ways to make the cookies without the apples making them soggy before it traveled into thoughts of the bills at the restaurant, Ralley's upcoming meeting, and Marco's family. When my phone rang, I was shocked to see I'd been on the treadmill for almost forty minutes.

Marco's face on my screen surprised me even more.

"Hey," I said, trying to control my breathing as I stepped off the machine.

"Weren't you done?" he asked.

"I lost track of time on the treadmill."

"What are you concerned about?" he asked, causing my breath to catch.

"How do you do that?" I asked when I knew I shouldn't have. I knew I should have simply answered the question rather than dig into how he knew me so well.

"Do what?"

"Read me…" My throat closed, and I changed the meaning mid-sentence. "Read people…so easily."

He was quiet for a long moment before he let out his response with a breath of air that felt like he'd had to force himself to answer. "I pay attention, that's all."

"Did the military teach you that?"

More silence, and I wondered if I'd crossed one step too far past the new line we'd drawn in the sand. It almost brought tears to my eyes, because I didn't want him to retreat because of it. I didn't want the stupid, mundane texts we'd been sending each other to stop, because they felt like the only thing I did for myself.

"My mom used to say I was good at it, too—seeing beyond what people were saying. But, yeah, my time with the Navy and with Garner Security has added to it."

"Navy? I thought you were a Marine?"

"I was a Fleet Marine Force corpsman. It's basically a medic. The Marines don't have their own. They use Navy personnel," he replied. His voice sounded pained, like talking about it was opening an old wound.

"You don't talk about your time in the military at all."

To be fair, he didn't talk about anything from his life.

"It isn't a happy memory," he finally replied. "I

choose not to dwell on it."

"That's how you know so much about anatomy, then?" I asked, trying to learn more but also trying to allow him to drift away from a topic that felt painful.

"Yes. At one point in my life, I thought I'd be a doctor."

It felt like Marco been built to be a protector. To stand guard, watching over people. But I supposed, if he'd been a doctor, he still would have had lives in his hands.

"When you got out, why didn't you go to medical school?" I asked.

"My priorities had changed. I needed…" His voice faded away. "I wanted different things."

I wasn't going to get him to uncover those secrets tonight. Not yet. Maybe not ever. But I hoped someday he'd trust me with even more of his truths.

There was a muffled conversation on his end before he came back. "Jonas has informed me he's going to waste away to skin and bones if I don't go feed him."

A boyish tenor spoke over him. "I simply said I was hungry."

A chuckle escaped me at the tease Marco had made as well as the response. An insight into Marco that no one but me had been given the privilege of seeing. Finding out about his foster brother had been one of the surprises our daily texts had provided, and this insight into him as an older brother flipped my heart more. Drawing me in. Enticing me.

I finally breathed out, "Have a good night, Marco."

"You too, Angel."

And then he hung up before I could really register the nickname. The sweet term of endearment that had slipped from his lips as if he'd said it a million times. My heart stalled and then started again at a clip that had nothing to do with my workout and everything to do with a serious man who was thousands of miles away.

Chapter Ten

Marco

THE THING THAT WRECKS YOU
Performed by Lady A

My heart beat wildly as I hung up, realizing the name that had slipped out of my mouth. The endearment that I hadn't earned the right to use. It was how I had her logged in my phone because she'd seemed that way from the very first moment I'd seen her, covered in snowflakes and twirling in the backyard at eighteen. I'd only been twenty-three, new to Brady's detail and Garner Security, but even then, I'd known enough to deny the immediate attraction I'd felt to the glowing apparition blending in with the snow. She'd seemed like she'd been sent from heaven to surround everyone in light, whereas I'd been covered in shame and regret from my court-martial.

As I'd watched her spin that day, she'd fallen to the ground and pretended it was on purpose, making snow angels. Arlene had hustled out the back door to check on her, and I hadn't understood why until later. I hadn't learned about her history and her parents' overprotectiveness until I'd spent months with Brady.

"Angel, huh?" Jonas said, drawing me away from my memories. There was a smirk on his face that I ignored completely.

"Are we ordering pizza or going down to the taqueria?" I asked.

"I guess the taqueria since we just had pizza yesterday? But no one's Mexican food is ever as good as Maliyah's or Maria Carmen's," he said.

I agreed. Maliyah may not have been Mexican, but she'd learned to cook all the classics in Maria Carmen's home, growing up. There was something in the food they made that was always missing from the meals I got from restaurants. The only food to ever come close was what I ate at Cassidy's place, which was decidedly un-Mexican but still had that missing quality. Like there'd been some kind of warmth and love infused into it while it was being made.

Jonas and I left the rental car at the house and walked the few blocks to a strip mall where Vazquez's Taqueria was crammed into a corner unit. The place was barely big enough to seat a couple of people inside, which didn't really matter because it was mostly known for its takeout.

We'd just ordered when a body slammed into Jonas, making my hand go for a gun that was locked away in the gun safe at Maliyah's. The tension left my body as I realized it was a teenage girl and not a bigger threat.

"Jonas!" she said before squeezing him tighter and then letting him go. She was a stunning young woman. Dark skin and soft spirals of black hair drifting away from her face with a volume that might seem untamed but instead looked like a masterpiece. Her brown eyes were large, warm, and framed in huge lashes. She was probably close to Jonas's age but had an aura of strength about her that made me think she'd be blazing trails in her not-too-distant future.

"Mel!" Jonas flushed a thousand shades of red at the physical touch and sort of jerked away from her.

The girl looked up at me and stuck out her hand, completely unfazed by Jonas's awkwardness. "You must be Marco."

I shook her hand, trying not to smirk. "Last I checked, that was me."

She laughed and then turned back to Jonas. "You really leaving for the summer?"

He shrugged, looking down at his feet. "Seems like it. But we aren't going yet. Not for a couple of days, right, Marco?"

I gave a curt nod.

"Carmella!" a voice growled behind us, and we flipped around to find a guy walking toward us. I wanted to call him a teenager because he couldn't have been more than eighteen, but he definitely had the swagger of someone much older. There was a look in his eyes that talked of knowledge beyond his years and a toughness to him that screamed from his veins. He was muscled, tattooed, and wore a tank top that showed off both. He had a beanie on his brown hair and a nose ring that glinted above a mouth framed in stubble.

He wasn't happy to see Mel with us. He draped an arm around her shoulder, pulling her up tight against him, and I saw her vivaciousness and energy slip away—submission that shouldn't have been there in anyone, let alone someone so young.

"Who's this?" he asked with a narrowed look in my direction.

I was pretty sure the guy was packing heat

underneath the tank top. The shape was barely perceptible from where it was shoved into his jeans at the front, and I suddenly wished for my guns that I'd stupidly left in the safe at Maliyah's.

"This is Jonas's brother, Marco," she said.

The boy-man didn't offer his hand.

"And you are?" I asked, lifting an eyebrow, widening my stance as I crossed my arms over my chest.

"What's it to you?" he demanded.

Mel rolled her eyes. "This is Artie."

"Arthur," he corrected her. He gave me a once-over and then dismissed me in a way I hadn't been dismissed in a long time, especially not from some teen punk who thought his shit didn't stink. "We gotta jam. Smokey expected us a half an hour ago."

She shifted, uncomfortable.

"You could stay and have dinner with us," Jonas offered, and when I looked at my foster brother, his eyes were hard, hands fisted tight, stance as wide as my own.

"No, she really can't, asshat," Arthur spoke for her in a way that raised every hair on the back of my neck.

"I think the girl can speak for herself," I said.

Arthur's eyes narrowed again, his hand settling on the piece hidden below his tank.

Mel seemed to read all the tension and put a hand on Arthur's chest as if to reassure him. "I'm coming. I just wanted to say hi to Jonas before he took off for the summer."

Arthur's eyes flew to Jonas, and some of the tension seemed to leave his shoulders. He lifted his chin in Jo-Jo's direction. "Yeah. I heard. Have a good vacation."

Then, he pulled Mel's fingers into his hand and started tugging her away. She looked back at us with a large smile and waved. "Bye, Jonas. Nice to meet you, Marco!"

Jonas deflated once she was gone.

"He's bad news," I said.

"That's what I was telling you. Who's going to be here for her when all hell breaks loose?"

I had no doubts that taking him to Grand Orchard was the right move now that I'd seen Arthur and Mel together. If he stayed this summer, unsupervised, as Maliyah healed, he'd be heading right into the middle of that shit, trying to protect a girl who seemed to understand what she was getting into. Would I like to pull her away from it? Sure. Would I like to shield her from the darkness she was bringing to her door as much as Jo-Jo wanted to? Damn straight, I would. But I wasn't her parent, her bodyguard, or her friend. She'd have to rely on those people to look out for her. I already had one too many people on my list to try and cover.

It didn't stop me from feeling guilty, though, which was probably only a tenth of what Jonas felt. He was quiet on the way home, quiet while we ate, and then said he was going to sleep, hours before I knew he really would.

"Jo-Jo," I said as his feet hit the bottom step. He looked back at me, and I spoke the truth. "I know you want to keep her safe, but there's nothing you can do for her if she's chosen this path. You being at her side is only going to provoke him to take things out on you both."

"So, I should just slink away? Hide like I'm afraid. Is that what you did? When your captain gave you that order and you refused?"

It hit me so hard in the chest that I was left speechless. I hadn't thought Jonas knew what had happened when I'd been court-martialed. I'd thought, at eight, dealing with his own transition into Maliyah's home and his past running rampant through his nightmares, that my issues had gone unnoticed—at least until Maliyah had her first takotsubo cardiomyopathy episode. Till I'd literally caused her broken heart.

When I didn't answer, he just stormed up the stairs away from me.

For the first time in my life, I wanted to talk about it. I wanted to seek solace from someone who might have actually understood what had happened. The choices I'd made. I laughed at myself sarcastically. Who was I kidding? What I truly sought was absolution. Forgiveness. I'd made a mistake that night. I'd miscalculated the strength of the anger and humiliation of the team. I'd thought my saying no would be enough to stop the ball from rolling downhill. It hadn't.

I hit call before I really realized it, aching for something light and good. Aching for a joy that filled the air when Cassidy O'Neil walked into a room.

"Hi, again," she said. It was the second time I'd called her tonight. What a moron I was, pushing forward instead of retreating. Loving the sound of her silky voice when I shouldn't. Just hearing it was like putting a salve over the wounds that Jonas had broken free. "Marco?"

I finally spoke. "Hey. Sorry. Were you getting

ready for bed?"

God, the thought did all the wrong things to me. Just like it had the first night here, when I'd texted and she'd said she was in bed but not sleeping.

"What's wrong? Is it Maliyah?" she asked, reading the bleakness of my tone even though I'd tried to hide it.

"Maliyah's good. At least, she was when we left her," I said, battling my emotions, trying to force them back behind the barrier, failing and floundering a bit.

I eased open the back door and sank onto the stoop. The noise of the city filled the air, even at night. A rev of an engine. A car horn. So far removed from the quiet of the orchards that I'd run through back in Grand Orchard.

My silence leached into the phone, taking her normally happy voice and littering it with the ache of my own when she asked, "Is it Jonas?"

It was, and it wasn't.

"He's gotten hooked up with some bad characters."

"Oh no. I'm sure that's hard for you. Especially when everything you do is so…honorable."

I closed my eyes against her words. "I would never use that word to describe myself."

"What? Marco, you have to be the most upstanding human being I know. Look what you do for all of us every day? Shielding us. Protecting us. Look at how you took on working out with me just because you saw someone who needed the help."

I wished my motives had been that innocent when it came to her. I'd wanted them to be that simple. Looking out for her. Helping her strengthen her muscles so Brady and her mom and everyone in her world would see her in the same shiny light that I did. But the truth was, I'd wanted to be near her almost as much as I'd wanted to help her.

"Marco? Talk to me," she said softly.

I groaned. This was ridiculous. I was acting like that fifteen-year-old kid I'd been when I'd first realized I was alone, crying and bemoaning my fate, wallowing in self-pity. That wasn't who I was.

"Being in Austin…just reminds me of things I don't want to remember."

It was her turn to be quiet for a moment, as if she was taking in each word carefully, considering them like she did her ingredients before mixing them into something new and healthy and delicious. I wanted to be mixed by her into something new that could sheer away the layers of my past and let me leave them behind.

"There's one thing that I've learned over the years in dealing with my condition," Cassidy said without an ounce of self-pity in her voice. "Pretending something isn't real won't ever help. It usually just ends up with a pile of broken skin and bones. Or… in your case, maybe hearts and souls?"

My chest felt heavy and twisted. I'd broken Maliyah's heart, and Cassidy didn't even know that, but she'd still used the words.

"Do you know what takotsubo cardiomyopathy is?" I asked.

"No."

"It's when stress puts so much pressure on the heart that it stuns part of it into not working. It's literally a broken heart."

She inhaled. "Is this what Maliyah has?"

"Yes. But it isn't the first time she's had it happen. The first time was when I was court-martialed," I told her.

"I can't...I can't even imagine you doing anything to have been court-martialed," she said, and my soul leaped at those words, wishing they were true. That I could be as bright and shiny as she imagined me. A knight in silver armor, carrying a sword to protect the kingdom.

"I deserved it, Cassidy. Don't ever think otherwise," I said, knowing I was being vague. Knowing that in not telling her the whole story, she'd be left to imagine the worst, but perhaps that was for the best. Maybe it would force her to push the barrier back up between us as I seemed unable to do.

"You'll never convince me of that," she said. "Even if you told me you killed someone, Marco, I'd know there was a good reason for it. That it was justified."

I snorted. I hadn't killed anyone. No one had died, even when Petty Officer Warren probably had moments when she wished she had. But after...I'd longed for the chance to mortally wound a few of them.

"I'm sorry I called. I shouldn't have. I'm not good company tonight," I told her.

"I, on the other hand, am really glad you called. I want to be here for you. Not only because you've done so much for me, but because...because that's what friends do for each other. Hold each other up when the other is falling down."

It caused tears to flood my eyes that I had no intention of letting out. I clenched my lids shut.

Fighting all of it. The emotions. The past. The way Cassidy's voice called to me and whispered things about a future I could dream about but never make happen.

Chapter Eleven

Cassidy

YEAH BOY
Performed by Kelsea Ballerini

My soul ached for days after Marco had told me about Maliyah, his court-martial, and the fact that he thought he broke her heart. The pain in his voice had traveled through me and lodged into my soul. The pain only increased when he returned to texting me instead of calling. I had a feeling it was to prevent himself from telling me more. From truly opening up to someone.

It weighed on me so heavily that it was hard to keep my cheery smile going. So much so that Brady noticed when he came by the restaurant's kitchen to drop Chevelle off on Friday.

"What's got you down, oh sister of mine?" he asked.

"Nothing."

"Don't lie to me. I'm not Mom," he said, leaning up against the wall, snapping his bracelets on his wrist.

"Mama, cookie!" Chevelle said, hands on the counter, standing on his tiptoes near the place where he knew the cookies were stored.

"Not until after dinner," I told him and handed him a slice of carrot that I'd been julienning.

"You've created a cookie monster," Brady said with a smile at Chevelle.

I tickled my boy under the armpits. "Are you a cookie monster?"

"Grrrrrr," he said, curling his little hands into claw-like shapes and tickling me back.

"Help, Brady, help!" I cried, sitting down on the floor so that Chevelle could attack me with ease. Little did he know that I wasn't ticklish.

"No way am I helping. You deserve all you get after the number of times you've flicked my ear." Brady's face broke into a huge smile.

Once Chevelle had tired of attacking me, he took himself off to the tiny, kid-sized table in the corner of the kitchen that was piled with coloring books just for him and these occasions when I had to finish up once Tristan or Brady dropped him off.

"What's really up?" Brady asked.

"Just a lot on my mind. The Earth Paradise offer, Marco, Chevelle." Marco's name slipped out before I realized it, but Brady narrowed in on it immediately.

"Marco? What do you know that I don't?"

"I just feel bad for him and his family, I guess."

"Family?"

My eyes widened, realizing I'd somehow let something slip that Marco hadn't told him.

"What did he tell you about his trip?" I asked cautiously.

"He told me he had to go home and take care of a

few things."

It broke my heart a little bit to know he'd left without telling anyone why he was really gone. Brady and Trevor were his friends just as much as they were his boss and coworker, and yet he hadn't felt like he could tell them these personal details of his life.

"Honestly, I didn't even think he had a family. I thought he was a lone wolf," Brady said.

I wanted to flick his ear and shove his shoulder but this time without the tease. With frustration that he could be so clueless. "He's worked for you for seven years, Brady. How can you not know he has a family?"

"Whenever I've asked, he's blown me off. We don't sit around braiding each other's hair and telling secrets."

"Remember that time you started braiding your hair?" I teased, trying to draw his attention away from Marco and the secrets I'd almost spilled unknowingly.

Brady rolled his eyes. "One time. It was one time."

I laughed.

Hannah skipped into the kitchen. Her paisley shawl flew out behind her, and one hand balanced the top hat on her head, making her look exactly like a miniature version of her musical hero, Stevie Nicks.

"Mom wants to know if we should walk home without you or if you're coming?" Hannah asked.

I wanted to laugh. There was no way Brady was letting his very pregnant wife walk home without him, regardless of the fact that they lived a mere two blocks away.

Which had me thinking of Marco again and the

way he protected everyone around him. And I wondered what had happened in the military to make him believe he had to be alone, shielding the world.

"I'm coming," Brady told her. He side-hugged me, kissed the top of Chevelle's head, and then they left with Chevelle shouting, "Bye, Nanah," after his cousin.

I washed my hands, finished cutting the vegetables, and then took us home.

♫ ♫ ♫

The weekend flew by as it always did with me working and Chevelle spending more time with my parents. With spring term officially over, he'd be spending most of his days with them now instead of Tristan and Brady.

The only thing different about my weekend compared to the rest of my days was the flow of text messages that had gone back and forth between Marco and me. We'd continued to check in with each other, asking about the things in our lives that had gone slightly off the rail. I'd ask about Maliyah and Jonas. He'd ask if I'd heard from Clayton—which I hadn't.

I'd just put Chevelle down and gone to put the latest trial batch of my salted-caramel apple cookies in the oven on Monday evening when I saw Marco driving into my parents' yard. My heart skipped a beat, and my body came alive, tingling as if he'd touched me. As if we were side by side with his penetrating gaze looking into mine.

I desperately wanted to run across the yard, fling my arms around him, and hug him until he lost his breath. I wanted to take the pain I'd heard in his voice when we'd talked and turn it into laughter. I needed him to know he had someone at his side who wasn't going to hold his past against him.

In truth, I ached to take the friendship we'd somehow crafted and grown over the last week and turn it into something more so that maybe, by the time Clayton Hardy showed up again at my door, Marco's words would be true.

Even as the hope blossomed inside me at the thought, I pushed it aside, reminding myself that Marco deserved more than the edges of my day. He deserved someone who put him first.

Knowing that didn't tame my body's reaction to him as he stepped out of the car with his dark hair gleaming in the last rays of the fading sunlight. His tan skin shimmered bronze even over the distance, calling to me just like his muscles did by rippling under a black T-shirt that gave a glimpse of his tattoo. Even when he wasn't on duty, Marco almost always wore black. I wasn't sure the man had another color in his wardrobe. Even his workout gear was the same shade.

I finished washing the bowl as the passenger door opened and another body emerged. Another male. Almost as tall as Marco but unlike him in any other way. He had light-brown hair, pale skin, and a lean frame. When he turned toward my house, I could see his face was much younger than his tall build would have you assume. The teenager, who had to have been Jonas, said something to Marco, and Marco laughed. An actual laugh. The ones that came so rarely that I kept them cataloged inside my heart like diamonds.

I ripped the dish gloves off my hands. Then, I grabbed one of the completed boxes of cookies and the baby monitor and headed out over my back lawn that needed mowing to the gate we'd installed leading to my parents' drive.

"Hey. Welcome home," I said softly, and both males' eyes settled on me.

Marco's dark ones took me in from head to toe, making my stomach swirl with need. Making my skin light up as if he'd touched me instead of just lingered over my workout gear hidden behind an apron. I flushed when I realized that, from the front, I might have looked like I had nothing on under the apron. A glance in Jonas's direction proved I was right, because his deep-green eyes widened, and his cheeks turned almost as pink as my own.

Marco took a step toward me, and his gaze was heated as it met mine. It was a steamy look that I wanted to be followed by him wrapping his strong arms around my middle and his firm mouth landing on mine. I wanted that so much the ache felt like it would leave my chest and brand itself on my face.

"Cassidy." Marco's voice was deep as always, maybe even a notch lower, and it made my skin break out in goosebumps. But it wasn't the 'Angel' he'd accidentally called me on the phone. That had been like hearing the gods call your name from on high.

"I made you cookies," I said, thrusting the box out. It wasn't really true. I'd made the cookies for the restaurant. It was my third batch that I was still trying to perfect. Caramel and apple dusted with salt instead of sugar. Using apples in cookies was always a challenge. They could end up too moist, doughy, but Marco was used to trying my experiments. He was my number one guinea pig, often arriving at night for our workouts after I'd just finished one of my test runs.

Marco took the box, and our fingers touched,

sending spirals of awareness through me and increasing the heat that pooled in my veins.

Jonas came around to the driver's side, crossed his arms, and stood shoulder to shoulder with Marco. There was a mere inch or two difference in their height. Jonas's lips quirked. "Who's this, Marco?"

Jonas's voice seemed to pull Marco from whatever spell had been cast over us. I sent the teenager a smile that caused his cheeks to flush even more.

"Cassidy, this is Jonas. Jonas, my…friend, Cassidy."

He hesitated over the word friend that we'd barely laid down between us. A word that should have been there long before this but was still new and had us trying to figure out how to fill in the meaning behind it.

I stuck my hand out to Jonas. He shook it, looking down at my outfit and then away.

I tugged at the apron. "Sorry for my ridiculous appearance. I was getting ready to work out but got sidetracked in the kitchen first."

Marco's lips twitched. An almost smile that flipped my heart.

"Cassidy owns a restaurant downtown and has some of the best food I've ever tasted," Marco told Jonas, but his eyes were still on me, sending me a message I wasn't sure he really intended.

Jonas laughed. "Wait till I tell Maliyah and Maria Carmen you said that. They'll be pissed."

"Language," Marco said, and he grabbed the boy in a headlock, knuckles rubbing the top of his head. Jonas groaned and fought the steely muscles that were sealed around him.

"Get off, you big goon."

The two struggled for a brief second before Marco released him. Jonas shoved his shoulder with a hand and then glanced at me and away again. The pink on his cheeks was still there.

"Let me get Jo-Jo settled in, and then I'll come over to work out," Marco said.

"Geez. Way to make it sound like I'm eight," Jonas groused.

Marco's lips twitched again.

"I'd like that," I said.

Then, I backed away and headed toward my house. I felt both their eyes on me as I walked away. It was so distracting I tripped over the back step and had to catch myself on the rail. "I'm fine," I hollered without looking back because I knew Marco would ask, but at least he wouldn't rush over and fawn all over me like Brady or Mom would.

"You are…I mean, glad to hear it," Marco's voice flew through the air, and when I turned back to see him, I could have sworn it was his turn to have red littering his cheeks.

My pulse quickened to an almost uncontrollable beat.

Inside the house, I took the last batch of cookies from the oven while continuing to clean some of the mess I'd made. I was almost done when the back door creaked open.

Marco was there, filling the space with his size and his aura and the smell that was nothing I'd ever experienced before him. Like a delightful mix of spices I couldn't quite figure out when I thought I knew them all.

The urge to hug him overwhelmed me again. To reassure him that whatever he'd been feeling over the last few days was valid and okay. I wanted him to know he didn't have to hide those emotions from me, but I didn't know how to take the friendly banter we'd had in our real lives and turn it into the something more that our phone calls had shared.

"I just need to glaze these real quick," I said, waving a thumb toward the rack.

"Don't you ever get tired of cooking?" he asked.

I smiled. "Honestly…not really."

He leaned against the archway to the living room, watching me as I moved about, whipping the caramel glaze into shape. I tried not to let the tremble his staring caused to show in my hands. We'd stared at each other a million times across a workout mat, but after all our more recent talks, this felt different. More personal, somehow. As if his gaze was sinking into my bones and spreading through my veins.

I brushed the icing lightly across the top of the cookies before sprinkling some sea salt on them. Then, I washed the bowl and threw the towel in the hamper in the laundry room off the kitchen all while Marco watched me.

"How does Jonas feel about having to come with you?" I asked.

His eyes traveled up and down my body. The apron was still hiding my shorts and most of my tank.

"After what I saw last week…I knew Maliyah was right. We had to get him out of Austin, but he isn't thrilled about it. I may have promised him some things I can't really guarantee."

"Like?"

"Time at the studio."

I laughed, and it caused him to frown.

"Marco, Brady would do anything for you. You realize that, right? He'd give Jonas his own album even if he had absolutely no talent."

Instead of making him feel better, this seemed to make him feel worse.

I took a step toward him but then remembered the stupid apron. I went to pull it off, but the string knotted behind me. I twisted, trying to pull at it, yanking, and having it tighten instead of loosen. Marco chuckled, the rumble coasting through the air, and before I could even really take it in, he'd moved to my side and was turning me with a hand on my waist so that he could see the tangled knot.

He bent to see the strings, and his warm breath journeyed across my neck and shoulders, making the goosebumps return. His hands stilled as if he'd seen my reaction, and I swore he inhaled a breath as if trying to catch my scent. My breasts turned taut, and my thighs clenched. It took everything I had to not push my hands into his thick black hair and tug his mouth to my skin.

His fingers worked the knot, and finally, the strings fell apart with the apron swinging away from my body. Only the rope at my neck kept it from hitting the ground. Marco's hands skated over both my arms as if smoothing the goosebumps, but it only caused them to increase. He pulled at the bow at my neck, and it came undone, falling completely. I caught the apron in my hands, turning to look over my shoulder.

"Thanks," I said quietly, our eyes meeting. Heat seared through us both. It wasn't one-sided, this craving I had. It filled him, too.

He reached up, tucking a strand of hair that had escaped my double buns behind my ear. His fingers lingered at the nape of my neck before landing on my shoulder. I ached for him to kiss me. For me to kiss him. For our mouths to devour each other. My eyes fell to his lips.

A little cry burst from the baby monitor. Chevelle calling my name.

I jumped back, Marco's hands fell away, and I tore my gaze from his to hustle down the hall to my son's room. He was standing at the side of his crib, looking down to where Hippo had somehow made it out of the crib and onto the floor. I picked the toy and my son up, hugging them to my chest.

"Mama's here, baby. I'm here."

I soothed and rocked him for a second, then he went limp in my arms, back to sleep. I put him in the crib, covered him with a blanket, and tucked Hippo next to him. He was almost too big for the crib. I'd need to move him to a toddler bed soon. I ran a hand over his smooth hair with love pouring from my veins, wishing I was a better mom—or at least, a less selfish one. Someone who would spend every minute of every day with him.

It was ridiculous to think it. My parents hadn't spent that much time with me. They'd taught at Wilson-Jacobs my entire life. I'd been in daycare when I was little, and I'd never felt unloved or unwanted. Quite the opposite, my parents had been there for every doctor's appointment, every fall, and every tear I'd shed.

When I came out of Chevelle's room, the lights in the bedroom Marco and I had converted to a home gym were on. I followed it to find Marco with his weights in hand and mine on the mat at his feet.

"Ready?" he asked.

I wanted to say no. I wanted to say, *'Let's go back to the kitchen, to that moment where a kiss had wafted on the air between us like never before.'* I wanted to force him to shed his secrets so that I could soothe him like I'd just soothed my son, but I didn't. Instead, I moved forward, picked up the weights, and said, "First one to a hundred gets to decide what we do next."

Chapter Twelve

Marco

KISS HER
Performed by Eric Van Houten

Jonas had given me shit about Cassidy as soon as the apartment door had slammed shut behind us.

"Now I know why you were so desperate to come back to Grand Orchard. She's *Angel*, right? Why didn't you tell us you had a girlfriend?"

I choked. "Cassidy is not my girlfriend. She's my boss's sister. A friend. A workout companion. That's it."

Jonas had laughed. "Sure…I can see how 'working out' with her would be worth it."

I'd cuffed him on the back of the head. "Don't be an ass."

"Maliyah is going to flip."

"Don't get her hopes up, Jo-Jo. Nothing is ever going to happen between Cassidy and me."

Then I'd left him to change, journey across the driveway, and enter the house of the woman I wanted more than I'd ever wanted anything in my life.

Almost kissing her in the kitchen had been a disaster.

Almost kissing her would haunt me for another twenty days. Just like the scent of her would and the way her skin had pebbled under my touch, making me think of just how tight her nipples would have been if I'd been skating over them instead of her arms with my fingers…and my tongue.

Chevelle had saved us. Saved us from making a mistake that would change everything. A mistake that might have meant removing myself from her world permanently, and I couldn't afford to do that right now. Not with Clayton Hardy threatening to show back up.

When she threw down her challenge to be the first to a hundred, I focused on the movements of the squat presses burning up my muscles instead of how good she looked bending and flexing. By the time we were done with our hour of workout, she was sweating, skin gleaming, and making me think of exactly what she'd look like underneath me or over me as we moved together in other ways. A different workout.

I almost ran from her then.

Trying to escape the images before I did something about them.

But they followed me home.

They haunted me through my dreams and were still haunting me the next day when I saw her enter *La Musica de Ensueños Studios* with Chevelle on her hip. I was in the Garner Security office, trying to concentrate on the update Trevor was giving me about The Painted Daisies, *The Exhibitor* reporter, and the information on Earth Paradise Distributions. It was Lance Ralley's name that finally dragged me back to reality.

"What did you say?"

"She's meeting with him at ten today." Trevor thrust his chin toward the studio across the street. "Brady and the lawyers are going over the contract he sent her with a fine-tooth comb. I haven't mentioned anything about the espionage lawsuit because you asked me not to until we knew more."

I glanced down at my father's watch that I'd worn since his death. It was five minutes to ten.

"Shit. What did you actually find out?"

"Hard to know for sure. He settled with the plaintiff."

"Did you talk to them?"

"They have a nondisclosure agreement in place. The woman said she wouldn't talk unless Lance approved it," Trevor replied.

I grabbed the paper Trevor was looking at with the details and headed out of the room.

"What are you going to do?" he asked, following me out the door. "We don't really know anything."

"She needs to know before she signs on with someone shady."

"Her or Brady?" Trevor asked, trying to hold back a smirk that reminded me of Jonas, who was spending the day in front of the TV with a game controller in his hand but wasn't really happy about it. I figured I had a few hours before he climbed out of the garage apartment and started exploring Grand Orchard on his own.

"Don't start with me," I groused and took the stairs two at a time.

I rushed across the street, barely escaping being

hit by a car, punched in my code at the front door of the studios, and stalked past the guard we had placed there. The control room was empty, along with the live room behind the huge wall of glass. I took the stairs two at a time, heading toward Brady's office.

I burst through the door, not out of breath, but probably more frazzled than I should have been. A half a dozen heads swiveled in my direction from the table at the back of the room. Cassidy was there, but Chevelle was missing, which meant he was probably with Tristan in her art studio down the hall. Brady was at the table next to his manager, Lee, who shoved up his dark-framed glasses on an ageless, tan face that blended perfectly with his otherwise dark complexion as I stalked in.

Lance Ralley, who I recognized from the picture in the workup we'd done on him, directed twinkling eyes in my direction, reminding me of a skinny Santa Claus without the beard. Friendly in a way that seemed counter to the intelligence we'd gathered.

The other men and women in the room had to have been the lawyers.

Cassidy's brows furrowed, confusion written on her face, but it was Brady that spoke first. "What's up, Marco?"

I made my way to the table and all but slammed the paper down in front of Lance. "Before Cassidy goes any further, you need to explain this."

Cassidy's mouth flew open. I knew I needed to get better control over myself, but there was no way I was going to stand by and let some schmuck take all her hard work and try to steal it away from her. Not on my watch. Never again would I let someone take advantage of an unsuspecting female.

Lance looked down, read what was written there, and didn't even flinch.

"I see you've done your research."

His voice was calm, not at all concerned.

"What is it?" Cassidy asked, reaching for the paper.

"It's a lawsuit I settled five years ago with Marsha's Muffins," Lance told her.

Brady was instantly on the alert, shifting from his nonchalant position to upright in a half a second, hand flicking at the bands on his wrist.

"What was the lawsuit about?" Brady asked.

"Marsha Deerborn accused me of corporate espionage."

"Come again?" Brady asked.

Lance ignored us all, looking to Cassidy instead. "Do you remember the day we first met? When I asked you if you'd created your recipes yourself or if you'd borrowed them from someone?"

Cassidy nodded.

"Well, that's because I had a very bad experience. An employee of mine created a muffin product for me. I had no idea that she'd done a stint at Marsha's Muffins as an intern. I had no idea she'd essentially used the same recipe as Marsha's until it was too late. Until it was in production and spread across the United States."

My eyes narrowed. I wasn't sure I believed the guy. There was just something tickling the back of my senses about him. Too friendly. Too accommodating. Too forthcoming. It hit me. He reminded me of my captain in the Fleet Marine Force. The one I hated. The one that looked like the boy-next-door but acted like Jack Nicholson. And even though my wariness likely had nothing to do with the real live man in front of me and more with haunted memories, I still couldn't help them.

Lance continued talking to Cassidy, almost as if none of us were in the room. "It's why you'll see specific clauses in our contract about you taking ownership for any patent, copyright, or trademark claims that come forward."

Cassidy raised her chin, pure confidence. "Everything I make is my own. No one can sue us for anything."

Lance smiled. "I'm glad to hear it."

He moved smoothly back from the lawsuit and into the contract they were proposing, drawing Cassidy's eyes to the presentation they had on the screen. It was a signal for me to leave, to stand outside and wait like my position as Brady's bodyguard expected of me, but for some reason, I couldn't make myself go. Instead, I leaned up against the wall, arms crossed, and listened as the talks continued. When I saw the amount of money he was offering her, my heart screeched to a halt.

It was staggering. Worse—or rather, even better for Cassidy—the amount he was offering for her recipes was only a speck of sand compared to the percentage of the sales he thought she'd receive when the products went live. She'd be able to pay Brady back without even sneezing. She'd be set for life. For Chevelle's life. She wouldn't have to work herself to the bone day and night anymore. Although, I couldn't imagine her not in the kitchen. Not when cooking and baking and creating were such a big part of who she was.

Thoughts of her in the kitchen brought back the memory of my fingers tangled in the apron string last night with her silky skin under my fingertips, with desire wafting between us that felt like it might devour us. But then, with a sudden twist of my stomach and a fierce pounding to my heart, I realized the truth. Cassidy O'Neil had always been out of my league, but this would lift her into a whole other universe.

There was no place in her life for a court-martialed corpsman turned bodyguard. I'd already known that, but I'd allowed myself to pretend over the last week. To be tempted by texts and calls that I never should have made and conversations full of caring words. Words that hinted at belonging. Words that had started to move our worlds closer together. This shifted us apart by leaps and bounds.

My mind was brought back to the room and the conversation by the mention of Texas.

"I'd like you to visit our production facility in Belton before you sign the final deal," Lance said. "You can see for yourself what we're trying to accomplish and meet the people I employ. I'm proud of the company and what we're doing for the world. If you gave us permission, I could have my product development manager work on your recipes before you came down. We'd have a clearer idea of what—if any—changes we'd need to make to them so they could be mass-produced. You could approve it all before signing in black and white."

Cassidy picked at the sleeve of the pale-yellow sweater she'd worn. It was so different from her T-shirts and workout gear but also a far cry from the suits in the room. I didn't understand why Cassidy was hesitating. She was being presented with a deal that could bring her more money than most people would see in a lifetime.

As if reading my thoughts, her eyes met mine across the room. I was hit in the stomach by the wariness there. It wasn't quite fear, but it was close. I felt like an ass because I'd stormed in, bringing her doubts. I suddenly wished I hadn't brought them to her door without digging more, but I'd just wanted to make sure she wasn't going into anything blind.

Lance pulled the glasses off his face, twirled them around, and said, "We need a couple of weeks to pull it all together, but you could bring your concerned friend over there with you."

It drew my eyes back to him and found his twinkling at me. I swallowed. Were my feelings for Cassidy so evident? I looked to Brady, but he was concentrating on the papers in front of them.

Lance continued, "You could even meet with Marsha yourself. Her facility is just up the road from mine. She'll tell you the same thing I did."

"I'm just the bodyguard," I said before I could take it back.

It drew Brady's eyes to mine, and Cassidy's fell to the table.

Lance chuckled. "That explains a lot."

Brady squinted at us, as if trying to catch on to the feelings and innuendos drifting through the room. Cassidy's chin came back up.

"That sounds like a good idea. The visit. Marco tagging along."

Brady's eyes narrowed even more, eyes drifting between Cassidy and me.

"Perfect," Lance said, chewing on the edge of his frames, hiding a smile.

One of the lawyers at the table spoke. "We'd like you to sign a letter of intent and NDA. It says that you won't agree to meet with any other companies before giving Earth Paradise a final answer, allows Earth Paradise to look at and play around with your recipes to ensure we can produce them, and gives you a small down payment. The remaining retainer for the recipes would be due upon signing the final contract."

"I'd like to give Cassidy and Brady a moment to review this before signing," Lee spoke up.

Lance nodded, rising, and two of the men in the room joined him. "Shall we come back after lunch, then? Say, one o'clock?"

Brady looked to Cassidy, and she nodded.

Lance and his team left the room. Once the door had shut behind them, Brady swiveled in his chair to look at Cassidy who was still staring down at the paper in front of her. "What's the deal, Cass?"

His eyes slid to mine, and I fought the desire to look away.

I hadn't done anything wrong. I hadn't kissed her. I hadn't touched her…except to claim her as mine to Clayton Hardy—which reminded me I needed Trevor to do some investigating on the asshole. I'd hustled down to Austin and lost myself in all things Maliyah and Jonas without telling him to run the check on Hardy. That had to happen—and soon.

Cassidy lifted her eyes and saw Brady staring at me. She swallowed and then punched him in the shoulder and flicked his ear. He leaned back. "Geez. Stop already. Those long fingers of yours are deadly."

I loved her long fingers. I loved thinking about them wrapped around parts of me that I shouldn't have wanted them near. I shifted, uncomfortable, hating myself for thinking about her that way.

"It's just...overwhelming. How am I going to manage this on top of everything else? Chevelle already gets so little of my time," her voice cracked, and it made my heart bleed because I realized how much guilt she carried around with her about being a single, working mother.

"This could actually give you more time with him," Brady said. "You could hire some more staff for The Golden Heart. You wouldn't have to be there from open to close. It would free you up some."

Cassidy shook her head slightly. "That's like you saying you're going to let someone else produce your album."

Brady's head tilted. "Honestly, it would be pretty close to what happens with my albums, Cass. I create the songs with Ava, record them, make sure what goes on the album is exactly what I want, but then I let everyone else take over. Alice designs the covers and the tours, Assad does his marketing thing, and Lee and Nick Jackson manage the distribution and rights. From there on out, I just show up and sing."

Cassidy curled the edge of the paper, deep in thought.

It was Lee who broke the silence. "If you want my two cents, I'd say take the down payment, sign the letter of intent, and go to Texas to check it out. Make sure these are people you want to tangle yourself with. Nick Jackson at Lost Heart Records is one of the most upstanding men in the music business. I wouldn't want to see Brady with many others. I know jack squat about the food business, and I thought Ralley seemed on the up and up, but"—he waved a hand in the direction of the paper I'd brought—"Marco seems to have uncovered a little dirt. I'd say do some more gardening. Make sure there isn't anything going to stick that you can't handle."

"I don't want this to bounce back on you," Cassidy said to Brady.

Brady looked shocked. "What do you mean?"

"You're my partner, Brady. Silent, but there. People know that. If we sign and things get dicey, it could hurt your image."

Brady was already shaking his head. "No. I'm not signing this deal, Cassidy. It has nothing to do with me. If you're really worried about it, let me remove my name from The Golden Heart as I've already tried to do repeatedly."

"It's your money," Cassidy breathed out.

"Was my money. I *gave* it to you. It was a gift."

She shook her head. It was an old argument between them.

Brady blew out a frustrated breath. "Fine, pay me back then. Sign the deal, and pay me off. Get my name out of it that way."

He stood up, stalked to the door, and then turned back. "Just think about it. Think about how you can change your life and Chevelle's with it."

And then he left, but not before shooting me a glare and a *what the hell* look.

I should have followed him out. Ten days ago, I would have, but now I wanted to be there so Cassidy had someone to talk to. Someone who only had her interests in mind. Someone who would listen just like she'd listened to me when I'd been plagued by my past and mistakes I couldn't take back.

Chapter Thirteen

Cassidy

BIGGER MAN
Performed by Joy Oladokun and Maren Morris

Brady left the room with a bang to the door that my even-tempered brother wasn't known for. The lawyers were scrutinizing the contract that Lance Ralley's team had left behind, Lee was watching me with a frown, but it was Marco's eyes that felt like they were burying themselves into my veins and had me the most unnerved.

"You know…he just wants to do something good with the fortune he feels guilty about having amassed," Lee said.

"That's what charities are for," I said, lifting my head.

Lee sighed. "But you're family. And family gives to family. He was ecstatic the day he talked to me about buying your building and helping you get started. He felt relief. Like he could *finally* do something for someone he loved."

Lee patted me on the shoulder and then got up to look over the contract with the lawyers. Marco moved from the wall to take a seat next to me, his presence finally aligning with mine in the way I'd ached for it to do since he walked in the room with a furious look and a glare directed at Lance Ralley.

"What's really holding you back?" he asked, fingers twitching as if he was going to reach for my hand and then changed his mind. He crossed his arms over his massive chest instead.

I didn't know how to explain it. There was a tugging low inside my belly, keeping me from jumping up and down and screaming with excitement at the offer. I was pretty sure it had nothing to do with Lance or Earth Paradise and everything to do with the unknowns I couldn't see. I searched Marco's face, wondering if I'd sound as ridiculous as I felt, but I finally just spoke the truth. "Honestly, I don't know. This feeling at the back of my gut, I guess. Stupid, right?"

Marco shook his head. "No, it's not. I'm a firm believer in trusting your gut. The times in my life I ignored it, I lived to regret it."

I had a thousand questions to ask about that. I wanted to know every single one of the times. I wanted to understand how they'd formed him into the honorable man who shared so little of himself with anyone, who said that the word honor could never be applied to him.

"Was it your gut that had you storming into the room and all but throwing the lawsuit in Lance's face?" I asked.

He glowered. "Yes."

"So…you'd go with me then? Look out for me with that gut of yours?" I don't know what made me push. I wasn't afraid of Lance Ralley. Uncertain…but not afraid. But knowing someone would be with me who was determined to protect me without smothering me… It was what I needed.

"I know nothing about any of it," he said. "I'm not exactly the right person to tag along." He closed his eyes, as if looking at me was painful, and it stabbed at my heart a little more than I could bear.

"I don't need you to know anything about recipes or food production or distribution. Like we said the other day, you read people for a living. That's what I need, and you're more than qualified to do that," I said honestly.

My words seemed to pain him as much as his had pained me. As if we'd learned enough to know how to wound each other, but not enough to know how to soothe it back over.

"Sounds like we have a few weeks before you need to go. We can decide then," he said quietly. It wasn't a no, but it wasn't a yes either, and yet I couldn't help my heart leaping at the 'we' that had flown from his lips.

I didn't respond, but my smile probably said what I was feeling without me needing to. His eyes crinkled as if he was having difficulty holding back his own smile. He got up out of the chair. "I'm going to go check in again with Trevor and then go back to the apartment to make sure Jonas hasn't blown it up, but I'll see you for our workout tonight?"

I nodded and watched him as he left. When I turned back to Lee and the lawyers, Lee was watching me with a thoughtful expression on his face that I couldn't quite read. Marco and I had just exhibited a friendship that no one had really been able to see before, even though they all knew we worked out together. In truth, it was a friendship that we'd just found ourselves.

I'd always been attracted to Marco, but what I felt now was so much deeper. Like something hidden in me was calling to something hidden in him, and I wondered if either of us would ever let those emotions be brought into the light.

♪ ♪ ♪

I signed the tentative agreement with Earth Paradise and headed to the bank to deposit the retainer check. I stared at the new balance on my account for a long time. It felt unreal. I wasn't sure I knew what to do with the money, so it would sit there until I did.

At home, the house seemed too quiet and closed in for all my feelings, so after Chevelle woke from his nap, I took him to the park, pushing him in the stroller. The first thing he wanted to do was feed the ducks because if there were animals anywhere nearby, that was where my boy was. Knowing this, I'd brought some vegetable scraps from the house, and he giggled and jabbered while flinging the pieces into the water. Then, we headed to the swings, which had always been my favorite thing growing up. I tucked him onto my lap and swayed us back and forth.

The day was bright and beautiful. Big puffy clouds littered the sky, and sunshine warmed me enough that I needed to remove the sweater I'd worn to the meeting, leaving me in a tank top and a long skirt dancing with flowers.

Chevelle laughed. "More, Mama. More."

He pointed to the sky, and I smiled, pumping my legs to take us a little higher but not trusting our awkward pose on the single swing to take him as high as I used to go as a kid. Swinging didn't require much balance. If you held onto the chains and swung your feet, you could float gracefully into the air without worrying about tripping or falling.

As it neared dinnertime, I rounded us up and headed back to the house.

I didn't see him until it was too late. Until I'd already parked the stroller at the base of the steps and taken Chevelle out. I had him on my hip, and as I neared the door, Clayton rose from the Adirondack chair tucked off to the side.

"Cassidy," he greeted, and his eyes took in every single part of Chevelle, as if weighing and judging him to see where he was falling short, all at the age of two. I reflexively turned so that it moved Chevelle farther away from him.

My heart banged inside my chest with fear and fury both driving me. I'd always heard the term "mama bear" when it came to mothers who tried to keep their kids safe, and I'd never really understood it until this moment. I hadn't had to. There'd never been anyone in our lives whom I'd had to shield Chevelle from.

"You're not welcome here, Clayton."

"He's got my coloring," he said.

He did. The dark brown of Chevelle's hair and the warmer skin tone was more Hardy than O'Neil, but that was the only thing I saw of his father in him. His eyes were mine. The wide, square jaw was my dad's Basque heritage. The almost dimple in his cheek when he smiled was all Brady.

I didn't respond. I was afraid I'd either cry or scream if I did.

"Can I hold him?" he asked.

"No."

"He's my son!" His tone grew fiercer.

I didn't want to have this conversation in front of Chevelle. True, he wouldn't have understood the majority of it, but I didn't want him to sense the emotions that raged through me. I brushed past Clayton, and my foot hit the edge of the welcome mat wrong, tipping me and Chevelle both sideways. I would have caught myself on the side of the house, but Clayton's hands steadied me.

"Jesus," he said. "You could have injured yourself and him."

My stomach twisted. It was the last thing I needed: him seeing my weakness. I brushed at his hands. "Get your hands off of me."

He withdrew them but not as fast as I'd have liked. I unlocked the door and set Chevelle down. "Go take your shoes off, Snickerdoodle. Mama will be right there."

I shut the screen but left the door open so I'd hear him and then turned back to Clayton. "I don't want to see you on my property again."

"You're not going to even let me try to make this up to you? To my boy? What's his name?"

"Do you remember the check you gave me?"

He blanched, and I could see he remembered it as clearly as I did.

"If I'd used that check you'd made out to Planned Parenthood, would you be here right now? Would you be trying to 'make it up to me'?" I used every ounce of sarcasm as I could on the words.

"But you didn't use it."

"Pretend I did. Pretend I did exactly what you

wanted me to do. You gave me that check and made it out to them because you wanted to make sure it was clear to me—and the world—that you weren't paying to support a baby. Isn't that what you said? You didn't want me to come back at you for more of your hard-earned dollars if I was *stupid* enough to keep the child."

He had the grace to grimace as I threw his words back at him. Harsh, cold, and calculating.

"We all make mistakes, Cassidy. I can do better. For you both."

"Except, I don't need you, Clayton. I can support Chevelle all on my own."

"Scraping by? I heard about the restaurant. The food industry is a drain on mom-and-pop places like that. You can't possibly be making money."

I laughed, thinking about the check I'd just deposited, but I didn't go there with him. It wasn't his business.

"Get off my property, and never come back."

"I don't want to have to go to court just to see my son, but I will if I have to," he said, eyes flashing because I continued to defy him. My heart sagged with a grief I couldn't explain at the thought of him getting some sort of custody over Chevelle. I thought I had a strong case. I'd kept the check he'd made out to Planned Parenthood. I'd kept the text he'd sent, asking me not to contact him again. But I also knew the courts were trying to be as favorable to fathers as mothers these days.

"Go. Away," I repeated.

"You're being irrational."

"I think she said to leave," a male voice said from

the steps, and we both flipped around to see Jonas standing there. He was dressed for running: AirPods in his ears, enormous sneakers on his feet, and sweat dripping down his face.

Clayton eyed him just like he'd eyed Chevelle moments before and Marco when he'd had his arms around my waist days ago.

"Who's this? A little young for you, don't you think?" Clayton said, glaring at me and Jonas. "What kind of house is this? With men coming and going constantly."

My face flushed at his insinuation. Especially since I hadn't had a man in my bed since him. Nearly three years of abstinence. Three years of denying myself human touch in the most intimate ways.

"How dare you," I blustered. "Not that it's any of your business, but this is Marco's brother."

"Are you going to leave on your own, or am I going to have to make you?" Jonas asked as he mounted the steps and crossed his arms across his chest in a stance that was so like Marco that it hit me in the pit of my belly. It caused my heart to swell for this teenager who was trying to protect me in just the way his brother would.

Chapter Fourteen

Marco

SHADE
Performed by Maren Morris

I rounded the corner of our street, sweaty and ready to hit the showers after the long run I'd taken with Jonas before joining Cassidy for her workout. Jonas and I had wound our way through downtown so I could point out the basics of the place: Cassidy's restaurant, Brady's studio, and the other shops that made up the quaint Main Street that drew tourists from around the globe, especially during apple season. We'd gone past the charming old stores and reached the more modern strip malls on the other side of town when Jonas finally called, "Give." I'd laughed and teased him but let him head back on his own, knowing what he really needed was time to absorb being miles away from where he thought he wanted to be. I gave him space and continued on for another half a mile before turning back.

I was surprised to see his tall frame on the steps of Cassidy's place when I turned onto the block, and my feet headed in that direction. I saw him mount the steps, and I heard him threaten someone, which raised the hackles on my neck.

It wasn't until I was closer that I saw the slimy face of Clayton Hardy as he stepped toward my brother. Clayton laughed darkly. "Cocky one, I see. You have me quivering in my boots."

"If you're not afraid of him, maybe you should be of me," I growled, taking the steps in a single bound so that I stood next to Jonas.

I had to give the man some credit. He didn't cower away. In fact, his eyes flashed angrily. The three of us standing off like some ridiculous television drama.

"Mama, wet," Chevelle's little voice broke through the tension. All our eyes went to the screen door where Chevelle stood with his stuffed dog, Hippo, in his hands. The animal was dripping onto the floor, and if the situation hadn't been full of tension, I would have laughed because I had a pretty good idea where he'd dropped Hippo. Instead, I continued to give Clayton my "fuck off" face.

Cassidy exchanged a glance with me, fear and frustration and fury floating through her, and then she turned to her son. "Did Hippo decide to use the potty again?"

She eased open the screen door and picked up Chevelle, wet animal and all. She didn't give any of us behemoths on the porch a second look.

"I'm not done here, Cassidy," Clayton said, and then he stormed past me, pushing my arm as he went by as if he could provoke me into striking him first. He'd love that—the angry boyfriend who was a physical menace to his child.

I watched him as he stalked over to a very expensive Jaguar—one I was surprised he could afford on a professor's salary. It raised more alarms. I really needed to dig into him more than I'd dug into Lance Ralley. If I hadn't had to fly to Austin, it would have been done already.

I looked to Jonas and clasped his shoulder. "Thank you."

"What is it with douchebags who think they have a right to tell women what to do?" he growled, and I couldn't have been prouder of him.

I opened the screen door, following the sound of Cassidy's voice to the laundry room off the kitchen. I was surprised when Jonas trailed after me, eyeing the very feminine house with curious eyes.

Chevelle was sitting on top of the dryer while Cassidy put Hippo into the washing machine with a load of towels. "He'll be okay. He's just going to take a bath. Remember last time. He came out of the dryer smelling brand new."

Chevelle looked like he might cry, and it tore a little at my soul to see him so sad. I reached around Cassidy and picked him up. "How about you show me where your Mama keeps those apple snacks while she takes care of Hippo?"

His eyes were huge as they watched Cassidy over my shoulder, but soon the cabinets blocked his view, and he turned back to me. He put his chubby little hands on my face. "Maco."

The kid made my heart about burst. His little hands on my cheeks and the way he couldn't say the R in my name was enough to almost kill anyone with cuteness.

"Yep, buddy?" My voice was deep with the feelings I had for him.

"Who dat?" he asked, eyes drifting to where Jonas stood in the kitchen's archway.

"That's Jo-Jo. He's my brother."

Jonas rolled his eyes. "Great, let's have the kid learn a ridiculous nickname, why don't we."

I grinned.

Jonas closed the distance, holding out a hand. "I'm Jonas, not Jo-Jo. And who are you?"

I wanted to laugh because it was obvious that Jonas hadn't been around little kids much more than I'd been before Chevelle had entered my world.

"I's Velle. I's two," Chevelle said, holding up two fingers.

"Two. Wow, man, that's old. Bet you can drive a car and everything," Jonas teased, and Chevelle giggled.

He pushed against my chest. "Car. I get car."

I put him down, and he ran out of the kitchen toward the toy box in the living room, digging through it.

Cassidy joined us in the kitchen. "Thanks for distracting him."

I eyed her up and down. She'd taken off the yellow sweater, showing off a tank top of the same lemony color that bared her shoulders and arms in a way that called to me to touch all her visible skin. She looked like a lemon drop cookie that would be sweet and tangy and addicting, which had me thinking of sliding hands and tongue over every inch of her.

She turned to Jonas, and before either of us expected it, she wrapped him in a hug, squeezing tight. I knew what that felt like. I'd had a handful of those hugs. As if she was embedding herself in your memories with the strength of the embrace. I hated that I was jealous of Jonas for getting one of them.

Especially when he'd earned it by defending her.

"Thank you," she breathed out. Jonas's wide eyes met mine over her shoulder.

Then, she let go and looked at us both. "Dinner is on me, gentleman. Thank you for getting rid of him."

"You don't owe us anything, Ang—Cassidy," I said, flushing at the almost slip up I'd done again. She smiled at me.

"Well then, stay because I'm celebrating the deal I signed and don't want to eat alone."

"I'm sure Arlene and Petri would be happy to celebrate with you."

I wanted to kick myself because it made her smile slip a little.

"You're right, but I'm not up to Mom and Dad tonight," she said quietly, and then the smile turned full wattage again, capturing my breath and holding it almost as if she'd hugged me. "It's lasagna, and you know you love my lasagna."

I did love her lasagna. I shouldn't have, because it was made with none of the things one expected of the Italian dish, but somehow Cassidy had made hers taste even better than the meat and gluten-loaded ones I'd known before hers.

"Let me shower, then I'll come help," I told her, easily giving in, and impossibly, her smile grew wider.

"Deal."

"I'll be back, and then you can have a turn in the bathroom," I said to Jonas, sending him a message that I wanted him to stay in case Clayton came back.

"I don't stink like you do. I'm fine," Jonas said.

I moved in, sniffed the air around him, and

pretended to gag. "You smell worse."

He stuck his tongue out in a way he hadn't done in years, and it eased the twisted pain I'd been holding tight in my heart for him. He was going through a lot with Maliyah, and Mel, and the crowd he'd merged himself with just to be there in case she needed him. Today proved just how much he would stand up for her. I needed to teach him a few moves.

I took off out the back door, determined to shower in the quick, military-efficient way that I'd become accustomed to. And I would have been back in Cassidy's house in less than fifteen minutes if it hadn't been for Brady's number lighting up my phone.

"Where are you?" he asked.

I was glad I could answer truthfully. "At the apartment. What's up?"

"That's what I want to know. What gives? How come my sister knows you have family in Texas and I don't, after more than seven years together? What was the deal with you and her in my office today? Are you sleeping with Cassidy?" There wasn't really anger in his voice, but maybe a layer of hurt.

"Wow. That's a lot of questions," I said in order to buy myself time while I tried to assemble all my answers. I didn't know how to feel about the fact that Cassidy had told him about Maliyah. Had she told him about Jonas as well? Not that I expected to keep him a secret while I was in Grand Orchard. I'd actually been hoping Brady would let him hang around the studio and absorb what was going on. Reignite his interest in music that I was pretty sure he'd put aside so he could be in an art class with Mel. He hadn't said as much, but I could put one and one together and end up with two just like anyone else.

Brady was as silent as I was, and it turned awkward.

"You're more than my bodyguard, Marco. You know that, right?" Brady asked, breaking the silence.

I sighed, rubbing my hand through the damp stubble of my hair. "Yes."

Ever since the Fiona Fiasco—as we liked to call the incident with the dead stalker—Brady had surrounded himself with people who meant something to him. People who could see him for the real person he was and not just a celebrity with a ginormous-sized bank account. It was important to him that everyone around him feel like they were family. We'd spent thousands of hours in each other's company. On planes, in cars, waiting behind the scenes in stadiums. I knew every little thing about Brady, Tristan, and Hannah. I even knew the moment they'd found out that he and Tristan were having a baby. I'd been the one to buy him the goddamn pregnancy tests—multiple because he'd wanted to make sure there wasn't another false negative. I'd walked into the pharmacy, bought a dozen of the damn things, and everyone in the store had looked at me like I was a pimp.

I hadn't really reciprocated when he'd asked about my life. Did I have a girlfriend? No. Did I miss my parents? No, they're dead. Did I miss the military? No. What was there to say to any of that without tearing at wounds that I'd carefully healed.

"What did Cassidy tell you?" I asked.

"Nothing. That she felt bad for you and your family and what you were going through. You told me your parents were dead," he said. The hurt leaked into his voice again.

"They are. She was talking about my foster mom, Maliyah. She was in the hospital."

It was quiet again as Brady took that in. "Did you think I'd judge you because you were a foster kid?"

"No," I responded automatically. Brady was the most down-to-earth celebrity I'd ever met. He didn't judge. Maybe because he'd been on the receiving end of it enough for his flirtatious ways, a highly criticized third album, and by a mom who thought he was irresponsible.

"So, why the big secret?" Brady pushed.

Because talking about any of it tears open all my wounds, was what I wanted to say, but didn't. Instead, I offered different words that were also true. "No secret. I just didn't want you to try and shove me out of the house during the holidays, which you would have if you had known about Maliyah and Jonas. They didn't need me to be there for them."

"And I did?"

"You need someone you can trust with you at those moments."

"I'd never want you to sacrifice your loved ones for me."

"Exactly my point," I said.

After another moment of quiet, he asked, "Who's Jonas?"

"My foster brother, so to speak. He came back with me from Austin."

"He's here in Grand Orchard? When do I get to meet him?" he asked.

I gave a half chuckle. "I'll bring him by the studio tomorrow. But I have to be honest, once he sees it, he's probably not going to want to leave. He'll likely ask you a thousand and one questions."

"He's a musician?" Brady asked, surprised.

"I think that's probably too strong of a word for it. He fiddles with a guitar, but he likes music in general."

"He's welcome anytime," Brady insisted.

"I appreciate that."

"How is…Maliyah, is it?"

"She's going to be okay. She's recovering from an issue with her heart and a minor stroke. She'll be in rehab most of the summer, which is why Jonas came back with me."

"How old is he?"

"Sixteen."

"The angst years," Brady joked, and I laughed.

"That's the perfect word for him right now."

Brady chuckled, said goodbye, and it wasn't until we'd hung up that I realized I'd been able to escape the discussion about Cassidy. Brady would realize it also, and it meant I'd better have an answer that dripped off my tongue when he asked again, but the truth was, I didn't have one. I knew what it should have been: a resounding, "Nothing." But even after knowing how wide the gap between our lives was growing, I found it almost impossible to stay away.

Chapter Fifteen

Cassidy

SOMEBODY LIKE YOU
Performed by Keith Urban

While Marco was gone, Jonas stepped up next to me in the kitchen, asking what he could do to help. When I gave him some vegetables to slice, he didn't bat an eye and used decent knife skills that had me curious about where he'd learned them.

"Do you cook a lot with Maliyah?" I asked.

He shrugged. "Off and on, but she said it was Life Skills 101 to know how to make a meal for yourself. She's big on eating at home versus eating out."

"It's better for you."

"Even if we were eating at your restaurant?" he asked.

I chuckled. "Well, my restaurant isn't your norm."

We worked in silence for a few minutes. The only noise was Chevelle making car sounds as he dragged one along the rug by the washing machine, waiting for Hippo to come out of his bath.

"Thank you," I said, and he stopped cutting for a

moment to look at me, cheeks turning red.

"Aw. This is nothing."

"I don't mean for cutting the squash, although that is very nice as well. I mean for stepping in back there on the porch." I'd already said the words—hugged him—but I wanted him to understand just how big of a deal it was to have someone willing to stand up for someone else.

His face flamed even more. "No means no. Leave means leave. I won't ever stand by and let someone be manhandled."

"I think Maliyah would be very proud of you. I know Marco was."

He rubbed at his cheek with the back of his hand as if trying to brush away his embarrassment. He went back to cutting.

"Marco says you're not his girlfriend." He shot me a look under his lashes.

My heart stutter-stopped. "That's right. I'm not."

"But he likes you, and you like him, right? So, what's stopping you from like…being together?"

My hand froze above the ramekin I was using to create the mini-lasagnas. Could everyone see us this clearly? The emotions and desire that wafted through us and around us like the winds were pushing us together? Or did it take an outsider, someone less used to seeing us, to realize it?

"Sometimes…liking each other isn't enough. Sometimes, it would just complicate things more than they should be."

I continued layering the chickpea noodles, homemade sauce, and vegetables.

Jonas sighed. "Relationships *are* complicated.

But I wonder if I'd had the guts to tell Mel how I felt before she started seeing that shit-for-brains, Artie, if we'd be together now. If she'd be…safer." His voice was full of teenage agony—lovesick—but there was also remorse.

I stopped and looked at him. "Being with someone just to protect them isn't a good reason to be in a relationship, Jonas. That's a sure-fire way for one or both of you to get hurt."

He glanced up at me. "Love's about sacrifice, right? You gotta be willing to give everything for the ones who matter most."

It was so deep and wrong and right all at the same time for someone so young to have voiced that it took me a while to respond. "If the sacrifice leaves one of you less…if the relationship is tilted and one-sided, it'll never work in the long run. Either the person sacrificing for the other will eventually be bitter about always giving, or the person being sacrificed for will feel like a burden. They'd feel guilty and doubt whether it was love holding them together or duty."

The washer buzzed, and I turned to go flip Hippo and the towels into the dryer and found Marco's dark eyes taking me in. We hadn't heard him return, but that didn't surprise me. Marco was stealthy when he wanted to be, and he knew my house well enough to miss the creaky boards on the steps and in the kitchen.

His hands were crossed over his chest, stance wide, as if he was expecting to have to fight an army of people. The smell of him washed over me as I got closer…spice and soap. His skin was red and glowing from the heat of the shower. My body ached for him. Wanted him so badly that it coiled through me whenever he was near and especially when he was looking at me like this. As if he wanted to shake me or kiss me or swear at me all at once.

"Excuse me," I said, sliding past him into the laundry room.

"Oh, good, you're back. I'm going to go shower," Jonas said and practically ran from the kitchen as if he'd sensed the sexual tension drifting between Marco and me and wanted nothing to do with it.

Chevelle had passed out on the rug in front of the washer. If I let him sleep, he'd never go to bed at seven-thirty, but if I woke him, he'd be cranky. I switched the towels and stuffed animal to the dryer and decided to leave him be. The floor wasn't comfortable. He'd wake on his own before long. I pulled one of the crib blankets from the shelf above the machines and draped it over him.

When I came back into the kitchen, Marco had picked up where Jonas had left off, cutting the last few zucchinis.

"There's a flaw in your logic, you know," he said. I loved how his voice filled a room. No matter the volume, it felt like it occupied the entire space. Powerful. Commanding.

"What do you mean?"

"You'd sacrifice for Chevelle over and over again, right?" he asked.

"Of course!"

"Will you ever feel bitter about it?"

"That's totally different than what Jonas and I were talking about," I said, grabbing the slices and finishing off the ramekins. "A parent is supposed to give everything for their child. They aren't equals. But if a couple goes into something assuming one is more than the other in some way, then it will always end badly."

He stepped closer to me, close enough that his thigh hit mine. Close enough that when he spoke, the warmth of his breath trailed over my skin.

"Is that why you've never had a serious relationship? Because you're afraid that your partner will always think you're less? That the scales are uneven? That you'll be a burden?" His voice sounded pained, filled with heartache that was all for me and not himself.

His words were partly true. Not completely. I hadn't had much opportunity to be in a relationship. There had never been a line of guys wanting to date Clumsy Cassidy. But I also would have hated feeling like I could never be enough. Or worse, have someone afraid to break up with me because they felt duty-bound to protect me.

I shrugged.

He captured my hands, bringing them to his chest and covering them with his own large ones. Solid and strong. But I could feel the wild pace of his heart beneath them. Like he'd run miles again. It matched the unsteady rhythm of my own beats.

"Clayton was a fool. Just like any man who can't see the brave, strong, passionate woman you are. You could never be less."

The words seared through my heart, burning, leaving a mark behind that would be hard to cover up. Hard to heal.

"I'm more than my hypotonia and an extra X-chromosome," I said in a voice that faltered.

He shook his head. "You don't have to be more than those things, Angel. They're just part of you.

Like your halo of blonde hair and your beautiful golden eyes."

I wasn't sure I'd ever be able to breathe again. The term of endearment falling from his lips along with the heat in his eyes. The look that said he wanted to devour me just as much as I wanted him to.

"Falling all the time isn't beautiful," I said and wanted to grimace. My statement wasn't a woe-is-me moment. It was a fact, but it could also have been perceived as seeking empathy I didn't want.

"It's sort of endearing."

My breath caught. I was going to be falling, figuratively and emotionally, if I didn't find my way back from the depths of his touch and his gaze.

"Endearing? That word seems so wrong coming from your lips," I tried to tease.

"Does it? What word would seem more fitting?" he asked.

"I don't know. I can't think."

That caused his lips to quirk. Not quite a smile, but an upward curl to them that made me want to kiss each corner.

Loud feet on the back steps drew us apart, reluctantly. Slowly. And as much as I had liked Jonas for defending me and Chevelle, I wished he wasn't there. I wished Marco and I had been able to finish lighting the candle burning slowly between us. That we'd been able to fan it into a flame that consumed us until it allowed us to throw away our cautiousness and just lose ourselves in the feel of hands and mouths and tongues coasting over each other.

Jonas didn't even register that we'd been tangled together. His head was bent to the phone in his hand,

Tripped by Love

a frown on his face as he let the screen door slam behind him.

"Everything okay?" Marco asked him, and he whipped his eyes up.

"Yeah. It's all fine."

But he didn't seem like it was. He seemed pouty and angsty, just like a teenager in love should feel. I hadn't ever had that. I'd skipped right around that phase of my life. I mean, I'd had a schoolgirl crush on the dynamic quarterback, like everyone else at our high school, but it hadn't been full of pining and the I'm-going-to-jump-off-a-bridge-if-he-doesn't-look-at-me kind of drama.

"Mama? Hippo?" Chevelle came out of the laundry room, rubbing his tired little eyes. I picked him up, sticking out my hip to give him a perch.

"Soon, Snickerdoodle. Let's play a game while we wait for Hippo and dinner." I turned back to Marco. "Want to put those in the oven for me and set the timer for thirty minutes?"

He nodded and turned back to the pans and the oven while I went into the living room with Jonas trailing me. I set up the Jenga-like game that used shapes and colors to identify which blocks to pull. To my surprise, both men joined us, sitting on the floor by the coffee table while we waited for the food.

The talk was light. Jonas asked about the restaurant, Brady, and his studio. I asked about Jonas's guitar skills and who his favorite bands were. Marco silently built and rebuilt the tower every time it fell with a quiet patience as he listened to us all jabber back and forth.

Dinner was full of the same conversations.

When Chevelle began to droop again in his high

chair, I said I had to give him a bath, and Jonas thanked me for dinner before taking off to the apartment, but Marco stayed behind. I grabbed Hippo out of the dryer, and Chevelle's face lit up like he'd seen Santa Claus. He brought the dog to his face, rubbed his nose in the animal's belly, and then sighed the most adorable little sigh.

"I'll clean the kitchen while you give him a bath," he said, waving a hand at the mess we'd made. Usually, I cleaned as I went, but I'd been distracted this evening.

"You don't have to do that. I'll do it after. I'm probably not going to work out tonight. I'm too drained." It had been a very long day. Full of highs and lows and swells of attractions. Full of joy and fury and desire I couldn't seem to tame.

"I got it. Go take care of Chevelle."

I stared for a long moment before taking Chevelle off to the bathroom, a strange ache circling through me as I wondered what it would be like to have this every night. To not have the full burden of a household fall on me. If I was still living with my parents, I could have that. Mom or Dad or both would fill in the voids, give an extra hand, but it didn't feel the same at all. Much like what Marco and I had been talking about earlier, the difference between a parent and partner was more than the mixed-up letters.

I bathed my boy, rocked him while reading a book, and then stuck him in his crib with kisses and snuggles. "I love you, Snickerdoodle."

He stuck Hippo up at me. I kissed the dog, snuggled him just like I had Chevelle, and then gave him back to my son. Chevelle's eyes were closed before I'd even switched off the light. I grabbed the baby monitor and headed out to the kitchen.

It was sparkling. Everything was put away, and the dishwasher was humming.

Marco was sitting in a kitchen chair, arms crossed, but his eyes were closed, and his chin was almost touching his chest. I wanted to laugh. It was like he'd fallen asleep just like Chevelle—while resisting doing so. He looked peaceful asleep. He always wore a sense of calm around him like a cloak, but there was something softer and sweeter about him this way. My chest expanded, filling with emotions I knew were ridiculous to have for a man I'd never kissed, who would probably never kiss me because, regardless of his words from earlier, I was a duty. An obligation. His boss's sister.

I touched his shoulder gently, and he jerked awake, arms going wild and almost smacking me in the face. I laughed as I ducked, lost my balance, and was surprised when he caught me with an arm around the waist, which had the opposite effect. Instead of steadying me, I teetered more in the opposite direction and ended up in his lap.

Both of our eyes went wide. Our mouths were mere centimeters apart. My butt was tucked up against parts of him that I swore went hard the instant I landed on him. Neither of us moved. We just gazed into each other's eyes as if cataloging the way our bodies felt folded this close together, touching in tantalizing and forbidden ways, determining who would be the first to call mercy and give. Stand up. Move away.

I didn't want to. I didn't want anything but to finish what we'd started earlier before Jonas had interrupted us. I needed to see what it felt like to be kissed by him. Claimed by him while I claimed him back.

His hand lifted, and his rough finger ran along my jaw, ending on my chin where he rubbed softly. "You have baby powder."

Flames licked through me, traveling from every place he was touching me—hips, thighs, chest, and arms—into my inner recesses. Melting them from solid to liquid like watching chocolate on a double boiler.

I moved slightly, drawing our lips even closer. His lids closed, thick dark lashes laying against tan skin. My eyes fell to his mouth. Solid dashes of red that always looked both firm and soft to me. I dropped my chin forward the remaining distance, giving in to the temptation but also holding back just a little so that the touch of my lips on his was a barely perceptible one. Almost a dare, screaming, *Push me away. Make me stop.*

He groaned. I felt it from his core, all the way up to his chest as it expanded and contracted with the sound. And then, he was devouring me. He pulled me with his hands so there was no remaining space between us, and his mouth thundered against mine. Pushing, sliding, gasping. And finally licking. Begging access that I gave with a little moan of my own that seemed to drown us both. The movements of our tongues were softer than the force of our lips had been at first. Seeking, learning, lavishing each other with tenderness, solace, hope. Then raging again. Demanding, seeking answers that only our bodies seemed to know how to give.

My body flooded with endorphins. Heat. Desire. So much that it ached. So much that I wasn't sure I'd ever feel cool again. I'd forever live in the blaze that

Marco was scouring me with, marking me for all eternity.

My hands ran over the short stubble that was his hair, the bristles soft and sharp all at the same time, the texture of them adding to the fuel growing inside me. His hands were locked at my waist, curving into the soft hollow above my hip bones as if he was afraid to move them. Afraid to touch more than just that one spot.

My body arched into him as our tongues continued to weave together. Oxygen was such an unnecessary thing while we consumed each other. He groaned again and then removed his lips from mine. He flung his head back, face tilted toward the ceiling. Eyes closed.

I knew I should have backed off. I knew I should have stopped, but goddamn it, I didn't want to. So, I teased his neck with a lick and a nip, and his hands convulsed, gripping me tighter for all of twenty seconds.

And then there was only air between us.

He'd picked me up and sat me down on the chair while he stood at the opposite end of the kitchen table. Gasping. Panting as I'd never seen him do, even in the midst of our hardest workout.

My body was alive, but the cool air of the kitchen was brushing against my heat, and soon, I was shivering. From the desire and the absence of his body. From the memory of his taste and feel. From the knowledge that he was going to say he regretted it.

Chapter Sixteen

Marco

HARD LESSON LEARNED
Performed by Kenny Wayne Shepherd

She'd tasted like heaven. Like the sweetest chocolate and a hint of cinnamon bleeding together. Like earth and skies, fire and wind blended into an intoxicating mix that would forever be scalded into my memories.

Tastes a man could lose himself in craving for the rest of his life.

I wanted her.

Not just wanted…I coveted her. Wished for her to be mine more than I'd ever wished for anything in my godforsaken life. More than I'd once wanted a military career. More than wishing I could undo the one damn night that had ended it all.

Her eyes were lit with the same flames blazing through me as she watched me from the chair at the other end of the table. *I dare you to stay*, those eyes seemed to be screaming at me. She'd gone all-in. She'd doubled down and gambled it all. But she shouldn't have risked it with me. I wasn't worth the potential loss.

If I had an ounce of honor or self-preservation, I'd walk out the door and never step foot inside it again. But I couldn't. Not only because of Hardy hanging around and threatening to come back, but because my soul wouldn't let me. It was shrieking at me to do as she silently demanded—to stay. But if I mentioned Hardy as a reason to do so, she'd be furious with me. It would be exactly the duty she'd spoken of before. Duty that she hated being, but it was a duty nonetheless.

I wouldn't—couldn't—listen to the snickering voice at the back of my head saying it was possession and not duty that called me.

Cassidy seemed to be able to read everything that went through me. Every word and thought that whispered inside my brain. Her eyes narrowed, and she rose from the table, steadying herself. I was as proud as I was regretful that I'd made her legs weak with our kisses.

She headed out of the kitchen, looking back at the last minute.

"I don't want your protection, Marco. I don't need it. I just want you."

And then she walked down the hall without a glance back.

♪ ♪ ♪

There was plenty of food for breakfast in my apartment, and yet I dragged Jonas out of bed at the crack of dawn to head into The Golden Heart Café. I'd tossed and turned on the pull-out couch in the living room all night after having given Jonas the single bedroom for the summer. I was used to the couch. I'd spent many nights on it while guarding Brady before he'd met Tristan and moved in with her. So, it wasn't the thin mattress or the frame poking through that kept me awake. Instead, it had been the kisses and moans that had followed me from Cassidy's house.

And now my body was demanding to see her again.

I was ridiculous enough to use my foster brother as a shield. I could have left him alone and gone to breakfast on my own, but I was afraid of what I'd do when I saw her again. Afraid that the flimsy barrier I'd try to reconstruct would melt away, and I'd wrap her in an embrace that would stun and surprise every customer in the place.

It wasn't Cassidy but Willow who seated us at a booth at the back of the restaurant. This wasn't unusual either. When Cassidy was at work, she rarely left the kitchen. Except, she always popped out to see me when I showed up, and today she didn't.

"What can I start you with this morning, Marco?" she asked.

"An extra-large coffee, the Spanish frittata, and the pomegranate coffee cake," I said. "Thanks."

"And for you?" Willow looked at Jonas, and my brother seemed dumbfounded. I couldn't help the smirk that covered my face. Willow was a beautiful woman, and Jonas was all teenage hormones.

"I'll have the same," he finally stuttered out after I kicked him under the table.

"Since when do you drink black coffee?" I said once Willow departed.

"Is that what I ordered?" he asked, dazed.

I was unable to contain my laugh. He glared at me before turning to take in the restaurant with the fountain in the middle splashing quietly and the windchimes dangling from the tree as it sprouted from the water.

"This place is pretty cool," he said.

I nodded. It was pretty amazing, just like the woman in the kitchen. I caught glimpses of her through the serving window in her normal whirlwind of action mode. But the hints of her weren't enough. My body was aching to see all of her…to see if she'd taste the same if I crushed my lips to hers again.

A girl drifted down the stairs from the second floor where the interconnecting door joined the restaurant to Brady's studio, allowing the artists to come to the restaurant without being assaulted by news crews and rabid fans. The woman was tiny and had black hair streaked with bright-blue highlights fanning around her face, hiding it. Even without seeing her clearly, I knew who she was—the youngest member of The Painted Daisies and the shyest, if you believed the media hype.

Willow met her at the base of the stairs, a to-go tray and a bag in her hands that passed from one to the other. Jonas's eyes journeyed in the same direction as mine, and he gasped as Paisley lifted her head to reveal the tiny, star-shaped birthmark near her left eye that gave her away to the world.

"Holy shit!" he said. It was loud enough to draw the eyes of the couple in the next booth but not loud enough to stretch across the place to the stairs.

My heart picked up pace, adrenaline kicking in as I prepared myself to fight off the crowd if my brother's reaction sent people flooding in her direction.

"That's Paisley Kim. Holy fucking hell…" Jonas

was almost hyperventilating.

"They're recording a new album at Brady's," I told him quietly as I watched the customers in the café for their reaction. Jonas's hands shook as he picked up the empty coffee cup on the table and tried to drink from it. "Am I going to be able to take you in there without you losing your shit?"

I was only half-teasing. I couldn't take him into the studio if he was going to fawn all over them and interrupt their session. My words brought Jonas back to reality and me. He brushed his hand through his brown hair that still needed a cut.

"Yes. Yeah…I'll get it together. But fuck! It's really her."

"Maliyah would be pulling you to the bathroom by the ear to wash your mouth out if she heard all the swear words you just dropped."

Paisley had disappeared up the stairs, and my brother's eyes were still stuck at the top where she'd disappeared into the studio. Willow dropped off our coffees in the to-go cups she knew I wanted and our meals all at the same time. She looked at Jo-Jo's stunned expression and gave a light laugh.

"I take it he saw our latest guest?" she teased.

I nodded.

"She's so quiet when you talk to her you'd think she could never sing a note—and especially not in front of an audience of thousands," Willow said.

"She's shy," Jonas defended her, which was sweet and comical all at the same time.

"You don't say," Willow offered back. She winked at me and headed over to the next table to ask if they needed anything else.

I shoved Jonas on the shoulder. "Eat, so we can go."

"Eat. Right. Food."

It did very little to ease my concern about him keeping it together when we went next door.

After a few minutes, Jonas asked in a much calmer voice, "You know she writes all their lyrics, right?"

I shrugged. I didn't. It wasn't my job to keep track of the band in that way. I knew which members caused the biggest ruckus and had the most rabid fans. I knew which one needed two bodyguards and which one barely needed one.

"She's got the strongest voice too, even though the critics are always praising Leya's smoothness or Fiadh's brogue," Jonas went on.

I'd finished the potato-and-onion omelet that Cassidy had perfected and enhanced with a spice I could never quite place and sat back to take in Jonas. He continued to ramble about the band, their strengths, and their weaknesses between bites. I was impressed by how much he knew. Hope eased through my chest that being in the studio today might help him forget—at least for a while—Mel and her problems back in Austin.

I flagged Willow down for the check.

"She says you know better than to ask to pay," Willow said with another saucy wink.

I groaned. I hated that Cassidy always covered my meals. It was the reason I didn't eat here as much as I wanted to and also the reason I always ended up tipping as much as the bill.

When I slid out of the booth, I headed for the

stairs with Jonas trailing me.

"Wait here. I'm just going to duck in and say thanks," I told him, inclining my head toward the swinging door to the kitchen.

I pushed my way inside and was hit with the sounds and heat of the space as the grill sizzled and Cliff chopped so fast his hands were a blur. Cassidy was at the large, free-standing mixer in the corner. She had a white apron layered over her T-shirt and a pair of black pants she rarely wore. I was certain Cassidy's wardrobe had more skirts than any other woman on the planet.

As if she'd sensed me come in, her head swiveled in my direction. I crossed over to her. "Thank you for breakfast, but stop buying my meals."

She rolled her eyes. "Charging you would be like expecting my parents to pay."

"I'm not family."

She flushed at my words, looking away as if they'd hurt her. My stomach twisted because the last thing I ever wanted was to cause her pain.

"Will you wait for me before you go home today?" I asked.

She looked back up at me with surprise in her eyes. "Why?"

"In case that asswipe is there again."

She grimaced because it was exactly the duty and protection she was adamant she didn't want.

"I can handle Clayton," she retorted. Then, she darted an eye around the room. "You haven't mentioned him to anyone, right? I don't want my family overreacting."

My jaw clenched. I didn't want to lie. Plus, her

family knowing could only be a good thing. There'd be more eyes looking out for her, but I also understood just how desperate she was to stand on her own without being guarded. I wanted her to have that, even though I was unable to ignore my own desire to keep her safe.

"I haven't said anything. They should know, but I won't be the one to tell them," I said.

Relief rushed over her face. "Thanks."

"He thinks I'm your…" my voice dropped to a whisper, "boyfriend. He'll expect me to be around. We should keep up the front so he'll stay away."

"I don't need to hide behind you or the stupid lie you told," she said, chin raising, glancing around the kitchen again.

"Please, Angel," I said, unable to keep the beg from my voice. Her eyes widened, nostrils flaring as we both agonized over the term of endearment I'd dropped.

After a long painful moment, she caved. "Fine. I'll text you when I'm done for the day."

It was my turn to feel the relief flooding my veins. "Thank you." My voice was guttural and deep. Full of things I shouldn't have felt.

She eyed me and then turned back to the dough in the mixer.

I watched her for one long moment before turning on my heel and heading out, wishing I hadn't screwed things up the night before. Wishing I didn't want to repeat the mistake of our lips tangled together. Wishing I could give her what she wanted most—to be loved without being shielded.

Chapter Seventeen

Cassidy

WE'RE NOT FRIENDS
Performed by Ingrid Andress

As always, my morning bled into my afternoon, the pace of the kitchen and the flow of customers keeping me from dwelling too often on the heated kisses the night before or the beg in Marco's voice this morning when he'd asked for me to wait for him before I went home. But as the crowd slowed and we neared closing, my brain wouldn't let go of either of those memories.

Maybe it was because I knew I'd be next to him again soon. Maybe it was because the more we stepped beyond the casual coach and trainee that we'd been, the more I craved of him. From him. I wanted the heat from last night that had scoured me from the inside out to be a part of my everyday life for as long as it lasted. For as long as we could keep the flame burning. It shouldn't have been wrong to want those feelings to linger and remain. I'd never had them before with anyone else. It seemed a shame to waste them. To let them go by the wayside and disappear as if they'd never been there to begin with.

But I also refused to be a job. A duty. I stood by

what I'd told Jonas. That would never bode well for a relationship. I wanted a partner as much as a lover. As soon as I thought it, I pushed it back away. It wouldn't be fair to him or Chevelle to start something when I had so little to give already. Marco had been right to walk away.

With that in mind, I steeled my resolve, knowing I'd see him in the studio as I headed up the stairs with a bus bin. I could have asked Laney to go get the plates and dishes we'd sent over to Brady's for lunch, but I was afraid I'd lose as many dishes as she brought back in her awestruck stupor over Brady and The Painted Daisies all in the same room.

Just as I eased through the interconnecting door, Tristan came out of the room that had been kept as her art studio during the renovation. *La Musica de Ensueños* used to be her grandmother's music store, but after she'd passed away, the store had struggled. Once Brady had come into the picture, and he and Tristan had fallen in love, they'd agreed to convert the store into a recording studio. It kept Brady in town more but also allowed my brother to do something else he loved—help other musicians.

"I miss Chevelle," Tristan said, placing a hand over her belly without even realizing it. Her words lifted my heart because it often felt like I took advantage of her willingness to watch my son.

"Give him a week of grandparent coddling, and he'll be wanting to come back," I said sarcastically.

"Grandparents are supposed to spoil and coddle. It's normal."

We paused at the top of the stairs inside the studio, looking down into the mess of bodies that mingled about the control room. *La Musica de*

Ensueños Studios wasn't nearly as large as other studios, so the bulk of the downstairs was taken up with the live room and specialty booths. A state-of-the-art mixing console was jammed in front of the glass window dividing the live room from the leather armchairs and couches shoved into the nooks and crannies of the space. It was cozy in a way that made it feel more home than business, and it fit Brady's personality as much as the café fit mine.

A smattering of fiddle and flute notes drifted through the air. While The Painted Daisies was labeled an alternative rock group, they'd taken the cultural instruments of each of the band member's heritage and blended them into a unique sound that had taken the country—and the world—by storm over the last year. The six females in the band pulled together Korean, Irish, Colombian, Indian and American cultures into this unique montage that was hard to imagine fitting together and yet did so perfectly.

Brady was at the mixing console with a tall, lanky man I didn't know standing at his side. Brady's ear was cocked, and his eyes were closed as he listened, but my gaze didn't linger with him long. In a room full of bodies, it was Marco's wide stance and all-seeing eyes that drew mine. He was up against a far wall, eyeing the door and the small reception desk that blocked the space from the entrance. My heart jiggled and sprang to life, pounding a tune that the flute and fiddle seemed to amplify.

My resolutions from two minutes before seemed to slip and slide away. As we made it to the bottom of the stairs, Tristan put a hand on my arm to halt me, dragging my gaze away from Marco to her.

"Can I ask you something?" she whispered. Her

tone was curious but calm.

I nodded.

"Is there something going on between you and Marco?"

My heart stutter-stopped, and I looked back at the man who'd somehow realized I was there. He was taking me in from the tip of my head down to my ugly, orthopedic shoes.

"Why do you ask?" I breathed out.

"Brady was going on about it last night. Saying something about Marco showing up to defend you like some knight in shining armor in the meeting with Ralley yesterday and how you're taking him with you to Texas." Her eyes remained curious but not judgmental.

"There's nothing going on," I said and couldn't help the slight tremor of disappointment that went through me and the flame that lit my cheeks thinking of our heated kiss in my kitchen.

"But you'd like there to be," she said gently.

"I'll never want to be with a man who only sees me as someone who needs protection—surrounded in bubble wrap. I get that enough from my family. I don't need it in a partner," I told her the easiest truth rather than the complicated layer of reasons that had me bouncing back and forth on a moment-to-moment basis.

"And his job is all about protecting people. It's what he's been built to do."

I shrugged, a weak smile hitting my face. "Yep."

"Protecting someone doesn't always mean you believe they aren't strong enough to do it themselves, Cass. Sometimes, it just means you love them."

It was something I already knew from a lifetime with my parents, but it still didn't mean I'd want it from a man I was involved with. She squeezed my arm one more time and made her way over to Brady.

I made my way into the room and started picking up the dishes and glasses. Before I could even register it, Marco had moved from his spot on the back wall to lift the bussing bin from my hands. I shot him a look of annoyance but didn't say anything. I didn't want to draw any eyes—especially not my brother's, if he and Tristan were already talking about whatever they thought might have been going on between us.

I finished collecting the items and started for the stairs. "Hold on," he whispered.

Then, he moved over to where Jonas was sitting. He'd been hidden by Brady and the man standing at his shoulder so that I hadn't even seen Marco's brother when I'd come down. Jonas had his eyes trained on the live room with a look of awe on his face that made me smile. I was glad no one had sent him away, even though The Painted Daisies was recording their top-secret album. Marco spoke quietly to his brother and then headed back my way.

We walked up the stairs, and I waited until we were out of earshot of the control room to talk. "He isn't coming with us?"

"Nah. If I took him away now, it would be like stealing candy from a baby. He's old enough to find his own way home."

Those simple words hit me hard. No one had ever treated me that way at sixteen.

"And I'm not old enough?" I tried to tease, but the words were backed with a frustration I knew he could read.

"If I wasn't worried about Hardy being there, I'd never insist on walking with you, Angel." I wasn't even sure he realized he'd let the term of endearment slip yet again. "You know how to take care of yourself."

I couldn't help the wave of relief that flew through me at his acknowledgement.

"I do," I responded. "Which is more reason for you to head back to your detail and leave me to it."

"It was time for Trevor to take over anyway."

We made our way through the hidden door and back into the café where there were only a couple tables with customers left. The closed sign had already been flipped on, and I could hear Cliff singing in the kitchen, which meant he was cleaning. I had a few more things to do before I could leave.

My feet had barely reached the bottom step when Clayton's voice called my name.

I sighed, turning to see him rise from a booth as he stepped toward Marco and me in a suit that screamed money and a watch that had to have cost as much as my professional knife set. Thousands. Marco moved closer to me, the air about me filling with the electricity that drifted between us and causing the hair on my arms to raise.

Clayton's eyes narrowed at us. "I've been talking to folks around town, trying to find out more about this behemoth. Imagine my surprise when I was told that Marco is your brother's bodyguard."

"Yeah. So?" I said, confusion drawing my brows together.

"He's *just* your brother's bodyguard. I don't understand why you both lied about this." He flicked a finger between Marco and me and then continued with anger and frustration filling his voice. "But he's clearly not the reason you won't give me another chance. He's nothing."

"Nothing?" Marco growled. Then, he surprised me by dropping the bus bin, whipping me into his arms, and placing his lips against mine. It wasn't a chaste peck on the lips. It wasn't a mere press of mouths to demonstrate his ability to kiss me. This was tongue and teeth and heat. Claiming me. Dragging my soul out from my insides and showing Clayton that he owned it. That I was his. All my resolve to keep the distance between us fled as I yanked his body into mine, slid my hands into his hair, and claimed him right back. *You're mine, Marco Hernandez. Mine,* I wanted to scream.

Clayton choked his disapproval. "Enough. Don't be crass."

Marco slammed me back against the wall, dragged his hands up inside my T-shirt, and clenched my waist. His warm, rough fingers dug into the flesh there, and it burned me like a flame in the kitchen. Searing across my skin, filling my veins, making it almost impossible to breathe.

"Jesus Christ," Clayton muttered. "And this is who my son is being raised by."

My eyes popped open, and fear filled my chest, ice filling my veins. The display we'd put on to prove a point to Clayton had backfired. I pushed at Marco's body, and he grunted his objection. But when I pushed again, he let me go, picking up my hand with his, squeezing to comfort me as if he could sense that something had changed in the two seconds we'd gone from hot to cold. His chest heaved as we both turned to Clayton.

"He isn't your son," I said, lifting my chin and shooting daggers with my eyes.

"My lawyers are drafting the paperwork to request a DNA test."

Shivers ran up my spine, a tremble shooting through me. "It doesn't matter if the DNA is a match, Clayton. He still won't ever be your son. Remember, I have proof of how little you wanted him."

"People make mistakes. I have a right to change my mind."

"You wouldn't be able to change your mind if I'd done what you wanted," I said, repeating myself from our talk on the steps of my house. Fear and anger drove my voice lower until it was a growl that matched the one Marco had given moments before for an entirely different reason.

"You're right. But it doesn't change the fact that he does exist, and I want to be a part of his life. I would have preferred to be a part of both of your lives, but now I remember why I didn't want you to begin with. You're cheap. An easy lay. A woman without direction, with a failing restaurant, who hides behind her brother's money."

Marco dropped my hand and shoved Clayton in the chest. "Don't ever speak like that to her again. Cassidy has more determination and class in one finger than you have in your entire being."

Clayton didn't back away. In fact, he laughed. "Truth hurt? Wake up, man, before she knocks herself up with your kid and tries to trap you, too."

Marco grabbed him by the shoulders and pushed him toward the door. "Keep talking, asshole, and I won't be able to stop myself from littering the ground with your blood."

"A threat? You're threatening me?" Clayton's eyes gleamed with satisfaction, straightening his suit once he'd steadied himself again.

"No," Marco snarled. "I'm promising you that if you don't leave Cassidy and Chevelle alone, it won't end well."

Clayton looked around the restaurant. One couple had ducked out while the exchange had been going on, but Laney and the last remaining couple were watching with wide eyes. "I'm sure everyone in here heard it. I'll be filing a complaint with the police. I'll be requesting the removal of this violent man from my child's life."

"You can try, but you won't succeed." It wasn't Marco who spoke. It was Brady, coming down the stairs at a jog. Fury on his face that I'd never seen on my brother before. That I didn't even know Brady had in him.

Clayton took in Brady with narrowed eyes. "Won't I? A musician with loose morals and a flood of deviants surrounding him isn't exactly the upbringing I expect for my son, and I think the courts will agree."

"You calling our two very upstanding, highly respected parents deviants, Hardy? I think they and the entire academic world around them would object to those words."

"A drop in the sea of destruction surrounding Chevelle," he said. He turned disapproving eyes at me. "And who names their son after a vehicle? I'll be changing that."

The entire time Marco, Brady, and Clayton had been sparring, my body had been frozen, horror stilling me. But when he disparaged the name I'd carefully chosen so that my child could go his own path, it returned the anger to me in a flood.

"Go ahead and file a complaint with the police," I snapped. "I'm going to file a restraining order of my own. I fear you may do something irrational. I fear for *Chevelle's* safety," I emphasized my child's name.

Clayton snorted. "I'm a respected lawyer and professor. I know my rights."

"You study business law, Clayton. Business. Not family law. But I can guarantee you, no court is going to hand you *my* son. Not when I show them just how little you wanted him."

"I'll keep repeating it if I have to: a man has a right to change his mind."

Marco crowded his space again, and this time, Clayton backed off. He threw one last, disparaging look in my direction and then left with the bell chiming behind him.

I sank onto the nearest barstool, head in my hands, trying to control the trembling and tears that threatened to overtake me as panic filled my blood.

Chapter Eighteen

Marco

HOLD YOU TONIGHT
Performed by Tim McGraw

The last time I'd felt this much anger toward another human being had been that awful night in the Fleet Marine Force. After I'd seen the violence inflicted because I'd been stupid enough to shut my eyes. I turned away from the door to see Cassidy with her head in her hands and her body quaking. I was at her side in two large steps with my hands running in circles along her back.

"It's going to be okay, Angel. I promise."

Her eyes whipped up, littered with tears but shock as well. Her look drifted to Brady, and I silently cursed myself. I'd forgotten he was there in the sea of anger and heartbreak I'd been feeling. When my gaze met his, it was grim, and I didn't know if the emotions behind them were directed at me or the asshole who'd just left.

"What the hell is going on?" Brady demanded.

"I wish I could tell you," Cassidy whispered. "I have no idea why he's decided to come back and terrorize me. There's no way he really wants Chevelle. He can't have changed that much."

My heart hurt for her, for the fear she must have been feeling at Hardy's threats.

Brady turned to the restaurant's last remaining guests who were still cowering in their seats. He gave them a charming smile and said, "We've got your meal, Mr. and Mrs. Anderson. We're so sorry to have put on such a show. Can we get you anything else?"

"No, thank you," Mr. Anderson said and took his wife's arm and left.

Brady then turned to Laney. "You're done for the day, right? We'll see you tomorrow."

Laney blushed and headed through the kitchen to clock out.

He'd cleared the room in his normal, suave way.

When it was empty, with only Cliff still singing cluelessly in the back, he sat down next to Cassidy at the restaurant's counter while I remained standing next to her.

"How long have you and Marco been…." He trailed off, suddenly uncomfortable.

Cassidy laughed. "Never. We're not."

And even though it was true, it stabbed at my heart because I didn't want it to be true. I may have kissed her to prove a point to Hardy, but once our lips had met again, it had been a feral claiming that had occurred. Me claiming her, and her claiming back. I knew it was a disaster in waiting. I knew I couldn't keep something so bright without somehow tarnishing it, and yet I still longed to be the one at her side, holding her hand.

"I saw you two," Brady said, eyes flitting to the

wall that I'd had Cassidy pinned to with my hands under her shirt and my tongue in her mouth. Where I'd been in heaven. In heaven with an angel.

"That was just pretend," Cassidy said. "Marco helped me by saying we were a couple the day Clayton first showed up trying to get me to give him a second chance. Today, he said he didn't believe us, so we convinced him otherwise."

Every word was factually what had happened, and yet I still wanted to deny them. I wanted to insist that we were exactly what I'd said we were. Brady's eyes landed on mine, taking me in and trying to read me. I kept my face impassive—void of emotions—but it didn't seem to fool him.

"That was some pretty good acting, then," he remarked.

Neither Cassidy nor I responded.

Brady snapped his leather bands at his wrist in thought. "I'll call Lee. We'll find the best damn family lawyer in the United States."

Cassidy sighed, closing her eyes. "Poor Lee. He's always bailing me out."

"I pay him to manage things in my life, Cassidy. And even if I wasn't paying him, I can guarantee you, he would be all over this himself. Lee wouldn't stand by and let anyone try and take Chevelle from you."

The words caused the tears Cassidy had barely been holding back to burst out. A sob escaped her as they fell down her cheeks. I knelt down, pulling her hand back into mine. "He doesn't have a chance. There's no way he can take Chevelle from you. Not with the proof you have."

Brady's eyes widened at my tender speech, and I swallowed hard. He turned back to Cassidy. "What's this proof?"

Cassidy explained about a check Hardy had written for the abortion, which made my stomach clench, and some texts and emails she had from him saying he never wanted anything to do with her again. Hardy had begged her to take the "smart" path and get rid of the child.

I wanted to toss the guy into the Erie and let the fish eat him.

Brady's jaw clenched as hard as my fist. "I agree with Marco. He doesn't have a shot, Cass." Then, he turned and headed for the stairs.

"Wait, what did you come by for?" Cassidy asked.

Brady looked confused for a second, and then his face cleared with a small smile. "Right. I came to tell Marco I was taking Jonas back to the house with me."

"You are?" I asked, surprised.

"The band is done for the day, and they're heading to their rental house. Tristan needs to put her feet up, so we're taking off as well, but Jonas had some great ideas for The Painted Daisies' songs that I want to poke around some more. They're fresh and unsophisticated, but interesting. I'll have one of the detail bring him back to my parents' when we're done, if that's okay with you?"

Brady looked at me, and it hit me in the chest that I was responsible for Jonas in a way I'd never been before. I'd always looked out for him, but I'd never been the parent. I'd never been the one who could deny a request.

"I think Jonas would slit my throat in the middle of the night if I objected," I told him honestly.

Brady chuckled and headed up the steps. About halfway up, he turned and looked back down at us with lips tilting upward. "And pretend or not, that was one hell of a kiss."

I couldn't help the snort that left me, and I was glad it brought a strangled half-laugh from the depths of Cassidy. Brady disappeared through the door, and I took his spot on the stool next to her, spinning it so that our legs were tangled together. Our knees and thighs blended into a united mess. A current of heat and energy traveled through my veins that made my blood pound out a tune full of yearning.

"I think we need to talk," I said, my voice deep, the desire to pick up where we'd left off showing in each syllable.

"I'm not a project…or a client. I don't want you hovering around, trying to surround me in cotton so I don't get hurt," she said, chin lifting.

I stared into her golden eyes, amazed at the power I saw in them every day, even in the face of her fear and sadness from what Hardy had just put her through. It wasn't anything that I hadn't already witnessed from her before, though. She fought every day to be the strongest person in the room.

"I don't think of you that way," I told her because it was the truth. I didn't. I might want to protect her. Shield her. And I'd never walk away if there was a chance that something was coming for her, but I also didn't see her as someone who couldn't stand on her own.

She looked down to where my hands were on her knees. I wanted to skim them up the sides of her black pants and find where the skin began. If she'd been in one of her typical skirts, my hands would have had easier access to touch her.

She let out a tumultuous breath, the sweet and spice of it taunting me to kiss her again. "I need to finish up. Go home. Put my arms around Chevelle."

I nodded, but neither of us moved.

"I have to tell my parents," she said, sighing.

"If they're going to have Chevelle all summer, it's the smart thing to do. You don't want Hardy to catch them unaware."

She grimaced. "I've never told them he was the father."

That hung in the air between us for a moment, and I could almost hear how much she hated the idea of telling them now.

"I'll go with you," I said quietly.

Her eyes narrowed.

I chuckled softly. "It isn't to protect you. It's because I know Arlene loves me, and she might not completely lose it in front of me."

Cassidy's lips quirked. "Protection via charm."

I stared into her eyes. "Maybe."

She reached up and ran a finger over my jaw. It flexed in response, my body tightening at the simple touch. "You're right. We do need to talk about this," she said softly.

"We do," I told her. My heart was heavy and light all at the same time. I wanted her. I wanted us and hated myself for it…for even having the audacity to think I might be able to make her my own.

"Give me twenty minutes to wrap up here," she said.

"I can help. Just point me to what you need done."

"You going to mop floors?" she teased.

"I did worse in the military," I said, and my heart almost seized. I didn't talk about it with anyone, and yet it had slipped several times with her.

Her eyes widened because I'd brought it up after telling her I didn't like to talk about it. I couldn't take the look she was sending my way, as if there was only good beating inside my chest. Half of me wanted her to continue to see me like that, but I knew I had to rip away her rose-colored glasses and allow her a chance to run before I drew her close. Before we tangled more than tongues.

I stood up. "Point me to the mop."

She stared for a long moment before directing a finger toward the supply closet.

She went into the back and finished the prep work for the next day while I mopped the entire restaurant. The simple job allowed me time to think of all the things I'd done wrong in the last week. All the things I couldn't take back and didn't want to. Brady should have hated me. He should have been asking for me to be transferred to another detail because I'd crossed the line. Instead, in his typical Brady way, he'd teased and taunted us.

I wasn't sure what any of it meant.

The only thing I knew was that the tastes of Cassidy O'Neil I'd had only made me wild for more.

Chapter Nineteen

Cassidy

TO HELL AND BACK
Performed by Maren Morris

Whenever I didn't have Chevelle with me, I walked the few blocks back and forth to the restaurant instead of driving. It saved the environment and was good for me, even after a day on my feet. As Marco and I headed home after locking up the restaurant, the late-afternoon sun beat down on us in full strength. The humidity dripped over me, thick and heavy—as heavy as my thoughts and my fears.

Clayton's threats were still terrifying, but a feral protectiveness had reared up inside me since he'd arrived in Grand Orchard. One thing was certain: he couldn't have my son. Not even occasionally. He'd wanted me to get rid of the baby before he'd even existed, so he couldn't claim him now.

As we walked, our silence wasn't uncomfortable, even when there was a layer to it of the things left unsaid. Things that needed to be discussed before we could go back to the smooth camaraderie we'd had before. I wasn't sure if we'd ever get that back completely. It made me sad, but it also made my heart skip because maybe we couldn't go backward, but maybe we could go forward. Replace what once had been with something more. Bigger. Deeper.

I still wasn't sure I should even attempt it, because I had the message playing on repeat in my brain that it wasn't fair to him, or Chevelle, or even me, when every minute of my day was already accounted for. But the ache to try was there. Momentarily, I wondered if we had to be all in or if we could have something that was there casually, but a piece of me recoiled at the thought because it felt too close to what I'd had with Clayton.

I'd barely opened the front door of my parents' home before my boy was throwing himself into my arms. "Mama!"

I held him close, kissing the top of his head, squeezing until it felt like the air had left both our bodies, and he giggled before squirming out of my grasp. He ran to the coffee table with his awkward gait and then back, shoving a paper at me. "Hippo's bruder."

It was a picture of a stick dog, and even though it was rudimentary and childlike, it was too good for Chevelle to have drawn. "Did you draw a picture for Hippo?" I asked with a smile.

He shook his head. "Papa give doggy."

I looked over to where my father was sitting on the couch with a book in his hand about the return of Latin to our modern world. He barely glanced up.

"Papa drew this for you?" I asked with a smile. My dad was definitely not known for his artistic abilities.

Chevelle nodded. "Real doggy. Real doggy home soon."

Chevelle was giddy with happiness, and I looked

at my dad, shocked. "You did not promise him a puppy, Dad. Did you? There's no way—"

"I bought one of the Romeros' Boston Terrier pups. For your mother and me," he said, hardly glancing up.

I stared. We'd had a dog when I was little, and when it had passed away, Dad had sworn he'd never own an animal again. It was too hard when they were at the house so little he'd said. So, getting one now was obviously because of Chevelle.

"Dad," I warned.

He laughed, finally putting the book down. "I can get a dog, Cassidy."

Mom came into the room at the same time, and she rolled her eyes. "Your father has completely lost his mind. He doesn't remember the potty training, the gnawed wood, and the destroyed shoes."

"He wants to spoil Chevelle," I said with a huff.

Mom laughed. "Yes, *cailín deas*. He does."

"A man should have a dog to take on long walks as he enters his sunset years," Dad said. Marco let out a surprised grunt of humor that drew both my parents' eyes. "Marco, good to see you."

Mom squinted. "What's wrong?"

I almost rushed out with my normal, "Nothing," but I couldn't.

I sat on the floor with Chevelle, drew him into my lap, and inhaled the soft scent of his baby shampoo. "Do you remember Clayton Hardy?"

Dad frowned. "The law professor? I remember what an ass…"

His eyes grew, widening as he took in Chevelle and then me. Mom hadn't figured it out yet even when she was the one to normally see everything about me first.

"He moved to Harvard, right? I think I heard something about him covering a course here at Wilson-Jacobs this summer," she said.

I swallowed. "He's…" I looked up at Marco, and his eyes softened, as if speaking to me. Encouraging me. Giving me strength. "He was the sperm donor."

I couldn't say he was Chevelle's father because he wasn't. He didn't have anything to do with raising my son, or loving him, or being there for either of us.

Mom gasped. "What?"

She sat down on the sofa next to Dad as if she'd lost all muscle control. As if she was the one with hypotonia instead of me.

"Cassidy!" My mom looked at me with surprise and disapproval but also worry.

I shrugged. "We met up a few times. What else do you want me to call it? What I told you before was true. He wanted me to get an abortion, and I refused. It was the end of my discussions with him."

"But now he's back?" Dad prompted.

I nodded. "He says he wants to get to know Chevelle, but really…really, he's playing at something else I don't understand yet. He doesn't want a child. He made that very clear."

Silence filled the room.

"People change," Dad said quietly.

"Not this one." It was Marco who spoke. Deep and gravelly. Anger in his voice that had been there when he'd all but tossed Clayton from my restaurant. When Marco had promised that if Clayton came near me or Chevelle again, he'd clean the streets with him.

Dad and Mom both looked at Marco with surprise.

"You know something we don't?" Dad asked.

"Trevor and I are digging, but at the moment, it's more instinct than facts," Marco said with a slight shrug. "He threatened Cassidy at the restaurant today."

Mom gasped again. Her hand reached for Dad's, and they squeezed each other tight. A unit. They may have disagreed over Brady and me in the past, over the way Mom had overprotected me and held Brady accountable for things he should never have been when it came to me and my health, but at the end of the day, they were always there for each other, holding each other up.

My heart ached. I wanted that so badly I could almost taste it. Someone on this journey with me. Next to me. Balancing me.

I was surprised when Marco joined me on the floor, as if he'd read my thoughts.

"I promise," Marco's voice was deep again, holding layers of emotion that I wanted to crawl under like a blanket. "He won't be able to take Chevelle."

"Don't make promises you can't keep," Mom's voice snapped at him, and it drew our eyes back to her. It was what she'd nagged Brady about the most—the promises he'd made and then broken. At least, she'd felt like he'd broken them when it was really just him living his own life as he should have been. I'd never wanted my brother to give up his world to hover around me.

Marco met Mom's gaze with an even one. "I intend to keep that promise, Arlene."

I jumped in before things got tense. "Brady's

having Lee find a family law attorney for me. I have… I have some pretty nasty messages from Clayton and a check for the abortion that I never used."

Mom's face twisted and fell. My father draped an arm around her shoulder and pulled her up tight against him.

"Why didn't you ever tell us this?" Dad asked.

I looked down, hugging Chevelle. "It wasn't exactly a moment I was proud of."

It made me think of Marco's words about his time in the military. It had wounded him in some way, turning something that should have been perceived as admirable into disgrace. I had my amazing son, and I'd never, ever regret him, but I could regret the person I'd let myself be in order to sleep with Clayton. Marco and I both had things in our past that were complicated. Twisted pieces of pride and shame hiding within us.

"I's hungry, Mama!" Chevelle said, wiggling from my arms and freeing himself from my grasp.

It seemed like he was always hungry these days. A growth spurt had to be coming. I couldn't even imagine what it would be like when he was a teenager, growing inches at a time. Turning into a man. I needed him to be surrounded by people who would show him what being a man should look like. My father and brother were good men. They would always be there for him, but he deserved his own father.

My throat closed on my emotions.

"Okay, Snickerdoodle. Let's go." I stood up and wobbled. Marco steadied me.

"Maco come?" Chevelle asked, lifting his arms toward Marco and making it even harder to breathe. Harder for my heart to beat.

Marco looked at me, all the things we hadn't said yet still drifting between us. "Yes, I'm coming, too," he said as he easily lifted my son into his arms. Chevelle pointed to Hippo, and Marco picked the stuffed animal up without question.

I saw my parents exchange a look out of the corner of my eye, but I didn't care. When I met their gaze, they'd hidden away whatever thoughts they'd had.

"I just wanted you to know, in case Clayton showed up here while you had Chevelle. He's not allowed to see him, okay?"

"Of course," my mother huffed.

"If he shows up and gives you a problem, call me," Marco said.

They nodded.

We headed for the back door and the short journey that would lead me to my house. My mom's voice halted me. I held back while Marco continued out the gate and toward my door.

"What's going on with you two?" she asked.

"He was there when Clayton showed up."

"You know that's not what I mean, *cailín deas*."

"I know. But I don't have anything else to say about it right now," I said, trying to keep both the hope and defensiveness out of my tone.

I didn't wait for a response. It didn't matter. This was one aspect of my life my mother would never be able to control.

♪ ♪ ♪

Marco and I made dinner together again, taking

turns entertaining Chevelle while we did it. After, Marco cleaned up the kitchen and went back to his apartment to change into workout gear while I put Chevelle down. He'd just gotten back when my son asked to say goodnight to him, and the sloppy kiss he placed on Marco's cheek about undid me. It clearly impacted Marco almost as much, because he kept his eyes closed for way too long. Almost as if he was holding back tears.

I changed and met Marco in the gym we'd built together, just like we'd done hundreds of times before, but we both knew it felt different tonight. Something had shifted. As if by silent agreement, we didn't talk about any of the things hovering over us. Instead, we pounded our bodies through a routine we knew like the back of our hands. One that had me dripping with sweat and Marco glistening. The time he spent with me working out was nothing compared to what he really put his muscles through in order to keep his body cut and chiseled. Normally, our workout came before or after at least another hour he did on his own.

After our last round, I sank onto the mat with my water bottle. I lay down and let the coolness of the vinyl sift through me. Marco sat beside me with his long legs flung out in front of him. He leaned back on his arms in a way that flexed the muscles. His palms were spread wide, and his pinkie was almost touching mine. If I moved ever so slightly, I could hook them together. Join us.

"Thank you," I said quietly.

He looked down at me, eyes drifting from my face, over the length of me, and then back. His gaze settled on my lips for so long it made them part as if he'd sent a message to them by telepathy. Finally, his eyes met mine.

"I haven't done anything," he said quietly.

I shoved his arm gently. "Don't be ridiculous. You know you helped me."

His gaze bored into mine. The air turned thick in a way it hadn't been while we'd been exercising. Maybe because the workout had been the old us, performing a song we'd played hundreds of times. This rhythm was new and unknown. Exciting and terrifying. I didn't want to lose him by pushing for more, but I also didn't want to go backward.

When he spoke, his voice was as thick as the tension that bounced around us. "I liked kissing you, but the truth is, it's better for me to be alone. I shouldn't have started something I couldn't finish. It's better if we remain...friends."

I rolled onto my side so I could look at him easier, propping my head up with my hand. I could see that he believed what he said. Believed he should be alone, as if he was paying penance for things he'd never admit.

"You know what I think?" I finally breathed out.

His dark eyes flashed with emotions—warnings and pleas mixed together.

"I think you like to believe you're a lone wolf. Maybe because of your parents' deaths. Maybe because of whatever happened to you in the military. But the truth is, you are built for family. The loyalty in you...the way you care about everyone around you, even when they don't belong to you...you're aching to make it real. To have what you lost. But you won't let yourself."

"Wanting it and deserving it are very different things," he said quietly, and as if he couldn't stop himself, his hand came up to push aside the hair that had escaped my bun, being careful not to touch my face or my neck. The tendril was the only thing that got to feel his embrace, and I was almost jealous of my own hair. Stupid. But the lack of touch stabbed me almost as much as his words did. My heart twisted for him because he thought he had to deny himself this. Love of any kind. I wanted him to have it, even if it wasn't with me. Even if I didn't get to keep him.

"What happened?" I demanded, wanting to know what had left such a huge scar on him. Had left him feeling like there could never be a way back to redemption.

"I don't want to tell you," he said. It was hushed and pained, but it hurt me in a different way—as if he couldn't trust me.

"Why?"

"Because you won't see me the same way," he said gently. "And I'm selfish enough to want to keep the stars in your eyes. I want you to look at me like you do right now. As if I'm the hero of the story. The knight who shows up on his steed whether the princess needs him or not. Even if it's just to pick up a sword and swing at her side."

I shook my head, and my hair gave up its war with gravity, tumbling down about me. I had so much of it that it rarely stayed up in a solitary bun. It was why I usually had two round cinnamon rolls sitting atop my head. Today, I'd been lazy, simply looping it into place with bobby pins that wouldn't stay and had slowly been springing free all day. Our workout had been the final trial. Marco wrapped a single coil around a finger, slowly drawing it closer to my cheek but restraining himself from the final twist that would have his skin touching mine.

"But the princess doesn't fall in love with the knight because he shows up, Marco," I said with all the confidence I could muster. "She falls in love because when the war is over, he takes off all the armor and bares himself to her. Because they share their dreams and their goals and their hopes and their fears. She might admire him on the battlefield, but she loves him when he's entwined himself into every part of her."

His finger fell to my face, crashing into my lips, running a thumb over the bottom one and tugging at the top as if they were fascinating pieces of art instead of pieces of a body that everyone had. They were mundane, really, but he seemed enthralled by mine.

"Do you know what a code red is?" he asked, voice raspy and barely audible it was so low.

I nodded. "Yes. Doesn't everyone? I mean, if you've seen *A Few Good Men*, at least."

He grimaced, eyes flicking from my lips to meet my gaze.

"That movie and my life have quite a few similarities."

"Someone died because of a code red you did?" I asked, trying to hold back my shock, because I didn't want him to think he'd been right—that I'd think less of him after he'd told me the truth. I wouldn't. I knew that with every fiber in me.

"No. She didn't die," he said. "And I didn't give the code red."

I was surprised by the female pronoun but equally confused by his denial. "If you didn't give the code red, why does it haunt you?" I couldn't help the thought that ran across my mind. "You didn't order it, did you?"

He shook his head, growing grimmer, but it only continued to confuse me.

"I refused to follow my captain's order. He wanted me…" He swallowed hard. "He wanted me to steal all of her clothes. To sneak into her barracks while she was showering. Take everything there and everything from her locker. Towels. Everything. He wanted her naked and humiliated."

Anger spiked through me—not at Marco but at the captain. The arrogance and pain he was willing to cause another human being.

"Why would he do that?" I asked.

"Retaliation. She was a corpsman like me, but with more seniority. We'd been out on a training op, and the captain collapsed in the field. She'd been the first one at his side as he came to. He was already embarrassed as shit because you don't show that kind of weakness in the military, ever, especially as a Marine. He'd said he had a heat stroke. She said he had a heart issue. At a minimum, it would have put him behind a desk, and at worst, he could have lost his commission. Either way, he was humiliated and angry. Pissed that she'd gone against what he'd said was wrong with him."

"What happened when you refused?" I asked.

"He was even more furious. Had me clean the latrines like I was back at boot camp and had me confined to quarters. He threatened to write me up for disobeying a direct order, but we both knew he couldn't without lying about the order he'd given."

He paused as if looking through me at some video on replay. Images that caused him pain.

"I'm still confused. Why on earth would this make me think less of you?" I asked.

"Because I saw them leave and didn't stop them."

I held my breath and then waited for him to continue as fear started to crawl through me. "There were some Marines in the unit—young and impressionable—who had idolized the captain. They were also arrogant and chauvinistic and hated that a female corpsman was there at all, let alone putting their captain at risk." He paused, shaking his head. "I convinced myself they were just going out for drinks. That it had nothing to do with Petty Officer Warren and the code red I'd refused."

He stopped talking completely, shutting down until I thought he'd disappeared altogether in the past.

"What happened?" I prompted, afraid to know and desperate to hear the rest so I could somehow soothe him. Grant him solace and reprieve.

"They attacked her...left her naked and battered...assaulted...at the foot of the flagpole."

"Holy shit!" My eyes widened, and I reached out to grab the hand he'd moved back away from my face. I curved my fingers around it and forced the palm to my cheek. "Marco, that is not on you."

"It is. If I'd reported the captain to the major... If I'd stopped them or followed them... Petty Officer Warren wouldn't have been hurt. It was my duty to not only protect people but heal them, and I didn't. I turned a blind eye, and she was hurt...physically, mentally. In every way possible."

Before I'd really registered it, I'd pulled away and was sitting in his lap so that I could hug him to me with his face embedded in my neck and my hair. I squeezed tight like I'd done with Chevelle earlier.

"You wanted to believe they were good people. That they lived by the same code you did," I said softly.

He didn't push me away. His hands actually found their way around my middle and spread across my back, gripping as if I was something he could hold onto in the middle of a storm.

"I stayed silent, and she got hurt because of it. As much as the military normally rewards silence, Petty Officer Warren was the daughter of a major general. Not many people knew it because she'd enlisted under her mother's maiden name to prove herself on her terms and not her dad's. But when he found out, he went ballistic. Not only did he want heads to roll because of what had happened to his child, but our politicians were desperate to continue fixing the image of our military. Because I hadn't spoken up, I was as guilty as the ones who'd actually laid their hands on her. I agreed. I pled no contest to the court-martial charges and was dishonorably discharged."

I turned to press my lips against his temple and continued to run my hands up and down his back.

"Maliyah was distraught when she found out I'd been court-martialed." His voice was deep and pained. "And even more so when I was discharged. That was when she had her first cardiomyopathy episode. I literally broke her heart."

My heart felt like it was broken as well, bleeding for him. This man who wanted so much to be everyone's defender only to have two females end up in the hospital because of things he felt responsible for. All I could do was hold on stronger. To show him affection so he realized this didn't change my opinion of him. He was still everything I'd ever thought him to be, but also somehow more because he'd shouldered this guilt and grief on his own for so long.

He was still the knight swinging his sword, but he'd also laid himself bare, and it did nothing but make the feelings I had for him grow

Chapter Twenty

Marco

BETTER THAN I AM
Performed by Keith Urban

Cassidy had her arms and legs wrapped around me and was holding me so tight that there was no space left between us. Like the hugs she gave Chevelle. I could feel the strength of her emotions in the hug. She should have been pushing me away, scowling at me for having let this happen to another human being, for causing Maliyah so much sadness that she'd almost died because a portion of her heart had stopped. Instead, Cassidy clung to me as if I'd been the one wounded.

She kissed my temple. Soft lips grazing my hairline, sending electric waves through my body that reacted to her touch, to her entire being tucked up against mine with her softly shaped butt cheeks pushing into my thighs and groin. Her core lined up against mine in a way that instantly made me go hard even as I tried to push the thought out of my head.

Her breath hitched as I grew harder. Even thoughts of all my sins couldn't stop it because I was completely surrounded by the scent and heavenly grace of Cassidy O'Neil. She put her hands on my cheeks, drawing my face up from where it had rested, cocooned in her neck, hiding in the shower of long hair that had fallen over me. Her eyes met mine. Heated. But also full of sadness and horror and something else I was terrified of naming. Something that echoed the feelings in me that I tried to bury.

"Marco...do you even know how breathtaking you are?"

My chest cracked open. I closed my eyes against the sight of her.

I hadn't expected her to run, because Cassidy wasn't someone to duck at the first shot, but I had expected my past to stick a fence between us. Barbed wire that was jagged and easily tore flesh and bone. I'd expected her eyes to be opened so that she saw a very flawed man instead of continuing to look at me with glistening eyes.

She leaned in and feathered a kiss along my cheekbone, grazing over my lips to the other side before coming back to land on my mouth. A soft kiss. As if she was trying to give me solace. Comfort when I hadn't earned it and hadn't told her the story to make her feel any of this. I'd thought it would push her away instead of drawing her closer.

But the simple, light kisses exploded the heat inside me, turning it into a thundering roar of a volcano spewing out, and before I could stop myself, I was devouring her. Biting at her lips, plundering into the soft recess of her mouth, seeking all of her. She didn't push away. She did the opposite. She consumed me back. Teeth and tongues and lips brutalizing each other as flames of longing coursed through us.

Her hips thrust against my groin, and it drove me nearly mad. I wanted her bare. I wanted to remove the last pieces of clothing that were holding us apart until there was nothing between us. Until I was filling her and making her moan.

My hands slid under the tank she wore as a top and bra combined, fingers finding a hardened nipple, caressing and flicking until she gasped. All the while, my mouth continued to take her air and make it mine. Her fingers danced below my shirt, gliding over my stomach, making my muscles contract beneath her touch, burning me. Branding me. Making me Cassidy O'Neil's in a way I'd never belonged to anyone before.

I dragged the strap of her tank down and finally left her mouth to slide tongue and lips down her neck. The salty taste of her sweat embedded with her natural scent, making me hungry for her as if I'd been starved for years. I'd just lifted one beautiful breast from its confines when my phone rang out, blasting through the room, bringing us back from the gates of heaven.

It was Jonas's tone. One I couldn't ignore.

I groaned, and to my surprise, Cassidy laughed. She fell away from me, and I missed the heat and scent and weight of her instantly. I reached behind us to the small cabinet in the room and pulled my phone down.

"What's up?" I asked, and even to me, my breath sounded uneven. Shaken.

"I didn't bring a key to the apartment. I can't get in. I thought you'd be here by now," Jonas said.

"I'm at Cassidy's, working out."

"Cool, I'll meet you there." He hung up before I could even tell him not to come.

"Jonas is on his way." I popped to my feet and glanced down at her. She looked even more beautiful than normal. Lips pink and raw, a flush to her cheeks that had nothing to do with our workout. She'd pulled up her tank, but it was unable to hide the hardness of her peaks. Hard, just like I was.

Her eyes landed on my groin, and she smiled. "You better do something about that quick."

"Quick is not my idea of fun," I teased, and she laughed as she rose from the mat.

She pulled a T-shirt out of the closet and tugged it on just as the back door slammed shut. I grimaced, hoping it didn't wake Chevelle. "Sorry."

"Chevelle sleeps through almost anything. It's good. I bang around in the kitchen while he's sleeping, too."

I was still fighting to get my body under control until I realized we'd never really settled anything between us. I'd simply told her my deepest, darkest secrets without resolving a thing. Everything deflated as my mind filled with Petty Officer Warren's broken and bruised body, regret and anger replacing the desire.

Cassidy poked her head out of the room and called out quietly, "We're in the gym."

Jonas loped into the room on lanky legs with a grin so large it took over his entire face. He stopped to take in the small exercise space and our sweaty bodies.

"Wow, I don't think I realized you had all this in here," he said.

"You're welcome to use it any time," Cassidy told him.

His smile grew impossibly wider. "Thanks. You all are so…fucking nice."

"Language, Jonas," I tossed out.

Jonas flushed a little. "Sorry. I just... You're all really cool."

I snorted out a laugh at his stunned expression. "You've been Brady-fied."

"Tristan calls that the Brady O'Neil Experience...although...maybe...never mind," Cassidy faded off, turning bright pink. My smile grew as wide as Jonas's, but he didn't seem to catch the innuendo that had drifted into Cassidy's words.

"He listened to all my ideas, Marco. He even said he thought they had a lot of potential. He wants Paisley and Deja to redo an entire song just because of how I'd said it would be better with a retro, seventies vibe until the flute and pipe joined in. He's having them change their song...because of me...because of what I said."

I flung an arm over his shoulder and ran my knuckles over the top of his head. "Nice, Jo-Jo."

He groaned and pushed me off. "You're sweaty and gross. And stop with the Jo-Jo. It makes me sound like a trained seal or something."

Cassidy chuckled and then stopped once she realized how serious Jonas was.

I picked up my keys from the cabinet and tossed them at him. He caught them easily.

"I'll be up in a couple of minutes. Cassidy and I have a few things to finish up," I said. Her eyes widened, falling to my lips and then trailing down my body before returning to my face.

Jonas was already walking out. "'Kay. I'm going to call Maliyah and tell her about my day."

"She'll love hearing about it."

He was gone as quickly as he'd come, slamming

the back door again and making me wince all over.

Cassidy took two steps toward me, and I fisted my hands, afraid that if I touched her, it would be hours before I was back at the apartment instead of minutes. She took in the way I was holding myself and stopped. She brushed a hand over her forehead, rubbing at a spot that wasn't there.

"I'm being selfish," she muttered.

"What? No—" I started, but she stopped me with a hand.

"The truth is, Marco, I want you so much that every single part of me is vibrating with it. It isn't just physical. It's like my actual being…my soul wants it, too. But right now…I barely have time for the restaurant and Chevelle. I have this huge thing with Ralley hanging over me, and now Clayton has shown up on my doorstep. I don't know how to give you the time you deserve and not drop something else."

"I don't deserve anything from you, Angel. Not one thing. This…"—I flicked a hand between us—"I knew it was wrong. I'm sorry I let us get carried away."

It hurt to say it, and I could see my words had struck at her as well.

"It isn't wrong, you big lunk. It's just really poor timing. I don't know when my life will get easier… I'm not asking you to wait around in the background, fiddling your hands while I try and sort things…but—"

"I'm not going anywhere. This is where I'm at right now. Here. With you and Chevelle. With Brady." I meant every word. I'd be there for them. That was my job but also where my heart wanted me to be. Thoughts of Jonas and Maliyah shot through me—parts of my life that I'd kept from everyone for so long and now was being forced to reconcile as Jonas merged himself into my existence here in Grand Orchard.

"You should have more than just the leftover scraps of people's lives, Marco. You deserve to be the center of somebody's world. I just…" She looked like she was going to cry. "I don't know when I'll be able to give you that. If I'll ever… Chevelle will always be first."

I reached for her because I couldn't not. I pulled her up against my chest, and she settled with her cheek to my shoulder. "Chevelle *should* be first in your life. He's your child. I'm not asking or expecting anything from you. We're adults who shared some damn good kisses. It doesn't have to be more than that."

"I want it to be more than that," she said, and it sounded so much like Chevelle's whine that I couldn't help the chuckle that rumbled through me.

It felt right to have her in my arms. Like this was how we were supposed to fit together in a universe full of pieces that didn't belong. Her curves and lines blended perfectly into mine. Our bodies easily aligned. Maybe it just took time for souls to line up as well. Or maybe they wouldn't ever fit the way our limbs did. But the truth was, I wasn't going anywhere, and neither was she, and maybe that was all we needed at this moment. The knowledge that we were both still here.

"Maybe this is all it can be right now," I said gruffly.

She didn't respond, but she pulled away slowly, and it felt like a Band-Aid being ripped away. Like losing skin and flesh in the process. It took every single ounce of willpower I owned to not pull her back. Instead, I picked up my water bottle and headed for the door. I looked back, wanting to say something poetic. Wanting to tell her how much she meant to me, regardless of whether we ever kissed again, but I didn't have the right words. So, I just nodded my chin at her like an idiot and left, knowing my dreams were going to be haunted with all the possibilities that we hadn't fulfilled.

Chapter Twenty-one

Cassidy

WITH YOU
Performed by Keith Urban

Three weeks flew by as my life shifted and changed around me, and I made plans to go see Ralley in Texas. It was like some weird before-and-after collage that wasn't quite fully formed yet. The routine that I'd shaped Chevelle's and my life around had shattered.

Regardless of what we'd both said after our heated kiss in the gym, Marco and I seemed to drift together more than ever. Before summer had hit, I'd see him at the end of my day for our workouts and occasionally for breakfast or when he was with Brady. Now, I saw him multiple times a day, but he hadn't kissed me again. He hadn't even come close, and it pricked at my heart, even though I understood it. Knowing that Marco was resisting because he felt like he didn't deserve the affection only made me want to show him how much he did. I couldn't, though, because what I'd said to him was the truth. I'd been selfish to start something when I didn't have the time to give him what he truly deserved.

So, while we were spending extra time together,

we also seemed to have taken a small step backward. I was seeing him more but touching him less. Marco and Jonas came to the restaurant every morning for breakfast, and they joined Chevelle and me for dinner almost nightly. Sometimes I cooked, sometimes Marco cooked, and sometimes we ordered in. But now there were four of us at the dinner table instead of two. Chevelle loved every moment of it because he had three people focused completely on him. Jonas was as sweet to my son as Marco was, playing and teasing and making him giggle. It made my heart throb and hurt—the image of a family we made when we were really nothing.

Jonas seemed to bloom before our eyes. Brady acknowledging him and his ideas gave him a confidence that he hadn't had when he'd first shown up. Whenever I went to the studio to bring lunch, Jonas was offering ideas right alongside Brady. The Painted Daisies band members and their team never seemed to sneer at him just because he was sixteen. Maybe it was because Paisley, the youngest member of The Painted Daisies, was barely seventeen.

Paisley's sister and leader of the band, Landry, was the only band member to look at Jonas with hesitation, and it was only when Jonas and Paisley had their heads bent together, arguing music and lyrics. It was as if she was unsure of whether to stop the friendship forming between them or to just let it ride itself out. After all, they would be leaving Grand Orchard before the summer was gone.

A couple of days before Marco and I were set to leave for Texas, I returned to the café from the studio, lost in my thoughts about all the things going right and wrong in my life, when a man in a suit approached me at the restaurant's counter.

"Cassidy O'Neil?" he asked.

I hesitated, but he didn't seem to notice. He simply stuck out a hand with an envelope. "This is a court order requiring you to provide a DNA test for your son."

My heart squeezed tight. Fear and anger floated through me even though I'd known it was coming. With shaking hands, I took the envelope, watching as he walked away before calling the lawyer Lee had found for me. It felt as if I was gasping for breath as I waited for Annabelle Green to pick up and as if I was drowning as I explained what had happened.

"We knew this was coming, Cassidy. It's easier to give in to this demand and establish biological paternity while making our case against his paternal rights and responsibilities," Annabelle said.

"But it's a slippery slope, right? I mean…once he proves Chevelle is his biological child, then he can file for responsibility and partial custody." My voice wavered as I tried to keep the panic from surfacing.

Annabelle's voice was hard as she came back. "He won't get rights, Cassidy. He's paid nothing in child support. You have the documentation where he made it very clear he wanted the child aborted and wouldn't take any responsibility beyond that."

She felt we had a strong case, but it did nothing to lessen the dread filling me as I left the restaurant early for the first time in the entire time I'd owned the place. It was just my luck that I left the building right as Marco was leaving the studio. I tried to duck away, but it was too late. He'd seen me.

He jogged the handful of steps it took to join me with a frown, looking from me to the restaurant.

"What's wrong?" he asked.

My voice was lodged in my throat. I didn't want to do this. I didn't want to inch Chevelle any closer to Clayton than he already was. I shook my head, trying to cover my distress, but Marco read it like he was good at reading everyone around him.

He touched my arm, a soft touch that about undid me, and a little sob escaped before I could help it. Without further comment, he wrapped himself around me. I leaned into his chest and clung on, shutting my eyes to hold back the tears that suddenly threatened.

"Talk to me," he said, his tone deep and quiet.

"It's s-stupid," I finally choked out. "I have to…take Chevelle for a DNA test."

His arms flexed, tightening, and his heartbeat kicked up pace under my cheek. The wave of energy and heat that always seemed to encompass us when we touched raced into existence, but instead of igniting me today, it felt like standing in front of a fire on a winter day. Comfort. Solace. I wanted to stay in his embrace until this entire nightmare blew over. But I couldn't. I'd made the stupid assumption that I'd never see Clayton Hardy again. The only thought I'd ever given the man was what I was going to tell Chevelle someday when he asked about the sperm donor who'd helped create him.

I pushed away from Marco, and he let me with reluctance. The heat trickling away. The comfort all but disappearing.

"It'll be fine. It's just a stupid cheek swab. It's not like it's going to hurt him. I mean, the vaccination shots have been worse. I'm just being ridiculous," I rambled a bit—nervous and upset and trying not to be either. Marco just stared. "Thanks for the hug. I'll see you later?"

I turned away from him and headed down the sidewalk. Instead of letting me go, Marco simply joined me, his long legs easily keeping pace with mine.

"Why don't I come with you," he suggested.

"You're busy. It's going to take longer in the waiting room than it will to get the swab done. I'm okay. Chevelle's okay." I said it to him but was reminding myself as well.

"I was pretty much done for the day. I was just going to do some paperwork at the office. It can wait. This can't," Marco said smoothly.

The offer and his insistence wrapped their way around my heart. My parents had always offered to come with me to Chevelle's appointments, but I'd never taken them up on it. I'd needed to show them, more than anyone, that I could stand on my own two feet while taking care of my son. I'd needed to prove that I wasn't falling over while trying to be a mom, and yet, today, I sort of felt like I was.

So, instead of telling Marco I didn't need his help, I simply let him tag along.

The skies were dark with the threat of an early summer storm that wasn't supposed to hit until this evening. It gave the air a heavy and full feeling that fit my mood. We walked in silence to my parents' house.

When I opened the door, it was to find that Chevelle had just woken up from his nap. He had Hippo tucked up against him and a sippy cup in his hand while he sat on my dad's lap. Dad was surprised to see me home so early and doubly surprised to see Marco with me.

"Mama!" Chevelle said, dropping the cup and holding his arms up for me.

I pulled him from my dad, kissing his cheek and the top of his head before squeezing him until he grunted and giggled. He laid his head on my shoulder and grasped the end of my shirt in his hand. I closed my eyes, letting the sweetness of him sweep over me.

"What's up?" Dad asked, eyes darting between me and Marco.

"I have to take him to the clinic for a DNA test," I said, trying to sound confident and sure, unruffled. I couldn't break down in front of him as I had briefly with Marco.

Dad frowned. "Is there a chance...?"

He trailed off, and if my heart hadn't been so heavy, it would have made me laugh because it was obvious Dad was uncomfortable asking the question that had run through his mind. Had I been sleeping with more men than Clayton? Could Chevelle be someone else's?

"No." I shook my head. "But because I didn't list him on the birth certificate, it's the only way Clayton can prove it."

Dad nodded, looking to Marco again, a curious expression on his face that I wasn't sure I could read. Was it approval or confusion or hope? Hope was the worst, because sometimes I let myself feel it too.

"Where's Mom?" I asked.

"She went to her office. She needed a book for some research she's doing over the summer."

Dad rose, and I kissed his cheek. "Okay. We'll be off, then. I'll see you tomorrow."

He nodded, and I headed for the door as Marco and Dad exchanged goodbyes. I grabbed Chevelle's diaper bag, and the three of us headed out. Instead of going to the Prius, I headed for the porch and the stroller that I had waiting there.

"You're not driving?" Marco asked, surprised because I usually did whenever Chevelle was with me.

"No, I think the air will be good for me."

He looked with uncertainty at the dark clouds and then pulled the stroller down for me. I settled Chevelle inside, tickled his neck, and said, "We're going on a little adventure to see Jaci."

Chevelle giggled.

Jaci was a lab tech at the clinic who I'd been friends with when I'd worked there as a nutritionist. Even though we rarely saw each other these days, every time I brought Chevelle in for vaccinations or lab work, she was the one to help us. She always had cookies for him when we were done, and I was thankful that he usually remembered that instead of the pain of the shots.

Marco was silent as we walked, listening instead to Chevelle jabber away to Hippo. When we walked in the door of the clinic, it felt like every eye in the room turned to us, and I realized for the first time what we must have looked like. A family. A little trio. My heart clenched again. I wanted that for Chevelle and myself someday.

I registered at the lab, and then we made our way to the seats in the waiting room. Marco's arm slid along the back of my chair as I sat with Chevelle and a book from the diaper bag in my lap. We flipped the pages, and Chevelle pointed out the animals, saying their names and making the sounds. Even though he knew the names and sounds, he still got a kick out of making the grown-ups say them.

Chevelle shoved the book in Marco's face and

asked with a sly smile, "Maco, cow. Sound cow?"

Marco didn't even hesitate, didn't look around embarrassed. He just belted out a low, growly, "Moo."

Chevelle grinned, turned the page, and said, "Pig, Maco. Pig."

Marco leaned forward until his eyes were even with Chevelle's, then he stuffed his face into Chevelle's neck, making snuffling noises that had Chevelle giggling hysterically. His tiny boy laugh filled the waiting room, and it clenched my heart while easing it all at the same time.

"Is that Chevelle's laughter I hear?" Jaci asked from the doorway. Her blonde hair was in a long braid, and her scrubs hid her pretty shape that had drawn eyes whenever we'd gone out together. It had been a long, long time since we'd done so. Maybe since the night I'd first made the mistake to go home with Clayton three years ago. Jaci had been the one celebrating my graduation with me that night. I swallowed.

We got up, leaving the stroller to be picked up as we came out, and followed Jaci into the lab. I sat with Chevelle on my lap, and Jaci uncapped the tube with the swab in it. I was glad she didn't ask why we were there for a DNA test, but her eyes did keep straying to Marco.

"Okay, my little chickadee, I need you to open your mouth and say *aw* for me. Can you do that?" Jaci asked.

Chevelle put Hippo over his mouth.

Unexpectedly, the tears I'd held back overwhelmed me. I didn't want him to open his mouth either. I closed my eyes, but it was too late. They leaked out, sliding down my cheek. Marco saw them like he saw everything I did. He stepped forward, looked down into Chevelle's face, and said, "Who do you think can make the loudest, longest sheep noise? Me or you?"

Chevelle giggled. "Me! Me!"

Marco smiled at him. "Okay, Snickerdoodle. On the count of three, these two ladies will tell us who won."

My chest tightened even more at Marco using the nickname I used for Chevelle. It seemed right and wrong and filled me with all things I couldn't and shouldn't want with the man.

Marco counted down, they both belted out *baas*, and Jaci went in for the swipe, tickling Chevelle's cheek. He laughed at her and pulled away, but the horrible task was done.

"I definitely think Chevelle won!" Jaci said with a wink.

"Cookie?" Chevelle asked, and we all laughed, my heart easing a little more.

It was over. I'd known it was coming from the moment Clayton had shown up in Grand Orchard, demanding he see my son, and now it was in the past. I just had to put my faith in a lawyer I barely knew, who Lee swore by, and a court that still favored mothers even if the tide was changing. What I wanted to do was put my faith in the man standing next to me who I knew would shield me from every dark force that ever came for me and my son.

That single thought brought me back to my senses with startling lucidity. I'd never wanted to hide behind anyone before. Quite the opposite, I'd fought against my mom's tendency to surround me in bubble wrap and keep me from the world. Keep me from falling.

This time…this time it was clearly too late. I'd fallen. Completely and absolutely fallen for a man who I knew I shouldn't want. For a man who had his own reasons for staying away. Good reasons, like his job with Brady and his troubled past as well as my obligations and my challenges that would never go away.

But as we walked out of the lab with Chevelle munching on a cookie and Marco pushing the stroller, I let myself pretend, for the length of time that it took us to walk home, that we really were a family.

Chapter Twenty-two

Marco

ONE CALL AWAY
Performed by Charlie Puth

Walking home with Cassidy from the clinic, my heart felt like it had been squeezed and pulverized down to a mere stump. The silent tears she'd shed as the lab tech had swabbed Chevelle's cheek had made me want to ruin Hardy. I clenched my jaw, promising myself I would continue to poke and prod into every corner of Clayton Hardy's life. I was going to uncover every tiny rumor about him and every single bad decision he'd ever made.

I wouldn't let him come into Cassidy's life and destroy her peace. Not when she'd worked so hard to earn it. To build a life for herself and Chevelle after he'd walked away without a look back.

I pulled the stroller up on the porch for her and followed them into the house.

As soon as Cassidy set him down, Chevelle ran for his blocks. That kid was a builder almost as much as he was an animal lover. I wondered what it said about his future. I wondered if I'd be around to see him turn into a man making his dreams come true. An ache hit me in the bottom of my stomach at the thought…at how much I wanted to see him grow and change and take the world by storm.

"You're staying for dinner. As a thank you for going with me," Cassidy demanded more than asked, and my lips twitched because we'd been playing this game for three weeks.

Jonas and I had been here almost every night. I wasn't quite sure how it had happened. I'd suggest bringing home takeout, or she'd insist the meal she'd planned fed four. I was grateful for the dinners together because I wanted Jonas to feel grounded in Grand Orchard. I wanted to surround him with good people instead of eating with just me, in silence, in an apartment that could hardly be called a home.

"You don't need to thank me. I didn't do anything," I told her.

She stared at me for a long moment. "I bet you'd like to believe that, wouldn't you?"

I didn't respond. Instead, I sank onto the floor with Chevelle, helping him assemble the tower that was growing by the second and would certainly topple before long. I could feel her gaze burning into me, watching me play with her son, and I wondered if the same forbidden thoughts flipped through her brain as mine. How right it felt for us all to be together like this.

"Are you okay watching him while I work in the kitchen?" she asked breathily, as if I'd sidled up to her, slid my hands under her T-shirt, and kissed her. I glanced up, and the look in her eye almost killed me. Soft and sultry, with hope neither of us could afford blaring from them. I was the coward who looked away first.

"I'm good."

She looked from me to Chevelle one last time before heading into the kitchen. The air had been different between us ever since I'd let myself indulge in kissing her. Since that failed restraint, I'd kept my hands to myself, and she'd kept her hands to herself, until today, when I'd wrapped her in my embrace as a way of comforting her. Every piece of me ached to kiss away her tears, which meant it was dangerous for me to be here.

Chevelle hauled over some of his cars and toy animal figurines to shove into the piles of blocks he'd stacked as if he'd built a garage, or a pen at a zoo, or some strange mix of both. I watched his dark hair as it fell in his eyes. If it had been blond instead of chestnut, it would look like Brady's hair, thick and shaggy. There was a lot of the O'Neil family in Chevelle. Square chin, dimpled cheek, long lashes. Ever since the day Cassidy had delivered him with me pacing in the hall outside her hospital room and Brady inside, holding her hand, I'd had one thought about him. He was beautiful. A perfect bundle of joy and sweetness, just like his mother.

The day she'd gone into labor, Brady had called me to drive them to the hospital, and I'd felt panic in a way I'd never known. I'd been desperate to get her to safety before something went wrong with her or the baby. Outside in the hallway, I'd fought every instinct I'd had to storm into the room and make sure she was okay when her grunts and cries crawled up my spine and made me bite my nails into my palms until they'd bled.

I'd known, even then, it wasn't normal for me to feel like that about a woman who wasn't mine, who was simply my employer's sister. A person I'd barely spoken to and yet somehow felt responsible for—wanted to be responsible for.

Those feelings were still there. Stronger than ever before.

I took out my phone and dialed Trevor's number while Chevelle played, and Cassidy banged around in the kitchen.

"Hey, have we gotten anything more in on Hardy?" I asked.

"Give me a second, and let me check," Trevor said. I heard papers shuffle and his fingers glide over the keyboard. "Well, hell. Isn't this interesting."

My face got dark the longer he talked. I'd never been a guy to play offense. To strike out first. I'd joined the military determined to be a corpsman. To heal and protect, not to shoot people or blow things up. But Hardy…he made me want to use my military training in a very different way.

I hung up with Trevor using a hand that shook. I made sure Chevelle was happily engaged with his toys and headed for the kitchen.

I froze in the entryway. Cassidy had the radio on. A country song about summer nights and taking chances was playing, and she was dancing to it as she moved around the kitchen, a basket of berries in one hand, the other moving wildly. Her movements weren't smooth or practiced. In fact, they were almost awkward, but they were also free and uninhibited. A moment of joy after her afternoon of sorrow. Her eyes were closed, and there was a soft smile on her face as she sang with the words. She had a pretty decent voice—another thing that the O'Neil family had in common.

Before I could stop myself, I'd swept into the

kitchen and joined her, pulling on her waist so she was tucked up against me, hand going to her free one, and spinning her around. My feet moved to a rhythm they hadn't since I'd danced with my mom in a kitchen in Austin. She'd told me I needed to know how to dance with a girl if I was going to ask one to prom. I'd been embarrassed and uncomfortable, and she'd made me laugh until my unease slid away. The memory was normally full of heartache, but today, as my feet moved with Cassidy's and she smiled up at me with wide eyes, I was grateful for it. For my mom. For the time we'd had together where she'd tried to make me a better man.

My chest ached at the thought. They would have been so disappointed in me.

My failures to Petty Officer Warren.

My failures to Maliyah.

But I refused to let myself fail Cassidy, too. Not when it came to Hardy.

The thing was, telling her what I'd just learned was going to take the soft smile she'd just given me and tear it away. It would put her right back in the sadness, frustration, and helplessness she'd felt while watching Chevelle get swabbed.

My feet stopped. She ran into me, stumbling a little. My arms tightened about her.

"What?" she asked, reading the change in me when I'd always been damn good at hiding my emotions from everyone.

"He's married," I said the words quietly, as if the softer I said them, the less they'd hurt.

"What? Who?" she asked, and then the realization hit her. "Clayton?"

I nodded, and her jaw dropped along with the arm that had been holding a basket of berries while we danced. It tumbled to the ground, and I held her steady with one hand while I leaned down to pick it up.

"That asshole!" Her voice was guttural and pained. "He came here saying he wanted me back...and he's fucking married?"

She turned and stormed toward the back door. I shoved the berries onto the counter and caught her. "Angel, where are you going?"

"You know where. To give him a piece of my mind," she said, defiance and fury raging in her eyes.

"To what end?" I said as fear for her climbed through me. What would happen if she confronted him like this? Would he strike her? Hurt her? My stomach lurched.

"Why is he here?" she demanded. "What could he possibly want with Chevelle? If he's married, why doesn't he just have his own child?"

"I don't know. Not yet." But there was a promise in my voice and in my soul that I would keep.

Cassidy pounded a fist on my chest, letting her fury and frustration from the day fly through her. "He can't have my son!"

I wrapped her up tight in my embrace as tears slid down her smooth cheeks again. I hated it. Hated that he had the power to make her feel this way. I kissed the top of her head and squeezed her as tightly as I could, until the air left us both, and we momentarily felt like one instead of two.

"You know what I hate?" she asked in a shaky voice as her tears slowed.

I shook my head, unable to speak yet because of

the waves of emotion that filled me.

"I hate that the person I let myself be when I was with him led him to believe he could just show up and I'd go running into his arms. That I'd be weak enough to take him back."

The thought of her in his arms did horrible things to me, filling me with dread and animosity and nausea.

"You've never been weak, Angel. If he chose to see you that way, that's on him."

We stood holding each other for a long time before she asked, "Is that where he got his money? From the wife?"

I looked down at her. "What do you mean?"

"His fancy suit and expensive watch. He could never afford that when we were…together. Harvard can't pay that much more than he was getting here, right?"

The information Trevor had read from our local guys in Boston returned to me. "From what I understand, he had to sign a prenup. He gets nothing if they divorce, but if there are children, he gets money to maintain the children's lifestyle. And if she dies, he can manage her trust on behalf of the kids."

She snorted. "She better watch her back." I didn't laugh as she'd expected me to, and she added on, "Wait, you don't think he'd actually do something like that, do you?"

"I've seen people do more for less," I told her the truth.

"More than killing?"

"What happened to Petty Officer Warren—having to live with it the rest of her life—that's like hell every day. Killing someone would almost be considered kindness compared to that."

We hadn't talked about what had happened in the Fleet Marine Force since the day I'd spilled my guts to her. Speaking about it now, when I brought Warren up as little as I brought up my parents, felt both painful and cathartic.

She pulled herself from my embrace, and I reluctantly let her go. She turned back to the mess of berries, bending to collect more of the ones I hadn't recovered.

She glanced at me with a frown. "I'm more confused than ever with what he really wants."

I hated the suspicion that jumped into my head. A suspicion I wasn't sure I could prove without breaking a few laws and violating some HIPAA privacy rules. But I would get to the bottom of this for her. There was no way I was letting Clayton Hardy take Chevelle from us. My throat closed at my mental slip. From *her*. He wouldn't take Chevelle away from her.

Chapter Twenty-three

Cassidy

I DO
Performed by Susie Suh

I fell into bed that night, exhausted in every single part of me. My emotions had drained me more than the physical challenges of my day. Even ending it by working out side by side with Marco hadn't brought me the peace it normally did. The entire time he was there, glistening as his muscles flexed and bent, my body had longed to lose myself in him, to forget everything in my world that felt like it was about to tip over. So, the strain of holding back had only added to my fatigue.

As tired as I was, my brain still wouldn't shut off. Memories of Marco's sweetness with Chevelle and me bounced about in my memories. The tenderness of those images dissolved into hatred as I thought about what Clayton was putting me through. I disliked feeling the hate almost as much as I disliked the man himself. I'd never allowed animosity to guide my life, not even when kids had teased me growing up about my awkwardness, or being tall, or struggling with my grades.

Tripped by Love

When I finally fell asleep, it was uneasy and restless.

I woke almost as tired as I'd been before I'd closed my eyes.

To my surprise, Mom didn't mention how I looked when she came over at five. She just hugged me, told me to have a good day, and settled with a book and the baby monitor on the couch, waiting for Chevelle to stir.

I headed to the restaurant, mind filling with all the things I needed to do before the trip to Texas the next day. I grimaced as I realized that at least the DNA test and Marco's revelations about Clayton being married had kept me from obsessing over everything that could go wrong with me leaving Grand Orchard for a few days.

I really didn't need to worry, though. Cliff and Willow were stepping in to cover my absence, and they knew the recipes and the management of the restaurant almost as well as I did. Willow was actually better at managing the front and the customers than I was. I didn't know what I'd do when she graduated in the fall and left to find work somewhere else. I couldn't think of that on top of everything else that had piled on me at the moment.

Instead, I spent the day prepping as many food items as I could, checking all the orders for the week, and creating long lists of reminders for Cliff and Willow. As the day ended and I moved on to preparing more bread when I'd normally be leaving, Willow grabbed my hand and said, "Enough already. We've got this. Go on your trip. Try to relax and maybe actually have some fun. You haven't been away from this place in two years."

She was right, but leaving the restaurant was harder than I'd thought it would be. Guilt filled me more than anything else. As if I was letting Brady down by stepping away. But the dread I felt about leaving the café was nothing compared to what I felt at the thought of leaving Chevelle. I hadn't spent one night away from my boy. Not one. My heart and throat seized.

As the three of us left the café, I said, almost to myself, "Maybe I shouldn't go."

Cliff's large hand landed on my shoulder, and I looked up to see his face twitching with humor. "Go, Cassidy. I've never burnt a joint down yet and don't plan on starting now."

"That isn't even funny," I told him but couldn't resist the smile I gave him back.

They headed off to their cars, and I wasn't even surprised when I found Marco stepping out of the studio to join me on the walk home.

"You're nervous about leaving it," he said quietly. I didn't know if I loved it or hated it that he read me so easily.

I nodded, even though it hadn't been a question.

"Because you don't trust them?" he asked.

Our shoulders brushed as we walked, and the heady sense of awareness filled me, pushing at the wariness I'd felt and replacing it with a different kind of ache.

"No, I completely trust them. Honestly, Cliff has years more experience than me, and Willow knows the café in and out. I just…I feel like I asked for all this, and Brady graciously handed it to me, and now…"

"You feel like you're walking away from your responsibility."

"Yes. But that makes it sound like I don't love it," I said quietly, and I shoved the little voice deep inside that wondered if that were true. "Or that I'm ungrateful."

Marco scoffed.

"I know," I said with a wry smile and shrug. "I think I'm just tired. I'll probably skip our workout tonight."

It felt like I'd skipped more workouts in a month than in two years. When I glanced at him to see if he'd object, I couldn't help but feel disappointed as he nodded. "Probably a good idea. Get some rest. It's going to be a long couple of days."

The reality of it finally hit me. I was going to Texas…with Marco. We were going to be alone together for several days. In planes and cars and hotels. I flushed, thinking of it. I'd booked two rooms at the hotel, but I'd be lying to myself if my mind hadn't wondered what it would be like if we only had one.

We turned the corner of our street and found Jonas sitting on the steps of my parents' place. His elbows rested on his knees, and his fingers were laced behind his head with his eyes trained on the ground. He looked devastated and so not the Jonas he'd become over the last few weeks that the difference was startling. He looked like I'd felt yesterday. Sad and angry and a little bit lost.

"Jo-Jo?" Marco asked. He'd mostly stopped himself from saying the nickname at Jonas's request, but it still came out here and there.

Jonas looked up, and his face shuttered, feelings

hiding behind a bravado that he'd probably learned from his brother or from the life he'd led before going to live with Maliyah at eight years old. I'd only heard tidbits of it from Marco because he felt like it wasn't his story to tell. There was a mother who was in jail and who'd really not been much of a mom to begin with but whom Jonas seemed to still love with all his teenage heart.

"I want to go back to Texas with you tomorrow. I want to check on Maliyah," Jonas said.

There was obviously more to it than Maliyah, and Marco knew it.

"Something happen with Mel?" Marco asked.

Jonas looked down before throwing his shoulders back, lifting his chin, and saying, "No."

If I could see through the lie, then Marco certainly did.

"I'm not sure it's a good idea for you to go on this trip. Maliyah is still at Maria Carmen's," Marco told him. "Plus, don't you have songs to wrap up with The Painted Daisies?"

Jonas looked slightly guilty, but then it washed away in a defiance that seemed all teen angst. "They don't really need me. I'm not some fucking musical genius like Brady or any of them. Hell, even little Hannah can play me into the ground."

"Language," Marco said, trying to tease, but when it didn't change Jonas's expression, he softened. "You're selling yourself short, Jonas. You may not *play* as well as them, but you're talented in a different way. You hear and see what the music should become. You've made a difference to their album. Brady said you're even getting song credits."

A flicker of something like joy sailed over

Jonas's face before it returned to remorse and heartache. "If you don't take me with you, I'll just go myself. It's not like I don't have money for a plane ticket. I need to see Maliyah."

"When I talked to her yesterday, everything was fine. Did something happen that I don't know about?" Marco asked.

Jonas shrugged. "No. She says she's fine. But you know her. She could be dying, and she wouldn't tell us."

I could feel Marco warring with himself. The debate was so strong it tightened the muscles in the arm that brushed against mine. The desire to protect the ones he loved from being harmed waged in him like a battle cry. But the thing was, he couldn't be there for everyone all the time. He couldn't shield them from the choices they had to make all on their own.

"I'm serious, Marco. I'm going to Texas with or without you." Then, Jonas got up and stormed past us to return to the apartment above the garage.

Marco ran a hand over his face. "Shit."

"Language," I teased, and he looked up at me with eyes full of heartache.

I did the only thing I could. I embraced him just as he'd embraced me the day before. An attempt to offer solace when the world was spinning out of our control. I spoke quietly, as if to a wounded animal. "If he's truly that worried about her, maybe it would be good for him to see her in person."

"It isn't Maliyah, Angel. It's definitely something with Mel. If I take him back now, it'll put him right back in the middle of the gang I dragged him away from."

"So, we all go together, stop by and see Maliyah and Mel and whomever he needs to see, and then he can come with us to Earth Paradise," I said quietly.

He looked at me like I'd said something amazing. Like I'd said he'd won the lottery or that heaven really existed. "What?" I asked with a small smile.

"Together," he said quietly. The word was a whisper on the wind that filled my soul.

I cupped his jaw, running a finger along it. "Together."

It was a promise I was pretty sure neither one of us could quite guarantee, but it was one I wanted to the very depths of my soul.

♪ ♪ ♪

It wasn't until we were on the plane, waiting for it to take off, that the real anxiety hit me. I wasn't a great flier to begin with. Maybe it was because I didn't travel much, like my country-rock legend of a brother. Or maybe it was just being in the air in a layer of thin metal and insulation that I had no way out of if it decided to take a nosedive. But even worse was thinking about what would happen if everything did go wrong, and I lost my life on a plane ride. I didn't have a trust in place for Chevelle or even a will stating guardianship rights should go to my parents or Brady. That terrified me because it might leave Clayton a hole to worm himself into as Chevelle's biological dad.

My hands squeezed the arms of the seat, and I tried to control my breathing that had turned erratic. Jonas wasn't aware of it because he had his headphones on and his head tilted against the window with his eyes shut, lost in whatever was dragging him down. But Marco definitely noticed. He pried my fingers away, turned them over, and kissed the palm. It was a sweet, tender move that brought us closer to the kisses we'd exchanged weeks ago instead of the familial-like camaraderie we'd established since then.

"Are you afraid of flying?" he asked, surprise in his tone.

"I just…Chevelle…" I shook my head over the jumble of words coming out of my mouth. "I don't have anything in place for him. And what if something happens…and Clayton—"

Marco kissed my palm again and then raised the arm of the chair between us so that he could pull me up against him. "Nothing is going to happen. To you or Chevelle. Not on my watch."

The idea that he could somehow float me to the ground if the plane crashed made me smile. "You got wings under that jacket?" I asked.

He smiled. "No wings. But maybe a cape."

I laughed, which was his intention. The plane left the ground, making my heart pound as it soared into the sky and took me thousands of miles from my baby and my restaurant. Chevelle was with Mom and Dad and the new puppy my dad was finally bringing home today. He would hardly miss me with the dog to keep him company.

For the first Monday in two years, I was nowhere near The Golden Heart Café or Grand Orchard. The restaurant was closed on Tuesday anyway, and I would only miss Wednesday and Thursday before returning. It was a mere three days of openings. It would be okay. The café wasn't going to fall apart in that short of a time. Just like Chevelle would be fine.

But the panic that had reared its head to almost

consume me wouldn't go away for some reason, dread taking over me, even as Marco continued to try and distract me by telling me about Maliyah, Maria Carmen, and the group of friends who'd taken Maliyah into their family with open hearts when she was a teen.

    I listened and smiled and tried to push the sensation away, all the time knowing it wasn't likely to disappear completely until I was home again, holding my son in my arms.

Chapter Twenty-four

Marco

BETTER THAN I USED TO BE
Performed by Tim McGraw

My throat was actually parched from all the talking I'd done on the plane, rattling away about Maliyah and Maria Carmen and the group that surrounded her, all in an attempt to ease Cassidy's worries. Even before my parents died and shit went to hell in the Fleet Marine Force, I'd never been a talker. I'd spoken to Cassidy more in the last handful of weeks than I'd done with anyone in months, including Trevor and Garner.

After all that, I still wasn't sure how successful I'd been at alleviating her worries, because she clutched my hand in a death grip as the plane landed and had a somber face as we found our way to the luggage claim to retrieve her suitcase. Jonas barely looked up from the stream of messages he was sending on his phone. His expression was even grimmer than Cassidy's. I wanted to fix things for both of them. To see only wide smiles on their faces. But I felt helpless to make it happen. Things I couldn't control were driving their lives.

"Want to talk about it?" I asked, shoving Jonas's

shoulder with mine as we stood by the baggage carousel. He'd grown at least another inch in the weeks he'd been with me. It seemed impossible, and yet the evidence was there before me.

He wouldn't meet my eyes. "There's nothing to talk about."

I remembered that feeling as a teen, especially being new to Maliyah's house and unsure of whether I could trust her. Would she duck and run if things in my world weren't perfect? I'd had three years to get through before I could be on my own, enter the military, and make a life for myself. I'd focused on that, keeping everything as perfect as I could on the exterior. But it had taken a toll. It was still taking a toll. I didn't want that for Jonas, and I certainly didn't want him to think he couldn't trust me.

"Jo-Jo…" He glared at me. "Jonas, you know you can tell me anything, right?"

His eyes met mine for a minute before he bent his head once more to the buzzing phone in his hand. "I know. There's nothing to tell, Marco."

When he continued to ignore my presence, my gaze moved back to Cassidy standing by the conveyor belt. She practically glowed. She wore one of her standard long, flowy skirts with flowers littered all over it and a gauzy loose tank that showed a skintight one beneath it. The light behind her outlined the curve of her breasts through the see-through material and made my entire body burn with a desire to touch her. She had her hair down today, and it hung well past her shoulder blades in thick, golden waves.

Like she'd somehow called to me, I'd already stepped toward her without even realizing it just as she bent to pull her suitcase from the belt. I pulled it from her grasp.

"I can get it," she said and blew out a frustrated sigh.

"I know you can, but you shouldn't have to," I said. "Let someone take care of you once in a while."

She snorted. "Like you do?"

My gut clenched as I thought about not only how right she was, but how it was likely the reason Jonas wouldn't let others help him either. I'd been a bad role model, and Maliyah was even worse. She never let anyone do anything unless she had no choice. Maybe it was a scar from our days in foster care when we'd had to count on ourselves and no one else. I had the least reason of any of us to be that way. I'd been in a loving home for fifteen years. I'd lived mere months in the true foster system before Maliyah had taken me in, and she'd never been anything but loving and kind. Still, it was there, built inside me—the need to count on just myself. To not be a burden.

I looked down into Cassidy's face. Her eyes still held the worry she'd been going through on the plane. I smoothed a thumb over the bend between her brows. "I'll try, if you try," I said quietly.

Her eyes widened.

"I mean it," I said. "What do you say?"

She swallowed and nodded.

We turned back to Jonas who was waiting with the backpack he'd carried on the plane thrown over his shoulder. I picked up my duffel that had seen better days, and we made our way out to the rental car agency before heading to Maria Carmen's house with heavy emotions filling all of us.

Whereas Maria Carmen and Maliyah had once

lived blocks away from each other, Maria Carmen now lived on the other side of Austin. She'd moved into a new development when the city had started to expand as the Hollywood folks invaded Texas and grew the place like a dam breaking across it. The fact that we were several miles away from Maliyah's neighborhood brought me a small comfort. It meant we were also farther away from Mel and her gang boyfriend. Hopefully, it would keep Jonas out of the thick of things.

Maria Carmen greeted us at the door. Her frame was as lean as Maliyah's. They were both wiry and muscled from the workouts they did together, but Maria Carmen had tan skin with almost black hair and deep-brown eyes compared to the lighter tones of chestnut and hazel that were all Maliyah. As different as they were, they were still sisters—soul sisters.

"*Mijos*!" Maria Carmen said, coming out the front door and wrapping first Jonas and then me in hugs.

"Let them go, *querida*, so I can hug my boys," Maliyah said as she approached using a cane and moving at a snail's pace. It was ten thousand times better than how she'd looked when we'd left Austin, but it was still a long way from the bundle of energy that she normally was.

Maria Carmen laughed and stepped back so Maliyah could drape her arms around both Jonas and me at the same time. She didn't hug often, but when she did, you could feel the love wafting off of her. She backed up and patted Jonas's cheek. "You've grown again."

He looked away with a bashful, careless shrug.

Maliyah looked behind us, and I moved sideways

to tug Cassidy forward. Maliyah looked her over from head to toe, and her face broke into a huge smile. "Well, aren't you just a beautiful sight. I have you to thank for keeping my boys so well fed, I hear."

Cassidy turned pink. "Well...I do like to cook."

Maliyah laughed and stuck a hand out. "It's nice to finally meet you, Cassidy."

Cassidy shook her hand. "It's nice to meet you, too. I've heard so much about you that it's like meeting a legend."

Maliyah looked surprised. "My boys have been talking about me? That doesn't sound like either of them."

Maria Carmen chuckled. "Maybe we can move the inquisition into the house, 'Li, instead of on the street."

We followed the older women inside. Music was playing in the background. Latin pop songs that seemed as much a part of Maria Carmen's home as the brightly colored walls and teak wood that she decorated with. She'd once told me that if she couldn't be at the beach in Playa del Carmen, then she'd bring it to her, and that was exactly what it looked like. As if you could step outside the back door and find the bright blue of the ocean hitting a sandy shore.

The place smelled like chilis, and when we entered the kitchen, there was a tamale assembly line laid out on the counter. Maria Carmen normally only made them for holidays because they were so much work. I wondered if it was because we were there or because we'd brought a guest that had her breaking out the masa and husks.

When I looked over at Cassidy, her eyes lit up seeing the ingredients. "I've always wanted to make tamales, but I was afraid I'd screw it up."

Maria Carmen beamed. "You've come to the right place. No one makes tamales like me."

"Way to be humble, Car," Maliyah teased.

Maria Carmen shrugged. "It's the truth. You know it as well as I do." She turned back to Cassidy. "There are two secrets to making tamales. One is in the masa itself, and the other is in how you cook them. Most people cook them too long, and they end up dried hunks of dust. Come on, I'll show you."

She waved at Cassidy to join her in the kitchen, and Cassidy's eyes grew. "You'd tell me your secrets?"

Maria Carmen laughed. "There are no secrets. It really is all in the execution. If you succeed at it, I'll be ecstatic because none of my children have perfected it. Someone needs to carry on the tradition."

"You don't even know me," Cassidy said quietly.

Maria Carmen winked at her, shot an eye at me, and then said in a conspiratorial whisper that wasn't a whisper, "That boy has never brought a woman home. I kind of think you're family now."

I could feel the flush that littered my cheeks and was pleased to see it covered Cassidy's also. Our eyes met, awareness drifting between us even though we were separated by an entire kitchen and three other bodies. Family. God, it hurt to think of Cassidy that way as much as I wanted it to be true—for her and Chevelle to be mine forever.

I pushed the thought away as quickly as it hit me.

Maria Carmen pulled Cassidy toward the counter, rambling as they washed their hands, and started work on the tamales. Maliyah stood next to me, watching while Jonas continued to pass his thumbs over his phone screen.

"You love her," Maliyah said so softly I had to tilt my head to hear her.

I looked down at her in surprise. Love. I couldn't even admit to myself how deeply I wanted Cassidy O'Neil, let alone bring up the word love. The only truths I knew were that I wanted her in every way it was possible to want someone and that the emotions she evoked in me were stronger and more uncontrollable than any I'd ever had.

She chuckled quietly. "Didn't realize it? It's written all over you."

She looked at Cassidy again, the joy and wonder on Cassidy's face as she learned about the art of tamale making from Maria Carmen. "She loves you, too. Even if neither of you has said it."

That stabbed me in the stomach, twisting my gut and my heart until I wasn't sure I could breathe.

"Don't panic," Maliyah said. "But also don't screw it up by doing something insanely Marco-like by thinking she deserves someone better. There is no one better, *mijo*. You are the best kind of man there is."

Her voice was filled with emotions, making a lump appear in my throat.

"It's wrong," I choked out at first. "She's my boss's sister. She's…" I couldn't even begin to verbalize what Cassidy was. She was a true angel. Not perfect, and I didn't have her sitting on some goddamn pedestal, but she was heaven-sent.

"She's perfect for you," Maliyah said as if I'd spoken the words aloud.

She didn't give me a chance to respond. Instead, she turned to Jonas, and in a move faster than he or I expected, she swiped his phone and tucked it into her pocket. "You've lived on that thing for a month I bet. Marco would never tell you to stop. Now, you're here with me, and you will give me your undivided attention for the next couple hours at least."

"*Tía*…it's important," Jonas said, frustration filling his face.

Maliyah lifted her cane, waved it around the room at the rest of us, and then put it back down before saying, "This is important, Jonas. The humans in your life who are in front of your face, caring about you on a daily basis."

"But—"

"You can have it back after dinner," she said firmly.

He looked like he was going to lose his shit, and I sent him a glare that he saw and looked away from. He grunted out an unhappy, "Fine."

We spent the next two hours working in the kitchen with Maria Carmen, assembling enough tamales to feed a small army. Because it really would be a small army who appeared on her doorstep once the extended family heard there was a gathering going on at her house. There didn't have to be an official invite. There didn't even have to be a reason for the crowd to assemble. Us being there and Maria Carmen having made tamales would be reason enough.

Cassidy laughed and joked with both Maria Carmen and Maliyah, the stress and worry of earlier hiding away. I was grateful to both women for giving her something I hadn't been able to give her in the last few weeks—a respite from the burdens on her shoulders.

The door started opening at four o'clock. People drifted in carrying dishes with them, and the noise got louder, the music almost disappearing under the thunder of the voices talking. People shouted across the room to each other, laughing and arguing with a friendly banter. Maria Carmen's home was always this way. Smiles. Joy. Family.

People greeted Jonas and me the same way they greeted all the others that came in. Warm claps on the back or pats on the shoulder. Teases and taunts that made Jonas and me both turn red and only increased the ribbing they gave us. We'd always been welcome here.

I was standing in a corner of the kitchen with a plate full of food that had all been homemade when Cassidy joined me with her own plate just as full. I shot the plate a grin, raising my eyebrow. "You better hope you have room for all that. Maria Carmen has only one rule: if you dish it, you eat it."

Cassidy smirked. "I may go back for seconds."

I laughed. There was nowhere to sit because the tables and chairs inside and out were full of bodies, so we both ate on our feet. My plate was empty before I even really realized I'd downed it, and to my surprise, Cassidy had kept pace with me. I took our empty plates and tossed them before returning to her. Our arms were almost touching, the awareness drifting between us again, coating me with a heat like a shot of tequila.

"It's amazing," Cassidy said, eyes drifting around the room.

"It really is."

She looked up at me. "Brady would kill you if he

knew you were skipping out on this to be with him almost every holiday. Your family must miss you."

It brought the lump back to my throat that had risen when Maliyah had said that I loved Cassidy and that she loved me too. I thought back to all the times I'd signed up to stay with Brady and his family over the years during the holidays. I'd gone home with him to Grand Orchard even before he'd moved there permanently to be with Tristan.

My reasoning had always been clear. Brady had needed me—or rather, he'd needed someone. I'd wanted the married guys on our detail to be with their partners. I'd wanted Trevor to be with his mother and his sister who counted on him in the absence of their dad, and I'd known that Maliyah and Jonas had this—a family so large that one body missing would hardly be noticed. But as I looked down into Cassidy's golden eyes, I also knew a truth that I'd never admitted to myself. I'd wanted to see her. To be near her. She may have only been eighteen the first time we'd met, but over the years, I'd watched her become this vibrant, strong, independent woman who'd captivated me. She'd faced every single thing life had thrown at her with a fiery determination that awed me.

"I guess…" I swallowed hard. "I guess I went where I needed to be."

Her eyes narrowed. "You aren't the only one who can protect Brady."

I shook my head. "That's not what I meant." A little frown appeared between her brows again that I tried to rub away with my thumb just like I had earlier at the airport. "I meant…that's where *I* needed to be."

It took her a minute to understand what I meant.

"Wh-what?"

My fingers found hers, twining them together. "You don't need me to explain it." My voice was deep, full of emotions.

"I...I just..." She stumbled over her words like she often stumbled over steps, and it frustrated her just as it did when she fell. "You can't possibly mean you were there for me."

"Why not?"

She laughed softly. "Marco, until two years ago, you'd hardly spoken ten words to me."

I chuckled and shrugged, bringing her hands up to my mouth and kissing the back in a move that was so unlike me, especially when I was in the middle of a crowd, in front of people who knew me, that it surprised even me. "I don't think it was a conscious thing, Angel. It just happened. Souls drawn to souls."

Maria Carmen's shithead of a Chihuahua bounded through the room, having been let in because someone hadn't shut the slider, and he ran into Cassidy's legs, causing her to wobble. I placed my hands around her waist and drew her up close against me. My heart was pounding a furious pace. One that hers returned. I could see it in the flutter of the pulse at her neck and the way the gauzy tank she wore rose and fell as if being blown by a breeze.

Her eyes fell to my lips before finding mine again. "Your words are beautiful, Marco. You need to use them more."

"Yeah?" I asked. "I've always preferred action to words."

I swore her eyes darkened with heat. With lust. With the same desire that was flooding me and made the entire room, the music, the laughter, the barking of the damn dog, all fade away until it became nothing but a muted buzzing.

"I've yet to see your best moves," she tossed back, flushing slightly at the brazen comeback.

My body burned. Ached to kiss her full on the mouth. To continue to lose the world around us and just focus on our bodies and hands. On our lips and tongues. On the need that was growing into a raging inferno inside us. I lowered my mouth to hers, merely a soft rub along the soft plumpness of hers, tasting the hints of chili that were on her lips but also the hints of sweetness that always surrounded her.

She brushed back with hardly any pressure. A simple kiss.

And yet it wasn't simple. It was loaded with feelings and unspoken promises.

A whistle near my ear drew my lips from hers, but I didn't look away. I was still caught in the golden glow that was Cassidy.

"Get a room, *mijo*, before you burst into flames in my kitchen, and Álvaro has to put it out with his fire hose," Maria Carmen teased, swatting me on the butt with a towel.

"We should get going," I said, watching Cassidy's face and not once glancing toward Maria Carmen. "We still have an hour's drive, and you have to be at Earth Paradise first thing."

She nodded, rubbing her thumb along my lips and only driving my desire to a level that could become embarrassing in the midst of the family surrounding us.

I reluctantly let her go. "I'll go find Jonas."

"Jonas is staying with us. You can pick him back up on the way to the airport when you leave," Maria

Carmen said, and it finally drew my gaze away from Cassidy. There was a twinkle in Maria Carmen's eyes matching the one normally in Maliyah's.

I frowned. "That's really not a good idea, *Tia*."

There was no way I wanted to leave Jonas long enough for him to get to Mel and the asshole who were surely the reason for all his anxiousness. Maria Carmen seemed to know more than I thought she did because she sobered slightly.

"He said Mel was coming here tomorrow. I promise we won't let him out of our sight."

I glanced toward Maliyah who was on the couch, laughing and joking at something Maria Carmen's nephew had said.

"If he causes her to worry..." My throat closed up. "She might not survive another episode."

Maria Carmen patted my arm. "We've got this, *mijo*. The family is here. That is what family is for. We'll guard them both with our lives. You just go do..." She glanced at Cassidy with a smirk. "Do what you need to do."

I wanted the time alone with Cassidy. Without her family or my responsibilities. My pulse pounded at the idea of it. She and I. A hotel far away from anything but the two of us. It was so wrong and right at the same time.

Plus, Jonas needed to see that Mel was okay. If she was coming to him, without the asshole in tow, that would be a good way for him to reassure himself that she was all right.

"Stop hesitating," Maria Carmen said. "Be a good boy and listen to your *tia*."

Cassidy made a garbled noise somewhere

between a laugh and a choke. When I glanced back at her, her eyes were full of the same humor that lit Maria Carmen's.

I sighed, and both women knew I'd given in.

I made my way over to Maliyah, bent down, and kissed her on the cheek. "We're taking off. *Tía* says that Jonas is staying. You good with that?"

Maliyah patted my face. "I've missed him so much. It'll be good to visit with him, even if it's only for a few days."

"Call me if you need me to come and get him," I said.

She nodded and then turned toward Cassidy who was slowly making her way through the room, saying her own goodbyes. It unlocked some secret part in my soul to see her mingling with them…with Maliyah's family…my family. I'd never really considered them mine before.

I found Jonas on the stairs, texting away again now that Maliyah had given him his phone back. I rubbed my knuckles on his head, and he ducked away with a grunt.

"Maria Carmen says you're going to stay here while Cassidy and I go see Earth Paradise. I hear Mel is coming by tomorrow," I said quietly.

He nodded, looking at me almost defiantly. As if I'd tell him he couldn't stay. I didn't want him to. I wanted him far away from whatever Mel would bring with her, but as Cassidy was so often saying to me, I couldn't protect them all, and he'd be here with the family.

I repeated my words to Maria Carmen. "Maliyah can't handle anything stressful right now, Jo—" I caught myself. "Jonas. If she has another episode, we might not get her back."

That thought twisted my gut with fear and sadness.

Jonas ran a hand through his too-long hair. It had needed a cut a month ago and was now curling in waves well below his chin. "I know," he finally said.

"If you need me, I'll come back. I'm only an hour away."

He lifted his chin. "I'm not a child, Marco."

God, but he was…and he should have been. He'd already had so much of his childhood stolen from him. What was the harm in staying a little longer in that momentary space before the full weight of adulthood landed on his shoulders?

"I know, Jonas. You're not," I said.

Cassidy found me and gave Jonas a side hug. We said our final goodbyes and left with the noise and music still pouring from Maria Carmen's house at ten o'clock at night on a Monday. It filled the air in a way that only family could.

I opened the passenger door for Cassidy, and she climbed in. When I got into the driver's seat, I risked a look in her direction, knowing I was full of emotions that I was struggling to keep hidden.

"Will he be okay?" she asked.

That lump in my throat returned. "I'm not sure. But I hope so—for Maliyah's sake as much as his own."

She reached across the console and squeezed my bicep.

I turned the car on and headed down the road with waves of hope and worry as well as love and fear cresting over me. Like the tides, each emotion came and then receded until I wasn't sure how I'd be left standing when they were done with me.

Chapter Twenty-five

Cassidy

JUST FOR NOW
Performed by Maren Morris

Marco was quiet as we drove north out of Austin. The city lights faded away into the suburbs that then faded away into the dark of a freeway with only headlights and taillights filling the sky. My body was still humming from the soft press of lips we'd exchanged in the kitchen. So light it could almost have been nonexistent, but instead it had been filled with fire and flames.

Seeing Marco in a home filled with people who knew him, who laughed and teased and sent love in his direction, had surprised me even after learning about Jonas, Maliyah, and Maria Carmen. Marco had been such a solitary figure in my mind for so long that it was hard to catch up with the idea of him being part of a family. I wondered if he even realized that they saw him that way—as part of them.

"Can I ask you something?" I threw out as we drove.

He looked over at me quickly and then back at the road. "Sure."

"What were your parents like?"

His eyes closed for a millisecond as if it still hurt, years later, to talk about them. To hear them mentioned out loud.

"My mom was a pharmacist, and my dad was an accountant. They both came to the States after Operation Just Cause. My dad was an orphan, but my mom had lost her family in Noriega's reign of fire. That was how they met…both helping the American government. My dad was tangled up in it the most, following some of Noriega's money men, so it wasn't safe for them there after it all went down."

The surprise hit me in the center of my chest. "They were heroes."

Marco laughed. "My dad would have objected profoundly, and many of his countrymen wouldn't agree with that statement either. But he did what he thought was right."

I waited, wondering if he realized how much of them he'd inherited. Like humbly denying the good they'd done.

"They were really good people and good parents," he said softly. "I never once doubted they loved me. We were a happy, normal, everyday family who went to work and school during the week and spent our weekends and holidays traveling. Dad wanted to see as much of the United States as he could."

There was a sadness in his voice that made my heart hurt.

"I'm sorry…I shouldn't have…"

He gripped my hand, raised it to his lips, and kissed the back much as he had at Maria Carmen's.

"No. It's been too long since I've talked about them," he said quietly, but the pain still radiated through him. I wanted to take it away. I lifted his hand holding mine and returned the kiss he'd given me. When he spoke again, there was a tremor in it. "We went to the fair that night. I was fifteen, so I would have preferred to be there with my friends, but I also didn't mind being with my parents."

"Maybe you would have preferred being there with a girlfriend?" I asked, lifting an eyebrow.

He chuckled. "I didn't have one, but there was a girl I'd been mooning after."

"Mooning?" I teased.

He shrugged with a self-deprecating smile and then returned to his story. "My dad won this huge bear at one of the carnival games. It was so big you couldn't even see my dad's head as he carried it. It was completely ridiculous. The more embarrassed I got, the bigger scene he made. He was actually waltzing with it as we walked out to the car at the end of the night."

His lips were turned up, thinking about it, and I could just imagine how red and embarrassed Marco had been. If my dad had done that when I was fifteen, I would have run as fast as my uncoordinated legs could carry me.

"What a great memory," I said.

His smile slowly faded. "It was. The stupid bear barely fit into the back of the Explorer. It was actually leering over the back of the seat I was sitting in."

"Leering?" I couldn't help but laugh.

"Yeah. Leering." His lips tilted up momentarily before disappearing again. "The semi-truck driver had fallen asleep at the wheel. He crossed the divide, flipped the semi, and it landed on the Explorer. I don't remember any of it other than the lights heading our way and waking up in the hospital pretty beat up."

I squeezed his hand that I still hadn't let go of.

"I'm so sorry you lost them," I said quietly.

His Adam's apple bobbed. "Me too."

We drove in silence for a long time.

"I know it's not the same, but you have a beautiful family with Maliyah, Maria Carmen, and Jonas," I said.

He nodded. "You're right. I've been lucky to have experienced two loving families. I didn't always see it that way, but it's true."

I didn't want him to dwell on what he'd lost even when I'd been the one to bring it up. Maybe more so because I felt responsible for making him sad, even briefly. So, I changed the topic, moving away from his family to mine. "I never doubted my parents loved me either. They fought every day of my childhood to make sure I had every possible chance at a so-called normal life. They were there when teachers tried to make me feel stupid, when I broke bones, and when I foolishly tried to run hurdles in track."

Marco gave me a surprised look much like the one I'd given him. "Hurdles?"

I laughed. "I *tried* to run hurdles. It was a ridiculous attempt with my hypotonia."

"I'm surprised Arlene let you."

I smirked. "She didn't know." My smile faded. "Then, she blamed Brady after I'd broken my arm, because she found out he'd signed the permission slip for me."

"Wasn't he at Juilliard by then?"

I nodded. "Yep, but I emailed him, begging him to sign it for me, and he did."

"He's a good brother," Marco said with a gruffness to his voice.

"He really is. He took so much of Mom's wrath for me as a kid, and then he made sure I could follow my dreams by funding the café and helping me buy the house." Guilt filled me as it always did when I thought of all the things Brady had done for me over the years.

"Helping you is a gift to him. You know that, right?" he asked.

I nodded. I did. Brady wanted to help us all. Wanted to take some of the money he'd earned and spend it on the people he loved. But it still didn't make it easier to accept.

"You're a good brother, too," I said to Marco.

He didn't respond for a long time. "I haven't really been there very much. When I have been, I…" He faded away.

"You were dealing with the events of your own life the best you could. You shouldn't beat yourself up over that any more than I should beat myself up over Brady's generosity."

"It's easy to say, but not easy to do."

I nodded, agreeing. In that way, Marco and I were alike. Feeling guilty for things we shouldn't have.

We were quiet after that. Both of us lost in our thoughts of our families and our pasts and things we couldn't change.

My phone buzzed, and I looked down to see Mom's face. I panicked, letting go of Marco's hand to answer it. "Hey, what's wrong?"

She laughed. "Now you sound like me, *cailín deas*. I just wanted to make sure you got to talk to Chevelle before I put him down. That is, if he ever stops following the damn puppy."

Her words didn't match her emotions, and I laughed.

"So, you've fallen in love with it already?" I teased.

She huffed. "Chevelle, come talk to Mama."

There was a scuffle, and then my boy's tiny voice came on. My heart swelled like it did every single time I heard him. "Mama. Dog-dog. Run. I's follow."

I listened to him ramble, told him I loved him and to be good, and then Mom came back on. She asked where we were, and I told her we were almost to Belton.

"I hope everything goes well tomorrow. Let yourself enjoy the moment. You've earned it."

My heart faltered. It wasn't like my mother had never praised me or that she didn't believe in me. It just felt like she was telling me something more. Something bigger. The truth was, I still didn't feel like I'd earned anything, even though it was my recipes that had attracted Lance Ralley's interest.

"I'll talk to you tomorrow," I said quietly.

We hung up, and the silence filled the car again.

My mind swirled with all the decisions I had to make and the responsibilities that followed me around. I'd been lucky to have my dreams come true, but the heavy weight of those dreams as they'd become real was even more than I'd expected. The non-stop work and long hours it took to make it all come together every day was never ending. I was tired. Exhausted deep in my soul.

Sometimes... Sometimes I wished for just a momentary break to recharge before diving back in. In two years, I hadn't had that chance. Tonight...tonight maybe I could let it all go. For just one night. Maybe I could just be a woman standing in front of a man who she wanted with every fiber of her being without caring about what came next. Maybe we could lose ourselves in each other, living in this singular moment instead of the past or the future.

"Where are you at?" Marco asked, drawing me back to him.

I took a deep breath and told him the truth. "I'm thinking about how long it's been since I've had a night all to myself. With no one to take care of and no kitchen or recipes calling to me."

He navigated an off-ramp and made several turns the GPS was shouting out in order to get to the hotel. It wasn't a five-star hotel. Just an average place where business people often holed up while traveling for work. I didn't even think it had room service. But it had clean beds reserved for us in separate rooms. Visions filled me again like they had earlier of us sharing a room. Except, this time I could clearly see Marco's muscled torso moving above me. Hands and bodies tangled amongst white sheets. It almost took my breath away.

"You've earned a night off, Angel," Marco said. That word "earned" filled the air around me for the second time, battling with my conscience. "You work harder than anyone I know. Treat yourself for the next couple of nights."

"Yeah?" I said as he pulled into the hotel and parked the rental in a slot not far from the lobby doors.

He nodded.

"You know what else I'm thinking?" I asked. He didn't respond, just turned the car off and looked at me as I continued. "I'm thinking about how nice it would be to have one room instead of two."

His jaw flexed, teeth grinding together.

"Cassidy—"

"Don't. Don't start spewing all the reasons we shouldn't. I'm bone tired of doing the responsible thing, aren't you? Don't you want, for just once, to do the irresponsible thing?"

He closed his eyes, blocking me out.

I leaned in and ran a hand along his jaw.

"Marco." His eyes opened, plowing into mine with heat and intensity. "Let's be bad together. Really, really bad."

Chapter Twenty-six

Marco

WHISKEY AND RAIN
Performed by Michael Ray

Cassidy's words spun through me, licking the flames back to life that had barely been subdued after the soft kiss in Maria Carmen's kitchen. It filled me with images of Cassidy's pale skin laid out below me and a glorious smile on her face.

Her hand on my jaw flexed the longer I took to respond. The desire and humor in her eyes started to fade into embarrassment. It had taken courage for her to go out on a limb like that, and I was being an ass. I was doing the one thing she hated most—someone protecting her when she didn't need or want it. I placed my hand over the top of hers as it rested on my jaw. My other hand landed below her chin so she couldn't hide her golden eyes from mine.

"I want you." My voice was gravelly in a way only she seemed to bring out in me. "I want you more than I've ever wanted anything in my life."

"But?"

"I can't do a single night with you. Or even two or three. I'm afraid that if we took that step, I'd never be able to leave your side. I'd be a greedy damn bastard, Angel. I'd want all of you."

Maliyah was right that I had feelings for Cassidy. They felt deep and unending, but I wasn't sure if it was love because I'd had too little experience with that emotion. What I did know was if I took her completely, I wouldn't be able to give her back to the world. I'd want her to be mine forever. But what I didn't know was would she be okay with it? Would she let me be there at her side every day? And what did that mean for me and my job and the world I'd carefully crafted?

She searched my eyes, an ache in them that hurt me just to see it.

"I'm torn in so many pieces right now, Marco. I don't know that I have anything else to give but a handful of nights." She said each word as if she hated them. As if she wanted to say something different but couldn't.

I rubbed a thumb along her lips, wanting to devour them again.

"I know," I said gently. She had so many balls in the air it was unfair of me to expect more, but I knew that was what I'd want.

The ache inside her eyes turned to a different fire—anger fueled by humiliation I didn't want her to feel for taking a brave leap.

She pulled away with force, yanked open the car door, and stormed out.

I followed, getting to the rear hatch just as she pulled her suitcase from it. She wouldn't let go of the handle when I tried to take it.

"I got it!" she snapped.

I didn't fight her. Instead, I grabbed my duffel, shut the back, and almost jogged to follow her. The rolling suitcase hit the curb at a weird angle as she hauled it up on the sidewalk, catching the wheel and causing her to lurch sideway. My hands were on her waist before she could hit the sidewalk.

I pulled her up against me. "Stop. Just fucking stop," I growled.

Her breath was coming in puffs, and her body was tense not only from the almost fall, but from the emotions flowing through her.

"Why are you angry with me?" I demanded.

She glared at me for a long moment before her shoulders sagged, and she pushed her head into my chest. Her voice was quiet, drifting down to the sidewalk, the muffled sound blending into the dark of the night with only the lights from the hotel parking lot surrounding us.

"I don't know. Maybe I'm angry at myself? Or both of us? Or life? You're beautiful. Your words are beautiful, and I want it all to be mine when I shouldn't. Irrationally...I guess I want you to say you don't give a damn about all the things in my life that you'd have to compete with at the same time I hate myself for wanting it when I know it wouldn't be fair to you."

I kissed the back of her head. "You misunderstood me, then."

She caught her breath, slowly pulling her head up until her eyes, shadowed by the competing night and streetlights, met mine. "What?"

"I just wanted you to understand what you were getting into. Regardless of what's going on in your life, how little or how much time you have for me, I want it. I want the little pieces, Angel. But like I said, if we do this…" My body came to life at just the thought. "I'm not going to walk away after a night or a handful of nights. I'm going to want to be the person waiting for you in your bed when everything you have to do in your day is done. I'm going to want to be the person you tell about the ridiculous customer, or the wild new concoction you thought up, or how Chevelle has learned a new word. I'm going to want to be the person who kisses you until you forget everything that happened in the last twelve hours so you have a few moments of respite before you start your day all over again. If you don't want that too, then you need to walk into that lobby, check us into the two rooms we've already reserved, and say goodnight to me at the elevator."

Her surprise and pain coasted over her face, followed by desire and fear. There was also hope and something I couldn't name before a little flare of anger returned. "How can you want so little for yourself? How can you stand there and say you're willing to just have the crumbs left at the end of my day?" she demanded.

"I'll take you any way I can have you. But I won't take you and give you back. That's the line I draw." It hurt to say the words, knowing that I could have shut my mouth and spent three nights in heaven with her, gliding together like we were meant to be. But I also knew myself well enough to know I'd never be able to walk away from her after. I couldn't go back to being her workout coach and her brother's bodyguard. I had to be hers. The man she was with or nothing at all. Even if being that man meant only having moments of her time. Even if I didn't deserve to even have those scattered seconds.

My heart was pounding in my chest. Loud and

strong. Adrenaline filling it as much as it had the night I'd watched the members of my unit leave the barracks full of snide remarks and jostling each other's arms. I'd realized it as a life-changing moment, but I'd chosen to ignore it. This was the same way. Life-changing. All in or all out.

"Marco..." her voice cracked. Tears filled her eyes, and I hated myself, wanting to take back what I'd said at the same time I knew I'd say them all over again if I had to.

I let her go slowly, making sure she was stable, and said, "What we are right now isn't going to change if you choose two rooms. We will always be this—friends. People who care about each other. I'm not going to stop working out with you, or finding out what that asshole Hardy is up to, or see you less than I do now. But if you choose one room, it *will* change us."

I walked away, leaving her standing in the glow of the streetlight, letting her consider everything I'd said. It was shitty in many ways. To put this on her when she already had so much weighing her down. Chevelle and Clayton, paying Brady back, Lance Ralley and Earth Paradise. I wanted to strip it all away. Make her forget everything but how good she could feel in my arms with my lips on hers, with our bodies tangled. But I knew the truth. I couldn't go back if we stepped into that space together, and she needed to decide if she could live with that...with me.

It wasn't like I hadn't had one- or two-night stands before. I knew how and when to get the release I needed. How to make sure my partner got more than the release they sought. I'd just never wanted more than that with anyone. But then, I'd never wanted someone like I wanted Cassidy.

The automatic lobby doors glided open, and I scanned the area. The music was low and unassuming, and there was a kid barely older than Jonas behind the reception desk. Instead of going there, I made my way to the lounge where a few people sat at tables in front of a bar. I threw my bag at the base of a stool as I slid onto it and ordered a beer. It had been a long time since I'd had a drink. Months. I'd celebrated with Brady after he'd told everyone the news that he was going to be a dad, and that had been a single glass of champagne.

I heard the lobby doors slide open behind me, and I knew without even looking up that Cassidy had walked in. I heard the suitcase rolling across the tile floor, heard the clerk greet her and her soft voice returning his, although I couldn't hear the words.

I'd just tipped the beer up to my lips when she joined me.

She wasn't smiling, and just that simple fact made my heart twist. When my glance landed on her hands, it felt like a knife had been sliced down my insides. She had two envelopes. Two sets of keys. Two rooms.

Her hand shook as she laid one of them on the bar top. Her eyes met mine, sadness in them. "I…I want to say yes to all of that. But it wouldn't be fair."

She turned away, and her voice got even quieter. "Goodnight, Marco."

She walked toward the elevator, pulling her suitcase behind her, and I watched before downing the beer, hoping it would put out the flames of desire and hurt and heartache. Hoping it would allow me to forget what could have been if I'd allowed myself to let go of my beliefs for one single night. But I couldn't. Not ever again.

♪ ♪ ♪

The alarm on my phone went off, and I groaned. My head was throbbing, and my tongue was stuck to the roof of my mouth like it had been glued there. Last night, I'd chased that single beer with half a dozen shots of whiskey before heading up to a room with a king-sized bed and no Cassidy. I'd stumbled out of my clothes and lay on the bed in my briefs, wishing I'd been wearing nothing and had pale skin lined up against mine.

Now, I had to get my ass out of the bed, into the shower, and meet her in the lobby to take her to Earth Paradise, all the while hiding the rips in my soul she'd made. I couldn't blame her. I'd made an unfair demand. All or nothing when we'd barely shared a handful of kisses. It had been ridiculous.

I groaned again. The room blurred as I sat up. I fought through the haze, dragged my body from the bed, and headed for the bathroom. I turned the shower on cold, stepping in and staying there until my body was shivering and my teeth were chattering, but the walls were clear, and the throbbing in my head had receded.

When I looked in the mirror, I saw deep shadows under my eyes. On a good night, I was lucky to get four or five hours of sleep, and even though I'd had more the night before, the alcohol had ensured it was restless. I went to shave and realized I'd forgotten my shaver in Grand Orchard. The dark stubble made me look unkempt and only accentuated the dark layers from my disturbed night.

I dressed, laced my boots, and found my way

down to the lobby and the coffee I knew I'd find there. What I really needed was something greasy or spicy to nip at the hangover still trying to pull me under, but food would have to wait.

My phone buzzed.

ANGEL: Are you awake? I knocked on your door.

ME: I'm downstairs getting coffee. Can I get you one?

ANGEL: Thank you, but I made one in the room. I'll be down in a few.

I leaned against a pillar, sipping the coffee, one hand in my pocket, while I watched the bank of elevators. Eventually, the doors slid open to reveal Cassidy. She was in a stunning pink dress I'd never seen her in before—high-waisted with a band that landed just below her breasts and emphasized their shape before flaring out softly over her hips to land midthigh. Her long legs were on display in a way she rarely showed them except when she was in workout gear. Her feet were hidden in nude ballet slippers with rosebuds along the toes. Feminine and floral, just like Cassidy always was, but she'd layered a blazer over the dress, so she looked much more business-like and older than I'd ever seen her appear. Her hair was partially up, highlighting her high cheekbones and drawing attention to her eyes, but the rest still spilled down her back in long waves. She was so beautiful it almost broke my already torn and battered heart.

My gaze stalled on the shadows below her lashes. She hadn't slept either. If I'd taken her up on her offer, we'd likely have had the same look but for a very different reason.

She joined me with a small smile.

I'd told her nothing would change if she chose to get two room keys instead of one. I'd promised her that, and I'd do everything I could to hide the disappointment I felt.

"Morning, Angel."

Surprise flickered across her face, as if she'd expected me to stop calling her Angel because of what had happened.

"You look tired," she said, eyes raking down my body and taking in my standard apparel of a black T-shirt, black pants, and black military boots.

"I can't say the same for you. You look…gorgeous," I told her. It wasn't a lie. Her beauty outshone her tired.

Her lips lifted slightly. "Thanks. I'm nervous. About meeting Ralley on his turf. It makes it more real somehow."

I wanted to pull her into my arms, kiss her soft lips, and reassure her that everything was going to be fine. If we'd spent the night tangled together, I would have been able to do that. I would have been able to slide my hand into hers and hold it as we walked out of the lobby and toward the rental car. But instead, we were silent, making our way shoulder to shoulder but not touching.

I punched in the address of Earth Paradise into the navigation system, and we headed in that direction with regret hanging in the air between us. Hers. Mine. Ours. And I suddenly realized I wasn't going to be able to keep my promise to her. Things had changed almost as much as they would have changed if we'd spent the night together, and there wasn't a damn thing I could do about it now.

Chapter Twenty-seven

Cassidy

LET'S MAKE LOVE
Performed by Tim McGraw with Faith Hill

Marco had been silent all morning as Lance had taken me around the plant. He'd introduced me to so many people my mind was a whirl with names and faces. As we'd gone through test kitchens, the production floor, and the storage lockers, he'd filled me in on the sustainable farms and eco-friendly companies they used. He'd even discussed, with great pride, the tiers of solar panels covering the parking lot and roof of the building that fueled the plant. It was all state of the art but also green in every way he could make it.

It was hard not to be impressed, but the truth was, I couldn't fully concentrate on it. My mind was stuck replaying a movie reel of Marco and me from the night before. My offer and his ultimatum. The choice I'd made that had sent me to a room by myself, tossing and turning, aching for things that I shouldn't have wanted and didn't know how to fit into my life.

Marco's words were the sweetest words anyone had ever spoken to me. The thought of someone never wanting to let me go once they'd had me…it was tantalizing. I'd nearly given in. I'd nearly accepted what he'd thrown down not only because I wanted to be able to lose myself in his skin and his scent, but because the idea itself—having someone at my side at the end of each day and as the sun rose each morning—was a dream I'd been longing to make real for some time now.

But it would have been selfish to accept it. It bothered me that he was willing to accept so few pieces of my time and my energy. It drove me nearly batty that he seemed to think it was all he deserved when, really, he deserved to be the center of someone's world. To have them be consumed by him.

I forced my thoughts back to Lance and the conference room he was showing us into. He introduced his product development manager, Sue Lee. She had an ageless kind of face, but her black hair had wisps of white in it. She was all business as she waved to the samples she'd prepared for me to taste with the slight changes they were proposing to my recipes.

"What do you think?" Sue asked after I'd tried all of them.

"I can't even tell the difference in the pomegranate and acai coffee cake or the cookies," I said before waving to the chorizo quiches. "But there's too much crust on these."

Lance grinned, and Sue frowned.

"What?" I asked.

"That's what I told Sue," he said.

Three more people came in, and Sue rose. "I'll go back and whip up a few more quiche samples. We may have to increase the size to more single-serving rather than appetizer to get the correct balance. I'll have a new version ready for you tomorrow."

She hustled out, and Lance turned to the new team who'd strolled in, introducing them as his marketing folks. They'd taken my Golden Heart Café logo with the tree of life in the middle and the heart shape carved into its bark, enhanced it, and placed it on white packaging rimmed with gold trim. It was beautiful and professional and made my pulse beat faster with both joy and nervousness at the thought of seeing my food being sold outside of just Grand Orchard. They threw out several different advertising ideas and slogans, and I sat in awe of it all while Marco watched me. I didn't need to twist my head to the side to know this was the case. His gaze burned into my skin.

I gave feedback, but I wasn't sure I'd be able to recall what it was. The team seemed happy with it, and they left the room all smiles.

"Let's have lunch in the company cafeteria, and then I'll send you over to Marsha's Muffins to meet up with her. We have a very good relationship now. In fact, we distribute for her everywhere except in the United States," Lance said.

He took us into the small cafeteria where groups of people were scattered around tables spread across the black-and-white-checked floors. There was a full kitchen and several line cooks behind the counter. The menu held some of the company's own products but also standard lunch counter fare you might find in a fifties diner.

There was an air of contentment in the cafeteria that was easy to read. I'd been in places where the atmosphere was loaded with tension and unhappiness, and this was the complete opposite. Laughter drifted about amongst the groups, and the few solo people had newspapers or e-readers in front of them, completely relaxed.

My hesitancy about Lance back in Grand Orchard seemed almost ridiculous in light of everything I'd seen today. I glanced at Marco, and he appeared as surprised by the cafeteria as I was.

Seeing our exchange, Lance smiled. "We're family here. Lunch is part of the compensation package, and I encourage people to take the full hour. Life is about balance, don't you think? I want my employees to be happy while they're working, but I also want them to know I don't expect this to be the entirety of their worlds."

His words hit me hard in my belly.

When was the last time I'd had true balance in my life? Physically, it had never been part of my world, but I should have been able to find it in other areas. I'd preached it to my nutrition clients before I'd been laid off. But other than with my food and meals, I'd never followed my own advice. I'd gone headlong into every activity I'd ever done with an obsessed focus. School. Nutritionist. Mom. Restauranteur. Even my workouts with Marco had been stubbornly executed on a daily basis as if I could only succeed if I gave it two-hundred percent.

"Cassidy?" Lance asked, and I drew myself back to the conversation.

I smiled. "Sorry, was deep in thought."

He smiled warmly, like a father to a wayward child. "I've thrown a lot at you, and I've been hovering around you the whole time without letting you really absorb it." He waved to the counter. "Order what you want, and I'll leave you two in peace for the day. Here's Marsha's address. She's expecting you at two o'clock. I'll see you tomorrow morning at ten, but you're welcome to call and chat if you have burning questions between now and then."

I took the card he held out, and then he sauntered out of the cafeteria, talking to people as he went. Marco and I ordered at the counter and then stood with some other employees, waiting for it to be prepared.

"Why don't you go find a seat?" Marco suggested. "There's no reason for us both to stand here."

I was going to object, but with Lance's talk still pounding through my brain, I was reminded of Marco's words from the airport coming back to me: *I'll try if you'll try*. It wasn't just balance I was lacking in my life. It was allowing others to take care of me without feeling like it made me weak.

"Thank you," I said softly and moved off to find a table in the corner near a window. My eyes were drawn to the summer storm that was brewing outside. My thoughts felt as heavy as the sky. Like they were going to burst out of me just like the rain.

I'd been worried that this deal would be yet another drain on my already limited time, but Brady had been right. If I got this deal, I could hire extra staff at the café. I might be able to focus on creating food rather than managing the day-to-day. While I loved the restaurant, I loved the designing and crafting of the food and menus even more. I would never have admitted that to anyone before. I'd barely whispered it to myself because it would have felt like I was slapping Brady in the face to say, "Oh, hey, thanks for spending gazillions of dollars on my restaurant, but I'm not sure I really want to manage it, after all."

The idea of just being able to create the recipes and menus while someone else managed the restaurant itself seemed to lift a weight from my shoulders, and I suddenly wanted to make this deal happen with every part of me. I wanted it not just for myself and for the time I might get back with Chevelle, or to pay Brady back, but I wanted it for the restaurant itself, which might grow even more with a team running it instead of just me. I could make Cliff head chef and hire Willow as a manager and assistant chef. We could get more kitchen help and more waitstaff to ease the load on everyone. We might be able to stay open for dinner, and I'd be able to give everyone a raise. Just that made my heart soar.

But more importantly, I might be able to take weekends off and spend extra time at home. When Chevelle started school, I might be able to be there at the end of his day. I could spend the nights in someone's arms and not feel like he was only getting the leftovers of me before I scrambled back out of bed at the crack of dawn.

"You're practically glowing. Where did your mind go?" Marco asked as he slid into the seat next to me with our food.

I smiled. My heart felt truly light for the first time in days. "I just realized how much I actually want this deal with Ralley to work."

His eyes fell to my lips before gliding away again.

"Yeah? No more queasy feeling in your gut?" he asked, and there was something in his tone, as if he was holding back, and I frowned.

"Do your Spidey senses not agree?" I asked.

He shook his head, glanced around the room, and said, "No. Not at all. If anything, I feel the complete opposite of worried. It says a lot about a leader when their staff is this at ease around them."

"But…"

"No but because of anything here with Ralley. No lingering doubts. The but is really because of you. Are you wanting this *for you* or are you only thinking about paying off Brady?"

"I'm not going to lie and say that it isn't one of the reasons. But it isn't *just* about the money or paying my brother back. This is about my life. What I want for me and Chevelle. What good am I to him if I only role model working myself to death without also showing him that it's okay to care for yourself? That it's okay to work hard for your dreams but that it's even more important to be there for the people you love most."

I wondered if he understood what I was insinuating, but then his hand froze halfway to his mouth with a fry, and his look turned heated. I flushed as my thoughts went back to the car, my offer, and the reasons I'd ended up getting two keys instead of one. I'd hurt him in doing it, but I'd thought it had been the right decision. I hadn't wanted him to accept less. But what if he didn't have to? What if I simply had more to give?

"Last night, you said something about being greedy…" I trailed off, having a hard time speaking while his eyes seemed to devour me. I swallowed and continued, "I realized I'm greedy too. I want Chevelle to spend more time with me than he does my family. I want…I want to be able to have a relationship with someone who brings me joy without them feeling like they only get the leftovers of me when I'm exhausted from working twelve hours a day, six days a week. I want"—I looked around the room—"balance."

Marco reached out and curled my hand into his. He didn't say a word but let me continue to pour every thought I had out. "For a long time, I've felt guilty because Brady gave me this amazing gift, and I didn't want to let him down, so I worked really hard to make it successful. But the truth is, Brady doesn't care about that as much as he wants me to be happy. And this…" I brought his hand to my mouth and kissed the knuckles. "This would make me happy."

Marco swallowed hard before clearing his throat and saying, "I don't really have balance in my life either. I've been all about my job for years. Maliyah and Jonas… They ought to have had more of my time and attention. There should be more to me than just working out and guarding Brady. I'm not exactly sure how easy it will be for me to change."

His admission both tore at my heart for him as much as it soothed me to know I wasn't alone in my obsessed focus on my goals.

"We're quite the pair of workaholics," I teased. "But maybe we can start our own Workaholics Anonymous or something. Maybe…we could be each other's sponsors?"

His lips quirked, one of the first times I'd seen his partial smile all day. "I don't want to be your sponsor, Angel. Sponsors can't end the day tangled in the sheets together."

His words filled my belly with desire. Thoughts of our skin merging and blending together. Of whispered moans and stroking fingers. My face flushed, and he saw it, reading easily where my thoughts had gone, and his face broke into a huge smile. The one that was so rarely on his somber face.

The one that was like the light breaking through the clouds and sending heavenly rays down to the ground.

We sat there, eyes boring into each other, for so long that it felt like the day had disappeared into night by the time we resurfaced.

"You done?" he asked with a wave at my plate.

I nodded. He shifted both trays together and took them to the garbage cans divided into recycling, compost, and trash—environmentally friendly, like everything else at Earth Paradise had been. There was no reason for me not to do this deal.

I grabbed my purse and headed over to join Marco at the door.

His gaze was full of lust as he watched me walk. My body burned to simply return to the hotel with him. To pull him directly to the SUV, drive straight there, and head to one of the two rooms I'd stupidly rented the night before. But I had one more meeting to get through before we could do that. I needed to meet with Marsha before I signed on with Lance and made my life over for the third time at barely twenty-five.

"Marsha's?" I asked.

He reached up and tucked a tendril of hair back behind my ear. "I'm here for you, Angel. Whatever you want to do."

I slid my hand through his arm, leaning my head on his shoulder, and flames licked through my veins at just the simple touch.

"I'm sorry about last night..." I said, throat clogging with emotion. "Sometimes, I just need time to realize the only thing in my way is me."

"At night, it's easier for our fears to take hold and

not let go." My breath caught at his admission, as if he, too, regretted how we'd ended our evening.

We made our way out to the car, heading down the road just a few miles to where Marsha's Muffins was located. The place was much smaller than Earth Paradise, taking up several suites in a business park. It hardly looked like a major food production facility. The receptionist took us directly to Marsha's office. It was a cluttered mess, filled with books and papers that seemed to burst from the file cabinets. Marsha was a short, dark-haired woman who waved us into chairs, confirmed everything Lance had said, and then basically said she was actually grateful Lance had come into her life even if it had started under contentious circumstances.

We left almost as quickly as we'd arrived, with a basket full of treats, and a feeling that Lance was a white knight, offering golden apples to those who needed it most. Taking little people and little products and thrusting them into a limelight they never would have seen if it hadn't been for him. I felt very grateful and fortunate that he'd stumbled into the café and liked my food enough to make this offer, but I was also proud of what I'd created, that he thought it was good enough to be sent out into the world.

As we left the building, the clouds that had been heavy all day finally opened up above us, sending a downpour in our direction. Marco and I fled for the car at a sprint. Rain, me, and slick pavement were never a good mix, and Marco automatically knew this. Before I could even object, he'd swept me into his arms, carrying me like a bride over the threshold. My first inclination was to grouse, but the truth was, I was apt to fall in this kind of situation. So, I gave in just as I had in the cafeteria, letting someone take care of me.

I leaned my head against his chest, taking in his scent and reveling in the flex of his muscles as he held on to me and jogged the rest of the way.

He unlocked the car with a beep of the remote and set me down on the passenger seat. We were both drenched from the mere yards it had taken to get to the car. Water dripped from Marco's thick lashes. The rain made them appear even longer and darker. They were beautiful lashes on a beautiful man. When he went to back away, I reached up, grabbed his neck, and pulled him in for a kiss. The sweet raindrops on his lips were cool against the heat of our mouths, and the contradictory sensations flamed the fire that was always ready to burst whenever Marco was near me.

He groaned against my mouth, opening to me and letting me taunt and tease him with my tongue and my teeth and my lips. His hand went to the back of my head and pushed me closer until our bodies were slammed up tight against one another, and the rain was once again pouring over me as I sat half in and half out of the vehicle. But we didn't stop. Instead, we continued tasting and touching as the intensity grew in and around us, until my nipples were hard and aching, and I could feel the length of him pushing against my naked thigh from where my dress had risen.

It was Marco who eventually pulled back, taking in our clothes that clung to our bodies and the water dripping from my hair. A small, deep laugh broke from him. Pride filled me because I'd been the one to bring him this moment of happiness when he seemed to have so few. He looked up at the sky, closing his eyes as the rain continued to spread over him. His long neck was tantalizing and tempting. I wanted to kiss every inch of it. To slide my tongue down it. To nibble and nip and make him moan.

"Take me back to the hotel, Marco," I said, as surprised to hear the deepness of my voice as I was the waver in it that had nothing to do with hesitation and everything to do with desire.

He drew his gaze back down from the sky to me, eyes flashing with the same yearning that raged in me. He nodded, shut the door, and came around to the driver's seat. We were quiet on the drive, my body trembling with anticipation. My heart longed to be closer to his. To feel the sweet bliss that came from truly belonging to someone—a feeling I'd never had with anyone else. I wanted to finally give in and just accept the idea that we could be together.

Chapter Twenty-eight

Marco

TAKE YOUR BREATH AWAY
Performed by Josh Melton

The rain never let up on the way from Marsha's Muffins to the hotel. The car smelled of it, earthy and damp mixed with the sweet aroma that was always Cassidy. My heart thudded in my chest with a military-like cadence—hard, fast, and never letting up. The rips and tears from this morning, when I hadn't been able to have her, were sealing back up. God, I wanted her. Wanted her enough to risk everything else in my life going to hell, including my job with Brady. I could find another security gig. But deep in my heart, I knew that all Brady wanted was the people around him to be happy. As long as I didn't hurt her, he'd be okay with it, and I'd be damned if I did anything to wound Cassidy O'Neil.

I pulled the SUV under the overhang at the hotel's entrance, and Cassidy looked at me, surprised.

"It'll keep you dry."

She laughed, looking down at herself. She'd taken off the sodden jacket, and her dress clung to every curve and valley. It accentuated everything I wanted to spend an entire evening worshipping.

"I think that train has already passed the station," she teased.

"Go up to the room, Angel. I've got to run over to the drugstore."

Her eyes widened a little as understanding registered. Her cheeks flushed, and then she leaned over the console and placed a kiss against my lips that made me want to drag her into my lap and lose myself in her right in front of the hotel.

"Hurry," she said and let herself out with a smile and a wink.

Goddamn.

I drove down the street to where I'd seen a chain store and jogged in, dripping water all over the place. I grabbed a shaver and a box of condoms and headed for the register. At the last minute, remembering the hotel had no room service, I grabbed some drinks and snacks in case we didn't leave the room as I hoped we wouldn't. I intended to make the most of this night with her.

This first night…

My feet stalled, and my heart almost gave out at the idea of having more than this night. Of having an endless number of them to lose ourselves in each other's skin. I shook myself into action, hurrying just like she'd demanded.

When I got back to the hotel, I realized I had no idea what room she was in because I hadn't really looked at her envelope the night before. I swung by my room, tearing off the dripping clothes and pulling on a pair of sweats and a T-shirt.

A knock came from the adjoining door, and my

hands stilled on the text I'd been about to send to her.

"Marco?" her voice came through the walls.

I unlocked the door to find her standing there in nothing but a towel, her skin damp and pink. I knew it was soft from the times I'd been able to touch her, even before our shared kisses over the last few weeks. Working out together for two years, there'd been plenty of moments when we'd touched, and the silkiness of her skin had usually tortured me for the remainder of the night.

She eyed my dry clothes and the plastic bags I had in my hand, a flash of uncertainty crossing her face. She backed up into her room, and I followed, setting the bags down on the floor.

"Let me just get dressed." She turned, and I grabbed her around the waist, dragging her back to me.

"Don't," I said gruffly.

I bent my head to her neck, trailing hot kisses along the smooth expanse, and my body immediately jumped to attention, straining against the sweats I'd pulled on. I continued my downward path until my lips hit the top of the towel. I carefully tugged at where she had the edges tucked, and it tumbled to the ground, revealing every single part of her. My breath caught, and my hands stilled as I took her in. Lean, yet curved perfectly. A small trail of stretch marks near her belly button from having carried Chevelle inside her. Skin marked with the beauty of her life.

"God, Angel. You're perfect. A damn masterpiece." She rolled her eyes, and I yanked so that she stumbled completely into me. "You don't believe me? Then, I'll have to spend the rest of the night convincing you."

I bent and took a breast, with the tip already pebbled, into my mouth, and she moaned. My hands traveled down her body, sliding over the smooth skin, curling into her soft recesses, and she gasped, hips thrusting into mine. I swung her into my arms and took her to the bed. I laid her down and hovered over her before returning my lips and fingers to her secret places.

She fisted my T-shirt, pulling at it. I paused long enough to haul it over my head and throw it aside before returning to my devotion of her body. Her hands gripped my shoulders, nails biting into me as my mouth found its way to her core. Her hips bucked again, and I smiled.

"Marco…God…" It was a sigh and a beg and a command all mixed together, and it lit me up, the flames reaching through me as I continued to softly pull her closer to the edge of bliss. Her entire body shivered and shook as waves of pleasure coursed through her.

I crawled up her body, finding her mouth and plunging my tongue inside it. Needing the sweetness of her all over again. Wanting to hear my name in that throaty tone repeatedly. Wanting to take her right back into the abyss.

Her hands wandered down my back to my hips, exploring the lines of me like I was exploring every inch of her. Our bodies moved together seamlessly as if they knew automatically where to touch and kiss and suck and bite and surrender to give the other the most pleasure. As if we'd been made to be this way, tangled together, two becoming one.

"You're wearing too many clothes, Marco," she whispered in my ear, sending chills down over me with the sweet heat.

"I'm afraid I'll lose control," I told her, meeting her eyes full of desire with ones that matched.

"So, lose control," she said softly. "Lose control, and we'll begin again."

My heart squeezed, and my dick swelled until I thought I'd explode without ever having been inside her. I groaned, moved off of her, and dug in the bag for the condoms. I slid my sweats down, and she watched with an unsteady breath as I rolled one on. I stared at her, amazed that she was mine. Amazed that I was actually getting to touch and taste this exquisite woman whom I'd craved for so long.

I closed my eyes briefly, trying to burn the image into my memory so it would last for an eternity. The moment when we let go of our former selves and became something new together. I eased back onto the bed, and she pulled me so that I landed on top of her again.

"I'm not glass," she said. "I'm not going to break. Please don't treat me that way." Every moment of her past caught up to her in those words. The family who'd tried to keep her encased in bubble wrap. Those who saw her as somehow less, broken because of a chromosomal difference in her DNA. She was different, but it was in a way that was stunning and breathtaking.

"Angel..." Her hands found me, sliding down and curling around my hardness. "Jesus."

I kissed her with a ferocity that came from deep inside me. Something primal and uncontrollable. Something I'd never let out of me before. An inferno that needed to be assuaged, and she met every lick and touch and shift of my body with her own. With oxygen and not water, flaming instead of soothing. Growing the intensity between us until I gave in and slid home. She gasped, biting the crook of my neck and collarbone, adding more fuel to the blaze.

We blended together. Force to force. Soul to soul.

I let go, and our bodies found their way home.

♪ ♪ ♪

We'd fallen asleep after the first round of lovemaking. My arms wrapped around her middle, her leg thrown over mine, and our hearts beating together. It hadn't been pretty. It had been more wild and savage than slow and rhythmic. But she'd been right. Letting go had been the right thing to do. Giving in had been what we'd both needed. Now, I could spend the rest of the night worshipping her like I truly wanted.

I let my hand trace the slope of her hip and waist, up higher to the swell of her breast, grazing the nipple until it hardened beneath my fingertips. I watched, enthralled with how the tan of my skin stood out against the pale white of hers. She gasped, drawing my eyes to her face. She was smiling. A wide grin that was so damn lovely it was hard to look at her without shielding my eyes from the brightness. She was magnificent.

We began our dance again. Lips, tongues, fingers, and palms discovering every nook and valley. Every dimple and groove. Every line of sinew and bone. A slower beat, but still pounding with drums and howls as if the wild in us was hunting for what it needed all over again. The pressure built until we were both gasping and panting with our bodies hungry for the release. When it came, it was an explosion of light and emotion that seemed to echo across the room.

I left briefly to clean up, and when I returned to the bed, she had a smile on her face that I'd never seen before. Sated and relaxed but also a happiness that seemed to come from the inside, taking over her entire being. As if her mind had suddenly stopped long enough to let her savor the moment. I tucked her up against me with her back to my chest.

"Are you okay?" I asked. Her fingers on my arm tightened.

"I'm better than okay. I've never felt so…so perfectly perfect."

I couldn't help the chuckle that rolled through me.

There were so many things we still had to figure out. So many things that this time together hadn't solved, but I didn't want to bring any of it up. Not when she seemed so quiet—so at peace—when normally she was a bundle of nonstop energy, with doubts and guilt and determination driving her.

My eyes drifted closed, and it hit me that I couldn't remember ever feeling this much peace either. When hadn't my brain been filled with a list of things to do and people I needed to protect? When hadn't I receded into haunting memories of things I couldn't change? This moment with Cassidy felt…dreamlike. As if we'd stopped time, freezing everyone and everything except for ourselves.

It was going to hurt to have reality come crashing back in, but I chose to forget it. I chose to simply think about how our hands were joined, and how her smooth legs were tangled with mine. How this felt like home more than any other place I'd ever been since my parents had died. As much as I loved Maliyah, I'd always held back something with her. From fear, or self-preservation, or just because I didn't know how to accept a family again. But this…with Cassidy. It felt like true belonging, and I could only hope that she felt the same.

Chapter Twenty-nine

Cassidy

MAKE IT RAIN
Performed by Thompson Square

We'd somehow shifted while sleeping. When I'd closed my eyes, I'd had my back to his chest, and our arms and legs had been wrapped together in knots. Now, I was facing him with my nose buried into his chest, drinking in the smells of him, but I was still locked to him by arms clamped tight, as if he was afraid I'd disappear.

Making love to Marco had quieted my brain in a way that nothing ever had in my life. My mind that was normally full of noise and a constant buzz of things to do was almost silent. Here, there was nothing but the desire to stay tucked up against him. To be lost in the sea of Marco.

My body was sore in such a delightful way. Marco had kissed and touched every single piece of me. Toes and ankles, calves and knees, hips and waist, elbows and shoulders. It was as if he'd been memorizing me with careful attention to every detail. As if doing so was the most important thing he'd ever done.

It brought tears to my eyes. To feel so…adored.

I'd been with two men in my life before this. My first was a college guy who'd been more friend than boyfriend, and whom I'd convinced that having sex was exactly what we needed to burn off our tension over finals. It had been awkward and barely satisfying for either of us.

Then, there had been Clayton. I may have made the first move, but he'd been the one to control our time together. I'd allowed him to command me because I'd thought that was what I needed—someone to just tell me what to do so my mind would stop trying to figure it out, so I wouldn't hear the whispered voice of my subconscious trying to tell me I shouldn't have been doing it at all. We'd had sex maybe a dozen times. Even though we'd both found pleasure, it hadn't been…satisfying. There'd been something missing from those acts for me. As if I'd held back a piece of myself even when I'd given him my body.

My time with Marco had been fiercer and wilder than what I'd experienced with Clayton, but it had also left me feeling complete. Whole. As if all my cracks that had ached to be found and healed had been. As if I'd been gone on a very long journey and finally come home.

Lips found the top of my head, kissing me gently. "You're thinking," he said, voice deep and guttural from both sleep and desire. He'd already sprung to life between us, pushing into my stomach. It made me smile.

I looked up into dark eyes framed in such luscious lashes it was hard to believe they were real. "How did you know?" I asked.

He gave a half-smile. "I could feel it."

I rolled my eyes but couldn't help smiling back. "Are you some Jedi warrior now?"

That brought a wider grin to his face. Lazy and almost shy. "Not Jedi...maybe a Cassidy warrior. Not attuned to the Force but attuned to you."

I couldn't help the laugh that burst out of me, but he didn't seem to care. I pushed against his chest, and he rolled onto his back with reluctance, his hand lingering on my waist as if he wasn't ready to let me go. I straddled him, and his eyes widened, taking in my tousled hair that spun around my breasts and the nipples that were already straining for him again.

"Goddamn, Angel. You're the most stunning thing I've ever seen."

"Language," I teased. "What shall I do with you and that mouth?"

His smile disappeared in a storm of desire. "Teach me a lesson, Angel."

I leaned forward, pushing his hands over his head and capturing his lips as the rest of my body slid against his. I whispered, "I'm not a punishment kind of person. I'm more a show-them-the-way-through-love kind of person."

He growled into my neck, hands pulling away from where I'd held them to find purchase on my waist, leading my core to his. Tangling ourselves together. We lost ourselves in each other again, but he let me drive the pace and the rhythm this time, going where I led, giving as much as he took but always stopping just a hair away from taking control from me. It was my turn to learn every inch of him: the dimples at his sides from layers of muscles, the beauty marks trailing around his belly button like a crescent moon, the scar on his left shoulder, and the tattoo of the Fleet

Marine Force on his bicep.

After we both had reached the peak again with soft cries and deep groans, we returned to earth and the bed as a tangle of bodies and limbs. Peace filled me once more. I wanted this with him. Over and over again. I didn't know how my body would ever stop longing for it now that it had tasted it. A new obsession.

My stomach rumbled loudly, and Marco chuckled. "Shall we go to dinner?"

It was late. The red lights on the cheap bedside clock read ten o'clock. "I'm not sure anything is open, and in truth, I'm not ready to leave the room yet."

He rose, used the bathroom, and then grabbed the plastic bags on his way back to the bed. He dumped out a sea of junk food onto the sheets, saying almost shyly, "It isn't what you're used to."

I got up and crossed the room, my naked body on display but not really minding when it was Marco's eyes that followed me. I grabbed the basket of pastries that Marsha had given us and brought it back to the bed.

"It's okay to have a junk food bender once in a while," I said with a smile. "After all, I definitely think our hearts got a good workout."

He grinned, kissed me gently, and then we reached down to tear open and share the stock pile of muffins, trail mix, chips, and bottles of water that were before us. It was the furthest thing from a Michelin-starred dinner you could get, but it was one of my favorite meals I'd ever had—eating naked with Marco in a hotel room in the middle of Texas.

When Marco opened a bag of hot Cheetos, I couldn't help wrinkling my nose. It was the only thing in the entire stack he'd bought that I didn't like. He smirked. "Not your thing?"

"The orange goop is slightly off-putting."

He looked at his fingers and then showed them to me. "These? You don't like these?"

I shook my head.

He moved his hand toward my face, and I laughed, pushing it away and bending backward at the waist to try and escape. My legs were wrapped crisscross in front of me, and I couldn't get far. Marco moved swiftly, sweeping the food and wrappers away from us before placing orange fingers on the swell of my breast where they left a mark.

"But look how much fun it is to clean it off," he said, voice low and deep as he bent his head to lick the mark away. Then, he left more trails of orange along my body that he proceeded to lap and suck and clean away. My breath was coming in pants again. Desire pooling through me. Flames flickering against my insides once more, ridiculously seeking another release after having already had more in several hours than I'd had in a lifetime.

I wrapped my legs around his hips, drawing him closer.

"I've changed my mind," I whispered against his neck, sucking on the lobe of his ear, happiness filling me at the little grunt of pleasure that escaped him.

"Yeah?"

"Hot Cheetos are now my very favorite."

And those were the last words we spoke for several more hours as our bodies found their way back to each other.

♪ ♪ ♪

A phone ringing brought me into the land of the living. I was still tangled in Marco's arms, but we both bent automatically in opposite directions to try and find the offending device. I came awake enough to realize it wasn't mine. The ringtone was completely off. I settled back down on the pillows while Marco moved to sit at the edge of the bed.

"Hey," he answered it quietly, as if to not wake me, which made me smile because it was obvious I was already awake.

As I watched, his body stiffened, back going taut, shoulders drawing backward as he listened to whomever it was on the other end. His muscles got tighter the longer he listened.

"What the hell, Jo-Jo?" he grunted out.

I sat up, moving so that I was right behind him, arms surrounding him, cheek resting against his back. He was so upset. I could feel him trembling with the emotions. Fear or anger, I wasn't sure which because I couldn't see his eyes. My heart pounded as worry flew through my veins. Worry for Marco and Jonas and Maliyah.

"I'm on my way. It'll be at least an hour, but I'm coming."

He clicked off and bent his forehead to the phone as his elbows rested on his knees.

"What happened?" I asked.

He lifted his head, slowly turning to me with a face full of guilt and fear. Self-recrimination. As if whatever had happened was his fault. My heart fell, hoping beyond hope that it wasn't Maliyah. That she hadn't had another episode that had left her in even worse shape.

"He's in jail. He was arrested," Marco croaked out.

My face fell, shock filling me. It was the last thing I'd expected to hear.

"What? Why?"

He shook his head and then was moving, pulling away from me and heading toward his adjoining room. I picked up his T-shirt from the floor, yanked it over my head, and followed.

"Talk to me."

"I have to go. Arrange bail. Get him the hell out of there."

"Of course. Let me get my things together." I turned back to my room, and he caught my hand, stopping me.

"You have to finish with Ralley. Sign the contract. I hate to take the car, but I need to get back. I'll figure out something for you—a way to get a rental delivered to the hotel." He was rambling, and I was sure it was exactly how his insides felt. Emotions flinging around inside him.

I wrapped my arms around his middle, stopping him. "Breathe."

His head fell to my shoulder, face nestled into the crook of my neck with big gasping breaths.

"I'm coming," I told him. "I don't need to be here to sign the contract."

He stepped away, face grim. "No. Stay. There's nothing you'll be able to do."

I squinted at him. "You said if we made love, that you wouldn't be leaving my side. I don't intend it to be any different for me. I'm going with you."

I rushed back into my room before he could argue. I threw everything I owned into my suitcase, yanked on underwear, a long skirt, and tied Marco's T-shirt in a knot at my waist. I needed the smell of him next to my skin to remind me of what we'd done in this room together. Of how we'd joined our lives and souls in a way that wouldn't end just because we were rushing to help his brother.

For the first time in my life, I was actually desperate to keep a protective bubble around me, shielding me from the rest of the world. But it was too late. Reality had crashed down around us.

Chapter Thirty

Marco

GLASS
Performed by Thompson Square

Cassidy and I had checked out and were on the road in less than fifteen minutes. I was kicking myself for letting her come. For not having stopped her from packing and joining me on this hell drive back to Austin. Not only because I wanted to drive at speeds that weren't safe—and I wouldn't with her next to me—but because I refused to let something in my world be the reason she lost her contract with Ralley. I wouldn't be the reason she lost the new dreams she'd been making for herself. Dreams where she had more time for Chevelle and herself…and me.

My chest constricted, pulling taut over my lungs and my heart.

I'd known better than to leave Jonas in Austin. Just like I'd known better than to let the assholes from my unit leave without following them all those years ago. When would I ever learn to trust my instincts? There were so many times in my life where I'd failed because of it. Nash Wellsley had been the one who'd truly saved Brady from his stalker. I'd been the clueless newbie who'd just stood on the sidelines while Brady's PR manager had been drugged and almost shot. I hadn't even been around the day some asshole reporter had threatened Tristan and caused Cassidy to tumble from the steps, chipping a tooth and scarring her brow. Every single time something bad had happened to people in my life, I hadn't been there.

I'd tangled myself with Cassidy, thinking I could keep her, wanting her more than I'd wanted anything for myself. But I didn't deserve her. I hadn't earned the right to keep anything good in my life that close to me. Not when I couldn't keep them safe.

But damn, the thought of not keeping her was like a grenade going off inside me.

Cassidy was quiet in the seat next to me as we raced down the darkened road. The night sky slowly washing into gray. Beams of light shimmering against the few remaining storm clouds and turning the sky into a watercolor painting of pink and orange.

"Are you okay to drive?" she asked. "You didn't get much sleep."

"I never get more than four or five hours," I replied before I could stop myself.

She inhaled sharply, my past and my guilt floating between us.

"Marco…this isn't your fault," she said quietly, reaching out to touch my arm. I flinched, and she drew back.

"I knew I shouldn't have left him," I said, swallowing hard over the lump in my throat. "That is one hundred percent on me."

I'd been distracted by Cassidy. By thoughts of us twined together. By ideas of love and forever-afters. I was a solitary animal. I'd just forgotten that. I'd promised her I wouldn't leave her, and yet that was exactly what I should have done. I should have accepted the single night she'd wanted and let her be. Even as I thought it, my body continued to revolt against the idea.

I couldn't look at her, but I saw her fists clench out of the corner of my eye.

"You can't protect everyone," she said with a growl to her voice. "That's just as asinine as my parents thinking they could shield me from every single fall growing up."

My teeth ground together, emotions filling me, and when I didn't respond, she just kept going, trying to convince me of something she'd never be able to succeed at.

"It stabs me to my core when Chevelle gets hurt trying something, like when he busted his chin climbing the steps at the studio. But if I didn't let him try, if I didn't let him fail, he'd never know how to pick himself up again."

"That's completely different. You'd never let him do something you knew could end up killing him. You wouldn't let him walk into a pool when he didn't know how to swim."

She didn't say anything.

"I knew he'd do anything to protect Mel," I grunted out. "Even walk into a gunfight with only his fists."

She inhaled sharply. "Was he shot?"

I shook my head. "That isn't the point."

She was quiet again for a moment, and then she said softly, "Tell me something. Have you ever stopped beating yourself up for not defending Petty Officer Warren?"

I didn't have to answer. It wasn't something I could ever forgive myself for. Something I could never forget. Not when Petty Officer Warren would live with it in her nightmares until the day she died.

"Do you think Jonas would ever forgive himself for not protecting his friend?" she asked. "Don't you see? He saw you torturing yourself over the exact same thing, knew what choice you would make if you had to do it all over again, and did what you would have done."

It stabbed at my heart and all the wounds deep inside me. I did wish I could do it all over again. Every single day of my life. And she was right. Jonas had seen me lost in those emotions. He'd lived it with me. But goddamn, I didn't want him risking himself for a girl who had chosen to put herself in harm's way. That wasn't what had happened to Petty Officer Warren.

"He could have called the cops. He could have called me. He had options."

"I'm assuming he doesn't really have a solid belief in the cops if his mom is in jail. And he wouldn't want you to get hurt because of him any more than you want him to be hurt because of you."

Everything she said made sense, but it didn't change the way I felt. It didn't change the guilt I had over leaving him in Austin when I'd known exactly what would happen. He'd needed me, and I'd left. Closed my eyes and driven away. As much as I'd thought I'd changed, I hadn't. I was the same selfish bastard I'd been when I'd watched the members of my unit walk out the door of the barracks.

We were silent for the rest of the journey. Me because I couldn't speak, and Cassidy because she was thinking. I could see her mind twirling even as she sat there.

When we reached Austin, I went straight to the police station, pulling into the parking lot and jumping out almost before the engine was off. Cassidy was at my side, trying to pull my fingers into hers, but I stormed off. I wouldn't be able to hold myself together if I lost myself in her tenderness or the admiration she still had glowing in her.

Inside, I explained to the clerk who I was there for, and a police officer came from the back. He asked us to step inside a room off to the side in order to talk.

"Did he tell you what happened?" the officer questioned me.

I shook my head. "Just that there was a fight, and he'd been arrested."

"They would have killed each other if my partner and I hadn't pulled them apart. Jonas had his hands around Arthur's neck. Arthur had a knife he'd lost somewhere along the way, but he was pounding into Jonas's side with his knuckles."

Anger flew through me as I realized Jonas was probably injured, and they hadn't taken him to the hospital.

"Why isn't he at the ER?" I demanded, glaring at him.

"EMTs were called, and they were both cleared." The officer took me in, eyes flicking to Cassidy and then back to me. I stepped in front of Cassidy as if to shield her from his gaze, which was ridiculous.

"What has he been charged with, and how do I bail him out?" I demanded.

The officer sighed, rubbed his hand on his temple, and said, "No charges have been filed yet because no one is talking. Neither of the boys. None of the gang members who'd been standing around watching. Not even the girl we think they were fighting over."

My stomach fell so hard I thought I'd throw up. He'd been in the middle of a gang circle. On his own. Fighting for his damn friend. Tears pricked the backs of my eyes. Cassidy put her arms around me from behind as if she could sense it, and I closed my eyes, fighting against the waves of emotion and nausea.

When I opened them again, the officer was staring at me with pity or sympathy. Something I didn't want. He sighed and said, "Look, he can't leave town anytime soon. Not until you hear from me that he's in the clear. But I don't think the district attorney is going to want to go to court over a brawl between teenagers over a girl."

I swallowed hard, and the officer went to the door. "I'll go get him."

Cassidy and I followed him out of the room, waiting in the hallway for my brother to appear. I paced back and forth, trying to calm down. Finally, the doors to the back opened, and Jonas appeared. I inhaled sharply. His right eye was swollen shut with a decent gash over it, the entire side of his face was bruised, his nose had clearly been broken, and there was blood crusted on his lip. In addition, he was clutching an arm to his stomach and limping as he approached. His clothes were torn and covered in smears of black as if he'd been dragged down an asphalt road.

Cassidy gasped.

My fury grew because he should have been at the goddamn hospital and not a police station. My body was trembling, and I was afraid to move in case I started breaking things. Even though he was nearly full grown, all I could see was the eight-year-old boy I'd first met on the steps of Maliyah's house.

Jonas's good eye blinked, tears filling them that he barely held back.

I took a step forward, then two, before I had my arms around him, hugging gently but firmly. "It's going to be okay, Jo-Jo."

We stood there in the middle of the hall, holding each other up the best we could, while regrets and failures drifted through both of us. And then Cassidy was there, wrapping both of us in her arms, and it felt like we were pulled back from the cliff and into the light. An angel rescuing the humans tortured by demons.

The automatic door slid open, and the air that had already turned humid and hot came in along with pounding feet. Jonas shoved at me, and I let him go, only to turn and see Mel storming up to my brother. Her face was dark with anger.

"Look at you! I hope it was worth it, Jonas!" she yelled at him.

Suddenly, I was pissed all over again because he'd defended her, and she had the gall to stand there screaming at him.

"Mel," he said, choking on emotions.

"I told you not to get involved! I told you I had it handled," she snapped. It was then that I noticed her eye. It was almost healed but still tinged with green and a hint of black. Enough color to know she'd been hit—and hit hard. "Go back to New York, Jonas. Go find someone else who *wants* you to treat them like some damsel in distress. That isn't me. Won't ever be me."

She stalked away to the counter and said in a voice loud enough to make her point, "I'm here to pick up Arthur Mason."

Jonas's face fell. Sadness and anger all mixed together.

I kept my arm around him and pulled him toward the exit. The last thing we needed was for round two to start when they released Arthur into Mel's care. Jonas looked back at the last minute, and when my eyes followed his, he was watching Mel as she bit her nails and paced like we had been just minutes before. She didn't look toward Jonas once. Her eyes were trained on the back doors.

Jonas choked, a croaking noise strangled deep in his throat, and I rushed him out of the building because I knew he wouldn't want to break down in front of Mel. In the rental car, he leaned his head on the back of the seat and groaned. In the rearview mirror, I saw tears slide down his cheeks that he quickly wiped away.

Cassidy and I exchanged a glance of heartbreak and sorrow.

I drove us to Maliyah's empty house instead of Maria Carmen's. There was no way I was taking Jonas to *Tía's* place while Maliyah was there recovering. She'd take one look at Jo-Jo, and her heart would certainly give out.

When Jonas barely held back a yelp of pain as he got out of the car, my heart jerked again. "Do you need a doctor?"

Jonas shook his head. "No. My pride and my ribs are both bruised, but that's it."

I let us into the house, and Jonas started for the stairs, but I held him back with a hand to the shoulder.

"I don't think so. Come into the kitchen. We'll get you patched up, and you can tell me what the hell happened."

He grumbled something under his breath but did what I'd asked.

"What can I do?" Cassidy asked, eyes wide as they ping-ponged between us.

"There's a first aid kit under the sink in the downstairs bath. Just down the hall to the left."

She nodded, and I followed Jonas into the kitchen. I grabbed a bag of peas and carrots from the freezer and handed them to him. "Put that on your eye."

He sank onto the barstool and then immediately sat up again, clutching his ribs. Cassidy came in with the white box, and I spent some time butterflying the cut over his eyebrow, checking out his nose and lip, and then wrapping his ribs as tightly as I dared. He didn't even yelp. Instead, he just bit his lower lip and took the pain. Even though I agreed with the EMT assessment, I was still angry that they hadn't taken him to the hospital. He'd heal. At least everything on the exterior would, and those were the only wounds I was equipped to deal with. I didn't know what to do about the gashes in his soul…not when I'd been unable to heal my own.

Chapter Thirty-one

Cassidy

JUST BY BEING YOU (HALO AND WINGS)
Performed by Steel Magnolia

I watched Marco as he tenderly took care of his brother. His big hands that had been all over my body mere hours ago were now gently prodding, trying to provide comfort and healing. It made my heart swell. He was full of grace and forgiveness for everyone but himself. I didn't know what to do with that, how to help him, especially when he didn't see himself as needing it. I knew that feeling. I hated when people tried to "fix" me. But Marco had a wound on his soul that hadn't healed right. Pain that he forced back onto himself every time he started to forget about the past.

"What happened?" Marco asked.

I moved behind them into the brightly colored kitchen, making myself at home in a way I hadn't been told to but needing to keep busy. I looked in the refrigerator and found it almost empty, which made sense when no one had been there for weeks. But there were enough ingredients for me to make an omelet or two.

"Mel called me before we left Grand Orchard. She was crying and said Artie had hit her…that he'd gotten mad when she wouldn't…" Jonas looked at me, swallowed hard, and then turned back at Marco. "When she wouldn't do stuff."

My stomach flipped, thinking of the beautiful girl at the station who'd been there to bail out the man who'd not only hit her but hit her because she wouldn't have sex with him. I wanted to rush back to the police station and drag her out with us. To save her… And if I wanted to do that without even knowing her, I couldn't even imagine how deeply Jonas felt about it. My heart tore a little on his behalf.

Marco looked grim, jaw clenching and unclenching.

"Why didn't you tell the police?" he asked.

"What the hell would they do? She's already slept with him. They're both minors. She just wouldn't…" His voice was full of anger and disgust, but then he stopped talking with a glance in my direction again. I tried to pretend I wasn't watching or listening, because I realized my presence was making him reticent to talk. Out of the side of my eye, I saw him make a motion with his hand and mouth, and I felt nauseated as I realized he meant that this Artie guy had tried to force the girl to give him a blow job.

"She came to see you at Maria Carmen's yesterday, right? Let me guess, you tried to get her to leave him, and instead, she got pissed and stormed out?" Marco asked.

Jonas nodded with a grimace. "Something like that. She said I didn't understand being driven by passion and love."

"Hitting someone because they won't do what

you want isn't love or passion," Marco said, and my heart soared because Marco was such an honorable man, even if he didn't see it in himself. "Trying to force someone to do something sexually is one hundred percent about power. It's the least loving thing you can do."

Jonas nodded. "I know. I basically told her that, but she said she loved him and that she was just going to let him stew for a few days before she went back to him. I was so…angry, Marco. At her. At him." He stopped for a moment and then kept going. "I knew he would be at Smokey's. I just wanted him to know…to know that someone was going to be there to hold him accountable for his actions if he tried it again."

Marco inhaled sharply. "You walked into a location you knew would be overrun with gang members, Jonas. By yourself. Without a weapon. Fucking hell, you're lucky to be alive."

Jonas slumped and grimaced, grasping his side. "I know. It was stupid. Really fucking stupid. I don't know what came over me. I was just so furious."

I slid the omelet in front of him and sat down next to him on another barstool.

"Being angry that someone you care about was hurt isn't stupid, Jonas. Wanting to keep them safe isn't either, but"—I glanced at Marco—"as I was just telling your brother, we can't always protect people we love from themselves and the consequences of their actions. We can't hold ourselves responsible for their choices."

"She deserves better than this life she's setting herself up for," Jonas said sadly, pushing the eggs around but then finally taking a bite. He winced as he chewed.

"Some people can't see beyond their own flaws enough to realize they deserve more." I met Marco's eyes with my own. His jaw clenched as if fighting his instinctive retort where he held himself to some ungodly standard. His arms were crossed against his chest, his stance wide. He looked every inch the military man he'd once been. Every inch the protector he wanted to be.

My eyes strayed to the clock on the microwave behind him, and I realized I needed to call Lance because he was expecting me at his office soon. I pushed myself up, went around the counter, and placed a kiss on Marco's cheek. "I'm going to make some calls. Let me know if I can help."

I felt both of their eyes follow me as I left, going back to the living room we'd walked through on our way to the kitchen. I called Lance's number, explained we'd had a family emergency come up but that I was completely on board. I asked him to send the final contract to Lee and the other lawyers. He seemed thrilled, and I would have been as well if I didn't have the tension from the other room hovering over me. If I didn't have Marco's regrets weighing on my shoulders.

I called Lee and Brady and told them I was going to make the deal, and it lightened my heart to hear how happy they were for me. I asked Brady to finalize the documents we needed in order for me to buy him out of his share of The Golden Heart, and he griped about me paying him back, but I held firm. I needed to do this for myself.

Then, I called my parents and talked with Chevelle for what felt like the hundredth time since I'd left him. He was excited, talking nonstop about the puppy still. It felt like he hadn't even missed me, which twisted my insides a little but also eased any remaining remorse I'd felt at having left him.

After I hung up, I walked over to the wall below the staircase. It was filled with so many picture frames that it was almost impossible to see the floral wallpaper behind it. There were photos of younger versions of Maliyah and Maria Carmen as well as group shots of the people I'd met briefly at the house the day we'd arrived in Austin. There were also pictures of Maliyah with a host of different children who must have been her foster kids along with ones with just her and Jonas or her and Marco.

My eyes lingered on an image of Marco in his military uniform, smiling and happy, before drifting to one with him, Jonas, and Maliyah in front of a Christmas tree. A lump formed in my throat as I found one of a teenaged Marco with two people who looked just like him: dark hair, tan skin, deep-brown eyes. The three of them had wide smiles on their faces. Marco had his dad's square chin and his mother's lush lashes. Even as a young teen, he'd been as tall as his dad, and they'd both towered over his mother.

Jonas passed by me, heading for the stairs, and Marco appeared at my side.

He waited until Jonas had pounded his way up and we'd heard a door slam above us before saying anything. "He's so goddamn lucky."

I wrapped my arms around his waist, leaning my head on his shoulder but still staring at the image of his family. "He is. Not just because he wasn't hurt worse. He's lucky to have you."

I touched the frame with Marco's parents in it. "They're lovely."

Marco's hand joined mine on the glass, his

fingers rubbing it. "They were."

It rumbled through his chest. Deep and filled with emotions.

"They'd be so proud of you, Marco. But I think they'd also be sad."

His chest stopped moving as if he was holding his breath.

"Look at this family you had waiting for you." I pointed to a photo of Maliyah and Jonas and him, and then to another with the huge crowd from Maria Carmen's that included Marco and Jonas as well. "Why did you deny yourself this?"

His breath finally came out as a burst of air. "Fear that I'd lose them all, too, I guess. And then guilt that I could have a good life when Petty Officer Warren's would forever be haunted."

"I'm not trying to belittle what happened to her, but acting as if she remained a victim, stuck in that moment, doesn't do her any honor either. Have you ever tried to contact her? To see how she's doing now?" I asked gently.

I could feel his heartbeat become erratic under my cheek. "No."

"Do you think if you knew she was living a fulfilling life it would help you?" I asked.

"What if she's not?" he choked out, and his agony ratcheted through me and became my own.

But I was also angry at him for persecuting himself for so long. For holding himself to this impossible standard of perfection.

"Would you have gone into a gunfight by yourself that night?" I demanded. "Just like Jonas? Maybe you could have told your superiors, right? But how do you even know if they would have believed you? Or if they'd have tried to stop it?" I couldn't keep the anger from my tone.

He moved a hand, tilting my chin up so that our gazes were locked. "What's your point, Angel?"

"What if, what if, what if. You could have done everything you think you should have, and it still might not have made a difference. You can't spend your life punishing yourself for being human, or for feeling afraid, or believing in the goodness of others. You can't spend your life alone." I said it with all the fierceness I could. "I won't let you."

His lips quirked slightly. "You won't let me?"

I shook my head. "No. You made promises to me, and I'm holding you to them."

He closed his eyes. "I shouldn't have made them."

"But you did, and you meant them. You don't want to take them back." I pushed my hand to his chest. "You love me, and guess what… I love you right back."

His eyes opened, searching mine, grief and joy and disbelief all mixed together.

"Say it again," he said softly.

"I love you."

He kissed me fiercely, the wildness of our lovemaking the night before finding its way back into us for the first time since he'd received the call from Jonas. The craving of our bodies to be one filling us again. We lost ourselves in the passion of lips and tongues and hands for a long time, until a door slamming above us brought us back to where we were as a shower turned on upstairs.

"I love you, too, Angel. I want everything…" His voice was raspy with the deep emotions. "I want you and Chevelle. I want evenings spent building block towers with him, and watching you think up strange concoctions, and ending our day tangled together. But you're right. I also have a family here that I've neglected for too long, and at the moment, I think I need to stay with them and make sure they are okay before I can even let myself think of having the life I want with you."

I nodded. "I know." I kissed him lightly. "Just like I know you realize I need to go home to Chevelle and the restaurant. But no matter how long it takes for you to settle things here, I want you to know I'll be waiting for you to come back to me."

A lump of emotions lodged in my throat. We'd just found our way to each other, and now we were moving apart instead of together. He had a family to care for, and I had a life to change. But I thought, if we both took care of the things pulling at us like weights in the water, that eventually, we'd float to the top together.

Chapter Thirty-two

Marco

LIFE AIN'T FAIR
Performed by Canaan Smith

Dropping Cassidy off at the airport was like sliding a knife through my stomach, especially when I knew she'd be gripping the arms of the seat, full of worry and fear as the plane left the ground. But she was right. I had to come to terms with the reality that I couldn't be there to protect everyone all the time. I couldn't be at her side and also be here for Jonas and Maliyah. I couldn't split myself in two physically, and instead, it caused me to be split emotionally.

I kissed her goodbye with the same fierceness and wildness that we'd come to find in each other. A burning flame that would never be extinguished. Then, I made a plea to a God I hadn't prayed to in a very long time that he'd keep her safe until I could be at her side again.

When I got back to the house, I made a few calls and then settled in to do some research. First, I had to figure out who Mel's parents were, because I knew that neither Jonas nor I would rest until we'd tried our best to prevent one asshole from ruining a vibrant girl's life. Then, I needed to do what Cassidy had suggested—check in on Petty Officer Warren. I didn't need to talk to her and risk bringing back those dark days, but I could poke around her life and see if she was really living or holed up in a dungeon of my making. I turned on my computer and used Garner's system for personal reasons for the first time ever in order to find out what I needed to know.

The data on Mel was easier to find than the information on Warren. I had to put out feelers that would take a few days to get back to me regarding the petty officer. It would have to do. It was a step toward burying my past that I'd held too close for too long.

I gathered the phone numbers I'd collected on Mel's parents and went in search of Jonas. I told him what I intended to do, letting him have a say because it would impact his life directly.

"She's never going to forgive you if I talk to them," I told him.

"I'll never forgive myself if you don't," he said quietly with a maturity and wisdom I wish I'd had at his age.

So, I placed the call, told her father what we thought had happened with her black eye, and how we were worried about her safety. Her dad was stunned. His silence was filled with anguish, but he thanked me before hanging up.

Jonas received a text from Mel almost immediately, saying he should never contact her again. He was heartbroken, and I still didn't know how to help him with that.

Instead, we turned our attention to the other woman in our life who needed our help—Maliyah. We made a united decision not to tell her the truth about what had happened with Mel, Arthur, and the fight. We simply told her that Jonas had gone back to the house to try and fix it up as a surprise, and then we spent the next three weeks doing just that. We painted the outside of the house, replaced the dried grass out front with xeriscaping, and fixed every loose faucet, knob, and handle inside. Finally, we converted the downstairs study into a bedroom and hauled Maliyah's things into it so she wouldn't have to navigate the stairs until she was ready.

After that, we brought her home.

She was beaming with pride and love as we pulled up to the house. Tears rolled down her face as she tugged us both in for a three-way hug, holding on longer than was normal for her. "I'm so lucky to have you boys."

She used her cane to mount the two small steps to the front door and then fluttered around the house, looking at everything we'd done with a smile that wouldn't leave her face.

My phone rang, and my heart flipped as it had every single time Cassidy had called me while I'd been here. We'd talked more apart than we probably ever had together. "Hey," I said.

"Did she like it?" Cassidy asked.

I sent her a picture of Maliyah. "What do you think?"

Cassidy sighed. "She looks so happy."

"She does."

"And how's Jonas?"

"Beaming almost as much as Maliyah because he got to do this for her, but he's nervous about school starting soon," I said quietly so Maliyah didn't hear.

"Mama, Mama, Mama! Look, I cook!" I heard Chevelle call in the background, and it made my chest ache. I missed him. I missed the way he buried his face in Hippo, and clasped Cassidy's shirt tight, and how he patted my face in greeting.

Cassidy burst into laughter.

"What?" I asked.

"He's covered in flour."

My phone beeped as she sent me a selfie. I stared at it, my heart filling my chest. Chevelle had his head resting on her shoulder, and his face and body were covered in white powder, but Cassidy was glowing. Her hair was down, swinging about her face, and she was wearing my T-shirt—the one she'd picked up off the hotel room floor and never given back.

"God, you're beautiful," I said.

She laughed again. "I'm exhausted, but thanks."

"How are things with Cliff and Willow?" I asked.

She'd been working with them to hand off a lot of the day-to-day management of the restaurant. It had been challenging for all of them in different ways, and Cassidy was still filled with guilt because of everything Brady had done for her that she felt like she was walking away from. I just kept reminding her that she wasn't walking away. She was making things better—for her and Chevelle, as well as Cliff and Willow, because they'd both gotten promotions and more money due to the change.

What we didn't talk about was Hardy, or the DNA test results they were still waiting for, or the call I was desperate for about Warren. It felt like we still had a few dark clouds hovering around us that we hadn't been able to banish yet.

We talked for a few more minutes, and then we hung up with I love yous hanging between us—not said—but still there. We hadn't said them again since that moment by the stairs, but the air was still full of promises we were trying to find our way back to. When I turned around, Maliyah was watching me with a curious expression on her face.

"What?" I asked.

"You're happy. I don't know that I've ever seen you that way."

My stomach twisted with my own remorse. She'd been so good to me, and somehow, I'd never let her know how much it meant.

I took a step toward her and hugged her tight. Like Cassidy had taught me. Until the air squeezed out of us both. Maliyah chuckled softly. "Careful, these old bones might not make it through that kind of grip."

"Thank you," I said, looking down at her.

She got all teary-eyed. "Nothing to thank me for."

"Yes, there is. Thank you for stopping the bleeding. For being there for me at both of the worst times in my life. I don't know what I would have done without you. I love you. I'm very lucky to be able to call you my family."

Tears fell down her wrinkled cheeks, and she patted my face. "You must be in love. My tough boy has become all maudlin."

Jonas ambled in on legs that seemed to have grown even more. He needed new clothes. Everything seemed to have stretched tight on him in every possible way. "Are we eating soon? I'm starving."

Maliyah and I laughed and made our way to the kitchen and the thousand containers of food that Maria

Carmen had sent us home with. We ate and laughed and teased. My heart expanded and swelled at the little family we were. People who loved each other unconditionally, regardless of our mistakes and our pasts.

After I'd cleaned the kitchen, my phone rang. It was Trevor. He was holding down the fort for me single-handedly, and I tried not to feel guilty about it. This had been the longest I'd been absent from my post since joining Garner.

"What's up?" I asked, stepping outside onto the back porch.

"So, we got some new information on Clayton Hardy and his wife," he said. The somberness in his voice raised the hackles on my neck.

"Tell me."

My heart fell as he told me everything. I finally understood why he was going after Chevelle. Understanding exactly what was at stake and hating him for it all the more. Also knowing he wouldn't give up easily. But I wouldn't let him take Chevelle from Cassidy. No way in hell.

I had to get back to Grand Orchard.

"Do you want me to tell her? Or Brady?" Trevor asked.

"I want to be the one to tell her," I said because I wanted to be there to hold her in person when I did. I wanted the news to be softened by arms that loved her.

"Okay..." He trailed off because I hadn't given him or Garner a return date yet, and this was obviously news that couldn't wait.

"I'll figure it out," I told him. "If something changes and I can't get there quick enough, I'll tell

Brady so he can break it to her."

But that wasn't going to happen. I'd been aching to get back to Cassidy and Chevelle even before this. Now, I had even more reason. My glance strayed to the half-torn-up backyard. Jonas and I were xeriscaping it just like we'd done the front while leaving room for the planters Maliyah needed for the herbs and vegetables she liked to grow. My mind reeled with how I could get it done quicker. Maybe if I enlisted some of Maria Carmen's family, we might be able to get it done in a day or two instead of the week it would take just Jonas and me.

The screen door creaked, and Maliyah made her way out, using her cane and the porch rail to sit on the steps next to me. We were quiet, but the sounds of Austin could be heard beyond the silence of her backyard. Cars and horns. The neighbor's music and voices raised in argument. The Katz's were renown in the community for their love spats.

"I want you to take Jonas with you," she said quietly.

I looked at her, surprise in my eyes. "What?"

She patted my arm. "Did you really think I wouldn't hear about what happened? The social worker called me the day he was hauled into police custody. He's my responsibility, you know."

My heart twisted, stomach falling. "Maliyah—"

She smiled. "I know, I know. You were afraid I'd have another episode, so I let you both have your little secret."

Silence settled down amongst us for a moment before she continued, "I realized after you tried to keep it from me that you both probably thought you were responsible for this. For my heart. I don't think I ever told you…I had an episode long before you ever came to me."

A wave of emotions flew through me. Relief followed by more guilt and then fear. Maybe I wasn't the one to break her heart first, but I also didn't know what I'd do if she was no longer around, if she died because of it, whether I caused it, or Jonas caused it, or her own body just gave out.

"I don't want them to put Jonas in a home if something happens to me," she said quietly, tears filling her eyes. "And I also don't think it's good for him to stay here. When school starts, he'll be drawn back into that world. Arthur and Mel are seniors, and he's a year below them on the food chain. They can make his life hell if they want to. I'd like him to have a fresh start. I've already started talking to the social worker about it. They'd let you take him."

I tucked her arm through mine, grabbing her hand. "Do you think he'll even agree to go? We can't make this decision for him. He's old enough to make it himself."

She seemed surprised by my words. Even a few weeks ago, I would have all but forced him into the car and the plane without giving him a choice, needing to protect him from everything that could come after him. But Cassidy had torn back my blinders. I couldn't save him from his own choices. I had to let him make them and just be there to pick up the pieces if I needed to. Like Maliyah had done with me.

"Can we tempt him with more time with Brady O'Neil and The Painted Horses?" she asked.

I chuckled. "Painted Daisies. The band is The Painted Daisies. And they won't be in Grand Orchard much longer. They're just about finished with their album."

"Damn."

"Language," I teased, and she smiled before getting serious again.

"He needs a male influence. He needs you."

"He's surrounded with male influences at Maria Carmen's," I said.

"It's not the same. You're the only one he considers a brother."

Hell, it hurt my heart at the same time as it filled it.

"Besides," Maliyah said with a smile, "he spends most of his time with Álvaro when we're there, and that man is the biggest playboy I know. You want Jonas to learn to treat women as interchangeable body parts?"

I chuckled, and she shoved my shoulder with hers, reminding me of Cassidy who was prone to do the same. My body was crying out to be with my angel again. In my mind, I'd seen myself, like a fuzzy dream, returning to Grand Orchard, but not to the apartment above the O'Neil's garage, but to Cassidy's bed. Without even giving it much thought, I'd seen myself getting down on one knee, putting a ring on her finger, and making her and Chevelle both my own. Could I return to her and ask her to accept Jonas and me both? To take our baggage and make it hers?

It was a big ask. To take two tormented men into her life while she tried to raise a son. I supposed instead of going all in, I could simply ask to date her…continue to see her in some way. I could find an apartment or house where Jonas and I could each have our own room so I didn't have to continue sleeping on the couch. But it left a bitter taste in my mouth because

I didn't want to be apart from her. I didn't want to just date her. I wanted Cassidy O'Neil to be mine. To belong to me and only me, just like I wanted to belong to her, completely and absolutely.

I tore myself from those images and thoughts back to the porch and Maliyah's questioning gaze. I'd just have to take it a step at a time. I'd talk with Jonas, get back to Grand Orchard, and figure the rest out from there.

Chapter Thirty-three

Cassidy

NOT LOSING YOU
Performed by Maddie Poppe

Marco and I had been apart for three weeks, but it felt like it had been a lifetime. He'd been busy caring for a family he finally realized he had, and I'd been busy handing things off to Willow and Cliff, hiring more staff, and finalizing the deal with Ralley. I'd also been busy avoiding Clayton every time I got a glimpse of him in town. Thankfully, he seemed content to ignore me as we waited for the DNA results.

The Painted Daisies finished their album and invited a kaleidoscope of business owners, locals, and the college staff to a closed reception at the Wilson-Jacobs theater to hear their new songs for the first time. They hired the café to cater some simple cocktail fare for the event, and while I'd designed the menu and sourced the ingredients, I'd let Willow and Cliff run with it. It was weird to not dig my hands into the actual production, but they were doing great. It was almost painful how easily everything I'd worked so hard at for two years could be done by others.

"You need a dress for the event," Tristan said as

she and I sat in her living room, watching Hannah try to teach Chevelle to play the piano.

I shrugged, thinking about my stack of long skirts and the pink dress I'd worn to Earth Paradise. None of them were semi-formal wear that the party called for, but something would do.

"You know, you could spend some of those thousands of dollars now tucked away in your bank account to buy yourself something nice," Tristan insisted.

Sometimes, it was hard to believe the zeroes that existed there now. The money had come with a whole host of new problems. How to invest it, how to keep it safe for Chevelle, and how to help my community. But it still didn't feel like it was mine to spend yet.

Tristan sighed, dragging herself up from the couch and waddling toward the stairs. "Come on. You can find something in my closet, I'm sure."

I followed her up the stairs. She had a whole section of her closet for items she wore to Brady's award ceremonies. She waved a hand at them and retreated to the bed while I flipped through them. They all felt too formal. Too not me.

"You're different since you got back from Austin," she said, and I almost laughed. Not one person in my family had asked me about Marco and me since I'd returned. Maybe because I hadn't appeared sad or upset that he was still in Austin. Maybe because they sometimes caught the tail end of our flood of phone conversations. Or maybe simply because I'd smiled more even without him here than I had in a really long time.

"What do you mean?" I asked, knowing exactly what she meant but pretending I didn't.

"There's a glow to you. A feeling of peace," she said. "So, Marco and you… You *finally* did the deed?"

I flipped around, mouth dropping a little. "Finally? What do you mean finally?"

Tristan laughed and came back into the closet, pulling out a lilac dress and holding it up to me.

"The entire town has watched you two make googly eyes at each other for years. There's probably even a few wagers about it," she teased then shoved the dress into my hands. "This one. I'm not sure I'll ever fit into it again."

She didn't say it with even a hint of regret, just the simple facts as she put a hand on her belly with a tender pat. I was taller than Tristan, but other than that, we had a similar shape and build. We'd both had children—and had the curves and marks to show for it—but neither of us were the type to hate our bodies because of it. In fact, after taking so long to get pregnant, the changes to Tristan's body were like a badge of honor to her. But this dress… It was small and fitted and would display my curves in ways I was unaccustomed to.

I pulled my T-shirt off—Marco's T-shirt that I'd found myself wearing more than I wore any other belonging of mine—and slid the dress over my shoulders before taking off my skirt as well.

"So, Brady thinks we…did the deed, too? What did he say?" I asked. I shot her a look when she didn't say anything, ready to defend the man I loved. God, my heart clenched at that thought—I loved him. So much that it hurt. More than I loved anything except Chevelle. Those two males owned every inch of me.

Tristan returned to the bed. "You know Brady. He wants everyone around him to be happy. He'd give his right arm and learn to play guitar one-handed if it meant both of you could have the love you deserve."

The tightness in my chest eased. Of course he did. My brother had always been the kind of person to wish only good things for everyone and gave freely of himself in order to make it happen. Whether that was a moment of happiness as he signed a fan's shirt, a unique present he found for his manager, or a gazillion dollars he gave to help his sister start a restaurant.

I looked in the mirror, feeling just a hair awkward about the amount of body I was showing. The tiny straps barely held up the scooped bodice, and it curved to my hips and slid down my thighs instead of flaring out like I was used to. The hem fell well above my knee, showing my white legs to the world. Pale like milk or snow. I wondered what Marco would think of it. I wondered how his hands and lips would slide over the exposed skin. Those thoughts made my cheeks flush and my legs quiver.

I sat down on the bed with her. "Truth is…Marco is… There's just a lot more to his life than he shares with anyone."

"Anyone but you," Tristan said sagely.

I nodded, bit my lip, and held back the secrets that weren't mine to tell. "So much has happened to him. I'm not sure he'll ever let himself be truly happy."

Tristan stared for a moment and then looked down at the wedding ring from her first marriage that she wore on her right hand instead of her left. She'd lost her Navy SEAL husband when Hannah wasn't even a year old, and it wasn't until Brady had stormed into her life, years later, that she'd allowed herself to believe she could love again.

"I obviously don't know what Marco has been

through. But I do know that it's easy to feel like we don't deserve love and happiness. Not when others…can't have that," her voice broke a little. "Even now…there are times when I think about Darren, and I feel so guilty it's like I can't breathe. But then Brady swoops into the room and makes Hannah laugh, or I see them with their fingers tangled together on the piano, or he wraps me in his arms and kisses me, and I know that this was supposed to happen, too. I just need the reminder sometimes. Maybe that's all Marco needs—someone to remind him that he's worthy of love."

I nodded, knowing it was true. Knowing Marco needed someone holding a mirror up in front of him and showing him all the pieces of him that were beautiful and deserving. I wanted to be that person, but I wasn't sure he'd let me. I wasn't even sure if and when he was coming back to Grand Orchard now that he was determined to stay and help Maliyah and Jonas. To help the family he'd ignored for too long.

Those thoughts were still with me two nights later when I entered the lobby of the theater that was already bustling with people. I slid a hand down the fitted dress nervously. I hadn't worn anything so formal since…maybe ever. I hadn't gone to prom, and both my high school and college graduation had seen me in my normal long skirts and plain blouses under my robes.

The only thing saving me from running back to the house and changing was the fact that I was still in flats. No way my clumsiness could be put on display in a pair of stilettos like the ones the band members of The Painted Daisies wore tonight. The six women were in a range of them from spiky, heeled boots to tall, strappy sandals, but they all moved around on them with the grace of ballerinas that I would never have.

I missed Marco even more tonight because I was attending this event alone. I'd never had anyone at my side for things like this before, but knowing what it would feel like if he was there almost made it worse. I made my way farther into the lobby, trying not to feel awkward and out of place.

My first instinct was to go check on the little spread of appetizers and cocktails that The Golden Heart Café had made, but I forced myself in the other direction. I had to trust that Cliff and Willow had it covered if I was determined to step away from managing the restaurant. So, I pushed myself toward the wall of murals Tristan had painted for the university. It was a series of keyholes, and as you glanced through them, you saw Grand Orchard in varying seasons and times of day. A mural that said there was more to people and life than what you could see with a glance. Like there was more to me or Marco than what you saw on the surface.

Brady found me and slung an arm over my shoulder. "I almost didn't recognize you. You look beautiful, Cass."

I looked down at his gray slacks and button-down. "You look like some banker took over my brother's body."

Brady laughed. "I know. Thank God I get to change to go onstage with The Painted Daisies."

The band was going to showcase some of their favorite songs off the album. Not a full concert, but a little taste of what was to come. Brady had done more than just produce the album. He'd collaborated with them on a couple of songs as well. Duets about love and life.

"Why are you over here by yourself instead of mingling with everyone?" Brady asked.

I looked back to where the band was hanging out with their team, Brady's team, and some of the locals. My parents were there as well as some of the other professors and the dean of Wilson-Jacobs. People I'd known my whole life and shouldn't have made me feel out of place. Should have made me feel at home, and yet I still felt empty and alone.

"I don't know. Just feeling…" I trailed off.

"Like you're missing part of your soul," Brady said quietly. My heart twisted. That was it. Ever since Marco and I had slept together, and then I'd left Austin, I felt like I'd forgotten a piece of me there. As if I wasn't ever going to be whole again until he showed up.

I gave a slight nod, unable to speak.

"Do I have to send Trevor after him?" Brady asked, half-tease and half-serious. I reached up and flicked his ear. He pressed his head to his shoulder. "Here I am defending you, and you're torturing me with those wildly long fingers of yours."

I chuckled. "He's coming back. He just has a lot to take care of."

"He doesn't have a wife and kids hidden away somewhere, does he?"

I laughed again. "No." But it was still a family he couldn't just leave.

"Brady, you ready?" His stage manager, Alice, came wandering over. Her dark hair streaked with purple was done up in curls, and her normally thick-framed glasses had been exchanged for ones that sparkled. Alice had been with Brady almost since the beginning—even longer than Marco. But I'd never seen her in a dress like the one she wore tonight. Below the black satin, she had on a pair of spiked and studded Demonia boots that fit her vibe perfectly.

Brady looked at me questioningly. I shoved his shoulder. "Go! I'm fine. I'll make my way over to Mom and Dad."

He frowned, and I reached up to flick his ear again, but he ducked away and turned back with a smile. "Fine. Fine."

He and Alice headed into the theater, and I started to move toward my parents, where they were talking with the dean, when a hand grabbed my wrist from behind, yanking me backward. I twirled around, losing my balance momentarily before righting myself and finding Clayton's scowling face staring at me.

God, was the man ever happy? Tonight, there was a pinched look to his eyes and a hallow to his cheeks, as if he hadn't been sleeping.

"I got the DNA results. He's mine," Clayton said.

I gave a sarcastic laugh. "Did you expect me to be surprised? I knew you'd provided the sperm to create him. I didn't need a DNA test to prove it."

That was all he was—a sperm donor. I would never acknowledge that he was Chevelle's "father," and I'd burn in hell before I said that he belonged to Clayton in any other way, shape, or form.

I yanked at my wrist, but he didn't let go. In fact, he squeezed harder.

"I just wanted you to know that I would have allowed you to continue to see him if you hadn't been such a bitch about things. But now I'm going to take him, and you'll never see him again. My investigator has proof that you left him to go fuck some guy who was dishonorably discharged from the military. The same guy you let around my son all the time. He spends less time with his own mother than he does with others. No judge will allow you to keep him when you're such a bad influence."

My first instinct was to slap him. My second instinct was to defend myself. I wasn't sure how he'd found out about Marco and me...he'd obviously had me followed. I wanted to laugh and cry because I hadn't been anywhere in two years. I hadn't spent one single night without my son until I'd gone to Austin. I'd worked myself to the bone to provide for him. I wanted to scream all of that at him. To tell him that at least I'd wanted Chevelle even before he'd been born, but instead, I glared.

"You'll never get my son," I said, venom and hate in my voice. I tried to free myself again, but he just dragged me farther away from the crowded lobby down the side hall. I lost my balance, my shoulder hitting the wall, and Clayton put his other hand on my shoulder to stabilize me. The touch burned me like acid, making me jerk back again, a wobbled mess of knees and limbs that would never coordinate right.

"Jesus, you can't even hold yourself up, let alone a child," he spewed at me.

My stomach twirled, nausea filling me just as Clayton's eyes went over my shoulder, narrowing at something. He let me go as another hand slid around my waist from behind. A hand that I knew like it was my own. The heat of it seared through the silk dress, and my entire body seemed to swell and sigh simultaneously. Goosebumps littered my skin as Marco's deep voice spoke near my ear. "Angel, is there a problem here?"

My body relaxed into him, my back tucking up against his wide chest, my hand going to his arm that I realized wore a suit jacket. I turned slightly, taking in a Marco I'd never seen before. I knew he wore formalwear when he went with Brady to award ceremonies, but I'd never seen it in person. He was stunning. A vision of muscled manliness that exuded power and authority. Control and honor.

"You're here!" My throat lodged with emotion, happiness and joy filling me. I reached up and kissed his cheek.

Clayton made a garbled sound that drew my eyes back to him, reminding me of his unhappy presence.

"This is what I'm talking about." Clayton stepped toward us. "I won't let my son be raised by someone spreading her legs for just anyone who comes by."

Marco released me and pushed me behind him in one smooth motion. He put his hand on Clayton's throat and shoved him up against the wall. Clayton struggled, and Marco's other arm went across Clayton's chest, holding him still. Marco wasn't squeezing Clayton's throat tight. He wasn't restricting his airflow at all, but I could tell there was pressure there. The knowledge that all he had to do was squeeze.

"You will not talk to her that way. Ever. In fact, let's just say you'll never talk to her again," Marco growled.

I put a hand on Marco's shoulder. "Marco…"

He ignored me as he glared at Clayton and barked out, "Tell her. Tell her why you really want Chevelle."

Clayton's eyes widened, and he tried to push Marco away again. But he had none of the muscle or training that Marco did. There was no way he was getting free until Marco was ready to let him.

"I have a right to my son!"

"You didn't want him, though. Not until you found out your wife couldn't have any children of her own, right? There's no way to get your hands on her trust fund unless she makes your child hers by adopting him. It's all about the fucking money, isn't it? You don't give a rat's ass about Chevelle."

Clayton's eyes widened, and he blustered. "You had no right to dig into my personal life!"

I stepped forward and shoved a finger into his chest by Marco's arm. "You had no right to have us followed to Austin."

Marco turned his head, surprise littering his face before it turned deadly again. He looked back at Clayton. "Trying to dig up dirt? It isn't going to work, Hardy. Cassidy O'Neil is a fucking angel. She's worked her ass off to provide for herself and her son, whom you walked away from. She may have fallen in love with someone who isn't worthy of her, but no judge in his right mind is going to see her marrying someone as a negative. Chevelle is in a stable environment, surrounded by grandparents, aunts, uncles, and a whole community who adores him. He'll have a stepfather who only sees him as the gift he is rather than something that comes with a price tag."

I gasped at Marco's words. We hadn't even talked about what would happen if and when he returned to Grand Orchard, and now he was there talking marriage and making Chevelle his. Talking as if he'd already asked, and I'd already accepted. My heart leaped and soared. He'd said he wasn't ever walking away, and while I'd understood that, the words he spoke were like hearing he loved me all over again.

To my surprise, it wasn't my parents who showed up at our side. It was Trevor with a stoic look on his face and dressed in the black uniform that Marco normally wore in his role as a bodyguard.

"Problem, Marco?" Trevor asked, widening his stance.

Marco stared down Clayton. "Depends on if this asshole is going to leave of his own accord, or if I'm going to have to toss him out."

Clayton tugged at Marco's wrist and the hand still wrapped loosely around his neck. "I was invited," Clayton insisted with a haughty tone that did nothing for his cause. "All the faculty were invited. I have a right to be here. Just like I have a right to my child!"

"Being invited and being wanted are two very different things," Trevor said quietly. "It's time you left, Mr. Hardy."

Suddenly, there was another male body at our side. Jonas stood there, mimicking Trevor's stance, dressed in a pair of slacks, a button-down, and a blazer that made him look older than sixteen. His hair was slicked back, accentuating his green eyes that were flashing warning signs in a face that was almost completely healed from his ordeal but still showed traces of it.

"Need help, Marco?" Jonas asked.

Clayton glared at the three men now defending me. "Surrounding yourself with more riff-raff, Cassidy? Did you know about this one's mother? Or his father?" He directed his chin toward Jonas. "The fight he got in while you were in Austin is just in his blood. If you insist on encircling my son with people with anger issues, taking him from you is going to be a piece of cake."

My body froze as panic crawled up my back. Marco squeezed ever so slightly on Clayton's neck, making him cough.

"I told you never to speak to her again," Marco said. Clayton's face turned beet red. Marco seemed to squeeze harder. "I'm going to let you go, and what I want to see is your feet heading for the exit. If they don't go in that direction, I can guarantee you won't like what happens next."

Marco waited for a second as if expecting Clayton to argue. When he didn't, Marco slowly let up. As he did, Clayton used his hands to fling Marco's arm away from him. Clayton moved around Jonas, never turning his back to us but heading a few steps toward the doors.

"You'll be hearing from my attorney," he stormed. He yanked at his suit sleeves, smoothed down the front, and then spun on his heel and walked out.

I was shaking from head to toe, but before my knees could give out, Marco was surrounding me in his arms again. My cheek went to his shoulder where it felt like it belonged. My hands went around him. I squeezed tight, and he squeezed back, the air leaving both of us.

Marco kissed the top of my head. A gentle, comforting kiss like I gave to Chevelle when he needed soothing. My eyes filled. I couldn't lose my son. I couldn't. For a brief moment, fear swelled through me before I valiantly shoved it aside. Clayton wanted me to be afraid. He wanted me to think I had to choose between Marco and my son so that he could have power and control over me again. But I wouldn't let him have it. There'd be no need to convince a judge, or anyone, that Marco was a good man when he clearly was that…and so much more. He was honorable and brave. Courageous and strong. I would be lucky to have him at my side, raising Chevelle with me.

Chapter Thirty-four

Marco

BLESSED

Performed by Thomas Rhett

I glanced toward Jonas, whose face was a grim echo of Trevor's. Flute music followed by drums filled the lobby from the open doors of the theater. The Painted Daisies was onstage. It explained why we hadn't drawn a larger crowd, why Cassidy's parents hadn't come running to try and rescue her.

She was shaking like a leaf in my arms, and all I could do was wrap her tighter in my embrace. To try and dispel the hate and venom that Clayton Hardy had sent her way. To try and reassure her that everything was going to be okay, even as my own doubts were running wild.

"Jonas, why don't you go on in with Trevor," I said to my brother, eyes meeting his and trying to express my gratitude for his showing up at my side. "I'm just going to stay here for a few minutes while Cassidy calms down."

A little snort escaped Cassidy's lips, and she said, "Me? Calm down? You're the one who almost strangled someone."

It brought a wry grin to Jonas's lips that matched my own. Jonas gave us one last glance before heading toward the theater doors. Trevor hesitated as if he wanted to say something but then just turned and followed my brother.

I loosened my hold on Cassidy only enough to scan her. He'd had his hands on her when I'd seen them. He'd been pulling her toward the hallway, and my vision had turned red as anger had flooded me. I pulled her arm up, eyeing her dainty wrist.

"Are you hurt?" My voice was garbled with emotions.

She shook her head, but I rubbed over the soft flesh gently, soothingly anyway. Then, I raised it to my lips and kissed it. Her lids fluttered shut before opening again.

"You're here." It was a breathy half-whisper. A repeat of the words she'd said when I'd first wrapped my arm around her waist.

I nodded. "I wanted to surprise you."

My gaze took in the shimmery makeup layered lightly over her face that was surrounded in loose curls tonight and continued down the silky expanse of her shoulders and chest that were on display above the curved line of a light-purple dress. A dress that was completely un-Cassidy-like in that it clung to her shape rather than swung away from it. My body reacted to it without thought, heat filling me, burning from the inside out. I ached to touch her. Kiss her. Pull the dress off of her and put my tongue and lips on every little groove and valley that I'd so carefully memorized in our single night together.

"Well, you succeeded," she said, drawing my eyes back to her face. "You shouldn't keep doing that."

I frowned. "What? Surprising you?"

"Telling Clayton things that aren't true. That you're my boyfriend." Her lips twisted upward. "That we're getting married."

My pulse raced. She'd noticed my little slip, then. I had a ring sitting in my bag back at the house. A ring I'd intended to propose with after I'd talked to her about Jonas being with me for good. But I couldn't do it now. Not yet. Not until we put Hardy behind us. Not until I could prove to myself that Jonas and I wouldn't take her life and trip it up even more.

"I told you, Angel, I couldn't let you go once I had you. But…" I glanced toward the exit where Hardy had departed. "But if being with me risks—"

"He isn't going to get Chevelle," she cut me off. "And he can't take what's ours and destroy it either. I won't let him."

What could I have said to that? To a woman so fiercely sure of me that she was willing to take this huge leap of faith to keep me at her side? I stared down at her sweet face, warring with the natural instinct I had to protect her by walking away and the desire to keep every promise I'd made about never leaving her side.

Without the right words, I did the only thing I could. I kissed her wildly, letting the flame leap into life between us. Letting the passion that had eroded both our defenses in Texas take over until there was nothing but us, our bodies, and our souls. The world around us faded away, our emotions echoed by Brady and Leya's voices singing about the agony of loving someone you couldn't have.

She broke our kiss with a small laugh. "I'd love

to kiss you until you believed me, but I think we need to go in."

Cassidy O'Neil amazed me. My angel had a strength that ensured she rebounded from any hits directed at her. Maybe a lifetime of picking herself up repeatedly from falls was the reason for it, but no matter the reason, she always got back up.

I took her hand in mine and led her toward the theater where we slid into a back row.

Brady was in full rock-star mode, prancing around the stage in ripped jeans and a "Ghost" T-shirt. It was the song that had truly cemented his success in the country-rock world years ago, and he wore it every time he started a new venture as if it would always bring him luck.

The long-legged, dark-haired force of nature that was Leya moved around him on the stage, mocking and flirting while she sang. Brady was all suave smiles, but every time there was a pause in his lyrics, his eyes drifted to the front row where Tristan sat almost bursting with their first child. Love bled from the look.

My heart ached with the same feeling. My gaze dropped from the stage to Cassidy. She had her eyes turned to the front. She was sitting in the middle of a darkened theater and should have been a shadow, but instead, I felt like she was glowing. Like a halo of moonlight had cast its rays into the room. Or the flares around the sun. Maybe the rings of Venus. A life force you couldn't look away from once it had caught your attention. I wouldn't let anybody—Hardy, myself, or anyone else that came along—take that glow from her.

The crowd erupted into applause as their song ended. Brady left the stage, and Paisley moved out from behind the keyboards to take the microphone from Leya. Each of the band members took turns singing the lead in their songs, and they all had decent voices, but it was their charisma and their talent with a range of instruments that had really rocketed them to the top of the charts in just over a year.

"Thank you all for being here with us while we celebrate our new album," Paisley said. Her voice was sure instead of the quiet shyness it normally was when she wasn't in front of a crowd. An oxymoron of sorts. "This next song was almost scrapped from the album altogether before someone came in and rescued it. I wasn't sure he'd be here tonight, but I see he snuck in while we weren't looking. I'm kind of hoping he'll help me sing it. Jonas? Care to join me?"

My body tensed, searching the aisles for Jonas's lanky frame.

I found him near the front, sitting in between The Painted Daisies' manager and Brady's PR manager, Assad. I couldn't read Jonas's expression from the back, but his shoulders had stiffened. They were pulled tight in the way he held them only when he was on the defensive.

Assad shoved him in the shoulder, and Jonas slowly rose to his feet. He made his way down the aisle toward the stage and dragged himself on top of it without using the stairs. The fiery redhead of the band, Fiadh, grinned at him and shoved a microphone stand in his direction. Jonas stared at it for a long moment before taking the microphone out, shrugging out of his jacket, and hanging it on the empty stand. Then, he inhaled and turned back toward Paisley.

She had on a pair of thigh-high leather boots, a mini-skirt, and a torn black and blue top that matched her highlights. She looked older than seventeen, and yet her expression was still somehow sweet. She seemed suddenly as nervous as Jonas when he eased up next to her. Even with her stiletto boots, she barely reached his shoulder.

"I'm going to fu—screw this up," he said into the mic before giving a wry grin to the audience. "I don't have the vocals for it."

"It's your song as much as it is mine now," Paisley said, and tears sprang to my eyes, knowing how much that meant to Jonas. He'd been through so much, and to have someone give him this... It was beautiful.

Cassidy's fingers tightened on mine, and she tucked her face up against my shoulder as if she could give me the strength I needed when I felt like I was going to fall apart.

Paisley gave a signal to Adria on drums, and the beat started slow, a pulsing rhythm that was picked up in Fiadh's Celtic harp. Paisley began singing, and it was as if pain ripped from inside her into the lyrics. Loneliness. Heartache. Misunderstandings. When she paused, Jonas joined in. It was rough and a little off-key, but his voice amplified the self-hate that rolled from the words. At the same time, Leya's sitar collided with the notes from Fiadh's harp, echoing the emotions of the lyrics. The song told a story of two people who thought they were worth nothing until suddenly their worlds collided. The conflicting instruments drifted from a banging contrast into a blended harmony, love filling the gaps that life had left in their souls.

It was agonizing and beautiful.

I wished I'd recorded it for Maliyah so she could

see Jonas in this light. I wanted everything the song promised for him. A way to shrug off the past and see the possibilities of his future.

God. I wanted that for both of us.

To lose the sorrow and regrets and see only the brilliance of what stood before us.

Like Cassidy shining at me in the dark.

I leaned in and took her lips in mine again. Too many emotions filling me. Too many things I couldn't say with words that only my body knew how to speak. She answered back, pushing her mouth against mine, tongue sliding inside, licking as if she was smoothing away the scars and burns. I returned the favor, trying to free her of the weight of Clayton and the fear he'd ground into both of us.

We would find a way. She would be mine, and I would be hers.

We didn't have another choice because, just like the song said, we would never be whole without the other.

Chapter Thirty-five

Cassidy

IT'S YOUR LOVE
Performed by Tim McGraw with Faith Hill

Marco had been overwhelmed with emotions while watching Jonas onstage, singing a song about heartbreaking pasts and the journey to redemption. I knew he could see himself as much as Jonas in the words. My entire body ached for him. For me. For the possibilities that the song promised.

I hated that Clayton's words had put even the slightest doubt in Marco's mind about our future. The one he'd casually tossed out about us getting married and him making Chevelle his own at the same time he was making me his. There was not one piece of me that held Marco's past against him. I hated that he held it against himself. Was there a chance that a judge would hold it against him? Maybe. Was there a chance that Jonas's past would throw some monkey wrench in it? I supposed there was, but there was no way I was giving any of them up without a fight. Without proving that we were meant to be a family.

That word caught in my throat.

My mind whirled full of hope for a future I could

see clearly now. One where I was twirled down a sidewalk with someone who finished my sentences, and where Chevelle was tossed in the air by a man who loved him. Where I had time to create and the restaurant flourished. To a future where I let one man stand at my side and pick me up whenever I fell because I knew it would never make me less in his eyes.

When we got back to the house, it felt empty. There was no little voice claiming my attention, no tiny body to snuggle with, because Tristan's friend, Stacy, who ran a charter school in town, had Chevelle and Hannah for us tonight. I missed my son fiercely, especially after having been away from him for the first time just weeks before, but I was also glad to have this night to wrap Marco in my arms, comfort us both, and kiss away his fears.

"Do you want to come in for a cupcake, Jonas? You've definitely earned it," I said with a smile. He turned a deep shade of red, just like he had every time someone had complimented him on his song with Paisley.

He shook his head, eyes sliding to Marco's and my hands twined together. "Nah. I'm going to call Maliyah and then hit the hay. I promised Brady I'd help them pack up all the The Painted Daisies' instruments first thing tomorrow."

"Brady or Paisley?" Marco teased, and Jonas flushed again.

He pounded a fist into Marco's shoulder and then headed toward the apartment above the garage while Marco followed me inside the house.

We'd barely made it inside before his strong arms had encompassed me, pulling me up tight against him.

His lips brushed against mine as he spoke, the words vibrating off of them. "God, I missed you."

Then, he was devouring me like we'd devoured each other in Texas. Hands and mouths nipping and gliding over each other. Clothes being shed as we wound our way down the hall to my room. When we landed on the bed, limbs tangled together, he paused, eyes glistening like black jade in the shadows of the room with only the moonlight filtering in through the drawn curtains.

"Angel..." His throat bobbed, emotion filling his voice. "I need to give you one last chance to walk away before I embed myself completely in your life. Jonas is a permanent part of my package now, and we're men with pasts that aren't easy. Clayton—"

"Is wrong. You're one of the most honorable, decent, caring men I've ever met in my life." I pushed my hands into the short strands on his head. "If we have to, we'll bring your family, Garner and Trevor—hell, the whole damn town—in as character witnesses. You weren't the one who attacked Petty Officer Warren. You aren't violent, and neither is Jonas. Defending people you love isn't a negative quality. I'd be privileged to have you both in Chevelle's life, showing him how men can have strength and beauty and kindness."

He rested his forehead against my chest, and I felt a tremble go through him as he fought his natural instinct to protect me—this time by walking away. His back was taut, arm muscles bulging as he poised to leave. Every line of him was cut and grooved, like gems carefully crafted to bring out the inner beauty of a stone.

"Make love to me, Marco," I said, lifting his face

so he was forced to meet my gaze. "Make love to me and show me exactly what you meant when you said you'd never let me go. Make me believe every word, and I promise, I'll do the same. Keep you. Forever."

He let out a low, guttural moan, half pleasure and half pain, before he captured my mouth with his. Searing into my soul the promises we were making to one another. Fingers trailing over hot skin, lips following the same path. My movements echoed his, every touch and caress returned with equal fervor. A battle to see who could show who how much they cared first. A battle to prove that this was the only place that we belonged. Together. Our remaining clothes disappeared as our bodies slid together, silk against silk. A twirl of limbs that needed to be joined. Two souls who only knew the true meaning of life and love when bound together as the moonlight surrounded them and the rest of the world disappeared.

♪ ♪ ♪

Marco's face was soft and relaxed in the early morning rays that shifted through the drapes. Not only did he seem at peace, but it was as if a burden had lifted from him. I didn't know if it would come crashing back down when he woke, if there would be responsibilities and regrets drowning him, but I would be there every day to ease them away from him. To remind him that he deserved to be happy, too.

He hadn't heard back about Petty Officer Warren yet. The inquiries seemed to go into a black void with nothing coming out of it. I'd encouraged him to look her up, and my heart clenched, hoping it hadn't been a mistake. I hoped she wasn't barely holding on to reality…or worse. I wasn't sure what it would do to him if he found out she was still struggling.

I shifted slowly and softly, gently pulling away so as not to wake him. I'd promised Willow and Cliff new items for the fall menu, and with apple season almost upon us, I had a handful of new ideas I needed to try out. I was almost disappointed when Marco stayed asleep, because I couldn't kiss him good morning before I left, but there was no way I was waking him—not when I knew he barely slept on most nights.

I showered, pulled on clothes that were so much more my norm than the lilac dress from the night before, and sent a text to Mom as I went, reminding her that Tristan was picking up Chevelle for me from Stacy's. Then, I headed into town at a quick pace. My feet were clad in my orthopedic shoes, hardly making a sound. The birds were just starting to come awake, soft twitters echoing down the road. The chill in the air had me shivering because I'd left without a sweater or jacket. Summer was leaving us. Before we knew it, there'd be snow on the ground and kids sliding down the steep hill at the back of the Wilson-Jacobs grounds.

Main Street was quiet with very few lights and even fewer cars. Sweet Lips's windows shone brightly because Helen and Belle were always there early, sifting sugar and flour into desserts the town adored. I stopped for a moment, taking in the entire street. Home. A place I adored. People who'd stood at my side, shielding me my entire life. I'd resented the protection for so long, while simultaneously loving them for it, that it had built a wall inside me. One I'd refused to let many people cross in case they saw the truth…that I felt weak…different…broken.

Today, I felt like the wall had disappeared. I felt at peace with acceptance settling over me. I had Marco to thank for that. I would always trip and fall, but hating it and begrudging the helping hands held out to me would only worm holes of discontent into my soul. Every time Marco had held out a hand, he'd backed it with words or actions that showed how damn strong he thought I was for getting back up. Strength came in many different forms. Mine was just wrapped inside a body that would always test my grit.

My smile was real and large as I unlocked the door of the café and was greeted with the sounds and smells of the kitchen abuzz with the morning prep. It twisted my heart a little to know that it wasn't me there, getting ready for the day. But it also filled me with a relief I felt in my bones. I didn't have to do it all on my own. I could take the pieces I loved most, keep those, and hand off the rest to people who could do it even better than me.

When I walked into the back, Cliff and Willow were laughing and joking, knives slamming into the surface as they cut and diced—a dance only chefs understood.

They both smiled and greeted me with a warm hello.

I turned on the radio, washed my hands, and joined them, picking up a peeler and a stack of carrots. "Everyone was raving about the food last night. Thank you for doing it," I said.

Willow beamed, and I almost thought Cliff blushed.

"Thanks for trusting us to do it," Willow said.

My throat constricted as emotion flooded me. I hadn't trusted many people enough to let them help, determined to prove I wasn't weak. I felt like the final burden was lifted off my shoulders, enhancing the peace I'd felt on the street.

We worked in silence that was only broken by the occasional smart-aleck remark from Willow followed by a gruff laugh from Cliff. After the new waitstaff and line cook showed up, I left them to run the restaurant and went to dig out my menus from last fall. I'd keep some favorites and add some new dishes.

The new waitress we'd hired, another Wilson-Jacobs student who Willow knew, popped her head into the kitchen. Ashley smiled when her eyes landed on me at the table in the corner.

"Hey, Cassidy, there's a woman here asking for you."

Willow wiped her hands on a towel. "I got it."

Ashley shook her head. "No, she didn't want to talk to the chef or the manager. She specifically asked for Cassidy."

Willow and I exchanged a look, and I gave a small shrug before following Ashley into the main restaurant. Ashley pointed to a table near the door where a woman in a white dress with red polka dots sat. Everything about her screamed wealth. From the way her brown hair was perfectly styled, to the expensive watch on her wrist, down to the Hermès bag hanging off her chair and the Louboutin shoes on her feet. She wasn't someone I knew, and I had no idea why she wanted to speak with me.

I made my way over to her, and she looked up when I reached her side. "Hi, I'm Cassidy. How can I help you?"

She eyed me up and down, a sense of power and privilege wafting off her as she did it. Her gaze traveled over my hair up in two tight buns, the T-shirt with the café's logo, my long skirt, and my sturdy shoes before coming back up to my face. She didn't frown in disapproval, but there wasn't admiration in her eyes either. In fact, there was a wariness to her expression that surprised me, as if I would somehow be the one to judge her.

"It's a pleasure to meet you, Ms. O'Neil. My name is Vanessa Van Der Hellig-Hardy," she said with a clip to her tone that was almost aristocratic. She offered her hand, but I refused it as her last name settled down around me and realization hit me. She was Clayton's wife.

She withdrew her hand, lips pursing slightly.

"I'm sorry. I don't blame you for not shaking it," she said. "Please, have a seat so we can talk."

She waved across the table, offering me a chair in my own restaurant. I tried not to let it irk me. I couldn't afford to lose my temper with her any more than I could afford to lose it with Clayton.

"I prefer to stand," I told her.

Her gaze met mine, and she sighed. "I see Clayton has done what he is so good at doing, which is riling everyone up around him. I'm sorry. It's awkward to talk with you hovering. Please sit."

I didn't want to agree. I wanted her to leave my restaurant, the town, and my life, but her apology wormed its way into me a little. I couldn't imagine being married to Clayton. I could barely stomach the thought that I'd let him touch me…more than once. That I'd let myself believe I wanted what he offered me, seeking self-confidence from someone else's approval. But he'd made me feel worse.

I sat down, and she smiled. It was a pretty smile,

softening the rigidness of her appearance, but there was a falseness to it that was easy to read.

"I quite admire you, Ms. O'Neil." This caught me off-guard, and she read my surprise with a soft laugh, explaining. "You haven't done one thing that Clayton wanted you to. You kept the baby, raised it on your own, and then refused to let him near it even when I'm sure he tried to be smooth and suave when he first approached you. Not many people seem to be able to say no to him. I certainly didn't."

My eyes widened at her admission, but I still didn't say anything. I had nothing to say to her. She could have been the nicest person in the world, and I still wouldn't let her spend time with my son. He wasn't going to be anywhere near her or Clayton.

She glanced around the restaurant and then back to the coffee cup in her hand. "When Clayton first spoke of you, he said... Well, he said some not very kind things. But then I look around, and I can see that this took effort and determination—especially while raising a baby. You've had help?"

I debated what to say. What would my lawyer tell me to do? Not share anything? But it was already well known that Brady had funded the restaurant and that my family watched Chevelle for me. I did have help. I was grateful for it. I was at peace with it now, wasn't I? There was no reason to hide it.

"Yes. I'm really lucky to have a family who supports Chevelle and me in any way they can."

She watched me as if she could read all the things I wasn't telling her. "Family is very important," she said softly. "I'm afraid mine will be ending with me."

The sadness in her eyes was real, and while it increased my compassion for her, it wasn't like feeling bad for someone who didn't have a puppy. I wasn't handing her my son just so she could play fetch in the park.

"What will it take, Ms. O'Neil?" she asked, and I frowned, not quite following her. She clarified. "Name your price."

Every ounce of empathy left me, replaced instead with a red-hot fury as I realized what she meant. I stood, hand gripping the back of the chair tightly. "Get out."

She continued staring at me as if I was a novelty. As if I somehow continued to surprise her. I wanted to take her coffee and throw it in her face. I wanted to have the strength to pull her from her chair by the back of her polka-dotted dress and toss her from the restaurant. I took in a deep breath, trying to stay calm and knowing there wasn't much more I could take before I lost it and yelled things that would be held against me.

"Maybe you don't understand," she said. "You can name any price you want for me to take your son off your hands. You'd still be given visitation rights. I'd see to it, regardless of what Clayton wants. We'd write up a contract to ensure it."

I couldn't even believe how calm she stayed while offering to buy my child. I'd never in my life felt such disgust, horror, and rage all at the same time.

"I repeat. Get out! Get out and don't ever come back. How dare you…" My voice shook with the emotions I tried to contain. "How dare you even… What kind of human being are you? What kind of mother do you think *I* am?"

She smiled, and this time it seemed real, as if my anger and disgust had somehow truly amused her. No, pleased her. I tucked my hands under my armpits in order to keep them away from her. To stop myself from scratching the smile off her face.

"Just as I thought," she said, and she stood, straightening her dress and pulling her expensive purse from the chair to set it on her shoulder. Her eyes sparkled with humor at my outrage when she landed them back on me again. "You're right, Ms. O'Neil. A real mother would never bargain with her child. Maybe if they lived somewhere unsafe and knee-deep in poverty and thought they could give their child a better life, but none of those things apply to you. I'm glad you did exactly what I hoped you would."

I could do nothing but stare, afraid of what I would say or do if I moved.

Her smile grew wider as she left a hundred-dollar bill on the table for a cup of coffee and then stepped toward the door. "Clayton and I will both be out of your hair. I'm divorcing him, you see. We really don't suit now that I know who he really is. Once there is no chance of him getting his hands on my money through a child, I can imagine his pursuit of yours will end. We both know he abhors anything messy that he can't control, and children are both of those things, aren't they? Messy and unpredictable."

She took two more steps and then stopped, looking back at me with a gentleness I would never have expected. "I didn't realize he came to Grand Orchard this summer for this reason. I'd told him I needed space, but I didn't even know… Regardless, I've found out in time to stop it all. I wish you and your son much luck." She looked around. "But you don't need it, do you? You already have everything you could want."

She was sad, as if she was missing something important in her life, and I couldn't keep myself from softening again. I felt sorry for her. Not only for being married to Clayton, but for her inability to have children of her own, and for being the end of a family line.

She grimaced as she read my emotions. "Don't feel sorry for me, Ms. O'Neil. I'm a survivor. I think you are, too. I'll pick myself up off the ground and keep going."

And with that, she left, the bell ringing as the door swung shut behind her. Out the window, I saw her walk into the street to a limousine that pulled up behind the parked cars. A driver in a uniform jumped out, opening the back for her, and she got in without another glance.

It took a moment for me to realize I was holding my breath. That I was still waiting for the other shoe to fall. But then relief started to filter in as her words really settled into my heart. She was leaving him. Marco had said the only reason Clayton wanted Chevelle was because his wife couldn't have kids, and he wanted to get his hands on her trust fund. And Mrs. Van Der Hellig-Hardy was right about Clayton. He didn't want a child screwing up the perfection of his world. It was why I had been completely baffled over his desire to have my son. It made sense that it had only been about the money.

I was still standing there frozen when Marco and Jonas walked in the door. Marco's eyes immediately landed on me as I stood there full of so many emotions that I wasn't sure which one was showing on my face. Whatever it was, it was enough for Marco to rush over and pull my hands into his.

"What is it?"

My gaze landed on the limousine in the street.

"Was it someone we know?" he asked.

"It was Clayton's wife."

Marco's eyes grew wide. "Are you okay? What did she want?"

"At first, she offered to buy Chevelle," I said with a weak laugh. His eyes grew dark and his face angry, but I rushed to continue before he could react. "It was just a test. She really came to say she was divorcing Clayton and that she thought it would end his pursuit of Chevelle. I actually feel…sorry for her."

We stared at each other as my words sank in. We were going to be free of one of the last burdens hanging over our heads. He smiled—the huge one that stopped my heart and reminded me of beams of light from the heavens. Joy radiated from him, meeting my own happiness as it burst from me.

Then, we were hugging each other, squeezing tight until the air burst out of us in a gust. He sent a dozen little kisses to the side of my head until I turned my lips, and our mouths found each other. The café was full. People were staring, and neither of us cared.

Jonas made a noise, and there was a round of applause that filled the air, and I thought I heard Floyd tell Irma she owed him fifty dollars.

I laughed, pulling back to smile up into his beautiful eyes.

"I love you," I said softly.

"I love you, too, Angel. With every piece of my battered heart."

"It's too early for this without coffee and food," Jonas said, but he was smiling. Marco reached out a hand, snagged Jonas's arm, and pulled him into our embrace.

Jonas squirmed at first and then just gave in, one arm going around me while the other went around Marco. He hugged us back, and my heart soared. I wanted to be one of the few people these two men counted on. I wanted to be their family. I wanted Chevelle to have them both in his life. My eyes filled just as my heart did.

Marco and I may have fallen down repeatedly in our lives, but somehow, we'd stumbled our way into each other's worlds and found love. A love that would help us back onto our feet whenever we tripped again. I was his, and he was mine. Nothing else mattered.

Chapter Thirty-six

Marco

H.O.L.Y.
Performed by Florida Georgia Line

I leaned up against the porch post, staring into the backyard at the mix of people gathered there. Tristan and her friend Stacy lay on lounge chairs, discussing the latest parental debate at Stacy's charter school. Hannah was twirling in the middle of the lawn along with Stacy's kids, waiting to see who would fall over next. Chevelle had already hit the grass on his back and was giggling as the beads of Hannah's shawl swung above him as she spun, and the puppy that Petri had brought home galloped over Chevelle as he tried to catch the fringe.

Jonas and Brady were in deep discussion about something on a sheet of paper spread in front of them on the picnic table. Jonas's passion for music—or rather, for helping others make music—had only grown under Brady's tutelage over the last month.

Arlene and Petri were oohing and awing over the new baby as Arlene bounced her in her arms. Aria was tiny with a cry that was equally little and yet somehow melodic. As if she was going to have the same kind of voice as her father and her sister.

Trevor and Stacy's husband, Jin, were arguing over the barbecue that I was supposed to be manning. I hadn't even argued when Trevor had taken the tongs from me. I wasn't a cook or a grill master. I didn't need to be when I had a chef living with me.

I'd just come back out of the house after having gone inside to answer an unknown number on my phone. The voice on the other end had constricted my heart—Petty Officer Warren. Cassidy joined me on the steps, wrapping her arms around my waist, and placing a kiss on my cheek.

"Who was it?" she asked.

"Petty Officer Warren."

Her arms squeezed tighter, as if worried that the call would send me into a spiral. But over the last few weeks, lost in Cassidy's arms at night and hugging Chevelle to my chest during the day, I'd already started to let go of the remorse, filling in the space with my love for them instead. My goal these days was to see how many smiles I could raise on their lips and Jonas's. The best way to make amends with my past was to dedicate myself to loving them and bringing joy to the people in my present.

"Are you okay?" Cassidy finally asked, my silence spreading worry into her heart.

I turned in her arms, looked into her eyes, and nodded.

"Yes. But I was okay even before she called. More than okay. You've shown me how to live again. Love again. Be human again."

Her throat bobbed as if holding back tears. She cupped her palm over my cheek and jaw.

"But I'm glad I heard from her," I said. "She apologized…to me."

Cassidy's eyes widened.

"She said she was sorry that I'd lost my position for doing the right thing. That it had bothered her even at the time, but she hadn't been able to really focus on anything but healing herself."

Years of self-torture didn't allow me to feel much more than a pinprick of relief at her apology. But in addition to my own realizations that I couldn't continue to live with my regrets hovering like a rain cloud, the words had helped.

"She has a husband and a daughter. A job with the Department of Defense. She said looking forward, building a new reality, was the only thing that kept her going. She hoped I could do that as well. But she also hoped I'd understand that she didn't really want to hear from me again. It was best for both of us to leave things where they were—in the past."

Cassidy hugged me fiercely. The way she always did. Until the breath left us both.

"I'm glad you heard from her," she said quietly.

I nodded, kissing her hair.

"Thank you," I said quietly. She looked up, a frown between her brows that I rubbed away. "I wouldn't have looked for her if you hadn't suggested it. I wouldn't have allowed myself to move beyond it. To turn my eyes to a future instead of replaying all my mistakes. You and Chevelle. Jonas and Maliyah. I want to be here fully for all of you. I don't want to be lost in those memories."

"You deserve a beautiful future, Marco," she said with a soft smile. My mouth found hers, and like it always did when we touched, it caused everything else to disappear. The backyard, the sounds of laughter, and the voices all faded away as I lost myself in the heavenly scent and feel of Cassidy.

She laughed against my lips, pulling back a little and shooting an eye in the direction of the audience we had in the backyard. But none of them had even noticed.

"I'm sorry Maliyah couldn't be here to help Jonas celebrate his birthday," she said quietly as we both watched Jonas and Brady's friendly argument.

My throat constricted a little because I missed Maliyah more these days than ever before. As if, in allowing my emotions for Cassidy to break through to the surface, it had allowed a whole host of other emotions to come tumbling out behind them.

"She's already called him half a dozen times today," I said quietly.

As if finally aware that we were watching him, Jonas's eyes landed on the two of us twined together on the steps.

"Don't forget that thing you were going to do," Jonas said with a sly smile.

My eyes narrowed. I didn't need the reminder. But I wasn't sure I wanted to do it on the heels of the conversation with Petty Officer Warren. I'd wanted to put some distance between that call and my future. But then I realized, it was the perfect time. What better way to honor Petty Officer Warren's request that we both move on than to solidify the next part of my life.

Once I'd found out that Cassidy was gathering her family to help us celebrate Jonas's birthday, I'd asked him if it would be okay to steal a little bit of his thunder. He'd just shoved a fist into my shoulder and told me he was surprised I hadn't already asked. After all, I'd bought the ring when we were still in Austin weeks ago. Maliyah had helped me pick it out. It was a platinum band with a glittering yellow diamond in the middle not only because it was Cassidy's favorite color, but because she was the sunshine to my rain. The beautiful rays that encompassed my world.

I'd intended to ask her to marry me as soon as Jonas and I had come back to Grand Orchard. I'd wanted to do it that first night, but then, I'd held off because of Hardy and his threats to use me and Jonas against Cassidy.

When he'd found out that his wife was divorcing him, Hardy had shown up at the café, furious. As if we'd somehow had something to do with his marriage falling apart. He'd ranted and raved and broken a cup. Willow had filmed the whole thing, and we'd submitted that to the judge with all the other evidence against him. In the end, we hadn't had to worry about it because he'd withdrawn his claim for parental rights. In fact, he'd signed them away and left Grand Orchard with his tail between his legs and a note from the dean of Wilson-Jacobs saying he wouldn't be welcomed back.

I'd never seen Cassidy as light as she'd been that day.

The lightness stuck around and had become part of our daily lives. One of my favorite times of day now was our family dinners. The four of us sitting around the table in Cassidy's kitchen with Jonas chattering away about high school or music, and Chevelle driving his trucks through his food or begging for Petri's puppy to spend the night in his room. We'd somehow found a routine. Her cooking and me cleaning up while she settled Chevelle down for the night. After dinner, Jonas would return to the apartment over the garage to do homework and play the drum kit he'd bought and was still figuring out how to play while Cassidy and I moved into the gym. We continued our old nightly workout routines, but we'd added a new layer to them, moving from the mats to the mattress with ease. With a fire that seemed to consume us both and had no sign of easing.

Jonas pounded his drumsticks on the picnic table, drawing everyone's eyes to him and bringing me from my thoughts back to the woman tucked up against me.

"Hey, everyone, Marco needs to make an announcement," he said with a wink.

Even the kids stopped their spinning to sit down on the grass and watch me. I swallowed, uncomfortable with the limelight. I was better in the shadows, standing behind someone. I'd gladly be Cassidy's shadow for the rest of her days.

Cassidy's brow furrowed as I pulled away and knelt down in front of her. Her eyes grew wide with a small smile tugging at her lips. She looked so beautifully Cassidy today with her hair swinging about her shoulders and her legs hidden in swaths of skirt. I loved that I knew every inch of what lay beneath it. Knew exactly how they'd wrap around me when we found our way to her room tonight.

As the fading sunlight bounced off the roof of her house, I swore a halo lit her up, making her glow even more than she normally did. My angel.

"I'm pretty sure the first time I did this, I did it wrong. You didn't think I was serious. You thought I was saying it as a way of keeping that weasel of a human from you," I said as my voice grew gravelly.

"I'm pretty sure there wasn't a first time, Marco," Cassidy teased. Her smile grew, and her eyes sparkled. "You made a statement as if it were true."

I flushed a little. Even though I'd told Hardy she

was marrying me to get him off her back, I'd also assumed that the words were correct. I'd imagined her saying yes because, in my heart of hearts, I'd known she would.

I pulled the ring from my pocket and opened my palm so she could see it.

"Angel...you may think you're the only one who does the falling around here, but it isn't true. I fell hard and fast the first time I ever saw you. And I fell even harder while watching you build your business, strengthen your body, and raise a child with charm and humility. You showed me a grace I hadn't thought I deserved, and you taught me to forgive myself for being human—"

"Wait, you're human?" Trevor scoffed, and Brady laughed.

Cassidy smiled, put her hand on my cheek, and said, "Ignore them."

I smiled as joy filled me. "I love you, Angel. With every single fiber and vein in my body. And I'm hoping you'll keep the promise you made to forever be mine by becoming my wife."

I took a breath, waiting for an answer as her smile grew, and the group of people gathered behind us became silent. She smiled, stroking my face with her long fingers.

"Yes, Marco. Yes, a thousand times over, yes."

I turned my head to kiss her palm and then pulled her hand from my face in order to slide the ring on. The family in our yard burst into applause. I picked her up, swung her around, and planted a new kiss on her lips. One that should have been light and soft because of everyone watching us, but instead became heated and deep because I didn't know how to kiss her without it consuming us as fire burned through our souls. We'd somehow found our way together through a sea of loss and heartache, and now we were bound together by love and family.

She was mine, and I was hers, and nothing else mattered.

Epilogue

Marco - Two years later

MY BOY
Performed by Elvie Shane

"Run, Chevelle! Run," I hollered so loud my deep voice cracked. Then, I chuckled as he went scrambling toward third base instead of first. He'd hit the ball off the tee all the way into far-right field, and the other team had to scramble for it, but my boy was running in the opposite direction.

There was laughter and screaming from the crowd behind us.

Chevelle tagged the base and looked back at me with the largest smile I'd ever seen on his face with his brown hair falling into his eyes under the helmet he was wearing. He jumped up and down on the bag as if he'd made a touchdown. One of the players from the opposite team walked up, tagged him with his glove, and said, "You're out."

Chevelle's face fell. "But I'm on base."

The kid was only one year older than Chevelle, who was barely four, but he sounded older as he rolled his eyes and said, "You went the wrong way, moron."

It only took a couple large strides for me to reach

their side.

"Jeff, we don't use words like that," I said to the boy. "Remember, we're all learning. That's the point of tee ball."

Chevelle looked up at me with his big eyes glistening. Damn. If he cried, I'd cry too. I held out my hand, and he slid his small one into it. I led him off the field toward the dugout, and when I risked looking into the stands, Cassidy was already making her way down the bleachers with one hand on the rail and the other on her swollen belly. A belly filled with our daughter who was sure to make her way into the world any day now.

I knelt down in front of Chevelle and unsnapped his helmet.

"Was I supposed to go to the other base, Daddy?" he asked, voice wavering.

My heart leaped at the name. Just like it did every time he said it.

"Yep. But we all make mistakes, Snickerdoodle. It's okay. It's how we learn." A lump hit my throat. I hardly ever thought of the mistakes from my past anymore. I was too busy filling my days with happy moments. With love and family.

This boy had become mine in a way no one would ever understand. He may not have had my DNA running through him, but I was his dad. He was my son. We were a family. He called Jonas his brother and Maliyah Grandma whenever we saw her—which was a lot. We flew to her, or she flew to us. Even with Jonas away now, she still came to Grand Orchard.

Cassidy reached us, placing a hand on my shoulder, bending slightly to catch Chevelle's eyes and saying, "That was an amazing hit!"

His chin wobbled. "I ran wrong and got out."

Cassidy nodded. "You did, but that doesn't take away from the fact that you had an amazing hit. You'll know better next time."

Chevelle looked from me to her as one of his teammates came up. "Chev, that was an awesome hit. I wish I could hit that good. Can you show me how you do that at practice?"

Chevelle's face lit up. He pushed away from me and ran off to the bench with his teammate in tow. I stood, and Cassidy wrapped her hand around my waist, having to tilt her body slightly to the side so she could tuck herself under my arm with her stomach protruding. We watched as the two boys chatted away.

"Thank you," she said quietly.

"For what?" I said, frowning.

"For showing him it's okay to make mistakes. For being everything he and I need. For loving us."

I kissed her, flames immediately leaping to life between us in a way that was completely inappropriate on the baseball field in front of half the town of Grand Orchard. She laughed as she pulled her lips away and would have taken a step back if my grip on her hip hadn't tightened.

"Angel, I'm only the man I am because of the two of you."

"The three of us." She smiled, bringing my other hand to her belly. "And I believe Jonas and Maliyah would have a thing or two to say about taking some of the credit."

I smiled at her.

"Maybe. But you were the one who shined a light into my dark and guided me out."

Her fingers ran along the stubble on my cheek. I was more unkempt these days. Not only because she liked the stubble, but because I didn't seem to have time in the mornings to shave. I usually stayed lost in her until the very last minute. Until Chevelle knocked on the door, or Jonas called, or Brady demanded my presence.

Her face turned from smile to shock.

"What?" My heartbeat picked up pace.

She looked down at her stomach. "Um. I thought they were just Braxton-Hicks, but…I think maybe we should head to the hospital."

My heart raced even further. I picked her up and headed for the opening in the field.

"I can walk, Marco."

I ignored her as I called out to Chevelle and the rest of the team, "Uncle Brady is in charge!"

Brady looked up from his spot at the bench where he'd been helping one of the little girls on the team slide on her helmet. There was panic in his eyes as they met mine. "What?"

"We're heading to the hospital. Can't stick around. The team is all yours."

A groan went up through the dugout and the parents on the bleachers. Brady may have been the town's biggest celebrity, but he knew squat about playing baseball.

"We'll meet you at the hospital when the game is done," Arlene called from the bleachers.

Cassidy and I exchanged a smile. It was a miracle that her mom wasn't galloping down the steps to accompany us. Arlene's hovering was lessening with each year that flew by. She seemed happy these days to turn care of Cassidy over to me.

I put Cassidy down in the passenger seat of our SUV and leaned down to kiss her. It brought back a memory of the time in the rain outside Marsha's Muffins when we'd devoured each other in a parking lot. When she'd demanded I take her back to the hotel and make love to her, and I'd given in—to everything. I kissed her so long and so fiercely that I felt the next contraction run through her body as I swallowed her moans.

I ran my hand through her hair, pushing the curl back from her face, assessing her pain. When the contraction eased, she gave me a small smile. Heartfelt, but a little panicky in a way I rarely saw her.

"You okay, Angel?" I asked.

She nodded. "But I think we should hold the kisses for later."

I took off for the driver's side, determined to get her and the baby to the hospital as quickly and safely as possible.

♫ ♫ ♫

I stared down into my daughter's eyes and was lost in love all over again. I hadn't thought my heart could grow any bigger than it already was from the love I felt for Cassidy, Chevelle, and my family. But this little being had proven otherwise. She'd taken my heart and swelled it until it felt like it was going to escape my body.

I lay propped up on the pillows in our bed with the baby snuggled against my chest and Cassidy tucked up against me with her head on my shoulder. The delivery had been quick and easy, according to the doctor, but then he was male, and I wondered if he had any clue what really happened to the female body in order to give birth.

Two days later, Cassidy was still finding her feet again. It allowed me to spoil her in a way she still rarely let me—or anyone—do.

Chevelle knocked on the door and then came bounding in with a piece of paper in his hand. He threw himself at our laps, and I had to hold out my arm to make sure he didn't knee Cassidy in the stomach.

"Easy, Snickerdoodle. Mama is still healing."

He nodded and squeezed himself in the space between Cassidy and me, which had been pretty much nonexistent. "I need to know her name so I can put it on my drawing," he said, shoving the crayon-and-marker-covered page at us.

We had dozens of images of us on the refrigerator because Chevelle loved to draw almost more than he loved animals or his blocks. The first time he'd included me in one with "Daddy" written above my head, I'd cried. Silent tears of thanks and joy. Sadness that my own parents weren't there to see it, but also grateful that I had this family.

The baby moved, a tiny finger wrapping around me, seizing my heart all over again. She was just Baby Girl for now. Cassidy had insisted she needed to get to know her daughter before coming up with something so permanent as a name, and who was I to argue with the woman who'd just handed me this precious little girl?

I glanced up and caught the image of the four of us in the mirror over the dresser. A range of tans and golds and shimmery whites that the rays streaming through the window set on fire. So different than the dark look that had been my family or the golden one that was Cassidy's, but still beautifully blended. Still beautifully whole.

I turned my head, catching Cassidy's eyes. Hers were shiny as if her emotions were also about to burst free.

"This. This is the best gift," I said quietly.

She nodded, and I leaned over to capture her lips as Chevelle wiggled and the baby mewed, and I thought I would never in my life feel anything as good as this again. This moment took everything I'd ever gone through and cast it away as if it was a life that was no longer mine. It was someone else's haunted memory.

My heart and soul now belonged right here in the present and in the bright future our love made possible.

♫ ♫ ♫

Want a little more of Cassidy and Marco? How about a little hint of what's in store for Jonas and Paisley? Download the FREE *Tripped by Love* Bonus Epilogue now:

https://www.ljevansbooks.com/freeljbooks!

Do you want to know what comes next for Jonas, Paisley, and the rest of The Painted Daisies? The epic, spin-off series two years in the making is finally here! With an all-female rock band and the alpha heroes who steal their hearts, these fast-paced romantic

suspense novels might just leave you breathless.

Keep reading for a sneak peek right here, right now.
SWEET MEMORY - SNEAK PEEK

Sweet Memory – Chapter One

Paisley

CRYING UNDERWATER
Performed by Dami Im

TWELVE DAYS BEFORE

Paisley's emotions roller-coastered back and forth from high to low as she watched the apple orchards on the outskirts of Grand Orchard come into view. Frenzied excitement spread through her, the anticipation twisting in her chest until it physically hurt. She was going to see Jonas again! For the first time in two years! Just as quickly as the happiness came, it was swallowed by doubts that turned her stomach. What if it wasn't the same? What if the easy banter they'd found in texts and an occasional phone call disappeared in person? What if she wasn't what he expected?

Paisley's finger pressed automatically into the

raised, star-shaped birthmark by her eye as a tap, tap, tap of metal against metal drew her gaze from the view outside the Escalade to her sister. Landry had her hands in prayer mode with the rings on her two middle fingers beating out a rhythm. Tall, thin, and willowy with a sharply pointed chin, enormous eyes, and black hair cascading past her shoulders, Landry had an almost fairy-like vibe.

"What's going on in that head of yours?" Landry asked, the huskiness of her tone a complete contrast to her fragile appearance.

Early in their career, a critic had said Landry's voice was better suited to life as a phone-sex operator instead of a singer. The intended cruelty of those words had turned Paisley's stomach even when they hadn't been directed at her. But not Landry. It had motivated her to prove him wrong. When they'd won their Grammy last year, her sister had sent the man a picture of her holding it with a middle finger extended.

"Nothing's going on. I'm fine," Paisley responded. Whereas Landry's voice was deep and husky, Paisley's was light and feathery—barely a whisper.

"Try not to get your hopes up, Paise. It's easy to pretend to be nice and calm and have your shit together in a fifty-word text." Landry's comment snagged at Paisley's doubts and irritation flared deep inside her.

Instead of getting into another one of their ever-increasing number of fights, Paisley bit her lip and pushed harder into her birthmark. She wasn't sure if Landry really didn't like Jonas, or if she just didn't want Paisley to have a life outside the band.

Landry hadn't objected when three-quarters of the songs they were set to record had come from her texts with Jonas. The lyrics put Paisley's heart on display in a very uncomfortable way. They'd exposed her underbelly to her sister and the band. What would happen when the world got them?

Paisley's chest squeezed tighter, a prick of ice spreading through her veins as panic started to bloom, but her sister's next words replaced the ice with fire.

"You deserve someone better than a boy who was arrested for assault."

"He was never charged!" Paisley exclaimed, crossing her arms over her chest and trying futilely to stop herself from pushing into her birthmark again.

"He has anger issues, Paise. Someone like that will never change, and I don't want to see you lying on the ground because of his shitty past," Landry said.

"Oh my God, you act like he assaulted someone for simply looking at him wrong. He got in a fight with an asshole gang member who was beating his friend. You should be applauding him for standing up for someone he cared about."

"He didn't have to resort to violence," Landry said, a hardness in her voice that made Paisley's stomach twist again.

Before this year, she and Landry had rarely been on opposing sides of an argument. Mostly because Paisley knew her sister was always right, whereas she was the girl who'd barely gotten her G.E.D. But her sister was wrong about Jonas. Nothing Landry could say would convince Paisley otherwise.

"Look. I didn't want to show you this before, but you really leave me no choice," Landry pulled her phone out and handed it over.

It took a minute for Paisley to figure out what it was, and when she did, she inhaled sharply. The picture was one she treasured. It was the entire band with her and Jonas front and center on the stage in the Wilson-Jacobs Theater after they'd finished recording The Red Guitar album two years ago. They'd put on a little show as a thank-you to the people of Grand Orchard, and she'd called Jonas up on stage to sing the song he'd been instrumental in helping her shape.

Normally, when she was on stage, she felt like she was going to puke, at least until the music and lyrics centered her. But when Jonas had joined her, wrapping an arm around her shoulder, she'd felt a steadiness she'd never felt before. Not even when Landry held her hands and pressed her cool metal rings into her skin to ground her.

But this version of the picture was all wrong. Where each of the band members' faces should have been, huge gouge marks existed, and scrawled over their bodies in red ink were the words, "I will make sure you're never happy."

"What is this?" Paisley asked as she shot a glance toward the front seat and their two bodyguards.

"An example of what his life can do to you."

Paisley's heart thumped fiercely in her chest, as the ice returned. Her voice was barely audible as she asked, "All of our faces are scratched out. All of us. How can you be sure this is about Jonas?"

"We haven't received another one like it since we left Grand Orchard. His past came calling and briefly caught us in the crossfire. He's bad news, Paise."

The cold was spreading through her, turning her body to stone. Jonas would be devastated if he knew about this. He'd take the blame and swallow it whole.

He'd stay away…

God, she didn't want that. She'd been waiting for two years for them to be together. She couldn't tell him, could she? But how could she not?

You're so stupid. I thought you were supposed to be smart. What happened to you? Is that mark from where they sucked your brains out?

The taunts circled through her head, making a new wave of doubt fly through her. As the chants repeated in an unbreakable circle, her finger pressed deeper and deeper into the star birthmark.

Her cell phone vibrated, and even before she picked it up, she knew who it was.

> *JONAS: Are you here? ***Excited GIF****

Her heart convulsed, joy at the thought of seeing him rippling over the fear and panic. She couldn't tell him. It would ruin everything. But there was also no way she could see him tonight like they'd originally planned because he'd take one look at her and know something was up. Just like he'd known when she'd called him from a roof top in Sydney.

Before she could respond, Paisley's phone went wild with a string of texts in the band's group chat.

> *FEE: Did Ramona get lost? I swear you should've been here by now.*

> *ADRIA: Don't mind her, she's hangry and missing you.*

> *LANDRY: We were only apart for a couple of days, Fee.*

Paisley and Landry were the last of the band to arrive after spending the weekend with their parents at their cousin's wedding. It had been a nightmare, renewing their parents' desire to see her and Landry settled with good Korean boys who had steady, reliable jobs, and intensifying the divide between Landry and their parents.

> *LEYA: She's got a whole girl's night planned. Pedicures and facials and romcom movies.*
>
> *FEE: It was supposed to be a surprise, Ley'.*

Even panicked and scared by what her sister had shown her, Paisley couldn't hold back the small smirk she sent Landry's way at the text exchange with their friends.

> *NIKKI: If you're not here soon, the food will get cold.*

"How much longer?" Landry asked their two bodyguards.

"Ten minutes tops," Ramona answered from the driver's seat while Dylan scanned the orchards as they flew by. These two muscled and honed guards were their personal detail. After the band's popularity had exploded while on tour, they'd had to double their security. Now, none of them went anywhere without a bodyguard in tow.

> *JONAS: It was the GIF, right? It was totally over the top, and you're now questioning the wisdom of seeing me*

again.

She swallowed hard. The ugly image on Landry's phone spun in front of her eyes again. She didn't know how she could see him and not tell him, and if she told him, he'd pull away because he wouldn't risk her in order to be with her.

> *PAISLEY: The GIF is exactly how I'm feeling. If anything, it proved just how perfectly in sync we are. I can't wait to see you. Unfortunately, Fee has a whole thing planned for tonight that I didn't know about and can't get out of.*
>
> *JONAS: Dang. Okay. Well, we've waited two years, so I guess twelve hours is nothing.*
>
> *PAISLEY: A mere blip.*

The toss and turn of her stomach continued, disappointment spreading through her. She wanted to see him. Almost desperately needed to. As if she wouldn't be able to breathe much longer if he wasn't there. No picture was worth not being with him.

She turned to her sister and said quietly with a certainty she rarely felt and even less frequently showed, "He works at the studio, Lan, but even if he didn't, I'd see him. He doesn't deserve to have his past held over his head any more than you deserve to have your bisexuality held against you, or I should have my dyslexia held against me."

Landry grimaced. "That's not even remotely the same. That's part of our DNA. His issues are about his choices."

Jonas's childhood had impacted him almost as much as their chemical makeup. It was why he reacted the way he did, but the set of her chin let Paisley know she wasn't going to change Landry's mind. Not today. Maybe never.

"Did you tell the others about it?" Paisley asked.

Landry shook her head. "No. It seemed unnecessary."

Paisley didn't agree, but she wouldn't argue with Landry anymore today. The one about Jonas was enough to make her chest hurt and her stomach feel like it had turned into a briar patch with the thorns darting into her intestines.

They were silent as they drove the last few miles to the mansion the townspeople of Grand Orchard affectionately called The Farmhouse. It was a sprawling, early-twentieth-century Victorian tucked between the apple orchards and the mountains with a wraparound porch and more rooms than you could count.

The best part of the property was the pond, aptly named Swan River for the bevy of birds that called the tules and cattails home. The smooth waters had cast a spell over Paisley the last time they were there, easing her anxiety more than the swing set in their childhood backyard ever had.

Ramona hung a left onto a long gravel drive in the middle of the apple trees and eventually the house with its white planks and black shutters came into view. Paisley's eyes immediately landed on the porch swing where she and Jonas had once sat arguing about bands and music and lyrics. Her heart jumped at the memories as well as the thought of seeing him again, a rhythm beating inside her that she needed to capture on her keys. A song called, "Anticipation."

When the car came to a stop in the drive, Fiadh was waiting for them on the top step. She'd added a layer of lilac to her dark-red curls recently, which made them shimmer as they danced about, as wild and fiery as she was. The sunlight glinted off her diamond-studded nose ring as a large smile spread across her face.

They were barely out of the car before Fee had scurried across the circular drive to wrap them in a hug, bouncing the three of them around like a pogo stick.

"God, I missed you," she said, the pale dusting of freckles on her face shimmering in the sunset.

"Fee, I can't breathe." Landry's grouse was half-hearted, and Fiadh just laughed, squeezing even harder before letting them go.

They moved from the porch into the house, and Paisley's pulse spiraled again as more memories flooded her. The darkly stained walnut staircase was where she and Jonas had sat discussing the track order for The Red Guitar, and the antique, claw-footed, floral couch was where he'd tickled her until she couldn't breathe as they argued about Pink Floyd. The fake British accent he'd used to critique it had made her laugh until her sides hurt. It hit her hard in the chest with a longing she could barely contain.

"I tried to get them to wait to eat, but Leya and Nikki feigned starvation." Fiadh said as she led them down the hallway into the renovated kitchen. It was a deep contrast to the old charm of the rest of the house. Modern and chic, it had stainless-steel appliances, marbled countertops, and gray, distressed cabinets.

"Damn it, get your hands off my fries, Leya!" Fee

groused, pouncing on the table and ripping the bag from Leya's hands.

Leya rolled her eyes and threw a fry in Fiadh's direction. Fee just laughed, brushing it away as Nikki, Leya, and Adria took turns hugging Paisley and Landry. When they were all tangled together like this, it was hard to tell them apart in the sea of black hair and long legs.

Their first album cover had played up their similarities. They'd worn white leather jackets with their backs to the camera. Only Paisley, who was a good eight inches shorter than the rest of them, and Fiadh, with her deep-red hair, had stood out. The rest could only be told apart by the daisies emblazoned on their jackets. It had been their manager's idea to emphasize the band's name by having each of them choose a different daisy type to represent them. Now, the flowers were painted onto their instruments, mic stands, and clothes in a way that made them almost synonymous with their real names.

"Please tell me there's a veggie burger in that mix somewhere," Landry said, flinging her purse with her Golden Butterfly daisy embroidered on it over a chair back at the large oak table.

Leya dug through the bags and handed a wrapped burger to Landry.

"You're lucky Nikki remembered," Leya said, one artfully shaped brow raising above her twinkling brown eyes, full lips, and cleft chin. "No one is used to you inheriting my vegan ways."

"Have I told you lately that I like you best," Landry said, pulling Nikki to her and kissing her cheek.

"Get off," Nikki said, pushing her away. She

hadn't straightened her hair today, and the dark coils sprung about her perfectly oval face while her dark-brown eyes sparkled with the same humor as Leya's.

Paisley sat down, grabbing a burger and fries from the middle. She'd put her phone face-down on the table, and it buzzed, vibrating against the wood. Even with no sound, she knew it was another message from Jonas, and her fingers itched to read it, but Landry's frown stopped her from picking it up.

Adria chuckled at Landry's glower. "You have to let our little girl grow up, Lan. Dating is just the first step."

Her comment made Paisley want to scream, both in joy and frustration. Maybe it was because she'd never made it to five feet tall that had them treating her like a little kid, as if her tiny size had halted her growth and held her in some weird, childlike limbo. But she also appreciated Adria trying to defend her, so she sent her a soft smile.

Adria winked in return, the signature wink the world swooned over making her bright-blue eyes sparkle. Her nearly perfect features, along with her model-like figure, had helped her win multiple beauty contests in her younger years.

"I'm a tiny bit jealous of Little Bit," Fiadh announced. "It's been too long since I hooked up with anyone."

"No one is getting hooked up. We're here to record another Grammy-award-winning album. That has to be the priority," Landry said, shooting them all a glare but settling the longest on her.

Paisley twirled a French fry between her fingers, the barbed thorns that had appeared in her stomach digging farther into the lining because, as unhappy as it would make Landry, she knew she'd be spending time with Jonas. As much as she could. She'd waited almost two years to see him. Twenty-two months. Nearly seven hundred days. She wasn't going to ignore him and the way he made her feel no matter what Landry said or the picture she'd shown her. She couldn't ignore him even if she wanted to. Her heart and body were already beating out a song of expectation, one that wouldn't stop until it peaked at a breathtaking crescendo.

Sweet Memory – Chapter Two

Jonas

IS THIS LOVE
Performed by Whitesnake

ELEVEN DAYS BEFORE

Jonas's fingers banged viciously on his knees bouncing under the kitchen table. The slightly nauseated feeling in his stomach had nothing to do with the way his four-year-old nephew was shoveling in chorizo quiche and dribbling it on the apron he wore over his tee-ball outfit. Normally, Jonas and Chevelle would be competing to see who could eat the fastest, but today, the waves of expectation churning through him made it impossible to think of eating at all.

"So, recording starts with The Painted Daisies today, right?" Cassidy asked, drawing his eyes to his sister-in-law as she stirred something sweet-smelling on the stove. Blonde-haired with light-brown eyes and pale skin, Cassidy was a fabulous chef and restauranteur.

Jonas rolled his eyes at her question but didn't respond. He didn't need to. She knew exactly what was happening today, and it wasn't because of the texts he'd been exchanging with Paisley Kim for almost two years or the fact that he'd been working at Brady's studio for the same amount of time. It was because his foster brother—Cassidy's husband—had been working for days on the additional coverage needed for the band's protection while in town.

Marco walked into the room just as Cassidy placed a plate in front of Jonas. It was a crepe with pieces of strawberries arranged to make a smiley face. There were chocolate chips for eyes and a dish of chocolate sauce off to the side. It was the breakfast she normally made Chevelle to cheer him up after he lost a game.

Marco chuckled, and Jonas rolled his eyes again before saying, "You're all ridiculous."

But really, his heart and eyes stung because it was sweet. It reminded him of how lucky he was to have so many people in his corner these days. If someone had asked eight-year-old him if he'd ever have this kind of family, he would have replied with a pained and emphatic, "No."

"Mama, I want smiley cakes!" Chevelle whined as soon as he saw Jonas's crepe.

Cassidy ruffled his hair and kissed the top of his head. "You need protein to help you hit another home run today. So, eat your eggs!"

While Chevelle pouted, Cassidy went back to the stove, and Marco joined her, sliding his arms around her waist and kissing her neck. It was a sickening display of ooey-gooey love that happened on an almost hourly basis between them.

Jonas passed the plate of crepes to Chevelle, whose eyes grew wide before his tiny face broke out into a huge smile. He was the cutest dang kid Jonas had ever met. Not that he'd been around a lot of kids before he'd moved to Grand Orchard with Marco, but still.

Jonas put a finger to his lips and winked at Chevelle, who shot a look in his parents' direction before diving in. Jonas watched as Marco rested his chin on Cassidy's shoulder and settled his hands on her stomach protruding from her dress. To Jonas, she looked like she was going to burst any day. It had been sort of mind-boggling and awe-inspiring to see how her body had changed over the last nine months.

But then, women in general tended to confound him, which only set his knee bouncing at a more furious pace as his thoughts returned to the one woman he was both excited and nervous to see again. The woman who'd been haunting his dreams and messages for two years. The woman who'd taken a broken and beat-up heart and slowly mended it with her friendship.

Marco let go of Cassidy and sat down at the table, eyeing Jonas and then his son, who was now covered in chocolate. Marco's lips twitched, but he didn't scold either of them. He was an even bigger sucker for the kid than Jonas was. Chevelle might not have been Marco's son by blood, but they were undeniably a family.

Jonas's knee hit the underside of the table as it bounced, making all the dishes clatter and bang. Three sets of eyes turned to take him in. Marco's were full of concern, the teasing all but forgotten.

"What's wrong?" his brother asked as his dark brows drew together, making him look more grim-faced Aztec than normal.

Cassidy shot Jonas a soft smile, coming to stand beside Marco and resting her hand on his shoulder. Marco's tan arm skated around her waist, drawing her closer, almost as if he didn't even realize he'd done it. Jonas's heart banged harder, wondering if what he felt for Paisley was anything close to what these two shared.

"Our Jonas is in love," Cassidy teased.

Marco's frown grew. Jonas wasn't sure what he felt could be considered love, especially when he'd never even kissed Paisley. But he was drawn to her and admired her not only for her beauty and her music but also for the strength she showed every time she stepped onstage. Only a handful of people knew how hard it was for her to do just that.

"Jo-Jo—" Marco started, but he stopped when he saw Jonas grimace at the nickname.

Marco rarely used it anymore. It made him feel like a child when he was anything but. He was going to be nineteen in a few weeks, which wasn't necessarily a full-grown adult, but he wasn't a fucking kid either. He wasn't sure he'd ever really been one.

"I know. I know. She's a fu—flipping rock star," Jonas said. "And I'm not in love. We're friends, and I'm excited to see her."

"You're excited to see Maliyah when she comes

into town. I don't think it's quite the same," Cassidy continued to tease.

Marco chuckled, and Jonas fought another eye roll. Comparing his foster mom to Paisley was as ridiculous as the smiley-faced crepes. Unable to take their knowing looks and his nervous anticipation any longer, he pushed away from the table.

"I'm going to La Musica. I don't know how late I'll be, but I'll text you." He ruffled Chevelle's brown hair as he walked past. "Have a good game, buddy. Remember to have fun and not keep score."

Then, he left, ignoring Marco's worried look while attempting to calm the knots churning in his stomach.

♫ ♫ ♫

To keep his mind occupied and his nerves in check while he waited for Paisley to arrive with the rest of the band, Jonas went to work wiring the mics in the studio's live room. He couldn't deny he'd been disappointed when she'd changed their plans the night before. He'd thought they'd have a couple of hours alone before having to face everyone. But now, their reunion would be during their first rehearsal. A rehearsal they certainly didn't need, but Brady had insisted on. He wanted to hear all the songs together before they started laying down the individual tracks.

The wiring wasn't complicated, but it was intense as the band was known not only for their unique lyrics and rhythms but the variety of instruments they played. Paisley was almost exclusively on the keyboard, but she could—and did—play guitar on occasion. Her sister, Landry, was the opposite. She played guitar most of the time and drifted to the keys to back up Paisley. Adria was their drummer. Nikki played a range of guitars, fiddle, and ukulele, but spent most of the time on bass guitar. Leya was known for a whole host of instruments from India, but she predominately used the baby sitar. And then there was Fiadh, who was probably the most musically gifted of them all with the largest range, including the piano, guitar, banjo, accordion, tin whistle, Irish flute, Uilleann pipes, and the Celtic harp. She changed instruments with almost every song, sometimes within the songs themselves.

Jonas purposefully left Paisley's keyboard for last, but it still didn't lessen the shock when he finally stood behind it, eyeing the soft-pink Sweet Memory daisy painted on it. His insides flopped and clenched as he rested a palm on the flower, remembering like it was yesterday the way his hand had felt pressed against Paisley's for a single moment years ago.

Before he'd come to Grand Orchard, he'd thought he'd been in love with his friend Mel. She'd been stunning and vivacious. Powerful and smart. The kind of dynamic personality you knew was going to end up going places. It had radiated from her, and he'd been caught in her bright, shiny rays from the day they'd met at age nine.

But after Jonas had left Texas, it had been his attraction to Paisley that had shown him how wrong he'd been. There was no way he could have loved Mel in a romantic sort of way if he'd been drawn to Paisley only days later.

Something about Paisley's quiet energy and soft voice pulled at pieces deep inside him. Every time they talked, it was as if he found a little more of himself. Add in the jolts of energy that drifted through him whenever they'd touched, and he knew he'd never really loved Mel.

There'd been plenty of times over the last two years where Jonas had wondered if he'd imagined everything he'd felt with Paisley. Maybe when he saw her again, all of those feelings would no longer exist, but he didn't think so. He thought they'd be a flame that would be hard to put out.

The door of the live room bounced open, hitting the padded wall, and Jonas's hand slipped from the keyboard, heart going from zero to sixty in a mere nanosecond. But it was only Paisley's sister, Landry, who entered. Her dark eyes glared at him, and the knots in his stomach returned. She'd never liked the bond she'd seen growing between Paisley and him, and while part of him understood it, most of him just resented it.

Landry flicked her long hair over a shoulder, glanced toward the studio's front door where the other members of the band were filtering in, and then stepped close enough to talk without the others hearing.

"If I had my way, you wouldn't be anywhere near my sister. Instead, I'll make this perfectly clear. Hurt her, and I'll end you," Landry hissed.

Jonas's eyes went wide, and his fists clenched, nails biting into his palm as he tried to control the immediate spike of anger that flew through him.

"I have no intention of hurting her," he growled back.

Fiadh bounced into the room with her riot of curls swirling around her face like that Disney character from Brave. She glanced between Jonas and Landry and rolled her eyes.

"Oh my God, Lan. Please tell me you didn't say

something already."

Landry ignored her, moving to the guitar Jonas had set up. She ran her hands over it, fingering the strings, adjusting and tuning it by ear.

Fiadh practically danced over to Jonas. She flung an arm around his shoulder and said, "Jonas, Jonas, Jonas. We love, love, love that you helped us create a Grammy-winning album, and we adore the way you make our serious Paisley smile, but we are very protective of our Little Bit. So, get it right the first time, okay?"

"Fee!" Landry snapped, her husky voice going down another notch before shooting Jonas another scowl.

He had to get out of the room before he did or said something he'd regret. He worked hard—with the help of a therapist and the boxing bag in Marco and Cassidy's home gym—to control his anger these days, and he couldn't let one person's dismissal of him undo it. Jonas shrugged Fiadh's arm off and stalked to the door, almost running into Nikki and Leya as they entered with to-go cups in their hands.

"Sorry," he said as he stepped around them. He felt their eyes on him as he hurried out of the studio and onto the sidewalk, hating that he'd let Landry get to him.

He leaned up against the building, fighting the well of emotions building inside him and letting the heat of the brick spread through him. He wasn't that kid from Austin anymore—neither the abandoned child nor the friend who'd been left behind. He was part of a family now. He was loved. One person's rejection didn't make him worthless, even if he had a long way to go before he was the man he wanted to be. He tilted his head back, closed his eyes, and let the warmth soothe him.

He breathed in deeply, pushing down the negative thoughts and the hollow ache of his past. He wanted to be in control when he greeted Paisley. He wanted to show her only the joy she'd brought him with a handful of texts and calls.

"Jonas?" The soft voice was barely a whisper on the wind, but it jolted him out of his thoughts and back to the sidewalk. He hadn't forgotten the glow that seemed to emanate from her like an angelic halo, but seeing her in real life, after two years of not…it hit him in the chest like an asteroid crashing to earth.

Her straight black hair was looped partially up, and a tendril had escaped, sliding over the soft arc of her cheek. Her lush, black lashes emphasized her brown eyes, making them stand out in her oval face. His gaze landed on her plush, pink lips, lingering there too long and making his body ache to have them pressed against his for the first time.

She was in tight black jeans that clung to her narrow hips, rising high on her waist where a purple crop-top revealed a tiny sliver of her stomach that called to him to touch it. Her tiny frame seemed even smaller now that he'd grown another four inches in her absence. Even in her heeled boots, she barely reached his shoulder.

She had her index finger resting on the star-shaped birthmark right below her eye, giving away her nervousness only to those who knew her best, and it was with a sharp jolt of pride that he realized he did. He knew her. Knew more about her than anyone on this planet—maybe even more than her sister.

Emotions flew through him. Happiness. Hope.

Fear. He'd been holding his breath so long, his lungs felt like he'd had the wind knocked out of them, and when he tried to inhale, the air sliced through him.

Her name got caught in his throat as the reality of her being there continued to overwhelm him. Sometimes the other band members called her Little Bit. Her sister called her Paise. He'd done both, but he'd used Paisley the most because she didn't seem like someone who deserved to have their name shortened. You needed to speak all her syllables to do her justice.

Every single stunning one of them.

Keep reading *SWEET MEMORY* now.
FREE in Kindle Unlimited
https://geni.us/PDSM

If you want to keep tabs on LJ' stories as she writes them and get exclusive content, giveaways, and more, then you might want to join her weekly newsletter, http://bit.ly/LJEmoGive. You can get all these FREE Flash Fiction stories when you sign up: https://www.ljevansbooks.com/freeljbooks.

Want even more teasers? Want even more chances at giveaways? Join her Facebook Group, **LJ's Music and Stories**, to chat with LJ on a daily basis.

Message from the Author

Thanks again for reading ***Tripped by Love***. At the beginning—if you even saw it—I told you I didn't want to fill your head with my social media sites and other books because I wanted you to read the story and then decide how you felt about me and my words. I hope you loved Cassidy and Marco's story of love and healing. I hope the mix of lyrics and story burned a memory into your soul that you'll think about every time you hear one of the songs from now on.

We talk about music, books, and just what it takes to get us through this wild ride called life a lot in my Facebook reader's group, LJ's Music & Stories. If you do nothing else with the links here, I hope you join that group. I hope that we can help ***YOU*** through your life in some small way.

Regardless if you join or not, I'd love for you to tell me what you thought of the book by reaching out to me personally. I'd be honored if you took the time to leave a review on BookBub, Amazon, and/or Goodreads, but even more than that, I hope you enjoyed it enough to tell a friend about it.

If you still can't get enough (ha!), you could also sign up for my newsletter (http://bit.ly/LJEmoGive) so that you'll be able to keep tabs on all my stories as I write them. Not only will you receive music-inspired scenes weekly, but you'll also be entered into a giveaway each month for a chance at a signed paperback by yours truly.

Finally, I just wanted to say that my wish for you is a healthy and happy journey. May you live life resiliently, with hope and love leading the way!

Thanks for reading my little story!
LJ EVANS
www.ljevansbooks.com
FaceBook Group: LJ's Music & Stories
LJ Evans on Bookbub, Amazon, and Goodreads
@ljevansbooks on Facebook, Twitter, Instagram, TikTok, and Pinterest

Acknowledgements

I'm so very grateful for every single person who has helped me on this book journey. If you're reading these words, you *ARE* one of those people. I couldn't be an author if people didn't decide to read the stories I crafted, and I'm oh so grateful for you.

These people need extra mention because I don't know where I'd be without them:

My husband, who means more to me than I can explain in one or a thousand sentences, has never, ever let me give up and has done everything he could to make my dreams come true.

Our child, Evyn, owner of Evans Editing, who remains my harshest and kindest critic. I'm so grateful to them for using everything they learned in getting their degree to shape my stories.

My sister, Kelly, who made sure I hit the publish button the very first time and reads all my crappy first drafts.

My parents who have been my biggest fans and bring my books to the strangest places to tell everyone they know (and don't know) about my stories.

The talented Megan Keith at Designed with Grace, who has been much more than just a cover designer, but also a friend, beta reader, and partner.

Jenn at Jenn Lockwood Editing Services, who is always patient with my gazillion missing commas and my hatred of the semicolon.

Karen Hrdlicka who ensures the final versions of my books are beautiful and for never getting tired of telling me "that" should not be my favorite word.

To the entire group of beautiful humans in LJ's Music & Stories who love and support me throughout the Internet kingdom, I can't say how much I adore each and every one of you.

To a host of bloggers who have shared my stories, become dear friends, and continue to make me feel like a rock star every day, I can't say thank you enough.

To the other independent authors including Hannah Blake, Stephanie Rose, Annie Dyer, Kathryn Nolan, Amanda Johnson, and Erika Kelly who have opened doors for me and been there through every paralyzing moment to push me forward.

To all my ARC readers who have become beautiful friends and always know just the right thing to scare away my writer insecurities.

And I can't leave without a special thanks to Leisa C. and Leanne J. for being two of the biggest cheerleaders I could ever hope to have on this wild ride called life.

I love you all!

Books by LJ

Standalone

The Last One You Loved
A single-dad, small-town romance

He's a small-town sheriff with a secret that can unravel their worlds. She's an ER resident running from a costly mistake. Coming home will only mean heartache…unless they let forgiveness heal them both.

Charming and the Cherry Blossom
A contemporary romance with hints of magical realism

Today was a fairy tale…I inherited a fortune from a dad I never knew, and a thoroughly charming guy asked me out. But like all fairy tales, mine has a dark side...and my happily ever after may disappear with the truth.

My Life as an Album Series

My Life as a Country Album — Cam's Story
A boy-next-door, small-town romance

Spirited athlete's Cam's diary-style, coming-of-age story about growing up loving the football hero next door. She vowed to love him forever. But when fate comes calling, will she ever find a heart to call home? Warning: Tears may fall.

My Life as a Pop Album — Mia & Derek
A rock-star, road-trip romance

Bookworm Mia is trying to put behind her years of guilt when soulful musician, Derek Waters, strolls into her life and turns it upside down. Once he's seen her, Derek can't walk away unless Mia comes with him. But what will happen when their short time together comes to an end?

My Life as a Rock Album — Seth & PJ
A second-chance, antihero romance

Growly, trash artist Seth Carmen knows he's better off alone. But when he finds and loses the love of his life, he can't help sending her a host of love letters to try and win her back. Can Seth prove to PJ they can make broken beautiful?

My Life as a Mixtape — Lonnie & Wynn
A single-dad, rock-star romance

Lonnie's always seen relationships as a burden instead of a gift, and picking up the pieces his sister leaves behind is just one of the reasons. When Wynn enters his life just as her world is disintegrating, their mixed-up pasts give way to new beginnings neither of them saw coming.

My Life as a Holiday Album – 2nd Generation
A small-town romance

Come home for the holidays with this heartwarming, full-length standalone full of hidden secrets, true love, and the real meaning of family. Perfect for lovers of *Love Actually* and Hallmark movies, this sexy story twines the lives of six couples as they find their way to their happily ever after with the help of family and friends.

My Life as an Album Series Box Set
The 1st four Album series stories plus an exclusive novella

In the exclusive novella, *This Life with Cam*, Blake Abbott writes to Cam about just what it was like to grow up in the shadow of her relationship with Jake and just when he first fell for the little girl with the popsicle-stained lips. Can he show Cam that she isn't broken?

The Anchor Novels

Guarded Dreams — Eli & Ava
A grumpy-sunshine, military romance

Eli's chasing a dream that he's determined to succeed at, no matter the consequences. He isn't looking for love, but when the free-spirited singer, Ava, breezes into his world, he finds himself changing his tune.

Forged by Sacrifice — Mac & Georgie

A roommates-to-lovers, military romance

Mac is determined to change the world. A life in politics is his future. The dream Georgie once gave up is finally in reach—a law degree. When her family's past makes his future an impossibility, they have to decide just how much they're willing to sacrifice for love.

Avenged by Love — Truck & Jersey

A fake-marriage, military romance

Travis's focus is on his Coast Guard career and his brother's future. But once beautiful, comic-loving Jersey crashes into his world in desperate need of medical care, he offers a marriage of convenience to help. But what happens when convenience turns to love?

Damaged Desires — Dani & Nash

A frenemy, military romance

Nash is all about honoring a promise to his dead brother, so accepting a challenge from the long-legged force of nature tempting him isn't in the cards. Not if he wants to keep his only remaining friend and stick to the code he grew up on. Several dares later, he has to decide whether to continue hiding in his past or face a new future.

Branded by a Song — Brady & Tristan

A single-mom, rock-star romance

Brady's come home to help the sister he left behind and find inspiration for a new album. What he doesn't expect is to discover his muse in a woman who's completely off limits and lost in the past. Can he help her find the strength to sing a brand-new love song?

Tripped by Love – Cassidy & Marco

A broody-bodyguard, single-mom romance

Cassidy is juggling her restaurant, a tiny human, and unrequited love. There's no time for her ex to try and derail her. Marco is determined to bury the feelings he has for his boss's sister, but that doesn't mean he's going to let the sniveling father of her child steamroll her. What happens when a little white lie changes everything?

The Anchor Novels: The Military Bros Box Set

The 1st three slow-burn romances + an exclusive novella

Guarded Dreams, Forged by Sacrifice, and *Avenged by Love* plus the novella, *The Hurricane*! Heartfelt reads full of love, sacrifice, and family. The perfect book boyfriends to kick off a binge read.

The Anchor Suspense Novels

Unmasked Dreams — Violet & Dawson

A second-chance, age-gap romance

Violet and Dawson had a heart-stopping attraction they were compelled to deny. When they're tossed together again, it proves nothing has changed—except the lab she's built in the garage and the secrets he's keeping. When she stumbles into his dark world, Dawson is forced to break old promises to keep her safe. But when the swells subside, will their hearts still be intact?

Crossed by the Stars — Jada & Dax

A second-chance, forced-proximity romance

Family secrets meant Dax and Jada's teenaged romance was an impossibility. A decade later, the scars still remain, so neither is willing to give in to their tantalizing chemistry. But when a shadow creeps out of Jada's past, seeking retribution, it's Dax who shows up to protect her. And suddenly, it's hard to see a way out without permanent damage to their bodies and souls.

Disguised as Love — Cruz & Raisa

A chemistry-filled, enemies-to-lovers romance

Surly FBI agent, Cruz Malone, is determined to bring down the

Leskov clan for good. If that means he has to arrest or bed the sexy blonde scientist of the family, so be it. Too bad Raisa has other ideas. There's no way she's just going to sit back and let the infuriating agent dismantle her world…or her heart.

The Painted Daisies

Interconnected, slow-burn romances with an all-female rock band, the alpha heroes who steal their hearts, and suspense that will leave you breathless. Each story has its own HEA.

Sweet Memory

An opposite-side-of-the-tracks, second-chance romance.

Trouble—that's what her sister calls him. But she can't resist, not even when his past threatens her world.

Green Jewel

An enemies-to-lovers, single-dad romance.

He did it. She'll prove it. Her body's reaction to him be damned.

Cherry Brandy

An opposites-attract, forbidden romance.

Being on the run with only one bed is no excuse to touch her…until touching is the only choice.

Blue Marguerite

A Hollywood-celebrity, frenemy romance.

She may have to work with him to save her sister, but he'll never have her body or heart again.

Royal Haze

An antihero, secret-society romance.

He was ready to torture, steal, and kill to defend the world he believed in. What he wasn't prepared for…was her.

Free Stories

https://www.ljevansbooks.com/freeljbooks

Perfectly Fine – FREE with newsletter signup
A Hollywood, second-chance romance

He's a charming, A-list actor at the top of his game. She's a determined, small-town screenwriter hoping for a deal. They form an unexpected connection until heartbreak ruins their future.

Rumor – FREE with newsletter signup
A small-town, rock-star romance

There's only one thing rock star Chase Legend needs to ring in the new year, and that's to know what Reyna Rossi tastes like. After ten years, there's no way he's letting her escape the night without their souls touching. Reyna has other plans. After all, she doesn't need the entire town wagging their tongues about her any more than they already do.

Love Ain't – FREE with newsletter signup
A friends-to-lovers, cowboy romance

Reese knows her best friend and rodeo king, Dalton Abbott, is never going to fall in love, get married, and have kids. He's left so many broken hearts behind there's gotta be a museum full of them somewhere. So, when he gives her a look from under the brim of his hat, promising both jagged relief and pain, she knows better than to give in.

The Long Con – FREE with newsletter signup
A sexy, antihero romance

Adler is after one thing: the next big payday. Then, Brielle sways into his world with her own game in play, and those aquamarine-colored eyes almost make him forget his number-one rule. But she'll learn…love isn't a con he's interested in.

The Light Princess – FREE with newsletter signup
An old-fashioned fairy tale

A princess who glows with a magical light, a kingdom at war, and a kiss that changes the world. This is an extended version of the fairy tale twined through the pages of *Charming and the Cherry Blossom*.

About the Author

Award-winning author, LJ Evans, lives in Northern California with her husband, child, and the three terrors called cats. She's been writing, almost as a compulsion, since she was a little girl and will often pull the car over to write when a song lyric strikes her. A former first-grade teacher, she now spends her free time reading and writing, as well as binge-watching original shows like *Ted Lasso, Wednesday, Veronica Mars,* and *Stranger Things*.

If you ask her the one thing she won't do, it's pretty much anything that involves dirt—sports, gardening, or otherwise. But she loves to write about all of those things, and her first published heroine was pretty much involved with dirt on a daily basis, which is exactly why LJ loves fiction novels—the characters can be everything you're not and still make their way into your heart.

Her novels have won multiple awards including ***CHARMING AND THE CHERRY BLOSSOM,*** which was *Writer's Digest's* Self-Published E-book Romance of the Year in 2021. For more information about LJ, check out any of these sites:

www.ljevansbooks.com
FaceBook Group: LJ's Music & Stories
LJ Evans on Amazon, Bookbub, and Goodreads
@ljevansbooks on Facebook, Instagram, TikTok, and Pinterest

Made in the USA
Monee, IL
15 September 2025

25791994R00239